*By Allison Pataki*

The Traitor's Wife

The Accidental Empress

Sisi

Where the Light Falls *(with Owen Pataki)*

Beauty in the Broken Places

Nelly Takes New York *(with Marya Myers)*

Poppy Takes Paris *(with Marya Myers)*

# The Queen's Fortune

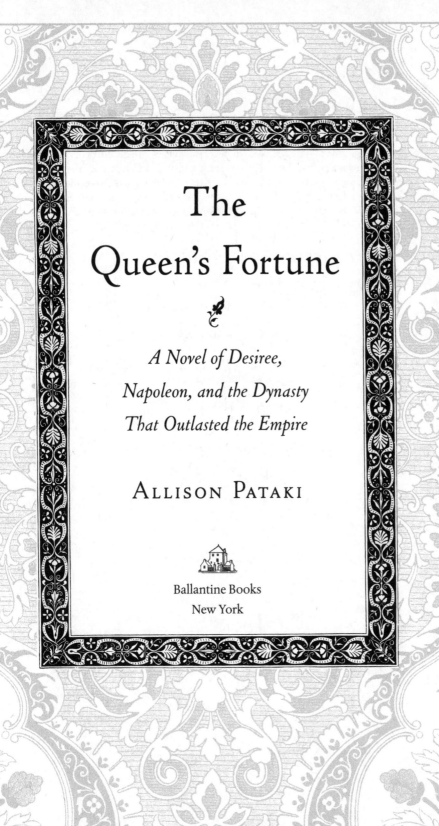

# The
# Queen's Fortune

*A Novel of Desiree,*
*Napoleon, and the Dynasty*
*That Outlasted the Empire*

### ALLISON PATAKI

Ballantine Books
New York

Copyright © 2020 by Allison Pataki

Published in the United States by Ballantine Books,
an imprint of Random House,
a division of Penguin Random House LLC, New York.

BALLANTINE and the HOUSE colophon are registered trademarks
of Penguin Random House LLC.

Hardback ISBN 978-0-593-12818-3
Ebook ISBN 978-0-593-12189-0

Printed in the United States of America on acid-free paper

randomhousebooks.com

2 4 6 8 9 7 5 3 1

First Edition

*Book design by Virginia Norey*

*For Lacy,*
*With gratitude*

# The Queen's Fortune

# Prologue

WHEN THE SNOW FALLS AT MIDNIGHT, BLANKETING THE empty cobbled streets, sugaring the gothic bell tower of Storkyrkan Cathedral, it becomes easy to imagine. For me, a girl from the south, where the breeze carried with it the warm seaside brine and the faint scent of the hillside lemon groves, the sudden appearance of these white flecks never fails to dazzle and disorient.

"*Kring kring,*" they all say. *Kring kring.* Round and round. It's one of the only phrases I've bothered to learn in Swedish: *kring kring.* "Round and round she goes, our mad old queen, riding through the snow and the midnight streets, imagining herself back in Paris."

I smile to myself, burrowing deeper into the plush seat of the enclosed coach, nuzzling my cheek against the silver fox fur of my cloak. How mistaken they are. I don't ride through the darkness of Stockholm, dazed by the snow, to imagine myself back in Paris. I don't ride through the wintry night to imagine him or his empire or the gold-emblazoned eagles or the brazen spire of Notre Dame, rising up from beside the Seine, a man-made finger of stone, defiant, poking the eyes of God.

No, no. *Kring kring.* Round and round I ride to see her once more: the girl whose name meant Desire. The girl from that other life, across the frozen sea and the war-scarred continent. *Desiree.* Before they renamed me, their queen, their Swedish mother, their Desideria.

I suppose he does appear in these midnight musings—I suppose they all do—but only as he relates to her, the girl he loved, the girl who brought the young, rough Corsican soldier to his knees. The girl he might have chosen. Could I have sated his hunger, rather than fueled it? Could I have prevented it all, thwarted the insatiable beast that would consume everything in its wake—his crown, his empire, his continent, his very life?

At night, encased in my snow-covered royal carriage, I think of her. The girl who might have saved him. Saved us all.

*Kring kring.* Round and round they go—these thoughts, these memories, these spectral phantoms who won and destroyed whole empires. A swirl of silk, steps gliding across the parquet of the dance floor. Dark and determined eyes, strong arms, the shifting colors of the officer's uniform. Crowns laid in place amid pomp and ceremony, only to be yanked off just as unceremoniously. Laughter, hers. His as well. Shouting and champagne toasts and song, always so many words. They've all fallen away, both the words and their speakers, and yet here I am. Only I remain.

They'll say what they will about me, their beautiful queen. Their cunning queen. Their kind queen. Their mad old queen. I'll let them. They'll put these words on me and they'll take others off. So many different cloaks and crowns and names have I worn. But not one of them can deny what I've known all along. I've known not only how to rule men and kingdoms—any ambitious schemer with an army can manage that. But me? I know something more. I know how to survive.

Even now, even when I sense that each misting of foggy breath might be my last, I know that I have one last chance to surprise them all. And so I shall. And it all starts with the fierce heart of a young girl whose name meant Desire.

# PART ONE

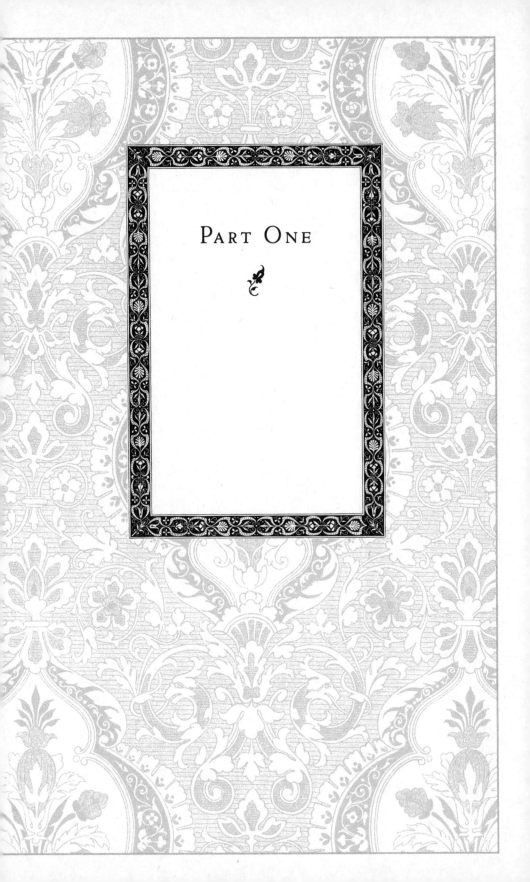

# Chapter 1

*The Convent of Notre Dame,*
*Southern France*
*Summer 1789*

S OMETHING WAS VERY WRONG. I COULD SEE IT THAT MORN-
ing in their pinched faces, the way the nuns flew up the corridor, their
heels clipping angrily against the cold, ancient stones of the abbey. Whispers skittering to and fro, hesitant and erratic, like the fragile flicker of the
candlelight that just barely illuminated their hurried steps.

My stomach growled and I pressed my fist into my gut, willing my
thoughts away from the hunger. "We haven't had a harvest this poor in
decades," the nuns kept telling us all summer long. Equal parts resignation
and censure, as if we'd somehow brought it on ourselves. "God is testing
our faith." God's test lasted for weeks, then months. Months that, to a hungry girl of eleven years, stretched out with the vastness of eternity. "We
must pray for the poor souls who are suffering. We pray for the poor, for
the hungry," the nuns told us each night at vespers, and then again at the
morning lauds. *The hungry?* I wanted to rail back at them. *Am I not starving?*
But I knew better, of course, than to answer the Sisters with anything more
than a doleful nod, eyes lowered piously to the floor. I didn't need my backside to ache along with my empty belly.

In the convent, the only place where we got enough food was the sick
ward; it was something we all knew as fact. When my sister, Julie, fell
sick last winter, laid up on a pristine cot, tucked in between crisp, white

sheets, I'd practically skipped through the halls to the nursing ward. I'd forced myself on her, pressing my lips to hers. *Like a stag in rutting season*, she'd gasped, her eyes wide with shocked and offended modesty as she chided me with one of Maman's well-worn scowls.

It had worked—I'd gotten myself gloriously sick, far sicker than Julie even. It had been two weeks of gluttonous eating, weeks of luxuriating in my warm cot, dozing even as I heard the bells chime for matins and the other girls, exhausted, stomachs empty and groaning for bread, shuffling down the dark halls to the freezing chapel for the predawn services. I'd stretched that illness for days, even after my throat had healed and my lungs had cleared. Not only had I lied, but I had lied in order to commit the dual sins of gluttony and sloth. I'd relished every minute of it.

But that morning, the morning when I was certain I was in trouble, it was not because I had feigned sickness. It was not because I had lied to get more food or sleep. No, that morning I had sinned far worse. *Thou shalt not steal.* I knew the commandment, and yet, I'd stolen. Perhaps not stolen—hidden. Sister Marie-Benedictine had been struggling across the yard during our morning recess when her wheelbarrow had toppled over, her dazzling supply of plump melons rolling across the small patch of parched, yellow grass. She'd enlisted us to help retrieve her bounty, but I'd stepped in front of one and kicked it quickly into a bush and out of sight. I'd just been so famished, and that melon had appeared so ripe and juicy—and so near. I'd felt a momentary pang of guilt, for Sister Marie-Benedictine was one of the kind ones, but my hunger pangs had quickly quashed that lesser discomfort. After Sister left, limping her cart across the remainder of the yard toward the kitchen, I'd enlisted Julie to help me move the melon farther from sight, tucking it away in the back of the yard. Our own treasure.

But someone must have seen. Someone had snitched, and now Mère Supérieure knew. I was certain of it. "Does it hurt?" I asked my sister as we shuffled down the long, dim hallway that led to our dormitory.

"What?" Julie asked.

"You know," I whispered.

Julie shrugged.

"The beating," I groaned, my voice betraying my panic.

"How would *I* know?" Julie frowned. Of course she would not know; she had never committed a transgression like this. Or, perhaps more accurately, she'd never been caught committing a transgression like this. She was far too cautious, her judgment far too sound. I had always been the reckless one.

"I just know they found it." I gnawed a piece of skin off my finger, the tinny taste of blood seeping into my mouth.

"Stop chewing your fingers," Julie scolded. Six years stretched between us, half my lifetime. Usually she was more a mother than a sister.

"Why else would they have disrupted our lessons and ordered us back to the dormitory?" I asked, certain of our fate, my hand falling limply to my side.

"Ah, the Clary girls, there you are. Julie. Desiree." Mère Marie-Claude raced toward us down the corridor, a flurry of white, her wimple fluttering around her face with each hasty step.

*Horror of all horrors!* Mère Supérieure, Mother Superior herself, here to administer our punishment! *God, I will never steal another melon, as long as I live. Please spare me your justice this once. I beg for mercy. Oh, Holy Mother, please intercede with your Son.*

But when I glanced back at Mother Superior's face, it wasn't anger I detected on her weary features. No, I knew that look, because it mirrored how I myself felt in that very instant; Mother Superior was afraid.

"Girls, your family has been notified to fetch you immediately and take you home, back to Marseille."

Neither Julie nor I spoke, so stunned were we by this sudden declaration.

"Fetch us?" Julie asked after a moment, my ever-dutiful sister forgetting the proper formality of speech in her confusion.

"Prepare your things at once," was all Mother Superior offered by way of reply. An image of my own mother's face, seared with anger—or was it her permanent disappointment?—blurred my vision. What would she say to this?

"Mother Superior, please." I fell to my knees, the unyielding stone floor receiving my joints with a vicious smack; I'd have bruises, to be sure. I ignored that, raising my hands in supplication: "The fault was entirely mine! I deserve to be sent from school, but not my sister. She played no part. I beg you to—"

"Hush, Desiree." Mother Superior lifted a long-fingered hand, her face stitching into an impatient scowl. "Quiet, for once, you foolish girl. You will return home, as will all the girls whose families can arrange for safe travel. The others . . . those whose families are abroad, well, we aren't certain how we shall . . ." Mother Superior exhaled aloud, an uncharacteristic display of some internal strain. "But never mind that. You girls are fortunate. Your family is close. They shall come and take you home, where you will be far safer than at this convent."

"But . . . take us home? Why? We are not on holiday." Julie's voice betrayed the same confusion I felt. Why were we suddenly unsafe here, in the convent? I wondered.

"War," Mother Superior said, her eyes softening, if only for a moment, as she saw our puzzlement. "You girls must pray. For . . . for all of us. And for France."

"War?" I repeated the word, incredulous. The sound was alien, the statement as outlandish as if Mother Superior were telling us that the Virgin Mary sat in the dining hall waiting to have bread and milk with us that very instant. "War with whom?" I asked.

Mother Superior frowned. "Ourselves. It's a revolution."

Julie took my hand, her palm clammy and cold, as Mother Superior continued: "The people have risen up."

The words I'd heard so many times in recent months raced across my mind: *We haven't had a harvest this poor in decades.*

Mother Superior's voice pulled me back to her, back to this dark corridor in the damp stone convent. "They seem to believe that the enemies come from the nobility and . . . and the Church. We are not safe here. They are sacking monasteries and setting fire to convents all over the country—stabbing priests, defiling nuns." She raised her hands, clasped them before her breast in a gesture of prayer. "But I've said too much. You girls don't need to know . . . I do not have time for this." She blinked, looking at Julie and then turning her eyes on me. "Go to the dormitory at once. Prepare your things. You shall leave this night. I shall pray for you." Her eyes held mine for a long moment, her expression seeming to indicate a mixture of concern and something else. Was it sadness? Or perhaps fear for my suddenly uncertain future? But then the stern woman pulled her shoulders back, straightening to her full height, and with that, Mère Marie-Claude turned and strode briskly away, offering not another word or backward glance in our direction.

"Revolution," Julie said in the nun's sudden absence, her voice barely a whisper. "Killing priests. Burning convents. How shall we ever make it home alive?"

I took my sister's hand and gave it a squeeze. "Papa will get us back safely. Or else Nicolas. Julie, don't worry, we shall be home by this time tomorrow." I sounded confident as I said it, and I was, so complete was my faith in our father and our elder brother. And besides, no matter how terrible the news may have been for our countrymen and our clergy, I could not ignore one glorious, welcome truth: at last, we were going home.

# Chapter 2

*Marseille, France*
*1794*

WHENEVER THEY BEGAN SHOUTING I'D SLIP OUT THE door, undetected but by Cook, whose sideways glance and barely perceptible grin always assured me that my secret would be well kept.

"Shh!" I lifted my finger to my lips, my eyes wide and imploring as I stepped delicately past the warm kitchen. Cook nodded, sniffed, and turned back to chopping her pile of fat yellow onions.

And so I did slip out the door that morning, humming to myself as I hopped through the doorway and into the gardens. There, I blinked, looking around. It always struck me as remarkable, a bit dizzying, really, to pass from the close and upholstered interior of our home—drawn damask drapes, muffled arguments, Maman's complaints of headaches—into the bright, fragrant refuge of our walled gardens. A sudden burst of color, the lilt of birdsong skittering along the mild air. I did not know then, would not understand until later, that it was a precious gift, and rare, to hear birds warbling all year long. To smell the earthy exhale of plant life, thick leaves unfurling under plump pearls of morning dew. But then, only a girl, I couldn't understand all that, even if I did have sense enough to savor my stolen hours in those gardens, where the warm breeze glided through the trellised hibiscus, carrying with it shifting slants of sunlight and the nearby cries of the gulls and the fishmongers, the horn blasts of massive ships pulling into port at our Mediterranean harbor.

There'd been much fretting since Papa's death just a few months earlier, but lately, it seemed to have worsened. Maman had come apart, the frayed edges of her nervous strain unraveling into outright panic, daily lamentations that we would surely follow Father's fate. "He did not die from the Revolution. He did not face the guillotine," our brother, Nicolas, would reassure Maman whenever she began her prophesying. Nicolas, seventeen years my senior and now our Clary patriarch, wore our family's fatigue and fear in the grim set of his jaw, in the rutted lines, newly etched, that crossed his brow. But he never lost his mild, reassuring calm, never snapped at Maman the way I would have, had I been in his trying position. "No tribunals have denounced us, Mother."

"Yet!" she'd answer, her cheeks mottled, her hands clenching and unclenching in a fitful rhythm.

A patient sigh from Nicolas. "Father's was a natural death, Mother."

"*Natural* death? Nothing natural about it," Maman would groan in reply, repeating the fears she'd voiced so many times: "It was the worry that felled him. The fear of the guillotine did it, sure as any blade. He knew we were all at risk." Whenever Maman began speaking like that, Julie would find my eyes with her own. *Not a word,* my sister's gaze would command. *Remain silent, and this shall pass.*

"We're far too wealthy," Maman moaned every day, her complaint a statement that a few years prior would have sounded absurd to any listener. "We've managed to survive far too long—they shall come for us."

I was young and naïve, a sheltered, coddled sixteen, but I knew enough to understand that Maman's lamentations weren't without reason; a madness stretched across our nation, a terror that pulled tighter than any hangman's noose. It was a rotten time to be alive in France, a time of fear so thick you could smell it in the streets, you could see it in the faces of those who passed. They'd killed both our king and queen, beheaded them in Paris before an angry mob, an ignoble fate previously reserved only for vile criminals and traitors. Louis and Marie-Antoinette, God's anointed vessels on earth—or so we'd always learned at the convent, before God himself had been banned from the nation, replaced by the Supreme Being—were now headless corpses tossed in the ground beneath a nameless grave, their rotting forms feeding the worms along with the petty thieves and other damned nobles. What had replaced them? The Committee, but more accurately, the Terror. We were to have no more nobility in France, no more of our ancient religion. Anyone who even whispered a kind word toward an aristocrat—or God—fell guilty under the new Law of Suspects.

So Maman held tighter to us these days, especially now that Papa was gone. My brother in particular; her eyes watched Nicolas with the ferocious love of a cornered she-wolf. She was convinced that the revolutionary tribunals—denied their justice on our rich papa by his sudden death—would enact their justice on his wealthy son and heir. We Clarys were of the *haute bourgeoisie,* the highest class of merchants. And though Papa had been born common, not of the noble class, his flourishing trade in silk and soap and coffee now belonged to Nicolas, and that made my brother one of the wealthiest citizens in the south of France. Wealthier by far than many of the aristocrats who had already lost their heads. This gave Maman much reason to fret and weep, and though Nicolas and Julie would try to console her, their efforts only seemed to further stoke her anxieties.

The best way that I, the youngest, found to navigate those trying days was to seek some small measure of refuge in my own solitude. I would hide, removing myself from their crying and cosseting, and so there I stood on that warm spring morning, my face upturned to the sunlight in our quiet gardens. I did not deny the Terror; I did not forget for one moment the fear that I knew reigned just outside our spacious family villa. I'd passed the city center and that dreaded new contraption—the guillotine—countless times when walking to the market or the seaside or to services at what used to be our church, now called our Temple of Reason. I'd smelled the sawdust that carpeted the ground around the executioner's perch; I'd seen the tumbrels carrying the damned figures to the square—or, worse, their lifeless, headless corpses away from it. I didn't deny the hell in which our countrymen and women were living. Even then, thinking of it, I shivered, my entire body trembling in spite of the warm morning sunlight.

And yet, I suppose I knew how powerless I stood against it all—how futile it would be for me, a young girl, to imagine myself of use in a time when even kings and queens were rendered powerless. I knew that Maman and Nicolas and even Julie had a far better chance of steering events in our favor, of keeping our family safe. I'd gleaned long ago that the best thing I could do for all of us was to stay out of the way and not add to Maman's list of lamentations. So that's what I did, there in the sanctuary of our villa's walled gardens, where somehow all seemed to remain quiet, undisturbed, and unsullied.

When I looked to the ground, I noticed the nest for the first time. It had rained the night before—hard, wrathful rain, the sort of storm that would have shaken this nest loose from the nearby juniper. I crouched low. There, beside the felled nest, I saw the shattered eggs, the shards of their shells a speckled blue, more perfect than our clear southern sky.

I leaned closer, my heart pierced not only by the shattered eggs, but by the perfectly whole nest right beside them, now empty. The nest had somehow survived the storm and the fall from the juniper, because the cozy space remained intact. I studied it, noting each twig woven with such care, a safe bowl from which to nurture and welcome and draw forth new life. A task of painstaking anticipation and preparation. Hope. The irrefutable fact of love. And then beside it, the shattered eggs, the worms already writhing all around, feeding off the wreckage of the lives no longer encased within. Where were the parent birds? Where would their love go now?

Perhaps one or two eggs remained, having survived the fall intact, I thought. I could find them and bring them indoors, where Cook would help me keep them warm and protected. Preserve those fragile little lives. My mind was bent toward that purpose, my hands scouring through damp earth, when Julie found me.

"Goodness, what is it now?" I heard her voice. "Head in the sky, hands in the dirt. Really, Desiree, must you always act like such a child, and today of all days?"

I turned, caught unaware both by Julie's sudden appearance and by the sting of her words. I sat back on my haunches, blinking up at my sister. "What is today?"

Julie ignored my question, waving a dismissive hand. "Inside. Maman wishes to see you."

My eyebrows lifted, a mild protest: Couldn't Julie cover for me, as she so often did? Couldn't she simply offer some excuse, saying she hadn't found me?

But Julie had no patience. "Desiree, now. You didn't hear any of that? Maman so upset? Are you really so oblivious to the world around you?" Her tone, the clear sharpness of it, served its purpose, and I rose at once, patting down my rumpled skirts, trying my best to shake the dirt from my lap.

"What's today?" I asked once more, but the question landed at my sister's back, for she had already turned and was hurrying toward the house.

Inside, the drapes were drawn against the bright sun, and a cool, eerie hush pulled tight over the large, empty rooms as Julie marched me through to the drawing room. There, in a plush armchair of upholstered cranberry satin, Maman sat, her legs propped on an ottoman, her entire frame drooping and lethargic. Even the features of her face sagged, weighted down with worry. There was no sign of Nicolas; he'd probably grown frustrated and excused himself.

"Desiree, my girl." Maman extended a hand, beckoning me toward her. That was unusual—it was Nicolas or Julie on whom Maman leaned, but rarely me. I edged closer, my steps hesitant as she took my hand in her tight grip. "My darling girl, perhaps you alone might be our salvation."

It sounded maudlin, even for Maman. I shifted on my feet, remaining silent.

"Our family needs you, my girl."

I turned from our mother to Julie. "Needs me . . . what for?"

"You must go to town," Maman said, and I was certain that my face revealed my shock.

"To town?" It was the exact opposite of what Maman had told us on every other day. *You are to avoid town. You are to avoid La Place. You are to stay away from the guillotine, avoid the crowds.*

"Yes," Maman said now, massaging a slow circle on her temple. "To the Hôtel de Ville."

"To the town hall . . . but why?" I turned to Julie, confused.

Mother began to weep, and Julie stepped forward, her voice hushed. "It's Nicolas," my sister explained. "He's . . . he's been arrested."

Mother's chest heaved with a loud sob. I stared at my sister, my eyes widening. "Nicolas—arrested?"

Julie nodded.

"Why?" I managed to ask, but I knew the question was foolish. Did one ever receive a proper answer to such a question these days? Why was my brother arrested? Why *not*? He was wealthy and he was alive in France during the Reign of Terror. He was the heir to a vast mercantile fortune. People were arrested every day for far less.

"It's worse than I feared," Maman said, blotting her face with a kerchief emblazoned with Papa's initials. "Your father, he's left us with more trouble than I knew."

I looked from Maman to my sister, confused by this.

"Your papa . . ." Maman pushed back against her distress, swallowing before she continued: "He had petitioned the crown, several years ago. He'd sent in the funds for a generous gift, along with a request for ennoblement. We were to . . . to become . . . noble. Before it all . . . well, before all of this." With that, Maman lost her last shred of fortitude, her face crumpling into her palms.

Julie stepped forward, pressing a hand on my shoulder, and I turned to my sister. "But I don't understand what it is that I might do?" I asked, my mouth going dry. "What can I do?"

"Maman believes that you have the best chance of success," Julie answered, her face softening as she took my hands in hers. "You are to go to the town hall and petition on behalf of Nicolas."

The enormity—the very futility—of this task struck me as absurd, stunning me a moment before I asked: "Me?"

"Yes, you." Julie nodded.

"You are to try first, my child." Maman fixed her gaze on me. "You are young. Look at you—hard would be the heart of the man who didn't presume you to be innocent."

I crossed my arms. "I cannot do it, Maman. I'm not . . ." My words trailed off even as my mind spun.

Maman frowned, impatient. "What is it, girl? Out with it."

"Only, it's that . . ." I said what I'd always believed to be the truth: "I'm not smart, not like Julie. Send her instead."

Maman raised her hands, swatting my words away. "Oh, what does wit have to do with anything, you foolish girl? You are *beautiful*, Desiree. More beautiful than Julie. You are to be sweet and soft and beseeching, do you hear? Look into their eyes in the same fearful way you now look at me—any man would leap to grant your wish."

My thoughts writhed in a tangled knot. Never before had Maman spoken in this manner. She did not mean to compliment me, nor to insult Julie, of that I was certain. She was simply desperate to have her son back; I could feel that, could feel the coiled urgency of her fear. But how was it that she thought *me* capable of this monumental task?

I looked down at myself. It was true that I was young and lovely—I knew it from the looks that the men now heaped on me in the street. Something had changed, only recently. Before, their eyes would pass over me, unpausing; I was just another coddled, well-dressed girl, ambling innocently up the street in the authoritative presence of Julie or Maman or perhaps Cook or Nicolas. But now when they looked, their gazes lingered, returning again and staying affixed, captive. I was not blind to the way their eyes traced the soft and curving lines of my figure, resting on my waist or my décolletage with something akin to hunger. I knew, too, from the way my brother frowned when he studied my silhouette, muttering under his breath, "Papa had to leave us in the exact year that Desiree turned into a woman?"

It had startled me how swiftly my body had transformed in just these recent months. There had been the arrival of my monthly courses, and then the gowns of my girlhood no longer fit, my newly ample bosom overspilling the top of my corset, my arms and legs turning plump and soft. When I looked in the mirror, my dark eyes stared back from the glass with some newfound power, my brunette hair falling in glossy waves around a face both alluring and yet slightly startled by its own appeal. Was I more beautiful than Julie, the sister six years my senior? Perhaps, I conceded. Yes. She had the same brown hair and eyes, but her figure was sharper, with angular edges where mine was supple and round. Her face, though it resembled mine as only a sister's could, was nevertheless longer and narrower, her features perhaps less pleasingly arranged.

And yet, I had no idea how to wield this newly acquired power, these potent but unfamiliar feminine charms. And certainly not in a task as monumental as the one set before me, the task of saving my brother's life. I turned to my sister, willing her to see these thoughts of mine.

"I shall come with you," Julie said, nodding. "I'll walk with you to the Hôtel de Ville. You shall speak, you shall lead the petitioning when we are inside, but I shall be with you."

"Good." I sighed, feeling a slight slackening of the tightness in my shoulders. "Thank you."

"And you will take this," my mother added, pulling a bulging silk purse from the folds of her gown and passing it to Julie. "Whatever the price, it does not matter. If that's not enough, you sign a bill of credit and you tell them that we shall deliver the rest. There is no limit, you understand? If the entirety of the Clary fortune must go to buying clerks and bribing guards, I do not care. Only bring me back my son."

Julie nodded, taking the purse from Maman before returning to my side. "Ready?" she asked.

I wanted to say no, but then Maman looked from Julie to me and I saw in her expression that I had no other choice. At long last, it was time for me, Desiree, to step in and take a part in the steering of my family's fragile fate.

Outside, the midday sun fell bright and hot, and we blinked beneath our bonnets as we exited our front gate, hands entwined. Our home was just steps from La Place Saint Michel, in one of the wealthiest quarters of the city and only a short walk from the Marseille town hall.

I'd known the streets of the Vieux Port, the old city center, my entire life, and yet the smells that pulsed throughout our town never failed to make their impact on a hot day. I rarely left the house at this time, the harshest hours of southern sunlight, the time for napping. I crinkled my nose against the onslaught of aromas as we wove through the crowds and the limestone buildings: fish and saltwater, horse dung, overripe fruits and vegetables spoiling on the tables of the outdoor vendors.

Just recently, other aromas had settled over our ancient port city as well; like so many others, our town now reeked of blood and sawdust. My stomach grew queasy as we approached the square, where the daily executions drew crowds of hundreds. I fixed my eyes straight ahead, away from the raised platform, away from the tall tower shape hulking under a cloth, its blade wiped clean after that morning's spectacle.

Instead I turned my eyes out over the horizon, toward the shimmering expanse of aqua-blue Mediterranean, its surface strewn with cargo ships, passenger vessels, and small fishing craft. I blinked against the sunlight and saw the massive stone structure rising up out of the nearby island, the ancient Château d'If—built as a naval fortress centuries ago but now functioning as a revolutionary prison. I felt the bumps rise to my flesh in spite of the warm day and turned away from that squat, impenetrable structure, willing myself not to think of the miserable wretches clinging to life on the other side of those thick stone walls.

Our port's other distinguishing structure, the massive Notre Dame de la Garde basilica, rose up behind the city out of the seaside cliffs, like some hulking creature perched atop our rocky shoreline. *No,* I thought to myself, *it's no longer a basilica. It's now a structure in the service of the State.*

We had not heard the ringing of Notre Dame's bells in years, not since a band of revolutionaries stormed the place and climbed its tower, seizing the ancient chimes and boiling them down to make bullets for the revolutionary army.

"Well now, citizeness." A gruff-looking man, his leer revealing gaps where teeth had once been, whistled from the other side of the narrow, stinking street. "Lookin' for something you can't get in those fancy drawin' rooms? I gotta blade for you right 'ere." He made a lewd gesture toward his breeches and I stopped midstep, stunned by the fact that it was *me* to whom he spoke. Such brazen vulgarity in broad daylight. And how dare he insult a Clary lady in such a way?

"Ignore him." Julie paused beside me, one hand clutching the money purse out of sight in the fabric of her skirts, the other hand squeezing my own. "Come. Now." She picked up our pace, spitting the words under her breath: "*Les cochons.* Pigs taking over this city."

We wove our way through the busy square, past the young girls in white linen bonnets who sold flowers; past the young men who milled around the square's benches, their loose breeches styled in the practically required *sans-culottes* mode of the revolutionary patriot, pamphlets and books in their fists as they debated politics; past the tired mothers with dirty faces, their hands lifted and begging for a *sou*, babies suckling or sleeping on their exposed breasts.

We approached the grand civic building, the Hôtel de Ville, where the tricolor flag of the Republic hung limp on this windless day before the elaborate baroque exterior. A row of tall arched windows flanked a cavernous doorway. My heart lurched in my chest, the enormity of my task slowing my steps. My sister noted my hesitation. "Come now. It's for Nicolas," she said, her voice low and determined.

We crossed the threshold from the bright Place into the government building. City clerks and government bureaucrats buzzed about the massive, high-ceilinged space without noting our entry. The air was cool, the hall filled with a sense of purpose. "Where do we go?" I turned to my sister, immeasurably grateful that she stood beside me. I had been inside this building only a handful of times, always with Papa, never for anything this significant.

"There?" Julie pointed toward a long queue, where petitioners—apparently from all across the south of France, based on the number of people—stood lined up before a window, a faceless bureaucrat apparently turning the wheels of justice from behind that partition, though it appeared he did so at a crawling pace.

"We won't see anyone until Christmas," I gasped, frowning at the interminable line. "Where is Nicolas?"

"I don't know, Desiree," Julie answered, her voice betraying a hint of frustration—or was it perhaps the same fear I felt? "I know nothing more than you do."

"Excuse me?" I turned to a nearby guard who stood before a side exit of the building. He looked at me, offering no reply. I continued: "Our brother has been wrongfully imprisoned, and we are here to post his bail. Would you be so kind as to direct us toward an administrator who sees to prisoner releases?"

The guard studied me, then Julie, then turned back to me. His mouth spread into a smirk as his eyes traced a clear line down the length of my figure. I clasped my hands in front of my waist, thrown momentarily off-balance by the bald, unmasked desire in his eyes. "You want my help, sweetheart, what're you going to do to get it?"

My mouth fell open, prompting this guard to snigger. Before I could stammer out a reply, Julie was beside me, her frame rigid in defiance as she declared: "We have means."

The guard turned to Julie, amused. "I guessed as much, based on the dresses." As he spoke, I could smell the sour-wine reek of his breath. "So did Citizen Capet," he said with a chortle, his street accent coloring the derisive nickname he gave to our dead king. "Fat lotta good it did 'im, eh?" He grunted out a laugh, scratching the groin of his stained trousers with a lone finger. "You'll wait your turn, citizeness, just like every other free man and woman." With that, he jerked his stubbled chin toward the long line of petitioners snaking away from the clerk's window. "Don't care if you got the fanciest gowns in the building. Just means some guard might want to get rich tearing 'em off your posh skins."

"Come, Julie," I said, tugging on my sister's hand, regretting that I had sought this brute's assistance. We shuffled away across the hall, eyes down, our resolve sufficiently battered by the hostile disrespect we'd seen so far.

"Look at the line," Julie said, toneless. We walked quickly across the vast interior space, not toward any particular destination—we simply wished to be as far away from that awful man as possible. "It's as you said, we shall be here for days and no closer to saving Nicolas. He could be tried and executed before we ever reach the clerk."

I nodded. I was so disturbed by all of it—by the glimpses of the prison and the church, by the guillotine, by the vulgar man in the street and now this vile guard, but mostly by the length of the line and our utter powerlessness to save Nicolas—that I did not even see the figure in front of me until I'd walked straight into him. Only the bulk of his body against mine plucked me from my troubled musings. "Oh, I am sorry, monsieur. I mean, citizen! I'm sorry. I wasn't looking where I was going." I kept my eyes fixed on the floor, fearful that this man might handle me as roughly as the others had.

His answer was entirely unexpected: "A lady need never apologize." The man's tone was completely devoid of hostility; his remark carried no hint of malice or lewdness. I glanced from under the brim of my bonnet up into a broad, unfamiliar smile. The face into which I stared was dark and ruddy, not attractive, but his large eyes appeared kind. The tension in my body slackened, just a bit.

"But then, a lady need never frown nor fret, either, and yet I see that you do both." His accent sounded foreign—Spanish, perhaps? Though he spoke with the authority of someone in charge, he wore loose breeches and a simple jacket, not an administrative uniform or government robe. The tricolor revolutionary cockade was fixed prominently to his jacket, pinned over his left breast. He stood tall and broad-shouldered, and he appeared older than I was, in his mid- or late twenties. But why did he keep referring to me as a lady, rather than citizeness? And who was he?

"Joseph di Buonaparte, at your service," he offered, answering my thoughts. His cap already in hand, he swept it aside with a flourish as he bowed deeply before my sister and then me. "And you are?" His eyes held my own and I saw a glint of good cheer, perhaps even mischief, as he asked the question.

"Desiree Clary," I answered, lowering my eyes as I offered a quick curtsy. My sister did the same beside me. "Julie Clary."

"Ah, the famed Clary girls?" This man, this Joseph di Buonaparte, repeated our family surname, clasping his hands together. "Daughters of the late Francois Clary? A fine citizen. A man who made this port city rich."

Julie and I exchanged a glance, and I could see that she wondered the same thing: *Who is this strange man with his easy smiles and his odd accent?*

"But please, you must tell me—what service can I render for the daughters of the late, great Citizen Clary?" he asked, eyes darting from me to Julie, then back to me, where they remained.

I stood still, temporarily mute in my incredulity. Julie took a step forward. "If you are in earnest, and truly willing to help, citizen . . . ?"

"A Corsican never offers anything unless he intends to follow through," he answered. "Unless, of course, he doesn't wish to. But that is an entirely different matter." He laughed, his eyes resting on mine, and I nodded, pretending to follow. Well, then, he was Corsican, at least that much I understood—the accent must have been Italian. But why did he speak as if he could actually help us?

"In that case, I shall meet your kindness with candor, sir. Er, citizen." Julie appeared to trust this strange man's gregarious manners, and she addressed him frankly as she related the story of Nicolas's imprisonment, leaving out the detail that Papa, a royalist, had made a generous gift to the crown just before the outbreak of the Revolution. Joseph di Buonaparte nodded knowingly as he listened, the confidence of his bearing not wavering in the slightest, even in the face of Julie's clear distress.

When Julie finished, he crossed his arms before his broad chest. Eventually, he nodded. "I understand," was all he said.

"We . . . we would be most grateful if in fact you could help us." Julie lifted the purse from her pocket, just enough so he could see it. "And we would be happy to demonstrate our gratitude."

Joseph cast a look around the massive hall before leaning close and putting his hand on top of Julie's. The gesture was overly presumptuous, bordering on improper, but there was no hint of lasciviousness or impropriety in it, simply an earnest concern as he said, "Please, Citizeness Clary, put away your purse."

Julie hesitated a moment, looking at his hand on hers, before heeding his request. "What you *can* do—" Joseph said.

"Anything," I offered, stepping forward, the hope evident in my tone. Joseph turned to me now as he spoke: "There is a nice café across the square. Why don't you ladies go and have a seat on the terrace? Order me a glass of something cold. Perhaps even a glass of wine. I promise you that, before this office closes for the day, you shall be walking home with your brother."

Julie and I looked from this man, this incomprehensibly kind stranger, toward each other. Was he to be believed?

Julie, surveying once more the interminable line of petitioners and apparently seeing no option other than to trust this Citizen di Buonaparte, looked from me back to him. "Sir, we put our hope in you. Thank you."

"You can thank me once I've brought him to you. Nicolas?"

"Yes, Nicolas Clary," Julie answered. "He was brought in this morning. We don't know where he's being held."

"Then I shall find out." Joseph di Buonaparte nodded, winking once at me. "Now, please, out of here. To the café! There are far too many rogues in this building masquerading as revolutionaries. No place for a pair of ladies."

Neither Julie nor I spoke as we sat at a table on the terrace, barely touching our cold lemonades. We were both wondering the same thing, I knew, and there was no need to voice the questions that neither of us could answer: Who was this Joseph di Buonaparte? Did he truly intend to help us? And, if his intentions were indeed to help, was he even capable of doing so?

The clock in the square marched steadily around the minutes and hours, passing teatime, until suppertime approached. The government offices would be closing soon. I shifted in my seat, my fingers restlessly smudging the sticky moisture that clung to the cup of my untouched drink. I was lost in my thoughts, a sequence of morose musings. I was thinking of Papa on the last days I'd seen him. Weak, in his massive bed, drifting in and out of fretful sleep. Maman huddled beside him, weeping and praying, even though our prayers had been made illegal. I was dreading the walk back home to Maman.

"By God." Julie's voice pulled me from my grim reverie, drawing my attention upward. "Look!" She pointed across the crowded square and I turned in that direction, my eyes darting past pigeons, students, housewives, dirty little children. There, two figures—one broad and tall, the other trim, well-dressed, familiar—emerged from the massive front doorway of the Hôtel de Ville into the early-evening light. They walked purposefully away from the town hall.

I gasped. "Nicolas!" Both Julie and I were out of our chairs in an instant, scrambling off the terrace to race toward our brother. I was the faster runner and reached him a few paces ahead of Julie. We both gasped for breath as we collapsed into his arms.

"Girls!" Nicolas welcomed our assault. I laughed, even as tears filled my eyes. "Nicolas, thank God."

"No, thank Joseph di Buonaparte," Nicolas replied, allowing Julie and me to squeeze him a moment longer. People passed by in the square, watching, familiar as they were with daily tears outside the town hall—

though such tears of joyful reunions were far less common than the other sort.

"Thank Joseph di Buonaparte indeed," Julie said, turning to our improbable new benefactor. "But how can we ever?"

The tall man bowed before us once more, his facial expression seeming to inquire whether we had dared to doubt him. Of course we had. And yet, here stood Nicolas.

"Are you . . . free?" I asked, my voice hesitant. I simply wished to take my brother's hand and pull him away from that building, away from those unseen prison cells, back into the safety of our family's walled villa.

"As you see me," Nicolas answered.

"Really?" I asked, hardly willing to believe it. "Clear of danger?"

Nicolas tilted his head toward me. "As clear of danger as anyone in this nation can claim to be."

I hugged my brother again and Nicolas allowed it. "And all because it appears that my younger sister has charmed the heart of an important man," Nicolas whispered into my ear, pulling out of the hug and pinching my cheek. Even had he not pinched my flesh, I have no doubt I would have flushed a shade of deep crimson, for I felt my entire face grow warm at the comment. *My younger sister has charmed the heart of an important man.* I swallowed, my eyes fixing firmly on the ground, away from the appraising stare of my brother, away from the expectant and eager smile of Joseph di Buonaparte.

Julie stepped in, mercifully. "It's more than we dared to hope," she said, her voice level. "And we insist that we must repay you, sir, for your kindness."

"Please, Mademoiselle, er, Citizeness Clary, away with the money purse! You insult my Corsican sense of chivalry."

"If not with money," Nicolas said, "then how?"

I allowed myself to look up at this and saw Joseph clasp his large hands, glancing from my brother toward me, then back toward Nicolas. Now even *he* looked slightly sheepish, as he fidgeted with the hat in his grip. "If it's not too bold . . . perhaps you might allow me to help you . . . escort your sisters safely home?"

Nicolas nodded with half a smile, sliding his arm through Julie's, leaving me unattended. "It would be our pleasure." Nicolas turned his gaze toward me, his eyebrows lifting. "Isn't that so, Desi?"

I stared at my brother, at his expectant expression, and then saw Julie, her own features arranged in a manner in which I could not decipher her thoughts, an uncommon occurrence between us. Then I looked to Joseph; so eager and hopeful was his smile. I did not want the attentions of this bold man—so much older, so very forward—on me, and yet I knew that we were indebted to his kindness, and it was clear what Nicolas expected of me. "Escort us home? Of course. Certainly," I stammered, breaking eye contact as Joseph strode giddily toward me, extending his thick arm for me to take. Together, the four of us turned our backs on the town hall and the crowded square and started toward home.

I'd never been escorted home by a man before, other than my brother or my father. At only sixteen, and coming of age as I had during a time of war, I had never been courted. Papa and Nicolas were both far too protective to allow it, and, besides, young men of my class, if not imprisoned or dead, seemed far too busy with politics these days than to waste time on trivial matters like flirtation.

But now, here I was, walking beside a man I'd known barely a few hours, following behind my newly freed brother as evening draped itself over the narrow streets of Marseille. I blinked, hardly able to understand all that had happened in just half a day. Nicolas and Julie clipped briskly ahead of us, a pace set by my brother, I guessed, in order to grant a bit of discreet distance between our two couples. I was uncomfortable on the arm of this relative stranger, shy and sheltered as I was, and thus grateful for the short distance back to our family's home. I was also grateful that Joseph babbled away at my side for the entirety of the walk, apparently happy to tell me his thoughts on Corsica and Marseille without any need for my reply. "The city is called Ajaccio," he said, describing his hometown. "You've never heard of it? Ah, but you must see it. Someday. The land! It's not unlike this. We also overlooked the Mediterranean. But never in my whole life did I see my mother buy olive oil or wine, we had so much of it on our family's land."

Ahead of us, Nicolas paused with Julie, turning as we approached the front gate of our home. "Citizen di Buonaparte, you must come in. Mother will insist on meeting my deliverer."

Apparently not one to decline any sort of invitation, Joseph assented with a hearty nod. "Indeed! I would like to meet the madame who produced daughters such as these."

"Careful, my good man," Nicolas said, flashing a good-natured smile. "I may owe you my life, but that does not mean I will sit by to witness flagrant flirtation with my sisters."

"But I'm Corsican!" Joseph bellowed. "I can't resist the opportunity to flatter a beautiful woman." Joseph's entire frame reverberated with his fulsome laughter, even as he held on to my arm and guided me through the gate onto our property.

Maman's joy at Nicolas's safe return was as excessive as her despair had been earlier in the day. She wrapped her arms around him as if she might never let go. She ordered the footmen to bring us champagne. As the evening outside darkened, she called for the candles to be lit and the French doors thrown open, allowing in the balmy air and the nighttime sounds of the gulls and tree frogs. "A toast," Maman said, lifting her glass toward the guest in our drawing room. "To a hero for our Clary family," she said, smiling broadly at Joseph, who was clearly reveling in Maman's attentions. All I wanted was to finish this glass of champagne, perhaps eat a quick bite of supper, and then slip upstairs with Julie, where we might discuss all that had occurred on this strange day.

But Maman, overjoyed at having her son home safely, appeared intent on chatting with our visitor, her rare interest in playing the hostess as surprising as it was inconvenient to me. She ordered that our flutes be refilled. "But you have an unfamiliar accent, Citizen di Buonaparte. Are you Italian?"

"Close, madame," Joseph answered. "Corsican."

"Corsican," Maman repeated, nodding slowly. "How . . . novel. I don't know that I've ever met a Corsican."

"There aren't many of us to meet," Joseph said, his easy, good-natured smile drifting from Maman to Nicolas to Julie, before finally resting on me. "It's just a small island of grapes and olives, after all. But it's home. Or at least, it was home."

"Rather as unstable there in Corsica as we are here, isn't that so?" Maman asked, ordering yet more champagne for our guest. I fidgeted, stunned by my mother's loquaciousness, her sudden interest in Corsican politics. Her spirits soared higher this evening than I'd seen them in quite some time—certainly since before Papa's death, possibly since before the Revolution's outbreak. Her motives were clear to me: after months of fretting that Papa's wealth and the favor of the nobility might mean our undoing, she finally believed that we had a protector in this di Buonaparte fellow, and she was giddy with relief. Dogged in her determination to solidify his good favor.

"Indeed, Madame Clary is not only beautiful, like her daughters, but also well-informed. The island is terribly unstable," Joseph answered. "And I fear that my family aligned with the wrong side. Hence, we are exiles. France is now home." Joseph said the last part as if he were trying to convince himself of that fact.

"Well, Joseph di Buonaparte," Maman said, her voice warm as she finished off her second glass of champagne, "Corsica's loss is our most fortunate gain—today you have been our deliverer, and you must allow us to thank you."

"Why do the Clarys keep insisting on thanking me? Does no one in France extend a favor without expecting some payment in return?" Joseph laughed at his own remark, and Mother waved a hand as she answered: "Ah, well, we are of the merchant class. You must forgive us our need to settle our accounts."

"Well, in that case, if a price is insisted upon," Joseph said, his smile suddenly turning bashful. "There is one thing."

"Please do tell," Maman said, an eyebrow arched, her entire expression expectant, poised to grant any request. None of us knew how, exactly, Joseph di Buonaparte had come into the power to see to Nicolas's release, but clearly Maman wished to keep him as a friend.

"Madame Clary, with your consent, please allow me to call on your daughter Desiree."

The entire room fell silent as Mother's eyes careened toward me, her mouth falling open. Clearly, this was not a favor she had been expecting. But then I saw it—the shifting of her features, the understanding of the opportunity, her surprise turning into an expression of visible delight. Julie shifted in her seat. Maman smiled at me before turning back to our guest. "Of course. You must come again. We insist."

"*Grazie!* Then I shall come tomorrow, perhaps at—" but Joseph's words were cut short, for just then we heard a strange shouting noise. The glass doors that ran the length of the drawing room were opened out onto the terrace and gardens, allowing a man's shrill voice to float to us indoors. "Come out here, *bastardo!*" the faceless voice cried from the street, and even though only one of us in the room spoke fluent Italian, we all understood well enough.

"Goodness." Mother blanched, looking to our guest, embarrassed. "What a thing to hear. I . . . I . . . don't know what to say. Usually, in this quarter, we don't suffer the indignities of the mob. Some student, drunk, no doubt."

"I know you're in there, *figlio di puttana,* you son of a whore!"

"Heavens!" Mother's eyes darted from Joseph toward my direction as she grimaced. "Desiree, shut the doors, would you? Nicolas, please have one of the servants inform the gendarmes. Some drunken troublemaker yelling obscenities around the entire neighborhood—it cannot be tolerated."

As I crossed the room toward the doors, Joseph lifted a hand and placed it on my arm. "No, wait, please." He stilled me and then stood, making his way out onto the terrace. There, he did the last thing I expected him to do. He raised his hands and, veins bulging in his neck, yelled out into the dark night: "*Bastardo, chiudi la bocca! O ti ucciderò!*"

Maman gasped. Nicolas frowned as Julie and I looked to each other, eyes wide. I had to clasp a hand over my mouth to stop the laughter. Then Joseph turned back to us, flushed, chuckling heartily. "He calls me a bastard, a son of a whore, but the fool doesn't realize that the same insults then fall on him."

Not one of us offered a reply. I could all but hear Maman's heart clamoring in her breast.

Joseph chuckled again, his round cheeks flushed. "It's nothing—only my troublemaker of a brother."

"Your . . . your brother?" Maman repeated, her warm, approving smile fading.

"Yes." Joseph nodded, replacing his cap on his head as if to leave, apparently unaware of the shock he'd caused. "We don't call him *Il Rabulione* for nothing."

Nicolas, whose Italian was far better than my own, repeated the nickname. "*Il Rabulione*. The Rascal?"

"That's right," Joseph said. "Always has been."

"Well, then. That's that." Maman gestured to Nicolas to see our guest out.

"The Rascal," I said, pressing my lips tightly together so as not to laugh at Mother's pained expression. It really had been quite an unusual day. "And . . . what's his real name?" I was impossibly curious about this young man who would stand outside the grand home of perfect strangers, hurling insults over their walls on the hunch that his brother stood inside.

"His real name is Napoleone," Joseph answered, turning as he reached the threshold of the room. "Until tomorrow."

With that Joseph bowed farewell, and my mother repeated her thanks one final time, but not her invitation for the next day's visit. Standing in the room now with only my sister and Maman, I turned once more toward the opened glass doors, beyond which darkness covered the gardens. I narrowed my eyes; in the faint glow of evening, I could make out our front gate. There, though almost entirely obscured by shadow, I could just barely detect the outline of a lone figure.

*What an odd name,* I thought. What had Joseph said? *Napoleone.* A most singular name. And, from the sound of it, a singular sort of man, too. I'd never known a Napoleone before.

# Chapter 3

*Marseille*
*1794*

THE BUONAPARTE BROTHERS WERE TO BECOME A SUDDEN, surprising presence in our lives. Joseph called early the next morning—earlier than expected—and he did not come alone. I sat on the bright terrace finishing my coffee, Julie and Maman at the table with me, when the startled servant appeared and announced our two visitors. Fortunately we were dressed for the day, even if not yet entirely prepared to welcome guests.

"Very well." Maman sighed. "Show them in." Under her breath, she added: "I wish he hadn't brought that dreadful brother along. And yet, we are to be charm itself, girls. This di Buonaparte fellow, somehow, has the power to keep us safe. We shall not squander that, understood?"

We rose as the two men entered, offering cordial greetings of welcome. Julie, I noticed, offered an uncharacteristically bright smile toward Joseph. My eyes went with curious interest toward the younger one. Napoleone, Joseph had called him. *Il Rabulione*. The Rascal.

"Please, would you join us?" Maman gestured toward two empty chairs.

"It would be our pleasure." Joseph nodded as he and his brother accepted. "I am so pleased to find you all looking so well after the events of yesterday. The Clary ladies outshine the Marseille sunlight this morning," he added with a flourish of his wrist as he removed his cap, the revolution-ary cockade visible on its front, just as it was on his brother's.

I took a moment to survey our visitors: the two Buonaparte brothers were entirely dissimilar in appearance, and, I suspected, in demeanor as well. Joseph was built tall and broad, his wide face spread in an open, straightforward smile. His brother, Napoleone, did not appear to possess the same ease in our company, nor the same general fluidity of manners. He appeared stiff beside Joseph, his short and narrow frame clad in a pris-tine military uniform. His officer's coat had a high neck and bright red collar, with freshly shined brass buttons down its front. Like his brother, he had dark hair, but his grew longer, falling on his shoulders, unbrushed, even slightly unkempt. His thin nose gave him the look of a Roman centu-rion, and his green eyes stared straight ahead, a surly expression with no attempt at a smile.

While I had no idea of their ages, I guessed that Joseph must be the older of the two. And yet, I noticed as they sat that Joseph seemed to look to his brother as if for cues. It was evident in how Napoleone chose his seat first and Joseph reacted. How Joseph seemed to wait for Napoleone until he sat in his chair.

I wiped my mouth, my face warming with embarrassment as I surveyed the place before me at the breakfast table with a heightened awareness of how it might appear to our guests: my bowl of coffee had a skin of murky white oil floating across the top from where I had dunked my buttered bread; scraps of soggy baguette, the remainder of my morning meal, seeped into mush on my plate. It all appeared so childish, so unrefined, next to this stern man in his officer's uniform.

"Can we offer you some coffee? Some brioche or tarts?" Maman ges-tured toward the platter from which we'd been picking.

Napoleone nodded his assent, making a sort of grunting noise as he reached for a brioche. Unvarnished, almost boldly and defiantly so, he bit vigorously into the roll and then, as an afterthought, tipped what was left of the brioche in Maman's direction. "Thank you, citizeness."

"I'm sure you're quite welcome," Maman said, barely masking her dis-taste. A person with genteel manners did not eat so hungrily in the presence of relative strangers, and ladies at that. I pressed my lips together, trying not to smile. Just then, Napoleone lifted his eyes and met my own. I was startled by it—by the intensity of his stare, by the magnetic pull of his dark-green gaze. I swallowed, my appetite for my remaining breakfast gone.

"You didn't meet him last night." Joseph gestured toward his brother. "Just heard his colorful words echoing across the neighborhood."

"Indeed," said Maman, shifting in her chair. Napoleone did not take that moment's opportunity to apologize for the previous evening's litany, nor, apparently, did he feel any shame. Maman cleared her throat, patting the silk folds of her broad skirt as this young man tipped his chin in my direction and said: "It is a pleasure to meet you." And yet, neither his expression nor his tone seemed to carry any pleasure. Meeting his eyes with my own, I felt as though my stomach might flip on itself.

"What an odd name you have," Maman remarked, glancing toward Julie with an eyebrow arched. Whatever gratitude or goodwill she bore for Joseph from yesterday did not appear to extend to his brother. "Napoleone. Is it . . . a Corsican name?"

"Italian." His voice was unique—softer than Joseph's, tinged with a silky quality. "From Machiavelli. You are familiar with his writings?"

"'The ends justify the means'—of course I'm familiar with Machiavelli," Maman said, a touch defensively.

"That was one of his assertions." Napoleone nodded, moving his eyes from me toward Maman. "And do you agree?"

Maman sat a bit stiffer in her chair. "Do I agree with what?"

"With the scholar, with Machiavelli? That a good result for the State justifies any means taken by its ruler, however ruthless?"

Maman shrugged, blinking against the brightening sun, against the intensity of this young man's appraising stare. "I'm sure I haven't put much thought into it. Certainly not this early in the day."

"Well, regardless—" Joseph interjected, but Napoleone raised a hand. "Quiet, Joseph." The older brother, surprisingly, obeyed. Napoleone continued, eyes fixed intently on Maman: "I consider it our duty, all of us, to put thought into such matters. We are, after all, free citizens suddenly in charge of our own fates. And tasked with building a new nation."

With that Napoleone turned his eyes squarely on me, and I forced my-self to return his gaze. I would not allow him to intimidate me with the intensity of his looks, even if I did feel a strange jolt run through me—a sensation entirely foreign, if not unpleasant. I was aware that Maman no-ticed our locked stare, as did the others. Finally, when Napoleone coughed, I allowed myself to look away, down at my lap, my hands running over the silk folds of the gown that pooled there. We always dressed well, even now in a time of revolution, given that our wealth was built largely on the silk trade. My gown that morning was of a rich raspberry silk, fitted tight around the bodice with a full, luxurious skirt. *Her head may be gone, but her power remains,* Maman often said of our dead queen and the influence she continued to wield over all matters relating to fashion.

Like most young French girls, Julie and I had grown up idolizing Marie-Antoinette, a queen known for her luxurious taste when it came to clothing, hairstyles, and jewelry. Her miniatures had been scattered all throughout our bedchamber. Of course, nowadays, one might as well sign one's own guillotine orders if caught possessing Marie-Antoinette's like-ness. But still, her mark on fashion lingered. We continued to dress in the lavish style of her ill-fated court, and on that morning, I was grateful for our wealth and our fully stocked wardrobes, for I noted how this young man, Napoleone di Buonaparte, studied my appearance, and I guessed from his attention that I met his approval.

Maman cleared her throat and Julie took up the efforts of hostess. "My brother, Nicolas, is not at home; he's gone to the factories to inform our workers of his happy release. Otherwise, I am certain he would reiterate the thanks that we all feel toward you, Joseph." My sister looked to our guest and I noted with surprise how she smiled, even appeared to blush.

Joseph returned Julie's gaze, preparing to reply, but he was once again preempted by Napoleone, who declared: "We were happy to help."

Julie looked from Joseph to the younger brother. "We?" she repeated.

Napoleone nodded, reaching for a second bun and biting into it before speaking: "My brother claimed the credit?"

I frowned, confused, as Napoleone jabbed Joseph's broad frame with an elbow, rattling off a slew of incomprehensible Italian before address-ing me: "I see that my brother once again basks in the sunlight of my connections. That's a Corsican family for you—you think *he's* unashamed, you should see how my sisters put me to work for them. Or Mamma! But I can't blame Joseph in this instance . . . who wouldn't wish to win the gratitude of the beautiful Clary sisters?" Napoleone smirked before elbowing Joseph once more. Gone was the confident and garrulous Joseph di Buonaparte of the previous day, so eclipsed was the large man by his much smaller companion.

"I'm good friends with the Robespierres, you see," Napoleone said, staring at me. "Augustin has become a champion of mine, and he has the direct ear of his brother, Maximilien."

"Maximilien?" Maman repeated the name. "Maximilien *Robespierre?*"

Napoleone nodded yes, as if friendship with the most powerful man in France—and the most feared, most ruthless prosecutor of revolutionary justice—was a mere fact to be served over morning coffee and brioche.

"And how . . . if I may be so bold . . . has it happened that the Robespierre brothers have become, how did you put it, your 'champions'?" Maman asked, her tone suddenly more hospitable, even if a touch incredulous.

"Ah, they call him the Boy General," Joseph said, speaking now, and his brother allowed it. "The Boy Wonder. The Prodigy."

Napoleone raised a hand. "You'll make me blush, brother." I noticed it then, the fleeting glance, just a flash, but Napoleone looked toward me, as if gauging my reaction. Then he clapped his hands, rubbing his palms together. "But, alas, Joseph, we must go."

"Already?" Joseph looked at his brother, disappointed but apparently willing to obey. Napoleone nodded. "Look at the hour. It's possible that word has come back."

Joseph shrugged. "My brother makes no allowances for social engagements. I was happy that he even allowed us to call this morning on our way into town."

"We have urgent business at the town hall," Napoleone said, rising.

"The Boy General?" Maman repeated the nickname as she rose from her chair. "A general, at your age?" Maman appeared impressed, even if still not entirely approving of this younger brother. "But you cannot be more than thirty years old."

"Twenty-four, in fact." Napoleone replaced the bicorn hat atop his head of dark, shaggy hair.

"Twenty-four! A general?" Maman eyed his uniform with newfound curiosity.

Joseph, who wore the civilian garb of loose pantaloons and a frock coat, bowed as he answered: "Ah, well, he is in fact a genius. And with our nation under attack from England and Italy and every crowned head in between, we need leaders, do we not?"

We walked the men to the edge of the terrace, and I noted with delight that Napoleone stepped in beside me. Leaning close, his voice soft, he spoke so that only I might hear: "My brother would not stop talking about you."

I glanced sideways at him, saying nothing, using my eyes to invite him to speak further. "I can see why," he added.

I bit my lower lip to slow the broad smile that threatened to burst across my face. I didn't know how to reply, but I needn't have worried, for Napoleone continued: "My brother is right. I have very little patience for social engagements, but I'd like to speak with you again. I will return this evening."

He said it as a statement, a point of fact; I had no opportunity to agree or disagree, for it was not a request. I offered a nod, but even that seemed unnecessary, for Napoleone, his gaze alert and probing, seemed to know already that I wished to see him again.

# Chapter 4

*Marseille*
*1794*

THE BUONAPARTE BROTHERS CONTINUED TO APPEAR REG-
ularly at our home. They were nothing if not men of their word.

Maman complained of a headache all that afternoon, so overwhelmed
was she by the events of the recent days. "What a disagreeable fellow, the
younger one," she said after they departed. "Joseph is blustery, but at least
he has a certain charm. Gregarious. But that younger one is surly in his
demeanor and uncouth in his manners. But I suppose we mustn't spurn
his friendship. . . ." She sighed. "He'll move on, soon enough, to some other
port, if he's truly the general he claims to be. Soldiers always move on." She
took to her bed for the rest of the day, and since Nicolas hadn't yet returned
from the workhouses, it was only Julie and me to receive Joseph and Napoleone when they called after supper.

It wasn't improper, given that Maman was at home and we were a group
of four in the salon, surrounded by servants buzzing throughout the
house, and given the fact that Julie, six years my senior, carried herself with
the decorum of someone twice her age.

"You are welcome, citizens." Julie stepped naturally into the role of
hostess, beckoning the men into the salon, where the last rays of the long
evening mixed with candlelight to give the large room a cozy glow.

"Maman is not receiving this evening, but she begs us to offer her sincere apologies, and her blessing that we may receive you both on her behalf."

I sat beside my sister on the silk settee, trying my best not to smile too broadly. It was all so unexpected, so dizzyingly exhilarating to have these men suddenly paying such ardent attention to us. They'd offered themselves as protectors, and yet now they seemed as intent on becoming suitors. *My first suitors*, I thought, my mind swirling with the languid evening breeze. I'd dressed with care before dinner—hoping that, in fact, Napoleone would return as he'd promised—selecting a flattering gown of soft lilac muslin, my brunette curls swept loosely back from my face and trimmed with pearls. Julie, I noted, had also dressed with care, selecting for herself a gown of pale green.

"Napoleone is unpleasant—I have to agree with Maman on that," Julie had said earlier as we dressed together. I didn't feel that way at all, but I didn't say so aloud. What she and Maman called surly, I found intriguing. What she considered uncouth, I considered a refreshing candor, a disregard for meaningless form and custom. It was funny, a bit odd even, that yesterday I had felt so shy under the gaze and attention of Joseph, and yet the following day, I longed to see more of his brother. Napoleone.

"But Joseph, he's awfully kind, is he not?" Julie continued. I turned my gaze sideways toward her. It was so unlike my sister to prattle about a man, to linger before the long mirror, fussing over the fall of her hair. Never, as long as I'd known her, had practical and proud Julie ever sought or welcomed the attentions of a gentleman caller—and there had been several interested suitors, given the size of her dowry.

And yet here she stood now, looking every inch the coquette, an unmistakable flush tinting her cheeks as she welcomed our guests, and I was certain it had little to do with the warm evening air.

"Can we offer you something to drink?" She leaned her head to the side, speaking to Joseph. My sister and I requested sherry, and the footman brought Napoleone and Joseph each a glass of port. Napoleone nodded a clipped thanks to the servant before his gaze swept the room, and I got the sense that he was capable of seeing things—noticing details with his intent green-eyed gaze—that none of the rest of us did.

The night was a pleasant one, and we opened the doors that led out to the terrace, where the sounds of the late-spring evening seeped in from the darkened gardens. "Might I suggest we take these outside?" Napoleone raised his glass. "The request of a soldier, you'll have to forgive me. I'm always more comfortable out of doors than inside these posh drawing rooms."

"I thought perhaps we could have some music," Julie said, gesturing toward the pianoforte. Diligent in her practicing, she was an admirably skilled player. I smirked, guessing that she wished to show this off to a certain older brother in our midst.

"But the sounds of a southern evening provide an accompaniment far more agreeable than anything we humans can produce," Napoleone said. My sister frowned; a gentleman should have picked up on the preference of his female hostess and quickly capitulated, but Napoleone either didn't understand her hint or didn't care to oblige it. "Joseph, shall we?" Napoleone gestured toward the terrace once more.

Julie blinked away her frown only when Joseph offered his arm to escort her toward the door. "Indeed." She nodded, slipping her arm through his, her music forgotten.

Napoleone offered me his arm, and I accepted it with a checked smile, wondering if he could feel the slight tremble in my frame. We walked out to the terrace in silence. "It is a good match, is it not?" Napoleone leaned closer to me, gesturing toward our older siblings, their backs turned to us and already making their way farther into the gardens. "I told Joseph that he would be well-advised to go after the elder sister." Napoleone said it with complete candor. "I have a knack for matters such as these. Probably because I understand human nature so well."

I looked at Napoleone, words evading me as I studied him closer. His features were delicate, his eyes alert and almond-shaped. His skin had a warm, honeyed complexion, the result of both his Italian heritage and a lifetime spent in the southern sun.

Was Napoleone di Buonaparte handsome? Perhaps not conventionally so—his frame was too narrow, his hair too long and unkempt. Though he kept his uniform immaculate, there was something unpolished, even a bit feral about his bearing. And yet, looking into his eyes, I found his features to be striking and expressive; I decided that his face was one that I would not easily grow tired of studying.

Realizing in that moment that I was staring too brazenly, I looked away, back toward my sister. Her figure glided along beside Joseph's into the dark evening, head tipped toward her companion in some conversation to which we were not privy.

"His agreeableness pairs well with her sincerity. And their ages match up better," Napoleone said matter-of-factly. I turned back toward him. His gaze was direct, determined, unabashedly so. "As do ours."

I felt my heart leap in my chest. I broke from his eye contact, staring instead around the terrace. The smell of jasmine floated on the night air, its perfume intoxicating, as a ship from the nearby harbor let loose its low, sonorous drone. Napoleone guided me off the terrace, and we stepped onto the soft grass.

"Do you play?" he asked.

"Pardon?"

"Piano. Your sister clearly wished to show her skills at the piano." So then, he had noticed. "How about you?"

"I play . . . though not very well."

"Then you must practice," he said.

I let out a small puff of a laugh, answering, "I suppose you are right."

He guided us, side by side, along a narrow path bordered by low shrubbery. "Mediocrity is never a desirable destination," he added. "At least, not when practice might transform mediocrity to competence, or even skill."

I nodded, considering my answer. *I prefer drawing,* I thought. Rather than the hours of technical practice required to master an instrument, I could take my parchments and chalks or watercolors to the seaside and draw for hours, sketching with only the colors of the landscape and my instincts as my guides. I wanted to share this fact of myself with Napoleone, and I was about to do so, but he continued before I could speak: "Of course, in some matters, all the effort in the world cannot make something of nothing. Like if one is simply bereft of intelligence. Or beauty. Or character. But even in matters such as those—intelligence, appearance, strength of character—a bit of effort applied might go a long way toward rectifying nature's deficiencies."

He was speaking so quickly, so decisively. "Joseph is a good man," he said.

"He does seem kind," I agreed.

"Your sister could not do better. He *is* kind. Agreeable. For most of our childhood he longed to be a priest. Until he learned what a hardship it would be never to marry. So now he longs to be a farmer instead."

I couldn't envision it—Joseph di Buonaparte tending olive trees in a vast field, sweating alone under a hot southern sun. No, a man like that belonged in a city, surrounded by crowds, flirting with the ladies and charming the men.

"He's nothing like me. He has no desire to be the soldier," Napoleone said. I enjoyed the velvety sound of his voice. I liked the way his lips rolled over the words, his accent foreign and pleasing. He made his sounds long and loose, his tongue as lilting with his vowels as the Mediterranean waves that lapped against the shores of his island home.

"He is older than you, isn't he?" I wondered why Joseph seemed to take his orders from Napoleone, if their birth order was what it appeared to be.

"By one year," Napoleone said, "but that has never meant anything."

"Oh?"

"No." He shook his head. "When Papa died, Mamma called me to his deathbed. She took my hand in hers, her face dry of tears. She looked me in the eye and said: 'Napoleone, you are the head of the family now.' That's the way it's always been between Joseph and me."

"How old were you when that happened?"

"Sixteen," he answered.

Sixteen. My age.

"I began my career as a soldier after that, graduating from the École Militaire here in France, finishing two years of study in just one year. I knew it would fall on me to take care of them all. Not only Mamma, but my sisters and brothers, too. Even Joseph."

"Was it always what you wanted—a soldier's life?" I asked, noticing the eager quality of my voice. I was fascinated by this young man, this Napoleone di Buonaparte, whose presence loomed so much larger over the space around him than his lean stature would have indicated.

"There was no other way for me," he answered. "It was clear from the very beginning: I was made for battle. In fact, I was conceived in battle."

"Oh?" I was highly aware of the way the bare flesh of my arm pressed against his own, covered under his uniform jacket.

"Papa and Mamma were both Corsican rebel fighters, part of the forces that in those days were encamped in the mountains, fighting against French rule of our island. I was conceived up in those hills. Mamma and Papa kept fighting until the very end. When it was my time to come, Mamma barely made it down from the hills and into our house, and she had no time to get to the birthing bed. I arrived on the rug by the front door, as she always tells me."

I gasped, lifting my hand to my mouth, grateful for the dark evening that hid my flush. "I've never been patient," he added, and I could tell from the way he said it that he smiled.

"And so you were born to a soldier in Corsica."

"Two Corsican soldiers. Mamma is as fierce as Papa."

"Two Corsican soldiers. But now you're in France."

"Yes. Papa eventually made peace with the French government on the island and we settled back on our family farm in Ajaccio. But I never lost the desire to fight. As a young boy, I would read everything I could on the great heroes—Julius Caesar, Alexander, Hannibal."

I nodded, vaguely familiar with those names, if not with the specific feats carried out by each of them. They were names of war. Names of men who had fought, long ago, just as men still fought in our day.

"Someday I will have my name in that list," he said.

I assumed this to be in jest, and I laughed, but I cut myself short when he continued to speak, with no hint of humor in his voice: "Only I won't hide like Caesar or Alexander did, behind the safety of my men and the lines. I will lead from the front, within the range of bullet fire."

"That sounds dangerous," I said. I had lost track of Julie in the large, shadowed gardens, but I didn't mind. Nor did she seem particularly concerned with acting as my chaperone.

"It is. But that's the idea. Fortune favors the bold. One doesn't win glory by hiding behind the lines. Why, during the Siege of Toulon, a British sailor ran a pike through my left knee in hand-to-hand combat."

I gasped, looking instinctively toward his narrow thigh, noting how he didn't appear to walk with a limp.

"Did that stop me? No. I killed the man just the same. Then I took a bloodied ramrod out of the hands of a dead man beside me and fired the cannon that would break the British chokehold on the port."

I blinked, my stomach going slightly queasy at such talk. And yet, I was undeniably intrigued. "But . . . how? How could you focus on the siege with a gash from a pike in your leg?"

He paused, considering his answer. "I have an extraordinary mind." I supposed that this, too, was meant as a jest, coming as such a flagrant declaration of his own aptitude. "I mean no humor in it," he said, as if perceiving my thoughts. "I do have a singular mind. I always have. In addition to my memory, I have this ability to be exceptionally focused. I can really only explain it like the drawers in a cupboard; I can open one drawer, deal with the matter to be found there, regardless of how large or small, and then set that aside, close that drawer, and move on to the next one."

We paused now, standing before the fountain in the backyard, its water bubbling in a soft gurgle, shimmering with a thousand fleeting diamonds as the moon shone down over its fractured surface. I turned to stare at the shadowed face of the man before me, this Napoleone di Buonaparte.

He returned my stare, his olive eyes alight in the glow of the evening. "That is how I know what needs to be done, and I do it."

I swallowed, unsure of whether he still spoke about his skills as a general, or perhaps something else. He said, "That is how I am able to focus, now, on my conversation with you, while I am in the middle of planning a major military operation."

"You . . . you are?" I said, trying to keep apace with his thoughts, even if he did make me feel as though I was caught standing on my back foot.

"Yes, that's why I was in such a hurry to get to the government offices this morning. I'm awaiting word from Paris. I've proposed a plan to unite the Army of Italy with the Army of the Alps and march into the Italian territories. After we've conquered those provinces, we will take Spain. It can be done. It should be done, for the glory of France. I'm the one who can do it; I await only the response from the Committee of Public Safety."

It was quite unusual to hear a man speak this way, laying forth the plans for such a vast military campaign—and, indeed, speaking about the very people who made decisions for our nation—in such a casual manner. "But until I hear from them," he continued, "I am stationed here. And I am going to court you, Desiree Clary." He said it as a statement, a matter of fact. As I was quickly learning, Napoleone di Buonaparte did not ask permission, nor did he make requests. He declared his intent and then he saw to it that his will became reality.

I was aware of some line that we were approaching. Or rather, Napoleone was approaching it, marching determinedly toward it, pulling me along. Did I wish for Napoleone di Buonaparte to court me? Yes, I did. Did it matter that I wished for it? Probably not. As I would come to realize, Napoleone was going to do what Napoleone decided to do. Those of us who occupied his orbit would soon learn that he had a pull to overpower all others; any challenge to his plans would only sharpen the blade of his will.

"But you are wondering why I've chosen you," he said, observing me, his fixed gaze probing my features, his eyes apparently seeing directly into the realm of my own swirling mind. I nodded, realizing that it was futile to try to hide anything from the inquiry of his stare.

"You are good, Desiree. You are earnest, you are pure. Do you realize how refreshing that is to a soldier? How rare that is in our world of revolution and discord? You are so many of the things I am not. I know myself, and I know what I need. And I need someone like you."

He took my hand in his, and I felt the ripple that passed from his flesh into my own. He smiled at me, a look as full with intention and purpose as it was with joy, and he raised my hand high in his own, gesturing skyward. My gaze inevitably followed the arc of our grip, and I stared up at a dark southern sky sewn with stars.

Then, as if on cue—as if the heavens themselves obeyed the commands of Napoleone di Buonaparte, the twenty-four-year-old Corsican refugee, the Boy General in the French army, a man with a plan to conquer much of Europe—a star careened across the sky, its tail scorching a crescent through the black firmament. Napoleone leaned closer, his whisper skittering along the rippled skin of my neck. "You see that?" he asked. "You see that flame that flies past, spreading light across its path? I am not a romantic man. I cannot offer you Joseph's constant chatter or easy laughter. I won't compose you poetry or woo you with sweet words. But come with me, Desiree, and you see how that star flies? You shall have the chance to do the same."

# Chapter 5

*Marseille*
*1794*

"MARRY HIM?" I GASPED, MY MOUTH FALLING OPEN. Julie was the least impulsive person I knew, which made the force of her news that much more shocking.

"Yes," Julie answered, meeting the astonishment on my face with her own level expression. "I've agreed to marry Joseph di Buonaparte."

"Does Maman know?" I asked.

"Yes, Maman knows." Julie turned back to the mirror, and I avoided her gaze, hiding the sting of it all—the fact that she and Maman had discussed, perhaps even planned, while I had been kept entirely out of the news.

Julie yawned. "I'm tired," she said. She sat at her vanity, brushing out her long dark hair. It was a warm evening and we were undressing for bed, having just returned from the theater with our two Buonaparte beaux.

"Nicolas approves?" I asked.

"He does," she answered.

"But . . . what do he and Maman think?" *Do they not see how hasty this is?* I wondered, though I did not say it.

"They are quite happy about it," Julie said, setting down her ivory comb. "Maman says it's a good thing to be aligned with a Buonaparte these days, and you know she cares for Joseph. Much more than she cares for—well, never mind."

*For Napoleone.* I knew my sister's meaning. I shimmied out of my un-laced corset and into my light sleeping shift, hiding my scowl.

"Come now, Desi." Julie's tone softened. "Aren't you happy for me? The older sister, the one you all worried would never marry?"

"I never worried you wouldn't marry," I said, my voice flat. Truth be told, I'd never thought much about Julie marrying at all. I'd never imagined she would leave, had never even considered that things could change. Julie was my sister, my constant, more reliable than even the rising or setting of the sun, since there wasn't an hour of the day or night during which time I did not have some awareness of Julie near me. With only my narrow, youthful understanding of the world, I'd never considered a scenario in which she would not be there.

Perhaps my face showed all of this, because my sister crossed the room and stood before me, her hands reaching to pull me into a gentle hug. "Don't worry, Desi. I shall still be your sister. We will always keep a place for you in our home."

*Our home?* So she and Joseph were already a "we"? And I was the guest they had agreed to welcome? I swallowed hard, forcing back the threat of tears. I would not cry, not when she was being so resolute about it all, so clearly treading cautiously with me, as if I were the emotional child whose eruption was to be anticipated and managed. I would be as practical, as mature as Julie was. I pulled away from the hug, leveling my chin as I looked at her. "When?" I asked.

"Soon. You know they are awaiting word from Paris on Napoleone's proposal for Italy. When Napoleone leaves for the capital, Joseph will go with him. If his brother continues to rise in the army, then Joseph could have a real chance at a career in the new government. He hopes to be a diplomat. He must be in Paris for that, beside his brother. And the only way I can go with him is if we're married."

My mind raced to take all this in, but my sister hadn't answered my question. "So, when?"

"Before summer's end."

"But . . . that's in a month! Surely you aren't going to marry someone you've only just met?"

Julie sighed and I bristled at the way she was clearly reminding herself to be patient—a patience born of pity, was it? I resented that.

"It is the best way, Desi."

"Why?" I asked, my tone biting. "How can you think that leaving home is for the best?"

"You know what it's been like at home. With Maman. Well, this could help things. Could help all of us. Joseph . . . he has connections but no wealth, and we have wealth but no protection. In aligning with each other, our deficits become obsolete, but our assets, united, become all the better."

I absorbed this, leaning away from Julie to lower myself onto the bed. She sat beside me, our bodies sinking slowly through layers of plush bedding. When she spoke, her voice was soft. "I'm not beautiful like you, Desi. Nor am I young. But I could not hope for better than Joseph. He is a kind man. He will be good to me, to our whole family."

"Well . . . why does it have to be so soon? Why can't you just wait a few years?" *Until I'm older and ready to be married as well*, I thought. But I didn't say it.

"Oh, Desiree." My sister patted my hand, turning to glance at her reflection in the mirror. "You don't know anything of the ways of men and women. There are certain things that . . . a lady . . . cannot do. At least, not until she's a wife."

I stood alone in the garden, the familiar space barely recognizable as I surveyed the scene. Maman had conjured our very own Eden at the Clary villa, with heaps of roses perfuming the air and hundreds of candles lighting the space. Joseph had ordered a massive arrangement of flowers delivered to our home for the wedding, accompanying the garlands of hibiscus and honeysuckle that draped the long banquet tables in the garden.

Nicolas had spent generously on both the wine and the meal. As night lowered around us, the air was redolent with the aromas of not only the flowers but also the feast—lamb and pork, saffron rice and stewed apricots, platters of whole fish, skin crisped, eyes and bones still in place.

The evening was balmy with just the slightest breeze, and though the seagulls cawed, though nearby the cafés of our busy harbor town filled with their nightly diners and revelers, we heard none of those summer sounds, for Maman had hired musicians for the night.

Nicolas had invited several of our family's most important clients, and he looked on, the *père de famille* now that Papa was gone, approvingly. Maman flitted about in her gown of midnight blue silk, tossing orders at the servants and accepting the compliments of the wedding guests. She'd been so nervous about a summer rain, but the night settled around us clear and comfortable, and the relief was evident in her broad smile.

The Buonaparte family arrived en masse just before the meal was served. I met them all: the younger brothers, Lucien, Louis, and Jerome. They all shared the same dark hair and languorous accents. They kept to themselves mostly, mingling only with the Buonaparte sisters, who were also in attendance. There were three of them: Pauline, Caroline, and Elisa, and they told me their names in quick succession.

I also met Mamma Buonaparte, the fierce Letizia, who entered the dinner party surrounded by her offspring. Looking at her, I guessed that she might have been beautiful once, perhaps in her youth, but her dark features were now sharp, scraped of all softness by age and hardship and the ruthless Corsican sun. She was quiet but civil with Maman, thanking her for her hospitality. I greeted her, staring into her unsmiling face, thinking that with her aquiline nose—much like her favorite son's—and stern, alert eyes, she might pose as a formidable matriarch of the former Roman Empire. "It is an honor to meet you, Madame Buonaparte," I said, lowering my eyes as I curtsied before her. She studied me with that probing gaze, and I instantly understood that this was another trait she had bequeathed to her son. I did not know what Napoleone had told her of me—or indeed whether he had told her anything at all—but I felt cowed as she returned my greeting, and then she turned to her nearest daughter and demanded a cup of wine.

With the Church having been carved up and stripped of all power, including that of blessing a marriage, Julie's wedding was just a quick legal affair at the town hall before the feast at our home. Fitting, as that is where she and Joseph had first met, just months before. Nicolas and Napoleone attended as witnesses, and I was to attend to Julie at the fête.

Of course the musicians began the night in the only way imaginable: a boisterous playing of "La Marseillaise," the anthem of our new Republic, given its name after volunteer soldiers from our own hometown sang it while marching on Paris. We sang along to the jaunty tune, men doffing their caps, women holding hands to hearts.

I felt a tap on my shoulder a moment after "La Marseillaise" concluded; I turned, already knowing whom I would find. Of course my eyes had been tracking Napoleone since the start of the feast. I'd watched greedily as he'd laughed with a sister—I believe it was the middle one, Pauline. I'd noted how he had waited solicitously on Mamma Letizia, bringing her plates of fish and cups of wine and slices of lemon cake. I'd relished seeing this other side of him with these women he loved, had even enjoyed the prick of envy that it had elicited in me.

"May I?" He held a hand toward me now as the musicians began their next set. I had barely placed my hand in his before he was guiding me forward into a swift quadrille. His steps were decisive and self-assured, if not entirely fluid.

Nearby, Joseph laughed, the sound of his joy soaring over the din of the partygoers and the music. "He is happy," Napoleone said, keeping his eyes fixed only on me.

"So is she," I answered. And she was; for that I was happy, too. But my heart did carry a pang of sadness, knowing that Julie would be gone that night. Nearby, to be sure—they had taken a modest but comfortable townhouse close to the square, only a few blocks from our neighborhood. But still, she would not be in our home, in the bedchamber we had shared since before my memories began.

"Mamma likes you," Napoleone said, his pronouncement pulling my thoughts from Julie. I stole a glance across the garden, where Letizia sat, scowling, flanked on each side by a daughter, two of her sons standing over her like sentries.

"She does?" I asked.

"She thinks you are a dear girl. From a respectable family."

I nodded. I supposed that was good.

"When you and I are married, I'll have my men fire a 101-gun salute before the feast," he said.

I would have tumbled to the soft grass, I was sure of it, had he not been holding me up, guiding me through the dance steps. *When you and I are married.* There'd been no proposal.

"How does that sound?" he asked.

I shook my head, looking into his green eyes.

"What is it?" he asked, his self-assured composure flickering for just a moment.

"At my wedding, I want something else," I answered.

"Oh?" He flashed half a grin, daring me to oppose him. "Pray tell."

I squared my shoulders, willing myself to speak my own mind: "I've heard that in Paris they have these new machines. They fill them with gas and they can fly."

"Yes, hot-air balloons," he said, nodding. "Indeed. I've seen one."

"You have? So they really . . . fly?"

"They really do. And if you want one at our wedding, we shall have one."

My eyes went wide. That was the second time in a matter of minutes that he'd said we would marry. Did he really mean it?

"But not yet," he said, his tone matter-of-fact. "I won't marry you yet. Not while I still await word from the Committee on my invasion plans for Italy. Not until after that campaign is concluded in victory. I wouldn't take the chance of making you a widow at the age of sixteen." He said it all with such decisiveness. It was settled. But like so many other moments, he had never even asked.

Did I wish to marry him? I considered the question a moment as he guided me through the dance steps. What did I wish—sixteen years old, dancing on the wedding night of the person closest to me in the world? Like everyone else in our fearsome, fragile world, what I wanted most was an escape from the Terror. I wanted my loved ones to survive. I loved my family, I loved my home—that, I knew.

But did I wish to remain at home, with Maman, now that Julie was gone? I knew the answer: no, I did not. Julie was speaking of going to Paris with Joseph and Napoleone; how could I stay behind in Marseille?

And now here was this singular, strong man, standing before me, telling me that I would go with them. A man more self-assured and powerful than

I had previously known possible. A man so much wiser in the ways of the world than I had ever hoped to be. A man who made plans, and knew how to act on them. The brother of Julie's husband. Just when it had appeared that my entire world would fall apart, he'd stepped into it—both he and his brother—and nothing had been the same since that time. Yes, I loved Napoleone.

And so I allowed myself to imagine even more—Napoleone and I joining forever, and my cleaving even more irrevocably to Julie and to Joseph, too. A new city, a new life. Our bond forged out of the strength of not just one union, but two. What could be better?

# Chapter 6

*Marseille*
*1794*

I HAD HOPED I WOULD STILL SEE MUCH OF JULIE AFTER her marriage, but I certainly hadn't expected her to appear back at home the next morning, before I'd even finished breakfast. I sat on the terrace with Maman, drowsily taking in my coffee, my mind and my movements sluggish from the previous evening's feast, from the fatigue of dancing late into the night. Maman looked triumphant but in need of a good rest. Even the gardens appeared tired, haggard from the spoils of the wedding festivities. But then I blinked in surprise, for there stood my sister before us, her eyes red and her face taut, her new husband standing beside her.

"Julie? Dear? Weren't the pair of you to depart for Nice this morning?" Maman and I both beheld the newlyweds with a shared look of concern; had their first night of marriage been so terrible?

Julie pressed her kerchief to her face, looking at me as she did so.

"Whatever is the matter?" Maman asked, looking from Julie to her new son-in-law.

"It's Napoleone," Joseph said, his voice hoarse as he took my sister's hand in his.

"What . . . what about him?" I asked, lowering my bowl of coffee onto the table as I slowly stood.

"He's been denounced," Julie said.

"Denounced?" Maman gasped the word. It was a fate only one step short of the guillotine—a certain path toward imprisonment, at the very least. "But he's close to the Robespierres," Maman said, as if to refute their claim.

"That's just it," Joseph said. "There's something much larger going on. My brother isn't the only one at risk."

Julie and Maman both went pale. I was certain that I did as well. I could not believe that I'd stood here in these very gardens just hours prior, dancing in his arms and speaking about our own wedding.

Joseph closed his eyes, running his large hand through his unkempt hair. He hardly appeared like a happy bridegroom on the morning after his wedding night. "I'd go into town to find out, but I fear the mob. Word from Paris is that Robespierre has been . . . killed."

Maman groaned as I collapsed back into my chair, my mind churning to make sense of this. Robespierre—our nation's de facto citizen ruler, the man who had overseen the executions of so many, even our king and queen—now dead? How mad could this nation possibly go? Who was left to be consumed if the rabid beast was now eating its own head?

"Not just Robespierre . . . his brother and Danton, Saint-Just, Desmoulins." Joseph rattled off the names we all knew so well—the names of the iron-willed and radical young men who had seized the reins of power, steering our government toward its ruthless policy of mass executions. "They are denouncing and killing one another. Paris is a bloody battlefield once more. Anyone close to them is at risk. And my brother was close with them, Augustin Robespierre especially."

"Where is he?" I asked. "Château d'If?" I offered the name of the nearby fortress that dominated our sea view, rising up out of the Mediterranean, an ancient and feared island dungeon.

"I wish he were that close." Joseph shook his head. "They've taken him to the prison in Antibes, Fort Carré. Do you know it?"

I shook my head.

"They have his writings to damn him as well," Joseph said. "He wrote some pamphlets in favor of the Jacobins . . . in favor of the Republic, really, but they are claiming it was to prop up the Robespierre government."

"So then, what is to become of us?" Maman asked, her triumph of the previous night turned to fresh terror. We were no better off for having aligned ourselves with the Buonapartes after all; in fact, we were now worse off.

"We wait," Joseph said. "It is all we can do. There is a general in Paris, Barras, who is leading this coup to oust the Jacobins from the government. He appears to be more moderate. Perhaps he will show leniency."

Julie stepped forward, placing her hand on my shoulder as she looked to her husband. "I would think so . . . for a war hero like your brother. And an innocent one, at that. He's committed no crimes against the nation."

Joseph sighed, crossing his arms. "We both know that neither service to the nation nor innocence is enough to save a man from the blade, my dear one." But then he turned to me, his tone lifting, the effort of this summoned fortitude visible in his weary expression. "Do not despair, Desiree. Not yet. My brother is beloved by his men; they would break down the walls of the prison and set him free before they'd allow him to ride a tumbrel to the guillotine. While Napoleone's men live free, there is hope."

Joseph urged us to rebuff despair, but Maman took to her bed. "We are ruined," she cried. "Just as I feared. I should never have been fool enough to believe that we could secure our safety by an advantageous marriage. Instead, we've now aligned ourselves with a family viewed as hostile by the government."

I found it increasingly difficult to be alone in the house with Maman. I took some refuge at my sister's home, though I knew from the twisting of her hands, from the pinch of her mouth, that she, too, was afraid—fearful that her husband would be arrested next. Nicolas was so preoccupied with managing Papa's affairs, and he'd taken a spacious townhome for himself closer to the port—in large part, I suspected, to escape Maman's daily carping—so I barely saw my brother, save for the occasional Sunday *dîner en famille*. When I wasn't at Julie's, I took off on foot. I walked the coastline, my fraught nerves propelling my steps along the craggy shore, like a sailor's wife haunting the limestone cliffs, eyes narrowed, fixed on the blue horizon in search of returning sails.

I thought of Napoleone constantly—he filled my daytime thoughts and prevented the sleep of my nighttime hours. If only I could have heard some word from him as to how he was doing—if only I could have visited, or even written him a note. But these were the days of revolutionary justice, and prisoners such as Napoleone were not afforded the luxury of correspondence with the outside world.

When I needed some task to occupy my restless hands, I drew. There by the water, I sketched my familiar coastline in chalk, hoping that my eyes would spot a ship's outline against the horizon, carrying Napoleone toward me and forcing me to scrap my work.

How could it all have fallen apart so suddenly and unexpectedly? I wondered. Just days earlier I'd been wrapped in my innocent bliss, newly tasting the sweetness of a first love, thinking that I might actually soon be married. And safe. And *happy*. He had spoken so surely—of love and of Paris and of a 101-gun salute at our wedding feast. And I had believed it all. In his presence, there had been no reason not to believe.

Yet there I stood—powerless once more. The person I loved was suddenly in the clutches of a cruel and random quarrel so much larger than we were. The man I had given my heart to was imprisoned in a medieval fortress, a dark and distant place from where we had no word. And suddenly, nothing was sure. Least of all his life.

The days passed in this manner. And then it was late August, a mild evening in the final days of summer. Dusk was lowering around the gardens, the first glimmers of starlight piercing the sky, and I sat outdoors. Maman had retired to her bed hours earlier, and I was alone. Passing time, knowing sleep would evade me yet again.

A movement on the far edge of the darkening gardens startled me from my gloomy solitude. My body stiffened instinctively before my mind caught apace; I wondered if my eyes were playing a trick on me, because there, in the murky light, a figure, narrow and lithe, climbed over the back gate and dropped down into our quiet yard. He didn't speak, though he stared at me, his face shadowed under his bicorn officer's cap. I sat motionless in my chair, awaiting some further clue. Was it really him?

He said nothing, simply waved me to him with an impatient hand. I rose, my senses heightened so that the call of a distant gull blared in my ears, the aroma of the nearby jasmine overwhelmed me with its heady perfume. I sailed toward him until he stood just a few steps away. "Napoleone?"

He raised a gloved hand to his lips, asking for quiet. His eyes flickered briefly toward Maman's window, where a lone candle leaked a feeble glow through the window.

"She's in bed," I said.

"And your brother?" he asked.

"He's taken a place of his own. Closer to the port."

Napoleone whispered when he spoke next: "There is someplace I wish to take you."

I nodded, putting my hand in his. I didn't look back, didn't consider going inside to rouse Maman to tell her I was leaving with Napoleone. This was my decision to make, and it took me less than an instant to decide. We walked silently toward the gate.

Outside, on the darkening street, a single military coach and driver awaited, and Napoleone held the door as I hoisted my skirts and climbed in. I swept the interior with my gaze and noted, with a pleased relief, that it was just the two of us. As soon as the door shut, closing us in together, I collapsed into his arms. "You're safe." I shut my eyes, burrowing my face into his chest as I clung to him. He had never kissed me, in all our time together, and yet now I heaped myself on him like an offering, begging him to kiss me, my face inches from his. "Thank goodness you're alive."

"I am," he said, patting my back, a restrained gesture, all the more so because of the complete unraveling of my own emotions. When he did not kiss me, I pressed my face to his starched officer's coat, breathing in the woolen scent, intoxicating myself with his presence after such an unbearable separation.

"I am alive, my dear girl," he said, his tone quiet, as if soothing a child. He lifted me out of his arms and held my eyes with his gaze. He looked tired, physically diminished somehow—his eyelids had a heavy, sunken quality. His hair was more unkempt than usual, matted to his head. His cheekbones were sharp crags, the point of his chin made even more severe without any extra flesh to soften the contours of his face. And yet, as weary as he looked, his green eyes were aflame, restless even. I felt my entire body drawn toward him, pulled, like the tireless waves dragged ashore by the unrelenting and overpowering tide.

"Where are we going?" I asked. I could see through the coach window that we headed south, the water on our right as we drove away from my neighborhood. In truth, I didn't really care where we went; I was happy simply to be in his presence.

And evidently, he had no intention of telling me. "It's a surprise," was all he offered. I tossed my head back, briefly shutting my eyes. "I'm not certain I can stand another surprise."

"This will be a happy one."

I exhaled an audible sigh. The coach began to pull us away from the sea, up a hill. I glanced at him sideways, a mixture of impatience and complete willingness to entertain this adventure of his. The air smelled of saltwater and the flower-laced breeze.

"You'll have to close your eyes now."

I balked, smiling coyly. "Is that necessary?"

"Entirely necessary," he said, pulling off the tricolor sash from his uniform jacket. "And in fact, I think I shall add this, for a bit of extra assurance." He covered my eyes with his sash, and I laughed, enjoying the elaborateness of this plan, whatever it was. "Napoleone di Buonaparte, do you mean to tell me that prison has made you into a romantic man?"

"Prison can claim no such credit. You, Desiree Clary, have made me into a romantic man."

My heart swelled at this declaration of his, and I found myself yielding to his plans for this nighttime ride. "And what of the driver, does he know where we're going?"

"Of course he knows where we're going. I'm an officer; I never set out on a mission without a well-thought-through plan, and my men are always prepared."

"Well then, General Buonaparte, if this is a mission, I suppose I am your target?"

He leaned close to me now, I knew this by the warmth of his nearby body, by the tickle of his words that landed on my neck: "You are the spoils, the treasure."

I wanted nothing more than to remain like this, close beside him and alone. I heard the steady *clip-clop* of the horses, felt the tilt of the coach, and I knew that we continued to climb the hill. With my eyes shut, my other senses grew ever more heightened, alerting me to the details of our surroundings: the thin mist of saltwater in the warm night air, the clatter of the carriage wheels on the hillside road, the nearness of his body beside mine in the coach.

Finally we halted, and Napoleone placed a hand on my arm. "I'll help you out."

"Can't I look now?"

"Not yet," he clucked, holding the sash in place so that my sight remained obscured.

I stepped blindly out of the coach, my hand in his, giggling as I leaned on him to guide me down to the soft ground. He walked me a few paces, the wind whipping my face, my skirts, my hair. I detected the faint and rhythmic roar of ocean waves shattering against the rocky shore far beneath us.

"*Et voilà*, now you may look." He lifted the sash and I opened my eyes, blinking into a vast expanse of velvety evening sky, the stars stitched across it like diamonds. Far below us spread the rolling expanse of sea. I gasped, for I knew this hilltop. "La Bonne Mère!"

"What?" he asked.

"Ah, it's what we locals call it." I gestured up, away from the sea, toward the massive shape of Notre Dame de la Garde that hugged the cliffside just behind us. "Our Lady of the Guard. That church is . . . was . . . believed to watch over all of Marseille. The Good Mother." It was an ancient hillside temple, fortified by ramparts and a massive drawbridge, once a house of worship for France's kings and commoners alike. Each year of my childhood, floods of pilgrims descended on Marseille from all over France, climbing this hill under the strong August sun to celebrate the Feast of the Assumption. Of course my family had taken part in those holy day celebrations—all of Marseille had. But all of that was in the past now, distant memory, beaten down and dulled like the rocks pounded by the ocean so far below.

"Or, rather, what we *did* call it. Until . . . of course . . . the Revolution," I clarified. No one prayed inside the walls of La Bonne Mère anymore, not since revolutionaries armed with pikes and pitchforks had breached the defenses and marched across the drawbridge, arresting the abbot and melting the ancient silver statue of the Blessed Mother. They'd dressed the statue of our Savior in a red cap and tricolor, the same uniform they put on the head of the disgraced King Louis in Paris.

"The bells no longer ring," Napoleone said, gesturing up toward the church tower. "They've been melted to make bullets."

I nodded. The clanging of the bells had long ago been replaced in our city by the slicing sound of the guillotine blade, the lusty cries of the crowds gathered in La Place. "But the tower still stands," he said.

"Tallest point in all of the city," I said, well-versed in my local lore.

"Come," he said, taking my hand, pulling me away from the coach.

"Where?" I asked.

"Up."

"Up? You mean . . . climb? The bell tower?"

"Ever been up there before?" he asked.

"Of course not."

"Best view in the south. Possibly in all of France. Come." He repeated the order, tugging my hand.

"How . . . how would we get up there?"

He flashed a wry smile, lifting a lone rusted brass key from his pocket. "Didn't I tell you? I'm an officer; I never set out on a mission without a thorough and well-thought-out plan." I didn't ask further, but instead allowed him to take my hand and guide me out of the breezy night.

Inside La Bonne Mère, the air was cool and dark, and the space still held within it the vestigial aroma of incense, burned so many times during its centuries as a house of worship. "I haven't been inside here in years," I whispered, and the sound of my voice echoed off the stone walls, stripped bare of their priceless trappings.

We crossed the massive transept, our shoes clicking against the ancient stone floor. The nuns and priests who had maintained this church and served our community had long ago been arrested or executed, around the same time that the stained glass windows had been shattered. I shivered, squinting around at the naked interior. There were no candles to light our step, but I knew that all of the precious holy relics and adornments had been seized and sold at auction. Some of the king's relatives had been imprisoned here for a time, earlier in the Revolution, before eventually facing the guillotine; they themselves had served as perhaps the least practically useful of La Bonne Mère's revolutionary spoils.

"Over there," Napoleone said, pointing. The tower was tall and grand, its winding staircase coiling upward from the far side of the church. Napoleone let go of my hand when we reached the stairs, ushering me before him.

I quickly grew short of breath as we climbed, my corset pinching against my lungs. When I paused at the second landing, he stopped behind me, granting me a moment's rest before urging me on again. "Almost there," he said, and I could tell that he did not gasp for breath as I did. This was not difficult for his thin, strong frame.

We reached the top after what felt to me like an interminable climb. I stood still, gulping in the salty night air and the view of our surroundings. "Worth our labors, was it not?" he asked.

From behind a balcony we had an open view, and we stared now, out over the entire world. I marveled at all that I could see: my city; the narrow, serpentine streets and alleys; the old port glimmering amid a tangle of flickering lights from taverns and homes and streetlamps and cafés. Château d'If loomed before us as well, the stone fortress rising up from the dark blue bay, an outline carved in black against the receding horizon of the Mediterranean. The sea unfurled before us, mirroring the vast expanse of stars and moonlight overhead.

"Is it not beautiful?" he asked, his body directly behind mine. I looked down, out over the sweeping view, but all I could focus on was his nearness. Would he finally kiss me?

"For eleven days, I was a prisoner, caged, staring out at that water." He put his hand on my lower back as he spoke. I blinked, forcing myself to hear his words, even as my senses thrilled at the press of his palm on my body. "Wondering at each sunrise if it would be my last. I told myself: the sea is forever, it existed long before I did. It shall outlast me. In a world where absolutely nothing is certain, at least that much is true."

I turned to him, weaving my hand through his. "How is it that you are free?"

He stared at me, his dark green eyes flickering with the lights of the southern stars and the rolling sea. "I should tell you that I arranged some gallant fight. Pirates and a stolen cannon, a swordfight on the ramparts. Is that what you are hoping for?"

In truth, I did not care how he had secured his freedom, only that he was near me. And would remain so. He studied me, his angular features arranging themselves in an appraising expression. "Are you happy I'm free?"

"Happy?" I let out a quick exhale. "That word is not enough."

He smiled, a rare sight. And then he went on: "My conscience is the only tribunal before which I will allow myself to be called. I was innocent. I knew it. The new men in power showed me leniency."

I lowered my eyes and whispered my confession: "I was so afraid."

"But you were brave. And that is more important."

Had I been brave? I did not know. I had not really had an option. But I liked that he saw strength in me.

He took my chin in his grip, angling my face upward. "You care for me?"

I nodded.

"You really do?" He seemed to need some further assurance. And so I decided to give it to him, freely. He had, after all, just called me brave, and I wanted nothing more in that moment than to be worthy of his affection. "I . . . I didn't even realize, until I thought you were gone, just how much I do."

"Then you will agree to something," he said.

I didn't ask what; I allowed my eyes to pose the question.

"You will be mine," he declared.

I swayed a bit, but his voice remained steady, as if I were one of his men and he were issuing a command: "Listen to me, Desiree. When I was in that miserable cell, I made a vow. I vowed to myself: I will never be at the mercy of those men back in Paris, fools, ever again. I will make my own fortune. I need you beside me if I am to do great things. If I am to *be* great. You . . . and Joseph. My plans for Italy will be dismissed now. Who knows what is to happen with this war, now that there is a new regime in power. But I will go to Paris, and I will discover what is next for me. I must be in the capital. But I won't leave without your word that you will follow. You will come to me, and become my wife."

I didn't really understand all of it, not fully. Not right then. I didn't yet know what such a life would hold. I simply knew that, having stood on this peak, I could not go back down. I could not descend to a lesser height of loving or living. I knew that life with Napoleone would be unlike any life I would have with any other man, unlike any other life I could ever imagine for myself. Life with Napoleone meant an existence lived out on a higher level—and that was what I now yearned for.

"Will you, Desiree?"

"Yes." I nodded.

"Say it," he commanded. "I need to hear you say it."

"Yes, I will be your wife," I said, my voice overpowered by the roar of the wind, by the distant shattering of waves against rock, by the tremor of my nerves. But I did say it, and he heard it.

"Then it's settled, Desiree." He made one quick nod of his sharp chin. "I am yours . . . I am yours for eternity. We make that vow, here, before the constant sea. No one can undo it," he declared.

He took my hands in his and I nodded my assent once more, feeling stronger, less shaky, in his grip. A thought flashed across my mind: I considered in that moment all those in my life whom I knew to be married, even in love. I thought of Father and Maman and the life they had lived together. I thought of Julie and Joseph. And then I thought: *Poor, limited souls!*

How pale their loves shone when held against the light cast by this young man who stood before me. They knew nothing of this sort of love, for they did not bask in the love of Napoleone di Buonaparte. With him, it was all so much more, because he was so much more than any other person I'd ever known.

Napoleone reached for me, took my frame in his grip, and pulled me to him. I had wondered whether he would kiss me, and now he did. He kissed me with a raw, unapologetic hunger. I'd never been kissed by another man—and now, I probably never would be—but I was certain that that didn't matter, for no other kiss could have rivaled his.

As so often seemed to happen, Napoleone led, and I met his command with a yearning assent. I assented as he guided my body down, as he removed his uniform coat and spread it on the cool stone of the bell tower floor to make a soft blanket. And then he laid my body on it, and his body was on mine. I kissed him without shame, telling myself that I was his and so, too, was he mine. I ran my hands through his hair, down his neck, over his back and his arms, exploring his skin and muscle. He was so thin in my arms, sinewy but strong. He responded to my touch with a soft sigh, and that emboldened me to continue to claim his body as my own, offering mine in return. He was feral in his own needs as his hands began to explore my body, seeking out parts of me that had never before been offered to another. He fumbled a bit with my gown and I laughed as I helped him, sliding the layers of fabric aside.

I gasped when he undid my corset and yanked my shift aside. I had never been so exposed to a man—to anyone—but my modesty melted away and was replaced instantly by a wave of pleasure as his mouth took over for his hands. "Desiree," he said, his voice hoarse. "The Desired One."

He was frantic now, tearing away silk and linen in order to draw the bare surfaces of our flesh closer. I thought back to Julie's words: *There are certain things that . . . a lady . . . cannot do. At least, not until she's a wife.* But here I was, all too willing. I was to be his wife, after all. He had said we were bound together for eternity. We'd made our vows to each other, and surely that was all that mattered.

Napoleone didn't ask; he took my body's movements, my low and steady hums of delight, to be my assent. And indeed my body welcomed his into mine. He shut his eyes, his face twisting with what I took to be pleasure, his movements quickly mounting in both speed and urgency. He groaned, ever more frantic, my body searing with both pain and the promise of some imminent bliss. But then, before I knew what had happened, he cried out in one long, breathless gasp. I lay under him, motionless, wondering what had gone wrong, as he collapsed on top of me, his surrender sudden and unexpected. He kept his eyes shut as his face went slack.

I felt a small tinge of disappointment as he rolled off of me, landing on his back on the stone floor. He sighed, half laughing, pulling a hand to his forehead, running his fingers through his matted hair. I pulled my shift up, concealing my breasts; it was an instinctive, quick gesture, one I made without even thinking, and then I wondered why I suddenly felt so ashamed, so self-conscious about being exposed before him, when only a moment before I had invited his touch.

We lay side by side in silence, our breath gradually slowing as the sea continued to besiege the earth far beneath us. I had no idea what to say, what to do. I felt thirsty, and my body ached. He looked toward me after what felt like an eternity. As he faced me, he slid his hand between my thighs. I resisted the urge to squirm under his bold, undaunted grip. It was my instinct to recoil all of a sudden, but I did not wish for him to know that. I did not wish to offend him. I remained still as he leaned close and placed one quick kiss on the top of my forehead, his hand firmly between my legs as he whispered: "I've conquered before. But that, my Desired One . . . was the best siege yet."

# Chapter 7

*Marseille*
*Autumn 1794*

NOTHING WAS THE SAME FOR ME AFTER THAT. I WAS changed—Napoleone had entered my world and overturned the way I viewed my place in it. I was, suddenly, a woman. A powerful, desired woman, and one who carried a secret.

Whenever I thought back to what we had done, to the intensity with which he'd touched me and kissed me and looked at me, the way his accent tinged his words as he called me *Desired One*, I felt newly dizzy. We had a secret that was ours and ours alone.

How did they not see it? I wondered. Maman and Julie. As members in their own right, how did they not detect that I, too, had become one of the initiated? Wasn't there suddenly some fever to my cheeks, an awareness to my expression, a sense of knowing that somehow seeped out of me? But I shared my secret with no one; I guarded it, hoarded it, savored it. Julie, too busy in her new role as wife, in her zeal to set up a household of her own, in her determination to have a baby, did not notice. Nor did Maman; perhaps Maman underestimated me. Still thought of me as nothing more than a girl. Perhaps she didn't know what I was capable of, the latent power that had suddenly uncoiled within me, the passions and promises that I could draw out of a man. And such a man as Napoleone, at that.

France, too, was in the throes of a sudden and drastic change. As a nation, we were as unstable as we had ever been since the overthrow of Louis and Marie-Antoinette. With Napoleone out of prison and the Buonapartes, for the moment, safe, we tried to make sense of the ever-shifting situation. The journals and newspapers were giving the recent chaos a name: the Thermidorian Reaction, labeled thusly because it had begun in the hot summer month of Thermidor on our revolutionary calendar. Beginning in Paris, it had been an uprising against Robespierre and his Jacobin friends, a backlash against the radicals who had made mass executions and public denunciations a matter of state policy.

By summer's end, the Jacobins were out—guillotined or fled—and a new government had solidified behind a group of moderates: advocates of the free Republic but comprising largely liberal landowners, pragmatic businessmen, even members of the nobility. They vowed to dismantle the dreaded Committee of Public Safety, proposing to replace it with a group of appointed executives and a national legislature.

"This is good, the new government, is it not?" I asked Maman as she and I walked to Julie's one afternoon for a visit. The days were getting shorter, the thick moisture of summer thinning into a pleasant autumn coolness, and I enjoyed the feeling of the gentle sunshine on my face. Napoleone had been gone the past few weeks, assigned to the camp in nearby Nice for training exercises, but I hoped for news from his brother when we visited Julie that afternoon.

Maman sighed. "I've given up trying to divine anything in this madness," she answered, weaving to avoid the young women who peddled flowers and spices along the port's crowded square. Not quite so hot and pungent, the autumn air smelled of saffron and lavender, of bread baking in the nearby *boulangerie,* and I found myself in a generous mood. I reached into my pocket and tossed the closest peddler-woman a *sou* that I had left over from running errands for Cook. Maman didn't notice but kept her eyes fixed firmly ahead. "Nothing has made sense to me in years. Sometimes I think it a blessing, your father's fate. That he didn't live to see his country come to this."

I knew from Napoleone and Joseph that the men now in power seemed to be less radical than the men they had deposed—so far at least. The daily public executions in our town square had, for the moment, been halted. And so I allowed myself to hope that perhaps our fear might at last subside, even just a little bit.

We arrived at my sister's home, a modest but comfortable townhouse, narrow and comprising four stories, of which my sister and Joseph occupied the bottom two. The rooms were not overly large, but they had gracious floor-to-ceiling windows and soft mint-green shutters. With no income yet from Joseph and just an allowance from her dowry, my sister employed only a few servants and an older woman named Selene to cook. The house had a walled garden in the back, and we found Julie there, sitting in the shade with Joseph as they drank lemonade. To my surprised delight, Napoleone sat with them.

"Desiree, Maman, hello." My sister glided toward us as both men rose. Napoleone wore his officer's uniform and he stood rigid, his expression unsmiling, as it so often was when he found himself in group company. Julie, on the other hand, appeared happy, as she usually did these days; she and Joseph were indeed a good match. "I'm so delighted you've come," Julie said. "Napoleone is here from Nice; isn't it a wonderful surprise?"

"Indeed," Maman said, but her tone indicated otherwise. She had still not warmed to him, even though she knew he was courting me. *Imagine if she knew the full truth,* I thought, recalling how he had told me we were bound to each other for eternity.

I curtsied toward my secret fiancé, smiling, ignoring Maman's displeasure. I hadn't seen him in weeks, and now, there he stood. The small garden suddenly felt warm, far too cramped for this many people; all I wanted was to be alone with him.

"Mother, I need to speak with you." Julie turned from me and angled herself toward Maman.

"Oh?" Maman eyed my sister.

Julie's voice was suddenly grave with concern as she said: "I fear my bedroom is not spacious enough for the armoire we currently have. Would you come inside—with Joseph—and give us your opinion on what sort of piece we might find to replace it?"

"*Replace* it? But that armoire is a family heirloom. No, no, no, you cannot be rid of that piece, my foolish girl. You must simply rearrange the other pieces in the room." Maman threw her shoulders back and nodded, ready to dispense her opinions. "I'll have a look."

"Oh, I knew you'd have an idea." Julie steered my mother away, beckoning Joseph to join, and I was certain she could sense my gratitude.

Now, with only the two of us remaining in the garden, I hurried toward Napoleone, putting my hands out. He raised them to his lips and kissed them, the hint of a smile softening his sharp features. "Desiree." He stared at me intently, and I resisted the urge to shift under the weight of his gaze. "You've grown more beautiful in my absence. It is hardly fair that the other men of Marseille should have the chance to appreciate your charms while I, a soldier, am stuck in the barracks."

I wanted to fold into him, to cover him with my kisses, to insist that no other man in Marseille would ever be the recipient of my charms—I saved myself only for him. But I restrained myself, sensing even in my youthful ebullience that a lady ought to hold back some of her overflowing joy, to allow a man such as Napoleone to indulge in a bit of competitive jealousy. Cocking my head, attempting a coy smile, I said: "Then I think it best that you not stay away for too long."

He liked that, as was evident in the way he nodded. "Sit with me?" He gestured toward the table and chairs.

I sat, refilling his lemonade and pouring myself a glass.

"I'm not sure how long we have alone, and there is so much I need to tell you," he said.

"Oh?" I took a slow sip, trying to look poised, careful not to spill any of the cool drink even though my hands trembled with excitement at this unexpected reunion.

Napoleone told me how he had been stationed in recent weeks at the barracks in Nice and that he'd just heard back from the new Parisian government on his proposal to lead the army into Italy. He had been correct—they had indeed denied his request. "Our national resources are depleted," he explained. "There are bread shortages across the country. Pockets of resistance—pro-monarchy communities—are erupting in fighting, and the army is being deployed to crush those revolts. The French people are exhausted . . . as hungry as ever, yet no nearer to any relief."

I listened, absorbing the news. Nearby, the horn of a ship droned, its bellow low and long in the harbor. "Well, then there is one bright spot," I said.

"What is that?" he asked.

"If not Italy, then you stay here with me."

He lowered his gaze, his finger rubbing a line through the condensed moisture on the outside of his glass. "I'm afraid not," he said after a moment, meeting my eyes with his.

I frowned, unsure of his meaning.

"I plan to go to Paris." From the way he said it, a declaration, I knew that he was decided.

"Paris?" That seemed, to me, like the worst place to be at the moment; hadn't he just explained to me the extent of our Republic's instability?

"Within this chaos and disorder lies opportunity," he said, noting my confusion.

"But why must you go already?" I hated how I sounded as soon as I asked the question—like a petulant child. But he was only just back from Nice. And *prison*. What of us? How would he court me for marriage all the way from Paris? He looked away, his stare landing on the burst of red hibiscus that climbed the nearby trellis.

When he spoke next, his words and his tone were direct, matter-of-fact, with no crack of emotion in his voice. "I will use this response from the government to go to Paris and speak to them directly. Introduce myself to them, now that they know who I am."

The joy of our reunion was suddenly gone. I shifted in my chair, glowering at my glass of lemonade as he continued.

"I am languishing here in the south, Desiree. With each day that passes, I am squandering the goodwill I acquired with my fighting in Toulon. Now is the time for a young man with talent and ambition to put himself forward; I need to be present in the capital, to pledge my loyalty to the new regime and seek out my next appointment. Perhaps I might find an older general to take me under his patronage and advocate for me with the new government. I am not sure yet—I only know that I would be a fool not to act during this time of change and upheaval."

"When will you go?"

He folded his hands on the table. "Soon."

"How soon?"

"I am here . . . to say farewell. I will leave this week."

My whole body sagged. Before I could form a reply, he leaned toward me, but he did not reach for me, did not put his hands on mine. "I've never concealed from you the fact that I feel called to greatness. In fact, I've been very honest with you about it."

I blinked, willing myself not to give in to tears. After a moment, I nodded, acknowledging this. "How long will you be gone?"

He shrugged his narrow shoulders, his face expressionless. "There is no way to know."

"I . . . I would go to Paris, you know. If we were married, I would join you as your—" But he raised his hand, shaking his head, speaking decisively before I had the chance to finish my thought.

"It's not safe for you just yet. I will go. Allow me to ingratiate myself with the men who now hold the reins of power. I will make a place for myself under this new leadership, and then I will send for you and my brother." As so often happened with Napoleone, it had all already been decided. Both for himself and for me. My only choice, it appeared, was to accept his verdict. But at least I knew I could trust him; I knew how badly he wanted Joseph beside him, and he had told me he would send for Joseph *and* me. I could trust in that and take some comfort there.

Muffled voices traveled out to the garden from the house—Maman was returning with Julie, and my sister was speaking loudly to give us warning. They were arguing over the armoire.

"We have so little time together," Napoleone said, leaning close to me, finally putting his hand on mine. "You won't spend it in a quarrel, will you?"

I shook my head, grateful at least for his touch. "Can I see you tomorrow evening?" he asked. "Come back here, tell your mother you are visiting Julie."

"Julie and Joseph plan to go out to the theater tomorrow evening," I answered, aware of the plans my sister had already made.

"Yes, they do," he said, nodding. "That's why you and I shall meet here."

Napoleone opened the door when I arrived at Julie's home the next evening, as if he'd been watching for my arrival. "Good evening," he said.

I thrilled, feeling as if I transgressed by walking into the quiet interior of my sister's home, even though I'd visited the place more times than I could count. But this was different; Julie and Joseph were out, and Napoleone and I were alone. We had not been alone, not entirely alone like this, since the night he had led me up the hill to Notre Dame de la Garde. I felt my face grow warm at the memory. Would the same thing happen this evening? I wondered. I was young, but I wasn't a fool; I was certain that he'd thought of it in inviting me here, where it would be just the two of us. Just as I'd thought of it in accepting his invitation.

Napoleone put his hand on my shoulder, pulling my attention back from my fidgety thoughts. "Have you eaten supper?" he asked. I nodded, even though I hadn't. My stomach had been a tempest all afternoon in anticipation of this meeting.

"Then can I pour you a drink?" he asked.

"Yes," I agreed. "Where is the cook?" I asked, looking around for the older woman who worked in my sister's home.

"I've dismissed her for the evening," Napoleone said.

I removed my bonnet and gloves as he fetched a carafe of wine and two glasses, and we made our way out into the garden, where the languid sounds of evening sailed across the air. He poured us each a drink and we sat in silence, serenaded by the hum of the city, of the breeze slipping through the trees, sticky with the scent of the nearby saltwater.

"Another?" he offered when I'd emptied my glass, and I nodded, accepting his refill.

"It is pleasant here," he said after a while. It was a statement, rather than a question, but the thought that came to me in reply was instantaneous: *Then why do you insist on leaving?* But I bit the words back, saying only: "Yes, it is."

"I won't miss it, though."

His words stung, the blunt candor of them; I was grateful for the evening, for the way the darkness concealed my frown.

"We are too far from everything that truly matters. Sea breezes and Mediterranean views are all well and good. Some soldiers would choose this, gladly. But it's a false peace—a siren's call. A beautiful but dangerous diversion."

I sipped my drink, not answering. So much of what Napoleone said came out sounding like a riddle to me.

"The only thing I shall miss . . ." His tone was different now. Emotion had seeped in—even longing. "The only thought that troubles me as I depart, Desiree, is the thought of being away from you."

I turned to him, seeing just the vague outline of his features in the muted glow of distant lights, the moon and stars shuttered behind clouds.

He reached for me, taking my hands in his. "Do you promise you shall be faithful?" His voice was tinged with a sudden urgency, and I wanted to laugh at his concern, at the absurdity of his wondering such a thing. I squeezed his hand, bringing it to my cheek and pressing his cool palm to my skin. "More than promise. I vow it."

"Why would a Clary trouble herself with a Buonaparte?" he asked, exposing a rare chink in his usually impermeable armor of self-assuredness. But I could hear what was surely there—worry. And doubt. He continued: "I'm a penniless man who has been imprisoned. A man without a nation, without powerful friends. Why would you choose me? I'm out of favor, with no hopes for any career advancement."

Maman had said the same thing earlier in the day, in her own way. A passing remark that she knew I'd hear. "We already have one Buonaparte; I think that is plenty for our family." I'd ignored the barb, clinging to my secret plans to marry my soldier as soon as he could send for me from Paris. Or, if Paris did not work out for him, I'd go to him wherever he was. *Yours, for eternity.* As constant as the sea. That was the vow we'd exchanged, atop the hill at La Bonne Mère.

I looked at him now, leaning forward in my chair, my own voice matching his urgency: "Napoleone di Buonaparte, you could be a farmer tending fruit trees and you'd still be worth more to me than any dignitary in the capital. Know that as you go to Paris: know that, no matter the outcome, I am faithful to you and eagerly awaiting the day when you can send for me to join you."

He pulled me out of my chair and lifted me into his arms. I was amazed at his strength, thin as he was. I heard the receding chorus of frogs and other night creatures as Napoleone swept me into the house, leading me into the spare bedchamber on the ground floor. There, without a word, he lay me down on the bed and I allowed it, meeting his kisses with a hunger that only seemed to fuel his further. I suppose I had known that the evening would lead to this; I suppose I'd even hoped for it. He clawed at my gown, struggling with its layers, groaning with impatience until I helped him. He had less trouble with the pieces of his own uniform.

I closed my eyes and stifled the urge to wince in the moment when our bodies joined. His movements were more rushed, more rough, than I might have liked. It was only a matter of minutes before his whole frame convulsed, collapsing over me, his slack mouth falling open. It was as it had been on the hilltop—hasty and brusque. Once more, I couldn't help but wonder if I had done something wrong. The ardor and attention from just the moment earlier were so quickly gone, and he pulled away from me, his gaze suddenly distant.

I lay there in the silence, questioning if there was supposed to be something more between us than simply these quick and curt couplings. I knew nothing else and thus had no way of knowing what to expect. Of course, I would never have dared to ask Julie, for I knew what she would say about my engaging in such behavior before any exchange of formal wedding vows. And so I ignored the itch of longing that throbbed inside me long after our lovemaking was complete; I pushed aside the desire I felt, the wish I had that Napoleone would continue to hold me, continue to love me. To put some tenderness or softness into his caresses. To keep me close even after his own ferocious needs had been so hastily and roughly sated.

He was scheduled to leave on the next day's tide. I felt tired and glum as I joined Julie and Joseph to see him off at the crowded port. Julie stood beside me, holding my hand, as the brothers said their farewells in hasty and muttered Italian. I noticed how Joseph stuck a fistful of money into his brother's pocket when they pulled apart.

When it was my turn to say goodbye, I remembered Napoleone's emphasis on bravery as a necessary character trait, and I forced myself not to cry. "You'll write me?" he asked, his voice firm as we embraced one final time.

"Of course," I promised.

"I won't become an afterthought? A jilted man put aside as soon as this ship pulls away and some other man comes calling at the Clary mansion?" He stared at me with his burning green eyes, as if appraising me one final time, probing for any flaw or weakness he might have heretofore overlooked.

I weaved my hands through his. "You, Napoleone di Buonaparte, could never be an afterthought."

The ship sounded its horn in warning, and Joseph helped his brother load his one trunk. Napoleone gave us a final wave before stepping onto the gangplank. As I watched his figure recede, a trim outline against the backdrop of the ship and wide blue sky, I allowed myself tears for the first time.

He couldn't see my crying at this point, and, besides, hadn't I been strong, like he'd asked? Well, now that he was gone, it was more than I could bear not to give in to the crush of sadness. I felt a sense of loss, and indeed of *being* lost, as I watched his shape growing smaller, replaced by a foreground of rolling Mediterranean surf. He had loomed so large over each of my days since he'd entered them, but now, his absence left me feeling unmoored. I wondered—I worried—whether I had perhaps forgotten how to be myself without Napoleone beside me.

And yet, even in his absence, everything in me and around me had shifted. My life had taken on a new orientation; Napoleone was the fixed pole at the center of the rest of my life, even though he was miles away, in a distant capital that I knew only in my imagination.

Napoleone kept me busy, even after he was gone. He'd left me with a regimen he'd designed, a course of study that involved music, reading, philosophy, and other subjects dear to his own curious mind. Not a particularly avid student in my own youth, I was nevertheless grateful for the distraction at first, relieved that I could apply my energy and focus to something that I knew would make my Napoleone proud. He'd opened a subscription to a musical journal in Paris so that I might practice the most current pieces on my piano. He urged me to practice my singing as well. He left me with a long list of texts I was to study: the writings of Rousseau, Montesquieu, Thomas Jefferson, Marcus Aurelius, and so many others. He urged me to write to him with my opinions on their subject matter.

*You must seek always to improve your mind, my dear girl,* he wrote in his first letter from the journey, posted while he was still aboard the ship carrying him north. *For I plan to be a great man, and so you must be the great woman who stands beside me. Imagine the pride I will feel when my fellow generals remark that my wife is a woman without equal, an enlightened citizeness of our Republic, one who can expound on the preeminent writings of political philosophy and theory.*

*In truth,* I wrote back to him, *what I'd rather do than spend hours reading or practicing the piano is to work on my drawing. And I've settled on the perfect subject: the Boy General, Napoleone di Buonaparte. I shall attempt to sketch your profile in pencil, with only my memory as guide. This will serve the double purpose of keeping my hands applied to the improvement of my art, while also producing a finished product that will provide much pleasure as I look on it.*

*A fine idea,* he wrote back to me. *But I suggest one change to your plan: when the sketch is complete, you must send it to me. I would like to see your artistic skill at work, and I would like to see what sort of likeness you render. Otherwise, I approve heartily of this idea, and am delighted to know that you will be spending hours thinking of my face, and not some other man's.*

I chuckled at this, pleased to read of my lover's jealousy. And then I saw his postscript:

*Only, be sure not to neglect your books, my dear Desiree. I still await your opinions on Rousseau and Jefferson.*

As the weeks passed and the autumn air grew milder, I tried my best to make my way through the dense tomes Napoleone had selected for me, but, really, once he'd made it safely to the capital, what I craved were the details of my lover's daily life in Paris. What were his lodgings like? What did the women wear in the city, now that Marie-Antoinette was no longer there to set the fashion for the nation and indeed for the whole continent?

Was dancing permitted once more at balls? Was it really true, as we read in the journals, that it was the new style to wear red strings around one's neck to imitate the effect of the guillotine?

Napoleone chided me gently when I asked about these details rather than discussing politics or music or philosophy in my letters. *Frivolity is destructive, and complacency is corrosive, and neither must ever be tolerated, my heart.* And yet he begrudgingly answered my queries, indulging my requests for gossip with the matter-of-fact accounting of his soldier's attention to detail: *Everyone is determined to make up for their sufferings, to make light of the hell which they have just narrowly escaped.* He told me about a ball he had recently attended with several other officers, one of the infamous *Bal des Victimes,* a Victims' Ball. *It is à la mode to have been imprisoned, only barely saved from death, to have lost a loved one to the guillotine. The women wear the red ribbons around their throats indeed. They crop their hair into the coiffure à la victime, the victim's hairstyle—shorn short, like the damned whose locks were clipped on their way to death.*

I read these details with a mixture of horror and curiosity. The Terror of recent years still seemed so fresh, so recent, a caged beast that might yet rise up and strike at any moment, but there in Paris, they made merry in the wake of it.

Napoleone, from his letters, seemed both disapproving and daunted. *Paris is one large flea market. The wealthy compete to see who lost more,* he wrote. *So, in that way, my poverty is fashionable, I suppose. And yet, the women who run the social calendars of this city don't truly have nothing, as they preside over their salons, seduce their wealthy lovers, host their fêtes in their grand drawing rooms surrounded by silk and champagne.*

Napoleone wrote to me of autumn and then winter, his words foreign as he described the shifting of the leaves, the first blanketing of snow. *I don't even wear gloves, as they are an extravagance for which I cannot pay. You, my Desired One, my summertime love, serve as a warm and pleasant refuge for my thoughts as I shiver here under a thin coat which I cannot afford to replace.* For me, a girl from the south, where the trees always remained in full leaf and the birds sang year-round, I could only imagine myself beside him, holding fast to his arm as we shivered, walking the quays of the Seine and watching the floes of ice that bobbed atop its surface. I wanted so badly to be there with him, to see what he was seeing, even if it was so terribly cold. I was ready to begin my life beside Napoleone, to leave my childhood in the south and embrace the adventures with which he'd filled my mind.

As the months strung together, I was slow to make progress on my pencil sketch. I'd begin each morning, only to spend several hours of frustrated work that usually ended in my tearing up the parchment and vowing to start anew the next day. The truth was, the longer we spent apart, the harder I was finding it to sit and conjure the finer details of Napoleone's profile. Nothing that I put on paper came close to recalling the image of the man who inhabited my memory. Watercolors of the sea and gardens proved far easier, and I found myself gratefully distracted by those projects, though I did not dare send them to my exigent lover.

He asked me about my progress, wondered when he would see my completed drawing, but I demurred, telling him it was not yet ready. He pestered me, also, about my music and quizzed me about my philosophy reading. But he did not speak of his military career or what his plans were for advancement. Did not mention when he would send for me. I did not learn until the spring that he had led a failed mission to try to recapture his island home of Corsica from the English. Joseph had known, but Napoleone had sworn him to secrecy, for fear that I would worry too much. I learned of it only once he was safely back in the capital, failed in his attempt, writing to me once more from his dingy rented room at the Hôtel de la Liberté.

"My poor brother." Joseph spoke to Julie and me on a rainy afternoon in Marseille. I was at their home, as I so often was those days, eager to escape Maman's headaches and my own restless melancholy. My sister was not yet pregnant, a fact that I knew upset her, but she and Joseph had a nice, gentle manner of speaking to each other, and Joseph, attentive husband that he was, remained solicitous of my sister's happiness above all else. He had made it clear that he saw me as a sister, a member of their family and one who was always welcome in the Buonaparte home.

But on this day, I could see as we sat down to luncheon that Joseph's mood was heavy. "It's Napoleone," my sister explained, serving me a slice of cold ham. "Joseph has had a letter from Paris this morning."

"And?" I asked, looking to Joseph, feeling the hastening of my own heartbeat. I hadn't had a letter that morning.

"He's miserable." Joseph sighed. He told me about Napoleone's recent loss to the British naval forces off Corsica. "He's disgraced. He lost several ships and had to abandon the mission. The Brits chased him across the Mediterranean. He returned to Paris humiliated and without any hopes for advancement."

"What has happened since he's returned to Paris?" I asked. Could a man be sent to the guillotine these days for failure to win a military campaign? Certainly we'd heard of it happening often enough in recent years—officers executed for any number of reasons, even in victory, and often-times without a trial.

"They haven't arrested him for it," Joseph said, assuaging my fears. "But they've reassigned him. To the Army of the West, under General Hoche."

I knew about the west, the area of France called the Vendée; Napoleone had told me about the pockets of resistance there. Royalist factions in and around Brittany were holding out hope of overthrowing the Republic and reestablishing the monarchy.

"Napoleone rejected the assignment," Joseph added.

"But . . . why?" I'd never known my fiancé to turn down a military assignment.

"He has no desire to move to some remote outpost on the Atlantic, where the only action he shall face will be to fire on Frenchmen. And so now"—Joseph shrugged—"he's without a place, even in his beloved army."

I hadn't known any of this; Joseph was giving me an unvarnished account so unlike what Napoleone ordinarily confided in me. He wrote to me that my letters were the brightest moments of his day, that I made up a full half of every aspiration he held for the future. But he'd never admitted to me any sort of pessimism about his place in the army.

And yet, even in his notes to me, I had detected a sort of restlessness, a lurking melancholy, a sense of unease, even if only veiled or obliquely hinted at. I knew that he struggled without enough money. I knew that he felt very much an outsider, excluded not only from the new administration, but from the festive aspects of Parisian society as well. But Joseph now painted a picture that was far less hopeful, even than Napoleone's bluntest notes to me.

"He has no hope for promotion if he goes to Brest and takes up a position under Hoche fighting the royalists. There's no glory in crushing your own countrymen. Plus, Hoche is young, about the same age as Napoleone. He's not dying or retiring any time soon. What can my brother hope to gain from his patronage?"

"So then, what does he plan on doing?" Julie asked. I knew that her own life plans were on hold while Joseph awaited his brother's next move. They, like me, had intended to go to Paris—they had put their hopes in Napoleone's plans to gain a position for himself in the new regime and send for us. But now, it all appeared so uncertain.

"For the first time in his life, I don't know that my brother has a plan," Joseph said, sighing, looking forlornly from his wife to his luncheon plate. "Currently, there are more than one hundred generals ahead of him in seniority. His hopes for elevation look unlikely. He's doomed to be standing still for a good long while, and there's nothing Napoleone loathes more than standing still."

Julie looked to me. "Well . . . what does he say to you about it?"

I shifted in my seat, glancing over at the clock on the nearby mantel when it chimed the new hour. "He . . . he has said nothing to me, just yet, about these recent developments." In truth, I had no idea when, if ever, he would confess these same troubles to me that he confided to his brother.

"He doesn't want you there while he's so miserable, Desiree," Joseph said. "He can barely afford to feed himself, let alone a wife. And, of course, with a wife, there's always the possibility of ever more mouths to feed, bodies to keep warm." Joseph drifted off, turning back to his plate. I knew that his intention was to bolster my spirits, to explain his brother's behavior, even though his words were having the opposite effect.

Julie's face was pale now, too, the topic of children in a marriage surely bringing to mind her own longing for a baby. I took her hand and gave it a silent squeeze.

Joseph went on: "He feels he has to be in Paris, to be near the seat of power, if he has any hope of grabbing an opportunity . . . if and when it might present itself. But he's penniless. They're not paying him a *sou* while he's not employed in an actual mission. He's got no salary, and yet he's supporting Mamma and our sisters, paying for our younger brother's training at the military academy out of his own scanty savings. He is hungry, wandering the streets of Paris without a friend. His lodgings are cramped, barely enough for him, and certainly not spacious enough for a wife. But do not believe he has forgotten you. If not for your love, Desiree, he might find himself in front of a passing carriage. He tells me as much, not infrequently."

My brother-in-law's words offered some small consolation, but I wished that Joseph—that *Napoleone*—would see that my attachment ran deeper than such material concerns. All I wanted was to join him, to be his comfort. I did not care that his boarding room was cramped, that his pockets were empty. But how could I tell him that without offending his pride? He wished to make something of himself, and he wished for me to believe in him while he did so.

And yet, it seemed that our hopes hinged on so many unknowns, on an opportunity that we prayed would someday present itself. Our future remained as blank and indecipherable as the pencil portrait I was trying—and failing—to sketch. I longed to go to Paris with Julie and Joseph, to begin the adventure for which Napoleone and I had planned. To start my life as a bride, with a home and a family of my own. But Napoleone was not yet ready to start that life with me.

I did not like feeling so stuck, so entirely helpless. I knew no other way to help my lover, so I prayed each night. Alone, in the dark, I called upon God and his Virgin Mother, even though the Church had been outlawed from our Republic and praying to Jesus or the Virgin Mother was illegal. I prayed, even though I had never been a particularly pious girl. *Please, dear God, please give my Napoleone the opportunity he seeks, so that he may distinguish himself. So that, in his greatness, he might finally send for me and welcome me to Paris, where I might fully become his wife.*

Hands clasped, I begged God to grant Napoleone some opportunity for greatness. I could never have guessed how resoundingly these silent entreaties of my heart would be answered.

# Chapter 8

*Marseille*
*Spring 1795*

I KNEW THAT MY SISTER HAD NEWS WHEN SHE AND JOSEPH invited me to a private dinner in their home. My usual habit was to simply stroll through their door, no matter the time of day, so for them to appoint a specific time on a specific date—surely they had something to tell me. I guessed that my sister was finally expecting a baby.

And yet, Julie's demeanor when I arrived to her home was not one of joy or excitement. I had dressed well for the evening, anticipating their happy news and an impromptu celebration. Perhaps Letizia and other members of the Buonaparte family might even be there, since a baby would mean joyous news for them as well. I longed for Napoleone but reveled in the idea that my sister's child would unite us even closer, being half his blood and half mine—just as our own children would someday be.

"Julie!" I hugged her when she received me in their small front foyer. The home smelled wonderful, aromatic with Selene's cooking, and I guessed it might be roasted duck. "Here." I handed her the bouquet I had clipped from our backyard, fragrant clusters of jasmine and honeysuckle.

"Thank you, Desiree," she said, taking the flowers absentmindedly, placing them down on the hall table without water or a vase.

I looked at her a bit closer, noting how she shifted from one foot to the other. I expected her to be out with it right away, but instead she ushered me into their dining salon with a taut smile. "Are you hungry?" Julie asked over her shoulder, her eyes avoiding mine.

"Oh, yes. I suppose."

"Good. Dinner is ready."

We entered the dining room where Joseph awaited us, glass of wine already in hand. But no champagne on the table, nothing that appeared to give the meal a celebratory aspect. "Ah, Desiree. Good of you to come." He helped us to our seats, and I noted the place settings: it was to be only the three of us, no other members of the Buonaparte family. The old cook entered just then, bearing a large platter of roasted duck with charred orange rinds.

"How are you?" Joseph asked as he received the platter and began to serve the food.

"I am . . . I am fine," I answered, accepting his gesture and passing him my plate for a portion of the duck.

"And Maman?" Julie asked.

"She's the same . . . she's fine," I said, narrowing my eyes toward my sister. "You saw her yesterday, did you not?"

My sister shrugged, smoothing the linen napkin on her lap. Then she glanced toward her husband. "We have news," he said, propping his elbows on the table, staring straight at me.

"Yes," I said, nodding.

Joseph took Julie's hand and announced: "We are moving."

I lowered my fork to my plate, looking from Joseph to Julie, my appetite for Selene's duck entirely forgotten. I said nothing. Eventually, Joseph added: "Leaving Marseille."

But what of their baby news? I cleared my throat. "Going to Paris? To join Napoleone?"

"No," Joseph said, stroking Julie's hand in his grip. "We will be moving to the countryside, to a farm near Saint-Julien."

I knew of Saint-Julien—it was just outside of Marseille, a rural region called "Les Olives" by the locals because of its plentiful olive groves.

"Olives," Joseph said, as if guessing my thoughts. "It will be the simple life for us—the land, the woman I love, and the family we shall build." He said it with such conviction. As if it was already done. Perhaps it was. And yet, my sister had not included me in any of her considerations, in any of their conversations.

Joseph must have read the disappointment on my face, or else he was simply a kind man, for he hastened to add: "Of course, you are our sister, Desiree. You are welcome to join us until . . . well . . . until my brother makes a decision on his future."

My mind raced to make sense of it all. "But what about Paris?" I looked to my sister. "I thought that the plan was for you . . . for all of us . . . to join him in Paris?"

"Yes, it was. Well, it's just that we . . ." Joseph paused, and I saw the meaningful look that passed between my sister and her husband. Only a flicker, a momentary exchange, but clear enough for me to catch it. I felt a stab of envy as I noted the gesture—as I considered all that was said and understood in that simple, intimate glance. My sister was not alone, regardless of the outcome of Joseph's and Napoleone's plans. She would not be left alone, but I might be.

Joseph's voice had a cautious, measured tone when he continued: "We are not certain what Napoleone plans to do at this point. Whether his future will indeed be made in the army, in Paris, or if he will have to . . . if he will choose to do something else."

I looked to Julie. She nodded, leaning toward me: "We can't wait forever, depending on something for which there is no guarantee. Of course, Joseph would have gone to Paris to serve in the new government, if in fact the opportunity had come up. But at a certain point, we must make our own plans, based on what makes sense for us."

So there it was: the lofty dreams of the Buonaparte brothers had been deflated. Napoleone had hoped to be a great general marching across Europe; his brother had hoped to ride that greatness to a position in our government. But now that Joseph believed that his brightest hopes for the future lay in planting olive trees—what did that mean for the man I was going to marry?

"But as Joseph said," Julie continued, picking up her fork and knife, turning her gaze to the roasted duck, "you are always welcome in our home, Desi. No matter what happens."

I feared how Napoleone would receive the news. That he would see it as I saw it: his brother had lost faith in their bright plans for the future.

But rather than despair or anger, Napoleone received the news with approval, an almost giddy enthusiasm. *It has always been the simple life that my brother has desired. First he wanted the priesthood. Now he wants his olives. If they will retire to the countryside, then perhaps we should as well,* he wrote to me, waxing rhapsodic about a rural life. *They will buy an olive grove, then we shall buy a château! I'll plant you a vineyard and we shall make our own wine. It could be as it was in Corsica—we shall never want for olive oil or grapes. We will have a brood of small Buonapartes to run riot over the entire neighborhood.*

I read and reread his words, allowing myself to see the picture he painted. Leaving Marseille, relocating to a farm in the country. It wasn't the future I had prepared myself for, the future that would take me to Paris. And certainly the life of a rural farmer's wife would be entirely different from that of an officer's wife. But Julie would be near, at least. And Napoleone seemed enthusiastic, more enthusiastic than he'd been in months. In a time when so many in our country faced futures far more bleak or hopeless, it wasn't a bad fate, I told myself. I even began to grow somewhat excited at the thought of seeing my Napoleone out of his uniform and atop a draft horse, clipping past his rows of vines.

But then as soon as I reconciled myself to our new idea, our new plans, he wrote again. This letter also pulsed with a frantic energy, but now my fiancé fixed on yet another target: the Far East. *With each passing day, I become more and more convicted in my belief that new lands wait to be discovered and conquered. I long to win glory for all of France. I intend to ask for an assignment to Turkey. The sultan's armies need modernization, and I might do for them what Lafayette once did for the rabble in the American colonies. Now that would be something—a veritable challenge. Imagine seeing the holy lands of Constantinople. Or India! I could acquire a post in the East India Company's army and come back rich as a rajah. What say you to that, my Desired One? Can you fancy yourself riding into some jungle camp atop a bejeweled elephant? I imagine that I might look quite dapper in the loose pantaloons. And you in a sari? Why, I simply must see it.*

As I completed the latest letter, I burst into tears. I couldn't even bear to share its contents with Maman; I knew how violently she would protest. And I myself didn't want to believe that Napoleone could really fancy such a fate for us, so far from France and the people we loved. I had agreed to move to Paris, or to the countryside—but India? And without even asking me before seeking such an assignment?

But I needn't have worried about that letter, either, for just a few days later, he wrote again: *I am working on a book about us, my darling. You are the beautiful Eugenie, a sweet girl of sixteen. I am the faithful soldier turned farmer, Clisson, who is forced to leave his vines in order to return to military service for his country.*

I lowered the letter, once more taken aback by his words. My Napoleone, suddenly a novelist? I read on, absorbing the excerpt he had included for my opinion. Clisson, the story's hero, meets a beautiful young girl in the company of her older sister. *Their eyes met. Their hearts fused, and not many days were to pass before they realized that their hearts were made to love each other. They felt as if their souls were one. They overcame all obstacles and were joined forever.*

Even as I considered these words, lofty and ebullient as they were, I couldn't help but worry that the real man, my Napoleone, was receding. It was all well and good that he could write such soaring lines about our love, about our fate being joined—but when would we in fact be allowed to live as such, as Julie and Joseph were? Why did he always seem as if he were waiting for something to fall into place before he could fit me into the larger picture of his life?

More so than these vague and impassioned words, I longed for what I saw in my sister's household: morning coffee and casual conversation over the newspapers, an uneventful supper in the evening. The unvarnished moments of life, the moments without ceremony, without lofty exclamation or abstract elegy.

Fortunately, Joseph and Julie seemed entirely willing to welcome me into the unvarnished moments of *their* married life, since I was not to have any of my own just yet. So I was at Julie's when we first heard the news of the uprising in Paris.

It was a cool, pleasant fall day in Marseille. Privately, we still referred to it as we had in former times—the month of October—but by the revolutionary calendar, we were to refer to it as Vendémiaire.

Joseph was out, in town running errands and seeking further news, but Julie had received that morning's journals, and so we read the accounts while sitting in her small salon, a rising sense of dread filling us both. Just a few months prior, the Parisian government had changed hands once again; I knew from the journals, as well as both Napoleone's letters and Joseph's remarks, that the new leaders were already drowning in debt and charged with unchecked corruption and incompetence. People across Paris were starving, no closer to having bread than when Marie-Antoinette had allegedly suggested they eat brioche.

From around the nation we heard fresh rumors that Austria saw our weakness and intended to resume its fight against our Republic, gathering troops along our borders with the hopes of putting a Bourbon—a relative of Austria's rulers—back on the throne. People simply wanted an end to the suffering and the chaos. Food on the table and order in the streets.

The royalists within the capital seized on this moment of unrest, taking arms and marching toward the government headquarters at the Tuileries Palace. Rather than following government orders to keep the peace, members of the National Guard had instead defected in large numbers, joining the crowds of rioters. Paris was once more a war zone. Who, we wondered, would win?

When Joseph finally returned home that afternoon, Julie and I practically pounced on him, hurling questions, demanding more news. The capital was overrun by warring mobs, he told us. The government had shut down, some members barricading themselves inside the Tuileries, others fleeing for the countryside. I knew that Napoleone had had plans to attend the theater this week—he had told me with pride how he had secured a free ticket from a colleague in the army, as he'd never have been able to purchase a ticket of his own. But surely he would cancel those plans, I reasoned with myself. Surely, he would do the sound thing and stay away from the heart of the city. Or would he? Scared for my fiancé, I voiced this fear to Joseph: "He'll be smart, he'll avoid the mobs, won't he?"

Joseph frowned, absentmindedly fiddling with the tricolor cockade on the lapel of his coat. "This is nothing new to my brother."

"War?" I asked, unsure of his point.

Joseph shook his head. "War, of course. But I mean riots. As a young man, he was stationed in Paris when the rabble first marched on the Tuileries. At that time, Louis and Antoinette were living there, under house arrest after being dragged from Versailles. The mob decided that even the Tuileries was too soft a sentence for their tyrants, so they stormed the palace. Overran the national guardsmen, who wouldn't raise their guns to fire on their countrymen, not even to protect the royal family. The crowd then marched with sharpened sticks and pitchforks up to the royal apartments, where they barged in on the king and his family."

I remembered this moment, of course. It had been before I knew Napoleone or Joseph or any of the Buonapartes, but every person in France had read of this stunning chaos in Paris. Never before had a king of France and his wife and children been treated so roughly—it had been one of the low moments before the Terror began in earnest.

Joseph continued: "With cannons pointed at his heirs, Louis was forced to put on the tricolor cockade and the red cap of the revolutionary and march out onto the terrace to wave to the crowds, like a dancing bear performing his steps at a circus. They hissed and jeered, hurled lewd insults at Antoinette."

I cringed, imagining the indignity. And then I wondered what any of this had to do with Napoleone and his current well-being in Paris.

"My brother saw it all," Joseph explained. "He was sitting across the street, outside on a terrace at a café. He recounted it to me, and I remember his disgust. Not only with the crowd, but with Louis's cowering. With the national guardsmen who stood idly by, failing in their sworn duty to protect the crown. My brother is no monarchist, believe me, but he does believe in might. He does believe in the importance of strong authority. He detests weakness, indecision, half measures that allow for chaos and anarchy. Leaders who bow to the rabble. So, my guess is that he is somewhere in Paris right now, advocating for a strong military response." Joseph paused a moment before adding: "The question is—who in Paris cares what a young man called Napoleone di Buonaparte thinks?"

I barely slept that night for fear that my Napoleone had in fact decided to go to the theater and, in doing so, had put himself in harm's way near the Tuileries Palace. I waited until dawn began to seep through the windows before rising from bed, dressing myself in the thin scrim of early light, and shuffling glumly down to breakfast.

Cook was just starting the fire, and soon the pleasant aromas of baking bread and coffee wafted from the kitchen into our breakfast room. I accepted coffee gratefully. Mother did not rise to join me that morning, so I sat alone with my impatient nerves.

Even if he wrote immediately, Napoleone's letter would not reach me for days. So, with no better way to pass the excruciating hours, I decided to walk to my sister's townhome. Outside, the crowds were already gathered in the square, my fellow citizens eager for news. The pace of guillotine executions had slowed in recent months, and I hadn't heard of one occurring that day, so I thought it safe to pause a moment. "Excuse me?" I sought out a young woman who held a babe in her arms. "What news from the capital, citizeness?"

She looked at me a moment, shifting her bundle before speaking with the slow, nasal drawl of the uneducated class. "Remember that young officer who lived here just a little bit ago? That Corsican fellow who'd fought at Toulon—the one with the odd name?"

My voice was faint as I offered: "General Buonaparte?"

She nodded. "Aye, that's the one."

"Of course," I said, feeling the blood drain from my face. "What about him?" The baby whimpered and the woman began to bounce, momentarily distracted. "Please," I begged, "what news of him?"

She looked back to me. "Seems he's made himself a right hero. Saved the Republic from a whole lot of rioters."

I steadied myself by placing a hand on her shoulder, and she looked at me askance, shifting her baby away from me. I removed my hand. "Pardon," I said, glancing around listlessly for a newspaper. "Excuse me . . . may I?" I asked an elderly man nearby. He handed me the paper in his hands, and I blinked at the words. There, in massive letters across the top:

NAPOLEON BONAPARTE SAVES THE NATION!

I noted the change in his name, the disappearance of letters, giving it a

French rather than Italian look, but it could only be my fiancé. I read on, the sound of the crowded square receding to a distant hum as my eyes devoured the words. I read how he had stepped forward in the midst of the army's paralysis and put forth a strong plan to crush the coup. How he'd hastily led a force of men to seize the cannons from nearby forts, bringing them into the capital. How he'd arranged his troops like an army preparing to mow down the enemy.

The picture formed in my mind as I read on. My Napoleone, uniformed, leading men on a frantic mission to seize the arms from around the city. Napoleone, atop a horse, ordering his men into neat lines, the center of Paris suddenly a battlefield he was determined to hold. Napoleone, green eyes aflame, ordering his troops to fire on the approaching mob.

All around me the noise grew, pulling me from my reverie. It was surreal, looking up from the paper and beholding the crowd. A group of men had hoisted the tricolor over the square, and now a small cluster of students stood cheering, fists raised in the air as they cried out, "*Vive Général Bonaparte! Sauveur de la République!*"

Napoleone had just recently told me that he did not wish to go to Brest to put down the royalist uprisings there, that he did not wish to fire on his fellow countrymen. Now, however, he had fired ruthlessly on French men and women, and he was being heralded as a national savior for doing so. What, I wondered, must he think of all of this?

# Chapter 9

*Marseille*
*Winter 1796*

"**P**ROMOTED? WHEN?" I ASKED, KISSING MY SISTER'S CHEEKS in greeting as I welcomed her and her husband out of the rain and into the drawing room of our family home.

"It's quite big news, in fact." Joseph slipped out of his damp cloak, handing it to the servant. "He's been credited with averting a civil war, and he's been appointed Commander of the Army of the Interior."

"Oh?" I tried very hard to bring a smile to my face, even as I wondered why my fiancé had not written to me of this news himself.

Joseph continued, warming his hands near the fireplace: "He's replacing General Paul Barras, a powerful man who seems to have taken Napoleone under his wing. Perhaps Barras shall be the friend—the patron—for whom my brother has been hoping."

I lowered myself into an armchair, folding my hands in my lap, falling silent as I considered this news. All winter long, as the damp and the breezes skittered off the Mediterranean, I'd been longing for word from Paris, but Napoleone had become very inconsistent in his writing. Whereas before he used to grow needy and covetous when I skipped even a day, begging me for letters, he now regularly went weeks without sending word to me. He rarely mentioned or apologized for his periods of silence, occasionally making offhand references to his workload and recent responsibilities following the coup. But now, with a promotion, it seemed that he'd be even busier.

I kept myself busy with my art and my reading, with visits to Julie and Nicolas, errands to help Cook and Maman, but I was no fool. After the part he'd played in crushing the attempted uprising of Vendémiaire, my fiancé had gone, seemingly overnight, from a man who could not afford a cup of wine in a café to being the toast of Paris, indeed of the entire country. He was referred to as "General Vendémiaire" and sometimes even the "Savior of the Republic." I knew that surely he was enjoying the sudden fame.

"With big promotions come big pay, too," Joseph said, lowering his bulky frame into the chair beside his wife. "Forty-eight thousand francs a year," he whispered, an offhand and perfunctory acknowledgment of the poor taste of discussing money with ladies. But Julie and I both gasped at this announcement. Forty-eight thousand francs a year! It was a sum that a year ago would have caused Napoleone to faint. Why, with such a salary, he could afford to hire a secretary to write daily to his fiancée, if he so wished.

What pained me the most, more than even my longing for his presence, was the fact that he did continue to write faithfully to his brother, even as he used his busy schedule as his excuse for neglecting me. Did he not realize that I was close enough to Julie—and therefore Joseph—to know how often he wrote his brother? To see how he still found the time and energy for detailed accounts of his outings to theaters and restaurants, evenings in the fashionable faubourg salons hosted by Paris's socialites?

One recent letter to Joseph, which Julie left out on the table in their salon, I managed to pilfer and read: *Everyone here appears determined to make up for what they have suffered; determined, too, because of the uncertain future, not to miss a single pleasure in the present.*

So then, I wondered, in what pleasures was my fiancé partaking?

When his letters *did* arrive at my home, they increasingly carried words of scolding or irritation. Gone were the flirtatious greetings and the affectionate teasing, replaced instead with a stern coldness: *You never told me what you thought of Rousseau, and now I am left to question whether in fact you even read the books I asked you to acquire. As I've said, not infrequently, these works ought to have an effect not only on your mind, but indeed, even on your very soul.*

What could I say to that? I longed for word from him, and then, when it finally came, it seemed like each letter was filled with mounting frustrations on his part over my shortcomings. He no longer asked to see any of my drawings, and I, feeling sure that my novice technique would draw nothing other than censure from him, had stopped offering to show him.

*Your previous letter, Desiree, contained several grammatical errors; I have asked you on more than one occasion to apply yourself to the improvement of your prose and to the formation of your reason.*

Oftentimes, I finished these critical letters in tears, feeling that my mood was worse on days when mail came than on days when it did not.

*You wrote to me of the concert you attended with your sister and Joseph—but what of your efforts to improve your own skills at the piano? Do you apply yourself? I think a woman's skills in music ought to be a priority; one must always be disciplined and aspire to greatness. For then, if mastered, music can have the happiest effect on the soul.*

But for all of his talk of the improvement of my soul and reason, he sought very little of my heart, and he gave me no mention of his. His tone grew colder, increasingly aloof, as the months progressed. He returned to addressing me with the formal *"vous"* greeting, which he had not used since our earliest acquaintance. It pained me to witness how Joseph took Julie's hand each day and spoke to her about all manner of things, addressing her gently as *"tu."*

It was as though he was slipping from me in ever new ways, daily becoming less recognizable as the man who'd sworn his love for me for all of eternity. The change in the spelling of his name became permanent; he didn't explain it to me—he simply began signing his letters as *Napoleon Bonaparte*, just as he was now known in the journals. I noticed all of these shifts with a mounting sense of discomfort, but I restrained myself from saying anything. Previously, I had teased him about any number of things, mocking him gently for the officer's formality with which he sometimes treated me, but now, I didn't even have the comfort to do that; I was frightened of how he might reply. I did not feel sure enough of my standing in his affection to tease him, even lovingly.

In late winter, he began to write vague remarks to me, troubling statements that seemed to carry some deeper meaning: *You know that my destiny*

*lies in the hazard of combat, in glory or in death. You must follow your own in-*
*stincts. Allow yourself to enjoy what is near to you.*

I always rejected such statements from him, writing back with warm
affection, hoping to thaw his encroaching coolness with increasing intimacy on my part. But my confident words belied the actual fears I har-
bored as I sensed his widening separation. I wished to join him in
Paris—and yet, he still did not invite me. Then, one day in early spring,
he began his letter to me with the impersonal and dispassionate salutation
of "Mademoiselle," rather than the usual "My Dear One," or "My Dearest
Desiree," or even simply "Desiree." I spent the remainder of the day in
tears.

Napoleon's dizzying rise through the leadership of the army meant that
he was suddenly a fixture in the newspapers. Columnists kept track of his
movements around the capital—outings in his fine new coach to the theater, evenings attending the fashionable balls or the stylish salons of the
Right Bank. I knew from the journals and from Joseph—and then from
what little Napoleon wrote to me—that he was in charge of keeping France
safe from domestic threats. He oversaw the wing of the government that
monitored the press and any potential dissident journalists. He was to
watch the theaters and the operas for any unpatriotic material. He kept his
ears alert at the high-society salons for potentially dangerous gossip or
discussion. He oversaw the purging of monarchists from within the government, and he ordered the closing and mass arrests of private clubs that
fostered anti-republican ideology.

It was a lot of work, but with a heftier salary came added comforts to
which he had never previously been entitled. He wrote to me of a new address: he would no longer rent a single dingy room, but instead he took a
spacious and well-decorated house for himself in the affluent Rue Chantereine, just a short walk from Place de la Révolution. He now had a coach
and driver to himself. And most shockingly of all, he suddenly began writing to me about his fashion—new boots, leather gloves, which he had earlier called a waste and superfluous extravagance. Cravats of silk and a
manservant to wash and set his previously unkempt hair. I read all of this
and wondered to myself: couldn't he certainly afford a wife?

I felt a considerable jolt of comfort when I did at last receive good news, some affirmation of the prominent place I still held in his affection: he'd had his book about us published, the one he had told me about in the earlier days of our courtship, *Clisson et Eugenie*.

Oddly, news of its publication did not in fact come to me directly from Napoleon himself. I was surprised, even if immensely proud, when I found out about it from Joseph, who'd had a copy mailed to him by his brother. And yet, I *had* been the inspiration for the love interest, the female heroine Eugenie—he'd even used my age and middle name in creating his character. So, surely, this was something.

I asked Joseph if I might borrow his copy to read it, and he obliged, admitting to me that romance novels held little interest for him and he had not yet looked it over. I hurried home, the book tucked tightly in my arms as if I clutched a precious babe, and I settled myself in the salon to read my fiancé's novel.

I'd seen passages already, portions of the book that he'd shared with me, eager as he was for my opinion and approval in the early days of the project. He'd acquainted me with the broad outline of the plot and the characters of his two lovers. And yet, as I read to the end of the novel, I found several stunning surprises—and I felt my dread hardening to a heavy stone in my gut.

It was not what he had told me. It was not what I had been expecting. It was not the inspiring, happy tale of love and marriage that he had initially promised to me. To begin, Clisson and Eugenie did fall passionately in love and were married. Their love only deepened when Clisson retired from the army and moved them to a prosperous farm in the countryside. But then, when the nation fell under attack once more, Clisson put down his scythe and kissed his wife farewell and nobly took up arms once more, selflessly returning to the army and the service of France. All of this I had anticipated. But then, to my utter horror, while Clisson is away fighting for his country, Eugenie shamelessly begins an affair with another man, forsaking the pure and faithful love of her husband. Clisson, upon hearing of this treachery, hurls himself heroically into battle and dies before the enemies of France.

I read it in one sitting. When I finished the book, its ending overwrought and tragic, I found myself too horrified for tears. I had stopped caring about the characters in the plot and through the last few pages had instead been fixated only on the thoughts and psyche of their writer; what had compelled Napoleon to write such a ghastly ending? If Clisson was indubitably based on Napoleon's own ideas of himself, then did he really believe me capable of behaving like the disgraceful Eugenie? Did he really have such little faith in women—in me, the woman whose name and character had inspired his Eugenie? Had he truly drawn on our love in writing of such an ill-fated union?

My entire frame was cold, and I began to tremble as my mind spun with more questions. Did Napoleon believe me guilty of some unthinkable betrayal? Or even capable of it, for that matter? But how could he—where would he have gotten such an idea?

I picked up the book, hateful object that it was, and raced out the door, back toward my sister's home. It was late, evening had come as I'd read, but I knew I could not wait through the entire night before speaking to them. Surely Joseph would have answers, would know *something*. At the very least, he'd certainly know more than I did.

"I need to go to Paris," I told Julie and Joseph as I barged, unannounced, into their small, candlelit salon. They'd finished supper and were sitting before a small fire, Joseph's head resting in my sister's lap as Julie read to him. No doubt they would retire to bed soon. They both looked at me with alarm as I entered, and then Julie noticed the book in my hand. My sister tapped Joseph, and he rose from her lap, sitting rigid beside her.

"How was it?" my sister asked, her tone wary.

"Have you read it?" I demanded.

They both shook their heads.

"It's horrifying," I said, my throat tightening around my desperate words. "I must see him. He clearly has the wrong idea about me. Someone has told him something dreadful."

Joseph sighed, and I noticed the look he exchanged with my sister. "What?" I asked, my mouth dry. "What is it?" I was fed up with other people knowing more about my fiancé, my life, than I did. I stared at Julie. "You must tell me."

"Will you sit, Desi?" Julie asked. And then, turning to her husband, she added: "Go and fetch wine, two glasses. My sister and I will have a drink while we talk."

Joseph nodded, hurrying to obey. I was left alone in the room with my sister. "Please, Desi." She patted the place on the sofa beside her, the place her husband had just vacated.

"What is it?" I slowly lowered myself to her side, my entire body feeling heavy. "Oh God, Julie, you do know something. What?"

My sister put her hand gently on mine, her face wilting. "He has invited us."

"Invited . . . whom?" I asked.

"He's invited Joseph to Paris; he's secured a position in the government for him."

I could feel the blood draining from my face. And yet, I clung to some feeble hope, staking my claim in the past words of Napoleon's, even if he had not repeated them to me recently. "Well then, I'll go with you," I said, sounding perhaps more certain than I felt. "Now's the time. For all of us. Isn't this what we have all been waiting for?"

Julie frowned, shifting in her seat, and just then Joseph entered with two glasses of wine.

"Thank you," Julie said. "Would you leave us a moment?"

Joseph deposited the drinks and promptly quit the room. My sister reached for a drink and brought it to her lips, draining the entire contents of the glass. She grimaced, pausing a moment before turning to me. "You know that Napoleon has had a rapid rise in the new government," she said.

I nodded. "Yes, of course."

"Will you have your drink?" She glanced at the full glass on the table.

I picked it up and took a sip. "What do you know, Julie?" I asked, my voice pleading.

"Nothing for certain, I promise you that. Only rumors. There are always rumors. It's nothing that Napoleon has said to Joseph, or of course I would have told you. It's just . . . what we read . . . in some of the papers."

I squeezed her hand. "Please, Julie. You must tell me."

She nodded, her shoulders sagging. "You know that one of his new responsibilities is to seize all private arms and weaponry . . . anything that royalist civilians might use to rise up against the government."

"Yes," I said. "And?"

My sister sighed. "This has put him in the path of all sorts of powerful families. Noble families eager to forfeit their arms in an effort to show good faith to the new government. It seems that . . . it seems that Napoleon has met someone, while performing this job."

"Someone?" I asked.

"A lady," Julie said, her tone tenuous.

I took a large gulp of wine, blinked back the tears that stung my eyes. "And? What is her name?"

"I'm not certain. I don't know much about her. Joseph will not tell me much, if in fact he knows more." My sister rose and crossed the room to a mahogany desk. There she pulled open the top drawer and retrieved a small piece of paper, a newspaper clipping. She walked back toward me and offered the paper. "This is all I know."

I glanced down, reading through a scrim of tears that blurred the words. It was a single sentence, a vague line in a society column: *General Bonaparte was spotted, dining at the exclusive restaurant Esprit de la Nation, in the company of one of Paris's most fashionable and desired hostesses.*

I read it several times, blinking against the threat of more tears, before looking to my sister. "All right. Well, it's dinner. It's not necessarily . . ." But my voice trailed off. I guessed that it was so much more. Combined with his prolonged periods of neglect, his cold words. His lack of affection or interest of late. The absence of his summoning me to Paris, even after he'd made a place for Joseph and my sister. I'd feared it for a long time in silence, and now I knew that my concerns had been well founded: I was losing Napoleon.

Within days, my fear turned into something more: heartache. My sister had seen only that one small column, a vague sentence she had noticed only because she scoured the Parisian society news. But one morning the following week, when I walked out to find a fresh newspaper, I did not have to scour any obscure columns. Because there, on the front page of a Parisian journal, in large and bold letters, was my fiancé's name:

"General Vendémiaire" Becomes "General Amour"! National Hero Napoleon Bonaparte Attends The Opéra Comique Accompa-

NIED BY HIS BEAUTIFUL MISTRESS, THE VICOMTESSE JOSEPHINE DE BEAUHARNAIS

I dropped the paper, my hands shaking, not even caring that I was in a public square and others might see my immoderate behavior. My heart clamored against my rib cage, each beat sending a fresh shudder of pain through my body.

What had happened to the man I loved? The man I'd trusted? I'd lost him. He'd demanded my promise to be as constant as the sea, and yet he'd left me as quickly as a retreating tide.

I no longer knew this distant, foreign person, this man who looked different and dressed differently and spelled his name differently. This man who would abandon me like this, behaving in a manner as cold and callous as if he owed me nothing, felt nothing for me. As if we'd made no vows. This man who would so callously break my heart, replacing me with a woman named Josephine.

# PART TWO

# Chapter 10

*Rue des Capucines, Paris*
*Winter 1796*

W HO WAS JOSEPHINE DE BEAUHARNAIS? IF I HAD BEEN desperate for news while marooned in the south, I soon found that Paris would provide me with more information than I could ever wish to know about the lady who had replaced me.

The capital was a city seduced, a population frantic for any gossip it could have about the dark-haired beauty—a widow of the Terror, a fixture at the city's most fashionable soirees, and, most importantly, the newly minted mistress of France's latest darling, the Boy General, Napoleon Bonaparte.

None of the journalists who wrote of "General Amour" and his new lover seemed to have any idea that I existed, that I was a girl named Desiree Clary from Marseille, and that, until recently, I had believed myself engaged to a young Corsican refugee named Napoleone di Buonaparte. It was as if that man had never existed, nor had the young girl who'd loved him and made her promises to him. I came to realize that this was because he'd never told anyone in Paris of my existence.

Since settling in with my sister and Joseph in their spacious Parisian villa on the Rue des Capucines, I'd been greeted with daily morsels of gossip having to do with the infamous socialite who'd taken my place.

Journalists and newspaper writers gushed about her, simultaneously enthralled and scandalized by her colorful past.

Originally a sugar heiress from the lush Caribbean island of Martinique, Marie-Josèphe-Rose Tascher de la Pagerie had come to Paris as a girl of seventeen to make an advantageous marriage to her much older cousin, the Vicomte Alexandre de Beauharnais. It had been an unhappy marriage from the start, but nevertheless one resulting in two children—a daughter, Hortense, and a son, Eugene. The vicomte had been a violent and lecherous man and had alleged that the children were not his. The Terror claimed his life, making Josephine a widowed mother of two at the age of thirty-one. She, then, was handed her own guillotine sentence.

Josephine and the children had survived by a matter of hours, spared at the last minute and freed from prison only after the shocking and sudden fall of Robespierre. During the reactionary period that followed the Terror—a time of debauchery and orgiastic revelry—the slender brunette widow had returned to Parisian society with unrivaled gusto, subsequently becoming a fixture at the most exclusive parties and events.

She was known as a quick wit and a charming coquette, and she'd soon come to preside over a small but influential clique of desirable women dubbed les Merveilleuses, "the Marvelous Ones." Every man in Paris longed to be invited to the fêtes and dinners attended by Josephine's circle of Merveilleuses. Rumors swirled that while food shortages persisted throughout France, the feasts at such ladies' gatherings were rich and plentiful, the champagne glasses never dropped below half-full, and the women had usually shed their sheer Grecian gowns by the time dessert was served. Journal writers joked, perhaps a bit longingly, that while the men of the Revolution had been dubbed sans-culottes—men without breeches—these women might be labeled sans-chemises: ladies without shirts. I blushed, reading about how these champagne-soaked gatherings devolved into bacchanal orgies among these society ladies and the powerful men whose patronage and protection they traded back and forth.

Josephine, a widow with a noble title and two children but absolutely no money, had become an intimate companion to several officers in the army before beginning an affair with the powerful General Lazare Hoche—a man she'd met while they were both imprisoned during the Terror. General Lazare Hoche. I knew that name: the same powerful young general to whom Napoleon had been assigned on the mission to crush monarchist uprisings in the west. During the earliest days of our separation, when his future had seemed so uncertain, Napoleon had refused to report to duty under Hoche, insisting on staying in Paris. *Well, apparently he had no qualms about sharing a woman with him,* I thought, my stomach twisting in a bilious knot.

After Hoche, Josephine took the even more powerful General Paul Barras as her lover. It was Barras who installed her in a beautiful mansion on Paris's Right Bank and assured her that she and her children would want for nothing. He was a rich man, and a generous one, and that generosity spread far enough that Barras was even willing to share his mistress—for right around the time that Barras left his post as Commander of the Army of the Interior, bestowing that role on his new protégé, the young Bonaparte, Josephine had begun appearing in public with the successor.

"Apparently she came along with the job," Julie said with uncharacteristic cattiness, her voice sour. It was a few minutes before the midday luncheon, and we were at home on the Rue des Capucines. Julie and Joseph's new mansion was quite comfortable, much larger than their home in Marseille, and paid for with the government position that Napoleon had secured for his older brother.

They had given me my own suite on the second floor of the house, complete with a small sitting room, a dressing room, and a spacious bedchamber, and I was grateful to my sister and brother-in-law for once again treating me as a welcomed member of the family, rather than the nuisance or tagalong I often felt like. I had moved with them to the capital just a few weeks earlier. Napoleon may have left me behind, carving me from his life without explanation or farewell, but I was not going to be cast aside by my sister, too. I'd begged, and then insisted, that she and her husband allow me to travel with them from Marseille to Paris, and they had eventually agreed. So had Maman. She trusted Julie and was fond of Joseph, and even she had agreed that it was time for me to seek a change from our shrinking Marseille sphere.

"But, won't it be painful for you, Desi? Being there in Paris, where you will see him so frequently?" My sister had never been overly fond of her husband's younger brother, but her opinion had plummeted since the news of Josephine had reached us. "You'll see his name in the papers each day, and his sallow face in our home. And her, too . . ."

"I'll be fine," I had lied. In truth, I didn't know how I would take it once I got to Paris; I hadn't seen him in so long, hadn't heard from him since he'd begun his relationship with another woman. But all I knew was that the thought of remaining behind in Marseille alone, without Julie, was more unimaginable than any alternative. Napoleon could deny me his invitation to Paris, he could cruelly rescind his offers of love *for eternity* without the decency of a proper explanation, but he would not deny me my sister. Or my life. Not when I was still so young and had only just awoken to the fact that I might have a future and dreams of my own. No, I would not be discarded or left behind.

I'd packed my trunks and ordered several fur-lined cloaks, and I'd moved with my sister to the capital as her husband answered Napoleon's summons. But now that I was here, in spite of my defiant talk and bravado, I did not know how it would actually go—though of course I had not admitted that much to Julie or Joseph.

I had not seen Napoleon since we'd reached Paris. Joseph had—he'd gone out to meet his brother immediately after we'd arrived. Julie and I had spent our days setting up the household and hiring a staff with the generous allowance that Joseph suddenly afforded his wife. In the afternoons, we would walk through the posh Right Bank neighborhood to the nearby shops along the wide River Seine, or we'd meander through the busy marketplace of Les Halles to peruse the colorful stalls, marveling at the cashmere scarves and muffs and fur-trimmed boots.

I was never at rest during these outings, in this city enraptured by the Boy General. Each time we passed beyond the front court and gated entry of my sister's property, I'd look about the street, wondering if I might catch sight of that familiar lithe figure. My breath stuck in my throat around every corner; perhaps he'd be rolling up the avenue in an army wagon, dispatching some message for the northern barrier. Or perhaps he'd be taking a leisurely stroll, arm in arm with her. Each row of the marketplace prompted a darting of my eyes, a fresh pang of fear that I'd meet the face I knew so well, the face I remembered with a painful mixture of anger and longing.

But today, I *would* be seeing Napoleon; there was no question about it. He was coming to luncheon at Julie's.

And he was bringing Josephine with him.

"I tried to say no," Julie said to me, her face creasing in apology. "I tried to arrange it so that it was just him, but Joseph overruled me."

"It's all right," I reassured my sister, attempting to summon a tone of indifference. "I shall be perfectly at ease. Time has healed me." I lowered my eyes, fiddling with the napkins on the table. When I looked up, Julie's expression was still one of concern. "It has," I insisted, a touch defensively. I swallowed. Then I added: "I now believe that he is a changed man and entirely unlike the man I had wished to marry."

Julie studied me, uncertain as to whether to believe me, before accepting my answer with a nod. "I believe you are correct in that, Desi."

We turned back to arranging the napkins, neither of us speaking for several minutes. I had no appetite for lunch, my stomach a thicket, but I helped Julie prepare the table. Eventually she broke the silence: "Joseph feels it's his brotherly duty to meet Josephine and accept her. Napoleon is devastated because Mamma Letizia and the sisters are refusing to meet her. Refusing to come to Paris, even, while Napoleon is taking up with her."

"Why?" I asked. The city seemed to wholeheartedly approve of its new golden couple.

Julie weighed her words, surveying the place settings on the table as she continued: "She hasn't always had the most . . . pristine . . . personal life."

I nodded; I knew of her relationships with other high-profile men in the military. Anyone could read about it in the journals. But Josephine was hardly unique in that—most of the women in her circle had taken just as many lovers, if not more.

"Apparently, Mamma Letizia thinks that Josephine is beneath her son," Julie said.

"Or," I said, "that Josephine has been beneath a few too many men who are not her son."

"Desiree!" Julie gasped, a scolding tone in her voice even as she let slip a smile. "Nevertheless, it'll be interesting to have a chance to see for ourselves. She seems to be causing quite a rift in the family, but Napoleon is smitten, apparently. And I do sincerely hope that you won't be too hurt by it all, Desi. But if you are, you must tell me. Now, do you like this pattern or should we put out the blue and white Limoges? Or perhaps the Nevers dishes would appear less formal? Oh, I don't know."

"I think the table looks lovely the way it is," I told my sister. Julie frowned, then turned to scrutinizing the silver around the five place settings. Never in Marseille would Napoleon's presence at a meal have made Julie the slightest bit apprehensive as a hostess; he had been the uncouth younger brother, ill-mannered, grateful simply to eat a proper meal. But here, in Paris, it was different. We were the outsiders, as unfamiliar with Parisian society as we were with the frigid, biting wind that skittered off the River Seine, and Napoleon was undoubtedly a powerful figure in this city. But even putting aside thoughts of our old Buonaparte companion, certainly the presence of Josephine, the undisputed queen of high society and leader of *les Merveilleuses*, was enough to put us both on edge.

Napoleon arrived as he always did, right at the appointed time.

When he entered the room, my entire body clenched, including my heart, but I forced myself to assume a casual smile, a mask of graciousness and cool hospitality. How many times had I imagined our reunion? Only every day since the moment he had left Marseille, embracing me on the dock, boarding his ship with just the one trunk and the promise that I would be his wife. And although I had spent the entire previous night tossing in my plush, oversized Parisian bed, anticipating this first moment back in his presence, nothing could have prepared me for seeing Napoleon enter the room with Josephine on his arm.

Gone was the skinny, sallow boy who had arrived in Marseille. His long hair, once greasy and uncombed, was clipped short and tight, trimmed neatly above the collar of his blue officer's coat. His sharp face of chiseled features, indeed his whole body, had softened, filled in; where once he had been wiry, sinewy, he appeared well-fed, his cheeks colored and full, his frame even a bit plump around the midsection.

But the greatest change I detected was in the intangible but irrefutable quality of his haughtiness. Napoleon had always been self-assured, even bold—it was one of the many things I'd loved about him—but now, as he stood with his chin jutting out, his hands resting squarely on his hips, looking around the room as if it were his domain to inspect, he appeared like someone twice his age. It was true that he now enjoyed power and wealth commensurate with a man twice his age, so perhaps this sudden self-importance should not have been a total surprise. Nevertheless, it was a change.

I could not resist studying the woman on his arm, either. Josephine entered beside him, and he helped her out of her fur-lined cloak before seeing to his own overcoat and bicorn hat.

She slid gracefully from her outer garment, revealing a tall, lean figure and a flowing gown of filmy lilac chiffon. It was Grecian in appearance, secured at her shoulders by two large diamond brooches and draped low over her décolletage, revealing the warm, bronzed skin of her bare chest and arms. She looked better suited to attend a summer garden party than a luncheon in the depths of winter, but she didn't appear to be cold.

I noticed how both Napoleon and Joseph stared, alert and motionless, as Josephine glanced around the room, greeting us all with a flicker of a coy, close-lipped smile, simpering with just the hint of a giggle. Her eyes, hazel in color and lined with dark lashes, landed on me, and I stood transfixed until I heard Napoleon's once-familiar voice. "My darling, you've met my brother Joseph, but allow me to introduce you to my dear sisters, the Clary girls. Julie is Joseph's wife, our hostess this afternoon. And her young sister, Desiree, is a cherished member of our family."

I was to be introduced as a *sister*? I felt the blood thrash in the veins of my neck, and I longed to cry out: *Sister? Is it common for a man to treat his sister the way you treated me? Or to speak the words you did, vows of eternity and fidelity?*

But I did not give voice to these thoughts. Julie's hand found mine, concealed by the thick brocade of our full-skirted gowns, and she gave me a steadying squeeze. I bit down against the words, hard, and I immediately tasted the metallic tang of blood in the back of my mouth, but I resisted the urge to say anything that would cause me to embarrass myself. I wouldn't let him do that to me. Not after everything else he'd put me through.

I drew my shoulders back and stood to my full height, which put me at eye level with Napoleon (though I did notice that he stood a few inches taller than I remembered, and I guessed that he had probably put something in the heels of his shoes), and I curtsied. I forced my features to remain calm as I said: "Good to see you, Napoleon. It's been ages." Perhaps he had grown accustomed to being called General Bonaparte at gatherings such as these, but I was not in the mood to humor his vanity.

I looked him squarely in the eyes; if there was any residual emotion or affection left in him—or even some remaining sense of obligation—I could not detect it in his features but for, perhaps, a fleeting flicker in his green-eyed expression. But then he cleared his throat, quickly patting down the hem of his officer's jacket, and any glimpse of sentiment was wiped clean. "Indeed," he said, putting his arm to Josephine's lower back. "And you as well, Desiree. You were a mere girl the last time I saw you. And now, you are a woman. You look as if you've been well."

I continued to stare directly at him, feeling certain that the fury I felt had stoked my cheeks to a deep scarlet. Before I could answer, he added: "Allow me to introduce you to the Vicomtesse Marie-Josèphe de Beauharnais."

"You are welcome here," Joseph said, offering a small bow.

Josephine brushed her bare hand along Napoleon's arm before turning her almond-shaped eyes first on Joseph, and then fixing them on me, offering a bright smile. "Please call me Josephine, especially since you are family. Everyone calls me Josephine now that Bonaparte has given me the nickname." She angled her face toward his, caressing him with her sideways, hazel-eyed gaze. "You do have a tendency to rename people, don't you, my darling? Or is it rather to remake them—in the image of your own mind?"

He wrapped his arm around her narrow waist, drawing her to him as if there were no others in the room. Though she swatted at his hand, she willingly yielded to his pull, allowing him to fold her willowy frame into his eager embrace. Making herself somehow smaller than him, pliant, even though I noticed that she was taller than he was.

"Now, now, my darling." She turned back toward me as she playfully slapped his roving hand from her waist. "We are guests, and I suspect our hosts are hungry."

"I'm starving," he whispered into her ear, though we all heard. "For you."

Josephine threw her head back in a quick laugh before leaning close to him. "So soon?" she cooed. Her soft voice had a languid, lilting quality—tinged by the accent of her island upbringing. "Aren't you ever satisfied?"

Now he looked as if he would devour her in our presence. "Never."

"Patience, my dear," she said, her tone indulgent as she gently shrugged him off of her. "Patience and you shall taste whatever you want." With that, Josephine turned a conspiratorial smile to Julie as if to commiserate over the insatiable appetites of their Bonaparte men. Julie merely looked on with the same speechless shock that I myself felt.

Josephine stepped forward then, leaving Napoleon behind as she took Julie's two hands in her own. "Aren't you both so lovely?" She glanced from Julie to me. "It is wonderful to finally meet you."

"And you," Julie said. I could tell that she felt shy in this new woman's presence. Back in Marseille, we had been considered among the most fashionable young ladies in the city, what with our family's endless supplies of new and expensive silk. Today, my sister, like me, had dressed for luncheon in the old style, in a manner that still paid homage to our dead queen—heavy brocade skirt, cinched and corseted waist, a column of bows up the front of the gown—whereas Josephine appeared like a figure plucked straight out of antiquity, a lady of republican Rome. I suspected that she did not even wear a corset, that there was only her bare skin beneath that one filmy layer of lilac.

"Shall we go in to luncheon?" Julie proposed, and we all nodded our agreement.

Josephine now took Napoleon's arm and I watched him escort her into the room. Was it her posture, I wondered, that distinguished Josephine from Julie or me? She carried herself with an effortless confidence; she appeared older than him by several years, in her mid-thirties I guessed. Nearly twice my age, I figured in my head. And with far more than twice the amount of life experience, from the sound of it.

Her face was undoubtedly beautiful, in a unique sort of way. While all throughout Paris I'd noticed that the fashionable, affluent ladies powdered their hair and faces to make themselves ghostly pale—even going so far as to pencil thin blue lines on their faces to give the appearance of veins through translucent skin—Josephine wore the sun-drenched olive coloring of her Caribbean upbringing proudly. She wore no pale *poudre*, or powder, on her face or in her thick chestnut hair, and she'd even rouged her cheeks to add *more* color to her already-dark complexion. Her wide-set hazel eyes were lined in kohl, giving her an almost exotic appearance, and she'd smeared some dark shadow, I guessed elderberry, on her eyelids. Perhaps, I thought, Josephine had realized that the white powder so en vogue among the upper classes—even now, when the Versailles nobles who'd first made it fashionable were long in their mass graves—would never fully mask her olive coloring and the effects of her colonial childhood and so she'd decided to embrace the opposite effect. She had enough social cachet to do so; I guessed that she might even be setting an entirely new trend, undoing what Marie-Antoinette herself had done.

As we made our way to the dining room table, Josephine swayed her hips slowly, and the diaphanous material of her dress rippled like water as the skirt fluttered around her ankles. It was then that I first spotted her ankles and noticed that she wore open-toed sandals! In Paris, in winter! They were leather, with complicated crisscrossing straps, reminiscent of what one might expect on a gladiator's foot in ancient Rome. I imagined Maman's horrified gasp. No lady that I'd ever known would have dared to wear such sandals—flaunting bare feet and ankles!—to a formal luncheon in another lady's home, no matter how warm the weather. It was especially unthinkable given the layer of snow on the streets outside. I turned to my sister, my mouth falling open, and noted that she had seen the same thing.

"Josephine has the most perfect little feet," Napoleon said, his eagle eyes catching the wordless exchange between my sister and me. "A childhood running barefoot over soft Caribbean grasses, not clopping around in too-tight heels. Isn't that right, my little Creole?"

She smiled through her blush, lifting a hand to her mouth before letting out a small giggle. "I'm afraid it's true. I just can't bring myself to squeeze my poor feet into those instruments of torture that you French ladies call shoes." Her voice was as warm and smooth as her skin tone, and her accent had a melodic cadence, no doubt from the island dialect on which she'd been raised. "Life is precious—so why should we suffer?" She leaned into Napoleon, resting her head momentarily on his shoulder before adding: "And for the same reason, I can't be bothered with a corset."

Napoleon looked to Joseph with a satisfied, proprietary smirk. "Josephine is an islander, just like us, brother." Napoleon then guided his lover to the seat beside his. I took my seat beside Julie, opposite my former fiancé, and Julie nodded to the footmen to begin serving the meal.

We lunched on a poached turbot with a lemon wine sauce and steamed potatoes. I had little appetite, nor did it appear that Josephine ate much from her plate. Napoleon barely looked at me throughout the meal, so solicitous was he of his new mistress. He refilled her wineglass several times; he leaned close to whisper occasional secrets into her ear; he asked her repeatedly whether the food was to her liking. He showed care and attention the likes of which I had never known him capable.

He had been taken with me—smitten by my fresh and youthful beauty, impressed by the grandeur of my home, cowed by the wealth of my family. He had felt an attraction to me, clearly, and probably even a real affection, given everything he'd said and written. But with Josephine, he was a different man. He had claimed to love me, but it was clear to all of us at the table that afternoon that he worshipped Josephine.

I noticed throughout the meal that Josephine smiled often, but rarely with her lips parted. The few times she did open her mouth to take small bites of her fish, she revealed fleeting glimpses of frightful brown teeth. She was a sugar heiress, after all, raised on a plantation where the stuff would have been present at every meal, and she'd clearly done lasting damage to her teeth as a result. *So she does have a flaw,* I thought with a small twinge of satisfaction.

Nevertheless, in her uniquely sensual way, Josephine had turned even that shortcoming into a tool of seduction, much as she'd done with her unfashionably bronzed skin. I noticed this throughout the meal: how she spoke with her lips close together, her voice low. One had to move closer to hear her words; in doing so, the unsuspecting listener couldn't help but catch the delicious scent of her jasmine eau de toilette, or the almond perfume of her thick, glossy curls. Feel the brush of her smooth, bare flesh. Catch a glimpse down her plunging, uncorseted neckline. She was a cat who lured her quarry ever closer without having to raise a paw.

We concluded the meal with platters of pungent cheese, then fruit that had been grown elsewhere than frozen Paris. I was ready to be gone from this room and this gathering. Napoleon was just finishing a recounting of an unpatriotic play he had recently ordered shut down when Joseph asked his guests if they would like a tour of his new home.

"Indeed!" Napoleon said, rapping the table. "I think it's high time I inspect these quarters of yours, make sure my government is giving my brother decent accommodations."

"I assure you, it is most certainly more than we need," Julie said, and I could see my sister balancing the split desires of being a gracious hostess to the man who employed her husband while not wishing to puff up Napoleon's ego any more.

"Well then, you'll just have to fill it with little Bonapartes," Napoleon said, nodding at his brother as if dispatching an order. My sister's cheeks blanched, and I shifted in my chair. "Well then, a tour," Napoleon said, rising from his chair, oblivious of the offense he'd given.

"My darling?" Josephine placed an ungloved hand on his arm, halting him. He looked at her, paralyzed by her touch, alert for whatever it was she wished to say.

"I'd like some air. I think I'll take a walk outside while you see the home." Her hazel eyes landed on mine across the table. "Desiree, dear, perhaps you would join me, since you are already familiar with the house?"

I was speechless and so was Napoleon. Eventually, he stammered, "But . . . you don't wish to stay with me?" He was a wounded puppy, stricken at the thought of even a moment out of her presence. She tilted her face at an angle toward his, demure, her voice soft and secretive as she said, "You know how often we will be back here, my darling. After all, he's your beloved brother. You'll give me the tour next time. But for right now, I'd like to ask Desiree how her trip was from the south. I remember what a harsh hostess Paris in winter can be for those of us girls who don't know the snow."

Napoleon was completely vanquished. He didn't look in my direction but simply nodded once, giving Josephine his blessing. She turned her gaze on me and said, "Then that's settled."

Did Josephine know about me? Was she aware of the role I had played in her lover's past? I was certain that she must have had an idea, for why else would she have singled me out for this stroll? She was beautiful and charming, but I suspected she was also quite shrewd, and that very little of what she did was *par hasard*—by chance, without a deliberate reason.

"Do you have a preference as to where we walk?" she asked as we exited Julie's door, her eager eyes fixed on me as if my satisfaction was her only interest in life.

"I'm still unfamiliar with the city," I answered, shaking my head. *And you are the one who invited me on this outing.*

She nodded knowingly, fluttering her thick lashes as she smiled. "Of course you are. Why, it took me *ages* to feel in any way at home here. I'll take you to an interesting spot; it's just down the street this way." We headed south, soon taking a right turn, and even though I was new to the city, I deduced that we were walking toward the river.

The afternoon was bitter cold, and our breath misted in front of our faces as we walked. "My!" Josephine shivered beside me. "Do you mind if I put my arm through yours? I get so cold, still."

I could not believe she had asked me to take such an outing, while the rest of our company remained warm inside the house. I glanced down at her inexplicable sandals. "Aren't your feet cold?"

"A bit. But it's not much farther. Just down this street." Her arm felt thin in mine. "Besides, whenever I feel cold, I only have to think of the frigid basement prison where they held us at Les Carmes. During the Terror?" She glanced sideways at me and I nodded to indicate that I understood. She squeezed my arm tighter. "But of course you and I would both bristle at a Parisian winter. We are from warmer climes. We have that, and so much else, in common." She said it as if we might have been sisters in our former lives.

"Do you miss Marseille?" she asked, her voice filled with what sounded like genuine curiosity.

I considered the question a moment before answering. "I miss my maman, and my brother. The sea. My childhood home. But I was ready to leave."

She nodded. And then I felt as if etiquette required me to return the question: "And you—do you miss your home?"

"Martinique, you mean?" she asked. "No. Paris is my home." It was a decisive answer, one that required no deliberation. When I said nothing, she added: "The air was warm. And filled with the salt of the sea, the fragrance of the tamarind and orange trees. But it was also filled with the smell of burning sugar. The screams of the slaves, the poor wretches. I remember once, when I was a little girl, one of the poor creatures got a hand stuck in the machinery of the *sucrerie*. I could hear him screaming all the way from the big house as the blades chewed him up."

I gasped, horrified, and she turned to me, her eyes studying mine. "I'm sorry. I've offended you," she said, her tone low.

"It's only that . . . I've never heard of such . . ."

"Slavery was an awful thing to witness. Worse perhaps for the soul of the slave owner than for the slave himself. That's a blessing of our Revolution, to be sure, that we've ended slavery in France. I tell Napoleon that all the time."

I nodded, less familiar with speaking about politics than apparently she was. We walked in silence a moment, and I wondered where she was leading us. When we turned a corner around a row of buildings, we faced straight into the knife blade of the wind. My feet ached from the cold even under my boots and stockings; surely hers had gone numb.

But her voice remained warm as she said, "I had a hard time adjusting to life here in Paris after growing up in the islands. So I can understand how you might be feeling, Desiree."

I very much doubted that she understood how I was feeling, but I did not wish to speak about it with her. She, on the other hand, seemed entirely eager to speak about herself with me. "I'm not even referring specifically to surviving the Revolution, you know. My husband . . . the viscount . . . I don't know what you might have heard? Or read."

I shook my head, as if to say I did not know much. Even though, of course, I had read some.

"He was a vicious man. He would beat me. He would lock me in rooms in his home and take my children from me for days on end. He once spat on me, hissing that I was 'beneath all the sluts in the world,' accusing me of debauchery when it was he who was bedding a different woman every night. I would hear him in there with his women, sometimes four at a time. A few times, he made me join in with them . . . but mostly, he simply locked me up in a separate room."

"That sounds . . . dreadful," I answered, my voice made tenuous by my confusion; why was Josephine confiding in me this way? How was I, a relative stranger, to respond?

"I was just a girl and I didn't understand. How could I? I was far from home, far from anyone who knew me or loved me or might have saved me. There were days when, truly, I thought he might kill me. Or wondered if perhaps I shouldn't do it myself, to end my misery before he had the chance. He was not well," she said, her voice low and toneless. "And yet, even though he insisted that I was no wife of his, even though he'd rage at me that I was a harlot and that our children weren't his, I went to prison along with him when the Terror began. As did our two poor children."

I nodded, overwhelmed by her story.

"Now, prison, that was something. Would you believe me if I told you that the walls of my cell were still covered in the dried blood and brains of the poor souls who had been massacred in that hovel before I occupied it?"

"No," I gasped, horrified at the grisly images swirling in my mind.

"Yes," she said, staring into my eyes as we walked. "I envied the mice and rats that scurried through our opened windows to eat the shit out of our overflowing latrine buckets. At least they could leave. God, how it reeked in there, of piss and blood and so much human misery. At night, I would hear the moans of the women who did their time à l'horizontale with the filthy prison guards. I'm talking about the widows of dukes, the wives of counts, spreading their legs like common street whores, each hoping to become enceinte with the baby of any gutter-rat guard who would take her. You know why? Because an expecting prisoner couldn't be sent to the guillotine until after her baby was born. That bought a girl nine months. We were all just doing whatever we could to stay alive another day." Her accent wrapped these vile words in her languid drawl, and I stared at her, shocked to silence by these unimaginable scenes she so candidly described.

I thought *my* time during the Terror had been harrowing, simply because Maman had been in a panic and my brother had been imprisoned and I'd had to walk by the city square where they carried out the daily executions. But, in fact, even though Papa had died in the midst of it all, I'd always been safe within the walls of my family's comfortable compound. Josephine now described a scene far worse than any hell I had ever known. *We were all just doing whatever we could to stay alive another day.* Of course, I wondered whether she herself had done these things she described—these ghastly things with the guards. But I'd never dare ask.

She sighed, pulling my attention back to her beside me, both of us shivering as we walked. "Then one day, I was told that I was being transferred to the Conciergerie the next morning. Of course, we all knew that the Conciergerie was the last stop for all the poor wretches on the way to the guillotine. Someone else came in and was given my bed. I was told I wouldn't have use for a bed starting the next day. I passed the longest night of my life on the filthy, piss-covered straw. Crying and praying. Wondering if my children, my Eugene and my Hortense, were beheaded yet. Wondering if in fact there is a heaven, and whether I would be permitted to go there. It certainly didn't feel as though God existed. It hadn't felt that way in quite some time. I watched as dawn came in through my cell window. I waited for the sound of the guard coming to fetch me. But then, that very same morning, we heard other news. Unexpected news. Men running up and down the corridors yelling that Robespierre was killed. His Reign of Terror was over. Can you believe it? I was to be set free. So, you see, I really am quite lucky, after all."

"Napoleon was imprisoned just after that," I said, recalling that time. My mind swirled with the images: dancing in the garden with Napoleon on Julie's wedding night, the very same night that Josephine now described as the longest, worst night of her life. That was the first time he'd raised the topic of our marriage. And then Napoleon's disappearance the next day amid the Thermidorian Reaction. Those interminable days when he was held at Fort Carré, memories of our feverish reunion and his fierce determination to ensure our betrothal.

My heart fluttered as I recalled all of it, and I decided to tell her these things. They were my memories, as real as my time with Napoleon had been, and I had a right to them, but just as I braced to begin, she cut me off, saying: "Yes, I know. Of course I know that." Her voice had a sudden edge to it, her sugary sweetness momentarily forgotten. And then, just as quickly, she smiled, her hazel eyes holding me with renewed warmth, and she turned to the street before us: "Ah, here we are." Her tone was light again, carefree.

"Look around," she said, waving her hand before me. I had been so immersed in our exchange that I had not paid attention to where we walked. Now we stood in a large, empty *place* on the Right Bank, where gracious buildings lined the four sides of the square, and a grand boulevard bisected its middle. "We know this place informally as La Place Vendôme, because the Duc de Vendôme used to have his palace here. He was the king's bastard. Then the Bourbons took it over, of course, and we had a grand statue of *Le Roi Soleil*, King Louis XIV, the Sun King." She looked to the vacant center of the square, wrapping her thin arms around herself, as if that might do anything to fend off the cold.

"That statue, of course, was smashed in the Revolution. This place smelled like blood; the entire center of the city reeked of it. No one wanted to live in this *quartier*, so near to so many daily executions. Buildings went vacant. They kept moving the guillotine in an effort to spare any one neighborhood from its horrible effects, but it was too late. This place was marked with death." She shrugged her narrow shoulders, her wide eyes scanning the area with a sort of detachment, perhaps recalling her own near-visit to this place.

"Now it's just a bare square—and no one seems to know what to do with the space. Napoleon has some ideas." She turned to me, her eyes alight and intent, suddenly fixed on our present once more. "But Desiree, why have you allowed me to prattle on like this? Talking about slaves and prison cells and smashed statues. And we've only just met. You must regret ever coming on this walk with me."

She studied me and so I stared back, noting the rosy hue of her cheeks in the crisp air. After a moment, I fidgeted under the attentiveness of her stare. "You're so beautiful," she said, flashing a sudden smile. "Just as he said. Round and healthy and innocent."

"Thank you," I stammered. I wasn't used to other women paying me such bold compliments, and I wasn't sure what to do with the invocation of the man whose love we held in common. "You . . . you are as well."

She smiled demurely, blinking her long lashes as she cast her eyes downward. "Innocent? No."

"Well, beautiful," I fumbled. I hated my girlish awkwardness, the fact that she made me feel as though I stood back on my feet, unable to catch up.

She reached forward and took my hand in her own. Her thin fingers were like ice, but her grip was unexpectedly strong. "I'm sure you guessed that I wished to speak with you alone."

My breath was a visible vapor between our two faces. "What about?" I asked.

"Napoleon has said such lovely things about you—he positively gushes at your name. He considers you and Julie to be his sisters. I think you and I shall be dear friends; I just know it." She gave my hand a squeeze, looking directly into my eyes. As she leaned close, whispering to me, I noticed a lone snowflake land on one of her eyelashes. "I wanted you to be the first to know of our joy. You and I shall be sisters soon, because Napoleon and I are going to be married."

# Chapter 11

*Paris*
*Spring 1796*

"WE SHOULD SEND OUR REGRETS. IT'S NOT RIGHT THAT you should . . ." Julie put a hand on my arm, asking for the third time: "Are you certain you will be all right?"

Before I could answer, Josephine swept into the room, her willowy figure draped in a flowing gown of white muslin, a tricolor sash cinched tight around her narrow waist. Her dark curls were swept back, with just a few strands of hair falling around her freshly made-up face. She spotted us across the dark-paneled room, obscured in dim candlelight, and smiled her greeting, "Ah, the Clary sisters!" She was one-half French revolutionary patriot, one-half Grecian goddess—and thus wholly the embodiment of Napoleon Bonaparte's most fervent fantasies for womanhood. And she knew it, of course. She had carefully honed every detail of her appearance in order to be so.

"I am so glad that you could make it. Thank you." She crossed the room toward us, where we stood with the surly registrar, a man who'd introduced himself with a frown and the name of Citizen Leclercq. We were on the upper floor of the drafty, run-down town hall of Paris's second *arrondissement,* just a short walk from the Avenue de l'Opéra. The registrar had offered us no chairs, so we shifted on our feet as Josephine approached us. Though the room was cold and dim, lit by only a few sparse candles and no fire in the hearth, Josephine's smile shone warm. "Napoleon told me: 'My darling, you shall have sisters there to attend you on your wedding night. I promise you that.' Thank heavens for the Clary girls."

Julie and I lowered our eyes, unsure of how to respond. Of course, we knew what had transpired—how Napoleon's mother and sisters had flatly refused to attend any wedding between their kin and Josephine de Beauharnais. "There are thirty thousand streetwalkers in Paris. You may have any of them you like. But why must you marry one?" Letizia had said to her favorite son upon hearing news of his engagement. Rather than deter or intimidate her lovestruck son, these comments had only elicited Napoleon's outrage and adamant defensiveness of his chosen bride. Joseph told us that Napoleon had railed at his mother and sisters in response, swearing that they would not have another *sou* from him until they accepted Josephine into the family.

Letizia had left Paris with her girls, shunning the wedding and sending Napoleon into a further rage. He had then stormed to Joseph's home, where Julie and I overheard him from the opposite side of the house swearing off any family member who disrespected Josephine. He called his mother a traitor and his sisters ungrateful shrews. He'd insisted that Joseph attend the wedding as his witness, ordering him to bring Julie and me to serve as Josephine's attendants and female family members.

Joseph had convinced Julie of the importance of her being there. Josephine's children were alive, having survived the Terror, but they were both away—the daughter being educated in a convent, the son at a military *école*. We were, as Joseph put it, the only family in Paris, dubious as our connection might be. Julie begrudgingly agreed.

I had been less willing. The idea of attending to my former fiancé's new bride—how could I be expected to look on, knowing that that was to have been my place? It was further evidence of Napoleon's complete callousness that he never spoke about any of it with me; he simply gave the order to his brother that I must be there and then assumed I would obey.

It was only my reluctance at putting Julie in a spot of further difficulty—the risk of placing her in the path of Napoleon's temper or financial retribution—that ultimately forced my hand. I knew she would take a stand for me, if that was what I asked. She'd demand that Joseph do so as well. But so, too, did I know that Napoleon was to be in her life forever, as her husband's closest companion. Even as his patron in government employment, it seemed. And I'd seen Napoleon's violent reaction toward those family members who had insulted Josephine; I was not fool enough to expect that he'd treat Julie with more care than he had his own beloved mamma.

Wasn't it easier to just swallow my misery rather than stoking anything further, prompting a potential rift between brother and brother, or worse, Julie and her husband? I would do this and be done with him. At least, that was what I hoped. And so there Julie and I stood, in the back room of the small office building on that early-spring evening, waiting beside the smiling bride.

And yet Napoleon, the ever-prompt and punctual soldier, did not come. Several hours passed. A few of the candles burned to their quicks and flickered out, casting the room into further darkness. Josephine adjusted the draping of her gown. She cleared her throat, restlessly fingered the curls that framed her face. She threw us sideways glances. But she did not speak.

The clock on the cracked mantel struck ten and still the registrar did not offer us ladies any chairs. Nor did he offer us refreshment, even a drink of watered-down wine or a broth to warm ourselves. Finally, after a gaping, unapologetic yawn, the man looked at his timepiece and then glanced at us: "This is more than I can bear. I am off to bed. Go downstairs and fetch a clerk if Citizen Bonaparte arrives."

Josephine's face registered alarm for the first time, her cheeks going pale in the candlelight as suddenly only Julie and I remained in the room with her, waiting. "He's been so busy," she said, casting a nervous glance from me toward my sister. "You know what he's preparing for?"

We both shook our heads.

Josephine nodded. "It's a secret. But I can tell you. The two of you are so kind . . . kind enough to attend to me here, where I have no living family." She lowered her voice, making us co-conspirators. "He's been appointed general of the Army of Italy. At last. What he's wanted since the earliest days of the Revolution. He'll finally march into Italy."

The news was stunning; I remembered back to the first days of our courtship—Napoleon's plans for Italy. His wish to march through those rich and disparate kingdoms at the head of France's columns. His plans had been rejected once, a casualty of a toppled regime. But now, it appeared as though he would realize his dream. "When . . . when will he go?" I asked.

"This week," Josephine said, her head tilting downward as she examined her fingernails. "I'll be a brand-new bride, left alone."

"So soon," Julie said.

Josephine nodded. "All the more reason why I shall look to you—as my family—to support and sustain me." Her smile flickered for an instant, feeble like the candlelight in the shadowy room. "I'm not afraid of Letizia. Mamma. Nor am I afraid of the sisters. Napoleon is furious with them, but I think that their opposition only makes him love me more." She grinned at this, her features suddenly coy. "In fact, my Bonaparte doesn't love me—he worships me. Never before have I known a man to—"

But her thoughts were cut short, because suddenly Napoleon appeared at the door, charging into the room with Joseph behind him. Barras, his mentor, the man who had given him Josephine, was there to serve as a second witness.

"My bride! My everything!" Napoleon held his arms wide, his face flushed and beaming beneath his ever-present bicorn hat. "The army demands my attention, but you, you have already conquered my heart." He strode toward her, sweeping her into his arms, her gown belling out as he hoisted her lean frame and twirled her around the room. Josephine giggled, his lateness entirely forgiven, and the assistant clerk was called up from the lower floor.

Julie and I stood to the rear of the room as Napoleon married Josephine. He presented her with a golden ring, the words To DESTINY engraved on the band. With the brief legal ceremony complete—as the Church still held no power to perform marriages—the bride and bridegroom prepared to sign the paperwork. As Napoleon had no birth certificate from Corsica, the clerk waived the requirement, telling him that a sworn oath in the presence of reputable witnesses would be sufficient.

When it was time for Napoleon to state his age, I noticed, with alarm, that he added a year and a half. "I am twenty-eight," he lied, giving his birthday as February 5, 1768. I knew his birthday to be August 15, 1769.

This date he offered would have made him only a few weeks younger than Joseph!

Next, Josephine, also lacking any official document, gave her birthday as June 24, 1768. This, too, I knew to be a lie, making her five years younger than in fact she was. She would have been a child at the time she birthed her own children. Why were they lying like this? I wondered. And then I understood—they were cutting the vast difference in years in order to appear the same age.

Joseph said nothing in protest as he signed the defrauded papers beside his brother. Josephine retreated to the corner of the room to admire her new ring. And then, Napoleon announced: "Back to my home! I wish to fête my bride!"

After years of waiting, I was finally invited to Napoleon's Parisian home, but only so that I could join him and the others in toasting another bride on his wedding night.

It was nearly midnight by the time our small party arrived at his large *palais* on the Right Bank. Napoleon nodded his approval as he surveyed the lavish dinner spread. "Champagne," he ordered, clapping his hands together. Servants appeared to hand us each a flute of chilled champagne.

I had no appetite as I entered the high-ceilinged dining room, where the long mahogany table groaned under porcelain platters heaped with oysters, turkey and chestnut stuffing, cheese, boudin pudding, stewed apples, and bowls overflowing with fruit and nuts. Josephine, rather than accepting the hostess's chair at the opposite end of the table, positioned herself on Napoleon's lap, sipping her champagne as she giggled, tilting her head toward his.

Josephine's dog, a small male pug named Fortuné, yipped and barked at Napoleon's feet, apparently jealous to see his mistress's attention diverted to another. "Fortuné the mongrel may not approve of me, but Lady Fortune has selected me," Napoleon joked to our table. And then he turned serious, lifting his glass in a toast: "Tonight, and all nights, I am the most fortunate of men. No one can possibly understand the delights of this woman." His hands roamed freely and unashamedly over her waist and hips as the rest of us fidgeted in our seats. I picked at a piece of turkey on my plate.

Napoleon, apparently, had no appetite, either. At least, not for the food. He twisted Josephine around in his lap so that she faced him as he said: "Now, my little Creole, what say you? Shall I make a wife out of you?" And before any of us could respond, Napoleon hoisted his giggling and compliant bride up from the table, sweeping her across the room in his arms. Before he crossed the threshold, he turned back, glancing at the table: "You all, stay. Eat. You are not to leave until the champagne is done and you are all thoroughly drunk. That's an order."

With the newlyweds gone, we turned back to our meals, no one speaking much. Joseph and Barras fell into a quiet conversation about the upcoming plans for Italy. Julie attempted to stifle a yawn. "I'm tired," she said to me, her voice low.

"As am I," I answered.

And then, from upstairs, we heard the dog barking. A muffled din as Napoleon could be heard yelling at the small beast. Josephine's soft voice as she tried to calm either her husband or the dog, or perhaps both.

"Sounds as though Fortuné plans to disrupt the wedding night," Barras said, chuckling to Joseph. Joseph leaned close and offered some reply, but he made sure that neither Julie nor I heard it. All we heard was Barras's boom of laughter in response.

A few moments later the chandelier over our heads began to quiver, sending a faint flicker of light across the dining room, the sound of tinkling crystal. And then we began to hear different noises—faint mewlings at first, muffled laughter. Then the sounds rose in volume—two voices, male and female, as Fortuné launched a fresh round of yips. I stopped chewing my dinner, dropping my fork. I looked at Julie, her round eyes and scarlet flush mirroring the mortification that I myself felt. Could it really be? More noises both high and low in register, more trembling of the chandelier overhead. Barras took a long sip of his drink, chuckling to Joseph as he muttered, "Little Corsican bastard wants to make sure we all hear how lucky he is."

I reached for my sister's hand under the table. "If you'll excuse me . . . I think I need to . . . I'm suddenly . . . a headache."

"Of course," Julie said. "Joseph, please have them fetch the carriage. Desiree and I will return home."

Joseph obeyed. As I rose from the table, saying my hurried farewells to the small crowd, I heard Josephine's sounds even more clearly overhead. I rushed from the room, my sister scrambling after me.

Julie held me close in the cold carriage as I sobbed. She didn't speak, nor did I, but my body could not help but give voice to my pain—heartache for what had once been, but even more so, mortification. Could there be anything more wretched than hearing the sounds of other people making love? I wondered. Especially when the man has made love to you? Especially when he was the only man ever to make love to you—and the only man whom you ever intended to love?

Several days later, the newlyweds summoned us back to their home to see Napoleon off for Italy. Letizia and the girls were still not in Paris, still not recognizing the marriage to Josephine, but Julie and I were expected to join Joseph. It was our first time back since their wedding night. At least he was leaving, I thought to myself. And hopefully for a long campaign.

Josephine appeared casual in a lemon-yellow chemise, a kerchief woven through her hair in the style of her native islands. Her eyes were red and puffy. Napoleon doted on her all morning as she reclined in an armchair, legs raised on an ottoman, a plush Smyrna blanket draped across her feet. The servants hustled around them both to load his trunks. Julie and I sat, drinking tea, as Napoleon told Joseph that he was fearful of what his abandonment would do to his wife. This only prompted further tears on her part.

"If only I could come with you," she said, reaching for her husband with limp arms.

"It is no place for you, my heart," he said, his fingers tracing the knot of the kerchief in her dark hair.

"But my place is beside you," she insisted.

He shook his head. "You shall have to be strong, my little Creole." Napoleon's tone was imploring but firm.

"I don't know that I can be," Josephine said, dropping her head into her hands as she erupted in fresh sobs.

I looked on, surprised. This woman had survived a cross-Atlantic ship voyage when little more than a child. A cruel husband's abuse, childbirth, and then the Terror. She'd emerged penniless, without connections, and yet she'd climbed to the top of Parisian society. Surely a temporary military campaign could not be so daunting to her? She'd be here, in a mansion, after all, with Napoleon's money and household at her disposal.

It was then that I realized it: as I watched them, the caresses and the words passing back and forth between their bodies, I realized that he loved the theatrics of it all. And so did she. When he wished to be the swooning, lovesick boy, she played the part of his temptress, his self-possessing muse. Now that he was the dutiful departing soldier, she was the suffering and faithful soldier's wife. Josephine managed and comported herself like a beautiful instrument, a work of art so perfectly attuned to the complex and shifting moods of its player—the man on whom she bestowed her favor. That man was now Napoleon, and he was rapt, powerless before her, even as he presumed that she was the instrument and he the handler.

We were all present in the room and thus forced to watch him take his leave of her. "You will be closest to my heart, right here." He slipped into his officer's coat, adjusting the miniature of Josephine that he had clipped onto the breast.

"Take me with you," she begged once more, rising from her chair as he stood.

"The battlefield is no place for you, my darling." He shrugged her gently off, pressing a hand to her tummy as he lowered his voice: "Especially if my little son is beginning to grow inside here. But know this, while I am gone, you shall be the constant object of my thoughts. To live for you, that is the story of my life now."

She nodded, fresh tears slipping from her eyes.

"Now, remember, my dearest little one," Napoleon said, preparing to leave the room. "If you do not write me often, every day, perhaps twice a day, I shall go mad, and I shall punish you when I return." He kissed her a final time, a long, slow kiss on the lips. "Now I must go." When he pulled away, her body seemed to lose its ability to hold itself upright.

"Joseph, come with me outside. Ladies?" Napoleon then directed Julie and me to take Josephine out to the back garden to avoid the sight of his departing coach. Fortuné accompanied us, his short, squat legs scrabbling to keep apace.

Within several minutes, we heard the wheels of the departing caval-cade. Josephine walked between Julie and me, her plump dog panting behind us. She appeared to regain her composure just a few moments after his departure, as her tears dried and her posture straightened.

"Your dog shall be happy to have your full attention once more," Julie said, in an effort to make some conversation.

"Indeed." Josephine nodded. "And Bonaparte tells me he is jealous that another shall be sharing my bed each night—even if it is only a dog."

Julie and I laughed, only because we felt that it was the polite thing to do. We weren't exactly certain how or when we had become Josephine's closest confidantes.

"You know," Josephine said, "the first time Bonaparte spent the night in my bed, just a few days after we met"—and thus while he had still been my fiancé, I noted with a stab of silent discomfort—"Fortuné bit him. Bonaparte was furious! Threatened to shoot the poor creature. But I told him that if he wished to join me in bed, he would have to make peace with my dog, for Fortuné has been my faithful companion far longer than anyone else. And I value loyalty above all else."

"It seems that they are learning to live peaceably together, ever so slowly," Julie said. I was grateful that she was making an effort, as I did not feel up for this conversation.

"Bonaparte agrees with me. On loyalty." Josephine hit the final word with added weight in her voice. Neither Julie nor I said anything. She continued after a moment: "That is why he is taking it so hard, the betrayal of Mamma and his sisters."

"They will come around," Julie answered. "Joseph said it is simply a matter of their running out of money, and then they shall—"

"He worries about me," Josephine said, cutting her off. "He worries what his absence will mean for me. How I shall hold up without his mother and his sisters here to support and sustain me." She shrugged her narrow shoulders. "But I told him: 'After everything I've been through, you think I need the support of a few jealous women?'"

Gone were the tears of a few moments ago. Gone was the weepy, clingy coquette who feared losing her soldier. There was a steely resolve under-girding Josephine's words now. She wasn't only speaking of Letizia and the sisters; she was warning Julie and me as well. These words were for anyone who would seek to threaten her place in Napoleon's esteem. As her husband was marching off at the head of the army, prepared for battle, poised to seize ever greater glory and wealth, Josephine, too, was prepared to fight her own wars.

# Chapter 12

*Rome*
*Winter 1797*

"THERE ARE THIRTY THOUSAND STREETWALKERS IN Paris." Mamma Letizia glowered, her Corsican accent thick with scorn. "He can take lovers, fine, but why did he have to marry one?"

Her three daughters laughed at this statement—bold, unhindered laughter, an indulgence in their shared revulsion at their newest family member. For, as much as the four Bonaparte women bickered and quarreled among themselves, there was nothing that united them like their mutual loathing of Napoleon's bride.

I threw a sideways glance toward Julie, whose focus was tilted down, seemingly preoccupied with the embroidery in her lap. It was hard for me to reconcile these criticisms of Josephine with the elegant waif of a woman I had met in Paris the previous winter. She'd been scantily clad, yes—inappropriately so, given the frigid weather—and yet she'd carried herself with a certain elegance. Even a level of dignity. Certainly in a manner different from the brazen and brash style of these Bonaparte women.

"A streetwalker would have been a better choice—at least a streetwalker would probably have been younger." Pauline Bonaparte snorted at her own quip. "Josephine is nothing but an old, used-up *horizontale.*"

None of the three sisters made any attempt at the embroidery in their laps as we sat in the large, airy salon of the embassy. Gossip was all the diversion they needed.

We were in Rome, where Joseph had recently been appointed France's ambassador to the Vatican. Maman, Nicolas, Julie, and I had joined him, as had his three sisters and his mother. I had been excited for our Roman adventure, eager to see the ancient capital along with my sister, to explore this eternal city of narrow meandering streets, art-filled palazzi, and festive outdoor cafés.

Josephine, on the other hand, had very conspicuously declined to join the family on the trip, even though Napoleon was still fighting in Italy and this would have put her much nearer to her husband. So far, in their months of marriage, they had spent only a handful of nights in each other's company—only those nights immediately following their wedding ceremony. Her husband had been away since that time, amassing an impressive series of victories that had won him even more fame and acclaim back in Paris. He had taken his armies across Italy and near to the Austrian stronghold of the medieval city of Mantua, and now Napoleon was poised to defeat the Habsburgs in a campaign that might finally push them back across the borders into their own empire.

"You know as well as I do why Josephine is not here," Caroline Bonaparte said now. It was the afternoon, and a soft, gray rain tapped the tall windows that lined the wall of the salon. "She's already taken a lover. It's common knowledge in Paris. Some dandy by the name of Hippolyte Charles."

Mamma Letizia threw her hands up in disgust, though I was certain that nothing her daughters could tell her would come as new gossip—the woman seemed to have more spies than even her son the general. "And *this* is the woman my son chose to marry? When he could have had any woman in France. He could have had her!" Letizia gestured her weathered hands in my direction. All three sisters nodded, mumbling their regrets as I kept my own focus on the nearby vase I was attempting to sketch.

It had become a common course of conversation, this deriding of Josephine; as much as Mamma Letizia and the Bonaparte sisters despised her, they seemed to approve of me in equal measure. Most likely, I reasoned, that was simply because I was not Josephine. I suspected they might have had a very different attitude toward me had I in fact become Madame Napoleon Bonaparte. And yet, since I had not, they filled their days with these frequent lamentations that their Napoleon had chosen Josephine instead of me.

"You'd probably be pregnant by now," Caroline said, delicacy not one of the stronger Bonaparte family traits. I often marveled to Julie that her husband was a diplomat—it was the last job I would have imagined for any of his siblings, or his mother.

"I cannot understand what he was thinking," Pauline continued. "She claims she cannot come to Italy in case she might be pregnant—that the trip would be too difficult. She thinks that fools us? If she were pregnant, she would know by now! She's not pregnant. She's too old. She's only thirteen years younger than you, Mamma!"

Mamma shook her head with fresh anguish. "Meanwhile, my poor son. All alone. A wife who refuses to visit. You would have visited, wouldn't you, Desiree? Of course you would. You're here."

I shifted in my seat, looking up from my sketch to glance at Mamma Letizia and then Julie. "It seems that Nicolas and Maman are having a nice time out on their tour. I suppose I'm a bit regretful that I did not join them." My mother and brother had gone to the Villa Borghese gardens, but Julie and I, not eager to walk in the rain, had declined to join them. Sitting here with the Bonaparte women, however, I was lamenting that decision.

"Gardens. Who needs to see another garden?" Letizia shrugged.

"You know what I heard?" Elisa returned to the topic of her sister-in-law. "Once, at a dinner party—this was before Napoleon, when she was still Barras's whore—she took off her dress on a bet. She stood there, naked as the day she was born, and weighed her dress to prove it did not weigh more than two coins!"

"All this talk of how the Revolution gave rise to the *sans-culottes*. I regret the day that it created the *sans-chemises*!" With that, Mamma Letizia coughed a wad of brown saliva into her nearby spittoon.

"I just hate to think of her back in Paris now. You know that with each victory Napoleon sends back to the Directory, they only exalt her more highly," said Pauline.

"Oh, I know it. It disgusts me. They call her Notre Dame des Victoires.

Our Lady of Victories. Meanwhile, she does nothing to support her husband." Letizia scowled.

"And what of her poor children?" Elisa interjected. "The son and daughter from the first marriage—Eugene and Hortense, I believe they are called. It's not as if *la horizontale* remains in Paris to be mother to them. Everyone knows she has the son at a military academy and the daughter at a convent. Imagine, leaving nuns to raise your daughter!"

I looked up from my drawing to exchange a look with Julie; we had been raised and educated, in our girlhoods, largely by nuns at a convent. But we said nothing of that now.

"And you know that our brother pays for both of the children at their schools. As if they were his responsibility. Meanwhile, she's feasting in Paris with her lover, laughing at Napoleon from afar," Caroline added, leaning forward. "Spending his money. She's renovating the house, you know?"

"I heard. Any time my poor son makes a little money, she spends it."

How much of this revulsion came simply from the fact that Josephine now received Napoleon's attention, his love, and his wealth, thus cutting into their own shares? I wondered.

"You know that she is redoing their mansion, and so far on the dining room alone, she has spent thousands. And her bedroom! Hear this! She's hired an artist to paint murals of swans and pink roses, and I heard that the cost has already exceeded—" Pauline stopped short when Joseph entered the room. He'd grown weary of their tirades, telling them, for Napoleon's sake, that they had better make peace with their in-law. That was the outlook that Julie was espousing, and therefore the one I was as well, but the sisters only seemed to do so when Joseph was present.

"Good evening, ladies." Joseph strode into the room. He kissed Julie, then his mother. Next he turned his attention on me: "Desiree, hello. Is your mother here?"

"No," I answered. "She's gone out with Nicolas."

He nodded. "Well, can I have a word with you?" He glanced toward his sisters and his mother, all of whom were, of course, paying attention to the exchange. "Perhaps somewhere private. Join me in my study?"

"Of course." I put down my sketching, glancing to Julie, whose expression told me she had no more idea than I did as to what this was about.

I followed Joseph down the long passage and into his dark-paneled study. "Will you please sit?" He gestured toward a heavy chair across from his own at the oaken desk and dismissed his attendant. I lowered myself into the seat.

"I've received word from my brother." Joseph carried himself with a new self-importance, I noticed, as if his brother's growing glory had spread to him as well. He was still affable enough, but he now had a habit of speaking with his chest puffed out, his chin jutting forward.

"Oh?" I had no idea what this could possibly have to do with me.

"As you know, he has been fighting like a fiend all across Italy."

I nodded. I read the papers. I saw how they were filled with articles extolling Napoleon's military genius and the many victories he strung one after the other. *Bonaparte flies like lightning, striking the enemies of France like a thunderbolt.* I suspected that Napoleon provided much of the language himself.

"He's finally decided that even he is entitled to a bit of a respite," Joseph said. "He will take some rest in Milan, and we shall go up to join him."

I still had no idea how this concerned me.

"While we are there, we shall meet the new French military commander of Rome, a man by the name of Duphot. General Leonard Duphot."

A small knot of unrest began to coil in my stomach as I waited for my brother-in-law to continue. "I'll let Napoleon tell it," Joseph said, lifting the paper before him, the letter from his brother. I saw Napoleon's familiar handwriting:

*Duphot has spoken to me of his desire to become engaged to your sister-in-law. I think it would be an advantageous alliance for her.*

I read the words, then I read them a second time, certain that my shock was apparent on my face as I lowered the letter and stared at Joseph.

"Now, don't look so stunned, my dear girl. He only wants what's best for you." I did not reply. My hands, I noted, were smeared with gray from my sketching. I rubbed my palm, saying nothing to Joseph.

"You are fortunate," Joseph said, his tone appeasing. "Your sister's marriage to me has connected you to the most powerful, beloved man in France. You would be a fool not to use our Bonaparte connections to make a good marriage. Duphot has wealth and power. He would be a good match."

I offered only a sharp exhale, a short sputter of incredulous laughter. Joseph went on: "And besides, Duphot already has a son, so you would not have much pressure. If you gave him one son of your own, he would likely free you from all wifely responsibilities. You could continue to live your life as you pleased."

My thoughts swirled, but I offered no response.

"What . . . what do you say?" Joseph asked, fiddling with the papers on his desk.

I took a moment before wondering aloud: "Won't I at least be allowed to meet him first?"

"Certainly!" Joseph rapped the table with his knuckles. "What do you take us for? You think we'd marry you off without allowing you to meet the bridegroom? Of course we wish for you to meet Duphot."

I suspected that Joseph expected some sort of appreciation at this, some thanks, but I was in no mood to offer any.

"Duphot shall join us in Milan as soon as he can take leave from his military duties. And he won't be the only one. Josephine has finally deigned to honor us with her presence." I surmised from his wry tone that Joseph felt the same dislike for his brother's wife that the rest of his family did. After all, as the keeper of family finances, he knew about the expensive swan paintings, the new marble tables, the rumors of her lovers and debauched parties. But he was the diplomat. He would never reveal his hand or risk alienating his brother. Perhaps that made him even more dangerous to Josephine.

"So, it is settled. We shall all be together in Milan, and you shall meet this new suitor," Joseph said. "Won't that be nice?"

The Serbelloni palace, where we arrived for our stay in Milan, was a staggering structure, grand enough to house an entire city. We arrived in the morning, mouths agape as our carriage pulled us through the tall iron gates into an enclosed courtyard. The palazzo's ground floor boasted a grand hall filled with marble columns and gold trim, crystal chandeliers, and a soaring domed ceiling, its dimensions and appearance worthy of an ancient temple rather than one family's residence.

But the most breathtaking aspect of this palace, the place Napoleon had handpicked out of all of Italy for his reunion with Josephine, was the flowers. Never one to overlook a single detail, Napoleon had ordered fresh-picked floral arrangements to cover every surface of the massive rooms. High doors opened out to terraces that led to the palazzo's vast, verdant gardens, where the flora had been planted and pruned with expert care. The air surrounding the palazzo hung heavy with the rich fragrance of thousands of lush petals.

Equally impressive was the way the palazzo was filled with art—rich oil paintings of the Madonna, scenes from the New and Old Testaments, references to the great scenes of ancient Greece and Rome. The rooms, large as they were, were stuffed with statues and busts, with scrolls and aged leather books. It was luxury, opulence the likes of which I had never witnessed, and I ambled slowly through one grand hall after another, absorbing each colorful scene with fresh wonder.

We arrived after Napoleon but before Josephine, and I noticed as soon as he greeted us that our host was irritated. I saw the tight set of his jaw, the quick manner in which he kissed his mamma before whisking Joseph off to a private conversation—and I guessed that he was not happy with Josephine's absence.

I settled into my suite, a small dressing room and a spacious bedchamber with paneled walls and tall mirrors, a large canopied bed, and floor-to-ceiling windows that looked out over the palazzo's forecourt. There, more carts continued to roll in, their wagons loaded with ever more paintings and statues. From where was all of this treasure coming? I wondered. And where did Napoleon intend to put it? As a small battalion of servants set out to arrange my wardrobe and personal items, I decided to go back downstairs to explore more.

On the ground floor, I entered a double salon, the high-ceilinged space vast and quiet, with only the sound of my shoes clipping on the marble floor. I noticed more *objets d'art* stashed haphazardly throughout the room—a harp, three bronze busts, several terra-cotta vases. I paused before a marble statue of a man, his head covered in a mop of thick curls, his muscular left arm raised triumphantly, a cape draped over his shoulders. What struck me most about this statue was that the man stood entirely nude, a thicket of hair swirling around his exposed manhood. I couldn't resist; I leaned forward for a closer look.

"Is he that impressive?" Napoleon's voice caught me entirely unaware, causing me to flinch as I looked up. He had entered at the other end of the large salon, and he walked toward me now. I felt my cheeks burn with a deep heat. "I was just . . . wondering. About all the art."

"Considering him for one of your models?" he asked, studying me. I shifted my weight. So he did remember my interest in drawing. "Perhaps that would be a more suitable subject for your study." Napoleon smiled, pointing toward a benign oil painting of a pastoral scene, sheep grazing as a shepherd snoozed nearby.

"Yes," I said, nodding in agreement. For a moment he had looked at me like the young soldier in Marseille. But he was no longer that man, I reminded myself with a silent rebuke. He didn't even have the same name as that young man. And so I cleared my throat, throwing my shoulders back as I asked: "Was all of this art already here in the palazzo?"

"No, I have collected it." Napoleon sauntered toward me, glancing from side to side at his trove. "Every city I sacked. Those Italian principalities— it's an embarrassment of riches. And now it shall all go back to France, for the glory of our nation. I plan to install it all in the palace of the Louvre."

I was surprised by his brazen seizure of this property, but even more stunned by how openly he admitted to it. "But . . . it appears to be priceless treasure."

"It is."

I narrowed my eyes, studying him. "Didn't they mind you taking it?"

"They had little say in the matter. They were vanquished, and I was the victor. Besides, we are the homeland of liberty, not those corrupt Italian doges and fat priests. They make a joke of such spoils. It is in France that we celebrate the ideals of antiquity, the ceaseless striving of man for self-improvement. It is in France where the great works of mankind belong.

And I am the leader who shall bring it there. I shall create in the Louvre a great palace filled with the world's best art."

Another voice interrupted us. "Napoleon?" Joseph appeared at the threshold of the room. "She has arrived."

We all knew to whom Joseph referred. Napoleon nodded, looking from me to his brother. "Good. I was going to be truly cross with her if she delayed my dinner."

We gathered outside as Josephine's cavalcade rattled through the front gates into the palazzo's massive forecourt. Six coaches, loaded with trunks and furniture, servants and gowns. Napoleon stood between his mother and Joseph, scowling, arms crossed: a general inspecting an approaching force.

I studied him as we stood there. Napoleon had grown downright plump—where the features of his narrow face had once been craggy and angular, they were now padded in soft flesh. The paunch of his once-narrow midsection hung over his belt, and his breeches were stuffed tight.

I did not know which coach carried Josephine, but a wigged footman hopped down from the rear one and opened the door. I felt my body go taut as Josephine emerged.

If Napoleon had grown thick around the waist, she, by contrast, had gained no weight; she was most certainly not carrying his baby within that slender figure. Napoleon's scowl deepened as he saw this. She stepped out, the feathers of her headdress grazing the top of the gilded carriage door as she emerged, her small pug, Fortuné, clutched in her bare arms. "Oh! Bonaparte, at last! You won't believe how taxing this journey has been!"

The servants descended on her cavalcade, beginning to unload her dozens of trunks, boxes of jewelry, gowns, silk pillows for her dog, and other personal items. She glided forward toward her husband, but Napoleon made no move to meet her, allowing her to reach him on her own. She collapsed into his arms, her voice soft: "I can't tell you how much I've missed you."

"Curious," he said, pulling back, unsmiling, from her embrace. "You've missed me, and yet you couldn't be bothered to write, let alone join me, until now? Barras told me he had to practically force you into the coach."

Josephine straightened, throwing a quick glance toward Mamma Letizia, then toward me, before she remembered herself. She fixed a calm smile onto her face, her hazel eyes sliding back toward her husband. "My darling Bonaparte," she said, pressing an ungloved hand to his chest. "Please don't tell me that after all we've been through to get to each other, you wish to quarrel? I could think of dozens of far more pleasurable ways to spend our reunion."

Whether this appeal softened his irritation I could not tell, for Napoleon's expression remained an implacable mask. He simply nodded to the attendants, gesturing for them to transfer Josephine's items into the palazzo. Then he took his wife by the arm and whisked her inside, not looking back toward any of us.

Dinner was not served until late, and Napoleon arrived at the table with Josephine, both of their faces strained. He seated her at the opposite end of the table and told us all to begin our meals.

"May I make a toast?" Josephine spoke, her eyes fixed on her husband. "To General Napoleon Bonaparte, the First Man of France."

"Hear! Hear!" Joseph agreed, raising his glass. Mamma and the sisters begrudgingly lifted theirs as well, and I took a sip of my red wine. It was full-bodied and smooth, the rich flavor a pleasant blend of fruit and spices. It seemed that artwork was not the only sort of treasure that Napoleon had plundered from the Italians.

"I think you've been drinking and eating quite well across Paris on my victories," Napoleon said, serving himself a thick slice of the roasted boar.

If the barb stung, Josephine did not show it, but instead she smiled sweetly and took a sip of her wine. Napoleon turned to his sister Pauline, who was seated to his right. "What do you think of the meal, Paulette?"

"Delicious," she said, preening at the use of the family pet name, nodding toward her brother as she accepted a slice of meat from him.

"I am glad that some of you appreciate the efforts to which I have gone to arrange a reunion for our family, a comfortable home for us."

Pauline turned and threw a sideways glance at her sister-in-law. Then, to my shock, she slid her tongue out, making a face at Josephine. I kicked Julie's foot under the table, and Julie's subtle nod told me that she, too, had noticed the insult. I couldn't help but turn to Josephine, eager to catch her response. Josephine returned Pauline's gaze, but her face remained expressionless, unfazed.

Just then a servant pushed the door to the dining room open, appearing with a massive platter of lobster, shrimp, and clams. As the man entered, the small pug Fortuné raced in after him. Upon spotting his mistress, from whom he'd apparently been separated, the dog let loose a frantic series of yelps and charged toward Josephine.

"Fortuné!" Josephine clapped, delighting in the sudden appearance of her pet. The dog ran across the room toward her. In doing so, he clipped the nearby servant's legs, causing the man to momentarily lose his balance. The platter of seafood in his hands tilted before careening to the floor, the porcelain smashing as clams and stewed tomatoes splattered the carpet. The dog, suddenly more interested in this available feast, turned from Josephine and pounced on the food.

"Fortuné, no!" Josephine rose from the table, running toward her small dog. The servants around the room gasped, hurrying toward the melee. Pauline shrieked. Mamma Letizia threw her hands in the air, screaming: "The lobster! *Dio mio*, what a mess!"

Josephine scooped up her barking dog. Napoleon rose from his chair, cheeks aflame, as he walked toward Josephine and the squirming animal. Fortuné yipped like one possessed, eager for release so that he might pounce once more upon the fragrant feast. "God help me, Josephine, I will lance that creature and toss him into the kitchen fires if you do not throw him out this instant!"

The dog growled at Napoleon, and Josephine tightened her embrace around his fat, writhing frame. "It was an accident," she said, her voice pleading even as her dog barked more defiantly.

"A far better accident would be if he were left outdoors tonight and the wolves made off with him," Napoleon roared. With that, Josephine burst into tears, fleeing the dining room as her dog continued to yip in her arms.

Napoleon stood alone where she'd left him. He glanced from his brother to his mother, who was muttering under her breath in inaudible Italian. He hovered, deliberating.

After a moment, Napoleon threw down his napkin, cursing in his native tongue as he turned on his heels and followed in Josephine's direction.

Those of us who remained at the table finished our meals in silence as the servants continued to clean the mess from the floor. There would be no seafood with the meal, that was clear.

It was Pauline who broke the quiet, and I could not believe that she, a few years younger than me, always spoke with such a brash assertiveness. "You heard what he said?" she glanced at Mamma. "She only agreed to come because Barras pushed her into the carriage."

Mamma nodded. "And now he sees that it's not because she's pregnant."

"Of course she's not pregnant—*La Vieille*, the Old Lady," Caroline said, looking to Pauline, who quickly showed her approval with a derisive snigger.

"I don't understand what they think is so wonderful about her, why the dressmakers in Paris fall over themselves to make gowns for her," Pauline said, sipping her wine. "She can't even afford to pay for them."

Elisa joined in: "She takes bribes, promises men back in Paris she'll introduce them to Napoleon in exchange for their money or credit."

Pauline crossed her arms, a pout turning her features childish. "I'm just as beautiful as she is. She's just more experienced than I am."

"You wouldn't want the sort of experience she has," Joseph said, his jaw tight. "Now that's enough. We've all traveled far to be here. We will finish what's left of this supper and then it's off to sleep."

After dinner, I climbed the stairs beside Julie, the servants snuffing out the candles behind us. As we neared the landing at the top of the stairs, we heard a muffled din, shouts coming through the thick walls from Josephine's bedroom.

"Come along," Julie said, taking my hand in hers and picking up our pace. I hurried beside her, but that's when I realized my mistake; it was not shouting that I heard coming from behind the door, but rather the sound of their lovemaking.

Neither Napoleon nor Josephine came down to breakfast the following morning, finally emerging only when it was time for luncheon. Josephine appeared at the table with a relaxed smile, her cheeks flushed, a red bandana tied *à la Creole* around her hair as her dark curls framed her face.

The meal was a quiet, uncomfortable affair. Joseph spoke about the gardens a bit, and Julie agreed that a walk through the palace grounds would be nice. We were in the less formal dining salon, and Josephine sat beside her husband, clearly ensconced in his good graces once more. They exchanged meaningful looks and whispers throughout the meal, their bodies angling toward each other, touching often, giggling about gestures that were transpiring between them beneath the table.

We finished our meal of poached salmon and salad, and Napoleon pushed himself back from the table, landing his hand on it. "Join me in the music hall?" He raised an eyebrow toward his brother. "Josephine wishes to play the harp for us."

We followed them into the large music room, where a harp gilded in gold leaf stood at the front of the room, a chair beside it. Other seating had been arranged in rows before the instrument, and I took my seat beside my sister and her husband. Josephine positioned herself beside the harp and smiled to her husband, collecting herself a moment before she began to pluck the strings.

The music began slowly, and Josephine shut her eyes as she played. She built toward a series of rapid scales, the ethereal, lilting melody prompting Napoleon to nod approvingly. Of course I remembered the words he'd once written to me: *A woman's skills in music ought to be a priority; one must always be disciplined and aspire to greatness. For then, if mastered, music can have the happiest effect on the soul.*

I'd never played an instrument for him. And he had never asked me to do so.

"Bravo," Napoleon said now from his seat, as Josephine's fingers moved quickly and skillfully, her lean arms working back and forth across the instrument's strings.

Elisa sat on my other side, and she leaned toward me to whisper: "They say she has some boudoir tricks from her skills as a harpist. *Zigzags*—some magic she works with her hands."

Pauline heard the comment and began to chortle, prompting Napoleon to throw a daggered look in our direction. When the performance was over, Napoleon rose, applauding. *"Magnifique!"* He turned toward us to make sure we all expressed sufficient appreciation. "Have you ever seen such skills?" We clapped politely, but Josephine looked only toward her husband.

He crossed the room toward his wife and placed a kiss on her lips in front of everyone. And then, hoisting her from her chair, he swept her into his arms and announced: "Now, my little Creole, how about a private performance?" With that, he carried her, giggling, from the room, and we did not see either of them for the remainder of the afternoon.

It was an unseasonably warm day, and the household was quiet as everyone retired to their siestas. Not tired, I had decided to explore the palazzo a bit, to examine the confiscated artworks and study more of the paintings Napoleon had gathered.

I walked alone throughout the ground floor, without even a servant in sight. Only the sound of the outdoor fountain traveled across the air through the open terrace doors. As I entered each room, I noticed that Josephine had left papers scattered throughout.

Letters, more precisely—letters Napoleon had written to her, going back months, to the earliest days of his Italian campaigns.

I knew his handwriting and I knew what it was like to receive letters such as these. At first I resisted the urge to look at them, noting how awkward it would be should someone find me doing so. But as I continued to cross the rooms, the letters kept appearing, left opened on tables and chairs and mantels, for all eyes to see. Josephine had been careless, but I suspected that it was intentionally so; after the public quarrels of the previous day, she wished to show all of us the extent of her husband's love, the depth of his affection, lest anyone believe her standing to be vulnerable.

Finally, I lost my resolve and I glanced at one of the notes where it had been placed on a marble side table. My heart clenched as I lost myself in the familiar slanted handwriting. I couldn't help but feel that my own letters had been part of a different lifetime, penned by the same hand but a different man—a boy, really. For though the penmanship appeared unchanged, Napoleon had never written to me with the depth of feeling that I now saw in his letter to Josephine.

The note began as somewhat familiar, with statements not much more effusive than those he had once directed toward me:

> *You are the constant object of my thoughts. My mind does nothing but imagine what you are doing.*

But then Napoleon's sentiments mounted in their intensity:

> *My incomparable Josephine! Away from you there is no joy. In the middle of business, at the head of my troops, you remain the single focus of my heart. You have robbed me of more than my soul, you have robbed me of my very liberty, for you are the only thought in my life.*
>
> *By what art have you entranced all my faculties? It is witchcraft, my dear love. To live for Josephine—that is the sole story of my life now.*

Then, surprisingly, the confident and self-assured Napoleon became suddenly insecure. Jealous, even:

> *If you loved me as I love you, you would write me twice a day. But instead you chat with your gentlemen callers and fill your precious mind with idle gossip. If you had any morals at all, you'd be at home thinking of your husband, living for him. A thousand daggers are ripping my heart to bits. The illness I feel when I imagine other men touching you . . .*

*To die without being loved by you ever again, to die with*
*my uncertainty, it is the torment of hell. My life is a perpetual*
*nightmare, I have lost all happiness if I have lost you.*

But then, just as quickly as he had turned fretful and jealous, he was once more conciliatory and loving, even apologetic. Fearful of upsetting her:

*A thousand kisses to you, my soul. My life. A kiss to the heart,*
*then lower, then much, much lower.*

He was tender, hopeful:

*I imagine you constantly, I see you with a round little tummy.*
*I would take care of you, see to it that you want for nothing.*
*Your comfort is all that matters to me in this life.*

His efforts to try to make her jealous struck me as plainly apparent, even juvenile:

*Five or six hundred beautiful ladies tried to charm me;*
*none had the sweet face which I have engraved on my heart.*
*I saw only you.*

And then, he turned toward language that made me blush, even though I was not the intended recipient. My mind raced; I could not imagine the man I knew speaking in such a way, and, yet, here he was:

*You know how I remember—and long for—my visits to your*
*little black forest. I kiss it a thousand times and wait impatiently for*
*the moment I will again be in it. To live within Josephine is to live*
*in fields of paradise. I would be so happy right now if I could*
*undress you. Kisses on your mouth, your eyelids, your shoulder,*
*your breasts. Everywhere, everywhere, everywhere!*

I looked up from the paper, my mind awhirl at this glimpse into Napoleon as such a devoted and impassioned lover. The letter quivered in my trembling hands and I knew I had seen enough—far too much, in fact. I lowered it slowly back toward the marble table. As I did so, I looked up into the mirror before me. It was then that I noticed her, standing behind me, reflected in the looking glass.

"You've found my letter," Josephine said, her lips spreading in a slow smile. "I'm so glad. I've been looking everywhere for it."

"Everywhere?" I repeated, incredulous. "But your letters are scattered all over. You can't have had to search too long."

Josephine shrugged, crossing the room toward me. She was in a simple gown of cream-colored chiffon, the low neckline embroidered in gold and silver stitching, her hair *en diadème,* the dark braid woven around her head like a crown. I noticed that her feet were bare as she padded across the Aubusson carpet. "Napoleon let me get no rest last night, and my mind is gone today." She reached me and put her hand on mine. Her flesh was warm, soft. "May I?" She arched an eyebrow, looking to reclaim the paper in my hand.

"Of course." I released it, my eyes looking away.

"Thank you." And then, her voice low, she added: "Of course, you know what it's like to receive such notes. He's such a romantic."

*I am not a romantic man,* he'd told me.

She glanced at me a moment longer, and then to the note in her hand. "Sometimes I feel as if he will go mad with his love for me."

I couldn't help but see, at this close distance, the warm, honeyed richness of her bare shoulders, her arms. Her skin was smooth, without blemish, and it smelled faintly of some floral fragrance, perhaps orange blossom.

She looked up now, drawing my eyes back toward her own. "You know, Desiree, we love having you around. We think it's so special, how close you are with Julie. And we both just wish to see you happily married." She put her hand on mine once more. "Your gentleman is going to arrive any day now. Duphot. I can't wait to hear what you think of him."

Did she know him? I wondered. But I wouldn't give her the satisfaction of asking.

"Give him a chance, that's all we ask. He's a skilled general. He's . . . seasoned."

It was a curious statement, and I wondered what she meant by it. But so, too, did I wonder whether this meeting with Duphot had truly been arranged by Napoleon, as Joseph had said, or by Josephine.

My thoughts were interrupted just then by a terrible noise in the gardens. It sounded like animals engaged in a mortal struggle. Josephine and I both turned our attention toward the open terrace doors. "Fortuné?" Josephine gasped, and she took off at a run toward the gardens, her chiffon skirt trailing behind her like streams of water. "No! No! Get him off my dog! Away, beast!"

I followed behind Josephine and quickly saw what she was seeing: a much larger dog—I guessed the mongrel must belong to one of the household servants, as I'd seen him slinking around the grounds—had Fortuné clapped in his sizable jaws, and he was shaking the small pug like the quarry of a hunt. Fortuné was writhing in the larger dog's mouth, squealing in a way that made me wonder how much longer he could survive such an attack. Even I, who felt no fondness for the pug, could not help but shriek in horror as I witnessed the struggle.

"No! Release him!" Josephine ran toward the melee, ready to throw herself on the ferocious beast, but Napoleon suddenly appeared with the cook, and he held Josephine as the cook stepped toward the dogs. "Make him stop!" she cried.

The cook succeeded in prying the pug from the mongrel's jaws, but by that time, Fortuné had ceased his protests. Josephine's cries alone filled the gardens. The cook looked down at the small dog, its body limp, its eyes vacant.

Now Napoleon released his wife and allowed her to charge toward her pet's slack frame. "No!" she cried, reaching for her little dog. "No! Help him, help him!"

But there was nothing to be done. Josephine wept, her face mottled and incredulous as she turned to her husband. "You must do something! Now!"

Napoleon shrugged as he looked at his wife, his expression apologetic but resigned. "Such is the way in battle, my little Creole. Either kill or be killed."

# Chapter 13

*Milan*
*Winter 1797*

DUPHOT ARRIVED AT THE SERBELLONI PALACE THE FOL-
lowing evening, in time to join us for dinner, and I immediately understood what Josephine had meant when she'd described him as *seasoned*.
General Leonard Duphot was old. Very old.

He sat next to me at dinner but spent the entire meal engaged in military conversation with Napoleon. That, to me, was a relief. I had little to
say to the man and guessed that he was older than my father would have
been, had he still been alive.

After dinner, Duphot asked me to join him for a walk in the gardens,
and as the eyes of the entire room looked upon me, I felt that I had no
choice but to oblige. I accepted his help with my cloak and then the offer of
his outstretched arm, and he led me through the doors out to the colon-
nade, where darkness had closed in. The gurgling of the fountain mixed
with the sounds of the surrounding city as we strolled along the narrow
pebbled paths. And then, from inside the house, a voice began to sing, and
I knew that Napoleon had asked Josephine to give the group another concert. I wasn't terribly disappointed to miss it.

We walked, Duphot and I, through a line of low-cut shrubbery. In the
faint light trickling out from the palazzo, I could make out the silhouette
of my companion. Duphot had been strapping in his youth, clearly, for he

was still strong, even at his advanced age. His military uniform fit well, and he carried himself with an upright dignity. But the hair at his temples was thin and white, and I'd noticed how he coughed several times throughout the meal, as if he had some discomfort in his lungs or trouble with digestion. How could such a man be my husband?

"When Bonaparte told me about you, I was intrigued." Duphot kept his arm on mine, guiding me along the path away from the palazzo. "You come from a respectable family. Clary. I knew of your father. Your dowry is not insignificant. And Napoleon assured me that you were pleasing to look at. He did not lie."

I glowered as I considered my reply; would it be foolish to accept such a compliment? Would Duphot perceive my courtesy as my tacit consent to his courtship? I didn't know. But before I could decide, he continued: "I shall show you the courtesy of frankness, Mademoiselle Clary. We both stand to gain much from . . . an arrangement between us."

I paused my steps. I could see through the dim light that he was staring directly into my face. He tilted his body toward me now. "I know that he's had you as a lover, but I won't hold that against you. Few people have been able to resist him, it appears, when he sets his will toward his objective. No matter what the objective."

I swallowed, lowering my eyes, mortified by all that this man knew and spoke of. He went on: "I shall give you the protection of marriage and my good name."

I saw a bench several feet away and walked toward it. "If . . . if you'll excuse me. I think I'd like to sit."

"Of course." Duphot followed me to the bench and we both sat down. He continued after several moments: "I won't require much from you. I already have a son. How old are you?"

My mind roiled, but I answered the question. "I've . . . I've just turned twenty."

"Ah, well then, my boy is just about the same age as you."

I grimaced at this. How could I become a wife to such an old man, and a stepmother to a gentleman of my own age?

"But you realize what this means for you?" he asked.

I shook my head. When Duphot spoke, his words were slow, the tone of a teacher patiently imparting wisdom to his pupil. "It means that I am not desperate for an heir. I already have one, and he is healthy and robust. Soon he shall have sons of his own, and my legacy will be secure. If you give me just one more child, I shall be immensely pleased. Grateful, even, and I would happily grant you independence." He paused, as if awaiting my murmur of appreciation. When I offered none, he continued: "I would be generous, too, in both material and behavioral matters. I will not govern your steps nor restrict your pleasures. I dare say, most beautiful young women would jump at such an offer."

I shifted on the bench beside him. Was the man proposing marriage or discussing the pragmatic exchange of market goods? Napoleon had once told me that he was not a romantic man, and yet his suit now seemed tender in comparison. Then, at least, we had both felt ourselves to be in love.

"Ah, but you wonder about the girlish notion of love?" I could hear from Duphot's tone that he was smiling, a patronizing smile, as if he knew so much better than I did. "Then let's be frank on that topic as well. Love is in no way essential to a successful marriage. At least, not strictly between husband and wife. You see, mademoiselle, I already have a lover. She has been with me for many years. I don't intend to give her up. So as I say— you'll be free as well." He put a hand on my shoulder. "So long as you take care not to get pregnant by another man, I won't govern how you choose to live your life. But hear my warning: I will not oblige carelessness. If you do fall pregnant with another man's child, I will not claim it as my own. I will not finance its upbringing or education. I will not protect your reputation in such an event. I am a reasonable man, a liberal man, an enlightened man, but I'm no fool, nor do I wish to be publicly cuckolded."

I was stunned to speechlessness, even as I felt my heart thrashing against my ribs. It was all too much to hear; I wished to flee from the conversation. From this place. This old man, this stranger named Duphot—I wanted to be gone far away from him.

How terrible, the things he was saying to me. But then, to be fair, he owed me nothing. I was young and naïve, but I was sensible enough to understand that, and to understand the times in which we lived. He'd just said he was a reasonable man, and all he was doing now was attempting to engage in negotiations from the viewpoint of reason, not the heart.

But Napoleon? The man who had once claimed to love me? He had actually sought to arrange my match to such a man as this? And Joseph had been party to it as well? Did they really care so little for me? I realized it then—I was a burden to them, my constant presence with Julie. Or perhaps I was a nuisance to Josephine. She was a self-assured woman, secure in her husband's favor, and I did not flatter myself in believing that she viewed me as a rival; but still, who enjoys having her husband's former lover spending every day in his presence? They wanted me married off, situated, settled.

Duphot continued, pulling my dreary thoughts back to the dark gardens: "I'll speak to your mother and your brother once we've returned to Rome. Do we have an understanding?"

I met his question with a query of my own: "Do I have a choice?"

He laughed, rising from the bench. "I suppose we can see what your mother says. But, really, Desiree, think about it practically. You're young. Your father is dead. You're not a virgin. And you're a woman—a woman whom the most powerful man in France hopes to see married. So, really, what is it that you were expecting?"

When that week in Milan was over, Duphot announced that he would escort me back to the Roman embassy along with Joseph and Julie. He would assume his post as the military commander of Rome, a position to which he had been appointed by Napoleon, and continue his courtship of me.

Mamma Letizia would depart for Paris along with her three girls, to a rented mansion that Napoleon had acquired for them near the Tuileries Palace. He and Josephine would be continuing on to Mombello, where he would plan his next stage of fighting against the Italians and their Habsburg allies.

"I wish to return to Paris," Josephine announced at dinner on our final night. "Life on these Italian roads does not agree with me. I had a fever coming here, and I feel sick just thinking about getting back in that coach."

But Napoleon would hear none of it; he flatly refused, insisting that he needed his wife's company, and so she sat in sullen silence for the remainder of the meal. We heard shouting in their bedroom later that night—shrieks, heavy groaning as if pieces of furniture were being jostled about—but I wasn't certain whether those were the noises of their disagreement or their ensuing reconciliation. Perhaps both. Either way, when Napoleon's cortege departed the Serbelloni palace the following morning, bound for his next Italian conquest, Josephine was seated beside her husband, and I was not sad to see either of them go.

Our small party arrived back in Rome shortly before Christmas. The winter there was much milder than what we had experienced in Paris, and I was grateful for that, but otherwise my spirits were low. I sought Maman out as soon as we returned to the ambassadorial residence and explained my feelings toward my *seasoned* suitor.

Maman, not surprisingly, saw the situation as pragmatically as Duphot did. "What is there to complain of?" she asked. Joseph agreed, taking up her side. Only Julie understood my perspective.

"How can I marry a man like him?" I lamented. "Old enough to be my father. And already in love with another woman?"

"Love has very little to do with it," Maman said.

"But you loved Papa," I argued.

Maman shrugged. "Little good that did me."

"Julie loves Joseph," I answered.

"You'll respect him with time," was all Maman offered in reply.

And so Duphot continued to visit our palazzo, and I was made to receive him each time.

Unlike our French countrymen, the Romans still venerated their church, and so Christmas was a festive and celebratory season in Rome. The household servants prepared a great Noel feast at our embassy lodgings, with endless servings of fish and chocolate desserts doused in liqueur. I, however, felt in no such celebratory spirit as we rode through the city to midnight Mass, the bells of St. Peter's Basilica ringing out their clamorous summons.

Rome, unlike France, still kept the old Christian calendar. In the days leading up to the New Year, the city roiled with feasting, wine pouring forth from the public fountains and large crowds gathering in the palm-lined streets to sing and dance and make merry.

We said goodbye to Joseph, who was being sent by his brother on a diplomatic mission to Parma in the north. Maman and Nicolas went out that afternoon to Mass to offer prayers for the coming year. In a sulk, I had flatly refused to go with them. Julie, showing solidarity and feeling glum herself over Joseph's departure, had remained at the palazzo with me.

That night, I heard the noise outside our gates growing ever louder, and I guessed that the celebrations of the New Year holiday were getting rowdier. Julie and I sat in the salon feeling sullen.

Night had fallen and the palazzo was quiet and dark, save for the few candles we had lit. It being the holidays, we had dismissed the servants, allowing them to return to their homes hours earlier to celebrate with their own families.

Julie was reading and I was playing a solitary card game, Patience, beside the fire. Outside, the shouting in the streets grew so thunderous that we both looked to each other. "Sounds as though some of them have had too much wine," I said, attempting levity, even though the noise was beginning to put me on edge. Not only the volume, but now the proximity of the voices made it seem as though several men were shouting from just below our windows. I crossed the room and peeled back the drapes. When I saw the scene before me, I gasped.

"What is it?" Julie lowered her book.

"They . . . there are men climbing the palazzo gates," I said.

"What? Why?" Julie rose from her chair and joined me at the window.

"*Morte ai francesi!*"

"*Tiranni!*"

"*Addio, francesi!*"

"*Figli di puttana!*"

Julie and I looked at each other, our faces expressing our shared horror. Even though the shouting was in Italian, the words were similar enough to French that we could deduce their meaning. These men in the streets weren't celebrating—they were protesting. And the object of their protest was the French occupation of their embassy.

"What . . . should we do?" Julie asked. Maman and Nicolas were still out. Joseph was gone to Parma. The servants had been sent away.

"Nicolas will be home soon," I said, my voice faint.

But Julie shook her head, pointing at the crowds. "Maman and Nicolas will never be able to ride in through the front gates. It would be madness to try."

"Let's go upstairs," I said. "Let's lock our doors."

I glanced once more through a sliver of drapery out the window: the men still climbed the gates, and now several of them had hopped over the wall into the forecourt. "Do they really mean to storm the palace?" I asked, my blood turning cold. It was just as the mob had done in France—making quick work of so many walled palaces and monasteries, even prisons. Had we survived the Terror in our own country only to now perish at the hands of an angry, drunken Italian mob?

Just then, a door groaned open, the sound coming from somewhere nearby in the darkened palazzo, and my entire body clenched. "Who's there?"

"Desiree?" A man's voice. I nearly wept—never in my life had I imagined it possible to be so elated by Duphot's arrival. "Oh, thank God you are here!" I ran toward him, my entire body slackening in relief. "But how did you get in?"

Duphot fixed his grim gaze toward the window, clearly aware of what Julie and I had seen. "I came in the rear gate, through the servants' alley. The mob is gathering at the front."

"Let's hope that Maman and Nicolas can do the same," Julie said. But Duphot shook his head. "No. It would be foolish to try to pass. I was alone on foot, so I could slip in. A coach would never be as lucky. They are incensed. Drunk, most of them, the fools. They are screaming things that make no sense. They think France is to blame for their hunger, while Napoleon only wishes to bring them liberty; their priests and princes steal from them every week, and then they blame our forces."

I took Julie's cold hand in my own, weaving my fingers through hers.

Duphot was quiet but angry, a stern and silent fury, the steely resolve of a battle-hardened veteran. "This is an insult to all of France. I will crush this before it mounts." He put his hand on the musket slung over his shoulder. "Stay inside."

With that, Duphot turned from the room and marched back toward the doorway through which he'd just entered. Julie and I charged back to the window to look out over the street below. The crowd was growing in size. After a moment, a figure strode out to meet them and I recognized Duphot. We could not hear his words, but it was clear he was shouting.

The Italian men began to shout back, hands raised, enraged faces illuminated by the torches they carried. Duphot's right hand hovered over the musket at his shoulder. Still, I could not hear his words, but I could see him growing more animated in his gestures.

Julie, beside me, breathed heavily. "What is he saying?"

"I don't know," I answered.

"He should come back inside now."

Several of the men began to shove Duphot, and he raised his arms to fight back. He was shouting. Then, one of the men reached for Duphot's weapon, and the old man tried to push him back. There were too many of them. Duphot struggled, but the crowd was closing in around him. We could no longer see his individual movements. Julie took my hand, and I felt in the clench of her icy grip that she shared my horror.

And then we heard it—the pop of noise ripping across the Roman night. We might have thought it was a firework, going off to celebrate the New Year, but then the crowd began to shout even louder, jostling and shoving like a swarm of mad beasts. And then another shot. And a third. And though the night was dark and the crowd was thick, both Julie and I knew immediately that Leonard Duphot was dead.

# Chapter 14

*Paris*
*Winter 1798*

WINTER STILL STRUCK ME AS AN INSUFFERABLY CRUEL season, with its bitter, ice-slicked wind and the oppressiveness of a low-hanging pewter sky. And yet walking remained the best way for me to find some small measure of solace from the whirling chaos of troubled thoughts that had followed me from Rome back to Paris. Julie and Joseph's home was lovely and comfortable, to be sure, and they had woven me into the daily fabric of their family life with warmth and hospitality, and yet I often found myself wrapped in fits of incredible loneliness. Bouts of restlessness and melancholy. Even in the grand rooms of their spacious villa, misery lurked all around me.

I had not wished to marry Duphot and I had certainly not been in love with the old man. Far from it. He had been a wizened general with a grown son, an established lover, and a second family by her. But that did not erase the horror I felt after having witnessed the man's violent murder. That did not mean that I did not see his death in my haunted thoughts, both sleeping and awake.

I'd left Italy immediately after that uprising, returning to Paris with my sister and her husband, but Paris did not feel like home, either. The nightmares that had begun in Italy trailed me back to the icy French capital. As had been the case during past seasons of trouble, walking became a sort of temporary refuge—a momentary distraction, at least. And so that January afternoon, I donned my thickest cloak and heavy fur cap and muff before taking off from Julie's home, hoping that the sights of the chaotic city might lure my thoughts into some much-needed diversion.

My walking routes were seldom planned, and I often found myself tracing a meandering route toward the Seine, where the silvery waters of the wide river carried all sorts of humanity and bounty from the farthest corners of our Republic and beyond. I'd stroll along the quays of the Right Bank, watching the boats dock, losing my thoughts as I saw the sailors and merchants unloading salmon and cheese from Normandy, lavender from the warm, sunbaked fields of Provence, barrels of plum-red wine from Burgundy. Here, with the wind gliding off the river, the air smelled cleaner than in the rest of the city center, where the narrow streets reeked of waste—human and animal—and the thick scents of cooking fires, damp wool, and so many unwashed bodies.

My restlessness on that particular January day was due to the evening's activity: a ball. A feast to celebrate France's recent victory over and peace with Austria. A grand ball to honor Napoleon and, therefore, his beloved Josephine at his side.

Of course with Joseph now firmly ensconced as Napoleon's constant companion and most trusted adviser, there was no way Julie and I, the other members of Joseph's household, could risk the offense of declining our own invitations, and so I would be forced to attend.

But I dreaded it. While our government, the Directory, was wildly unpopular, Napoleon's star continued to shine ever brighter. He was credited with restoring both glory and peace to the ravaged nation. The pair of them, Napoleon and Josephine, had returned from the Italian front at the head of one massive and never-ending victory parade—with entire towns coming out to cheer them, allowing Napoleon to plunder ancient churches and palaces so that his cavalcade grew ever more loaded down with priceless treasure and art.

And yet, as ebullient as the crowds had been along the way, nothing could match the frenzy with which the city of Paris welcomed its favorite adopted son home. Now that he was back in Paris, the city had decided to change Napoleon's street from the Rue Chantereine to the Rue de la Victoire. Victory Street. The Boy General was also being called the "Son of the Revolution," with the beautiful "Lady of Victory" beside him. And now, even though half of Paris was starving, without bread or firewood in the dark winter months, and even though Josephine had spent nearly half a million francs renovating and redecorating their mansion, the Bonapartes were throwing themselves a lavish, government-funded ball.

I dressed for the evening in a rich gown of sapphire blue, rubies sparkling in my hair and around my neck. Joseph escorted both Julie and me to his brother's grand home, where five hundred other guests were set to arrive in coaches and fiacres.

Joseph gasped as we entered the courtyard. "Brilliant, he's done it," he exclaimed, explaining the scene before us. The courtyard had been arranged to resemble an army camp, replete with uniformed soldiers and campfires in tableaux, along with cannons and warhorses. "To give all of us an idea of what our boys faced on the front," Joseph said, as he ushered us through the snowy scene and toward the wide front doors.

We entered the mansion, its high-ceilinged hall warm compared to the cold night. The grand rooms were ablaze with candlelight, the walls covered in fine art—just a small portion of Napoleon's spoils from Italy. Thousands of fresh flowers filled the large, crowded rooms with their fragrance, mingling with the scents of the ladies' perfume and the platters of aromatic food heaped along the banquet tables. Napoleon had once complained to me of being spurned by Parisian society, and yet all of the capital's most important citizens had turned out this evening in his honor. Recently returned nobles and high-ranking military officers mingled with society hostesses and members of the government, all chatting amid a forest of live trees, hundreds of which had been arranged in potted soil just for the occasion.

Joseph pointed out our nation's Foreign Minister, Charles de Talleyrand, who held court on a broad, winding staircase at the center of the hall, its banister wrapped in vines of fresh-clipped myrtle. "But no sign of him, just yet. I'm sure they wish to make their grand entrance once all the guests have arrived."

I knew that Napoleon was never late—at least, never intentionally so, and neither Julie nor I needed to question to whom Joseph referred when he mentioned "their grand entrance."

And they did appear shortly thereafter, entering through the wide front doors and into the bright, crowded hall. Josephine stood at his side in a simple gown of diaphanous white chiffon, her chestnut hair framed by a diamond tiara that looked unmistakably similar to a crown. Her face was, uncharacteristically, blank of its usual smile, her mouth with a pinched quality. I knew that she spent more on makeup alone than what most workingmen in France earned in an entire year, and so I found it curious that tonight, on such a grand occasion, she had not made her face up to its usual resplendence. She fixed her pale gaze straight ahead into the crowd, but not toward the husband beside her.

The packed room fell silent upon their entrance, all giddy and ebullient energy turning to eager attentiveness as the instruments ceased their playing. Even the crystal of the champagne flutes seemed to stop tinkling. Hundreds of guests turned to the military man, draped in his medals and tricolor sash, the famous bicorn hat atop his head.

Napoleon's eyes swept the room like a general appraising the positions of a battlefield, and I got the impression he was cataloging the face and name of each individual present, determining, even among these throngs of hundreds, who had dared decline his invitation.

A young woman had entered shortly after them, her own narrow frame draped in a simple gown in the same style as Josephine's. "Hortense. Josephine's daughter from the dead viscount. Napoleon's stepdaughter," Julie explained, whispering in my ear. Hortense appeared not much younger than me—I put her at about fifteen or sixteen—and I was struck once again by the difference in age between myself and the woman Napoleon had chosen over me.

Talleyrand went toward the pair first, appearing to savor every moment of this political theater. He welcomed Napoleon and told him that the orchestra had prepared a special song—to honor him but, in fact, to honor Josephine as well. With a nod, the nearby conductor lifted his violin bow, and the musicians took up their instruments.

It was a jaunty melody, militaristic in tone, and the singers soon joined in, delivering the lyrics that had been prepared especially for the occasion. Josephine's taut features softened, and soon she was donning an appreciative smile at the lyrics written in her honor: *"By tending to his happiness, you honor the obligation of France."*

Dinner was not served until late in the evening, shortly before midnight. By that time, the guests had enjoyed plenty of wine and champagne, and the mood was a festive one.

Napoleon took up his place at the head of the central table, with Josephine at his side. She fidgeted with her fork, eating little, while Napoleon tucked into the feast with gusto.

Talleyrand made the first toast, lifting his glass as he said: "Tonight, especially, we honor the citizeness who bears the name most dear to the man who brings our glory. The dear companion to France's conquering hero. To Josephine!"

The room erupted in approving cheers and Napoleon nodded slowly, glancing to Josephine, who offered a demure nod toward the Foreign Minister. But her characteristic radiance seemed somehow diminished this evening. I wondered if anyone else noticed.

The buffet was as decadent as the rest of the evening, but I had little appetite for the rich food. There was an endless spread: salmon in cucumbers and dill, sole in white wine, small tender hens heaped with rosemary and onion, potatoes baked in Gruyère, and soft, warm varieties of fresh-baked bread, clusters of grapes, and platters of olives.

After the feast, Talleyrand announced that our honored General Bonaparte had given us yet another gift—one of which even we Parisians were not yet aware. A new diversion, a risqué dance brought straight to us from Austria known as the *waltz.*

Napoleon and Josephine began it, their bodies entwined in unabashed proximity, and she began to smile more easily as he swept her across the parquet floor to the triple-time melody.

Outside, fireworks burst across the wintry sky, brightening the night as they spelled out *Vive la république.* It was past one o'clock in the morning by the time Napoleon found us. Joseph, Julie, and I stood drinking coffee and enjoying a small plate of desserts. "Ah, brother, I see you've found yourself the most beautiful ladies in the room." Napoleon smiled at me, his eyes roving freely over my figure before resting on the cinch of my waist. I felt my spine go rigid. It was odd, I thought, that Napoleon stood here, flirting with me; he hadn't flirted with me since Marseille. Why was he not pinned to Josephine's side, as he usually was?

"And I see you've thrown yourself a lavish party. One fit for a king, dare I say?" Joseph made the statement like a well-intentioned joke, not one with dangerous insinuation, and his brother appeared to take it as such. Napoleon gestured toward the walls covered in artwork, the banquet tables heaped with platters that servants kept refilling. "Everything for the glory of France. Winning is all for nothing if one does not take advantage of success."

"I toast to that," Joseph said, accepting another glass of champagne from a servant. I accepted a flute for myself, as Julie declined. She was still hopelessly eager to become pregnant and thus limiting all food and drink that was too rich.

"There's the man of the hour. What did they call you—the Son of the Revolution?"

We all turned upon hearing the deep voice, the accent thick and languid, reminding me of my home in the south.

"Ah, Bernadotte!" Napoleon offered a bright smile to the tall, dark-haired man who had so suddenly appeared. "And what do they call you? Sergeant *Belle-Jambe*? Sergeant Beautiful Legs?"

The man, Bernadotte, shrugged off the moniker with a half smile. "I put it down as desperation—there were too many men longing for a view of a nice pair of legs if they had to remark on my own."

"But we do have to admire them," Napoleon said, gesturing to the man's long, strong figure, his legs clothed in the tight-fitting breeches of the French officer.

"I'd rather offer my admiration elsewhere, to one more worthy." The man, who stood more than a head taller than Napoleon, turned his dark gaze directly on me. "Would you mind introducing me to your companions?"

"Of course"—Napoleon shifted—"where are my manners?"

"You're a Corsican; I just presumed you never had any," quipped the newcomer.

"That's something, coming from a hot-headed southerner like your-self." Napoleon laughed, then turned to us. "Ladies, please allow me to in-troduce one of my best sergeants, an incorrigible Gascon but a fine soldier nonetheless, Jean-Baptiste Bernadotte."

"One of *your* sergeants, eh? I don't know whether to refute your intro-duction based on that, or to accept it due to the other generous compli-ments mingled therein."

"You did serve under me in Italy," Napoleon said.

"I did a great deal more against those Germans than simply serve under you, young man." This Bernadotte smiled broadly, flashing a mouth full of straight, white teeth—they were startlingly nice, in fact, a rare sight. "When our Bonaparte here needed assistance against the Habsburgs in Italy, I marched my men through blizzards and over the Alps to help him out of a bind."

"You are a valiant soldier and a hero to France, there's no denying that, now mind your mouth for once and meet these ladies, Bernadotte," Napo-leon said, turning to us. "This is Julie Bonaparte, wife to my brother Jo-seph. And this is Julie's sister and my dear old friend, Desiree Clary."

Both men looked at me now, but I met the eyes of Bernadotte, who said: "Hardly *old*, Bonaparte. Mademoiselle Clary, a pleasure to meet you." He took my hand in his and placed a quick kiss on top of it, keeping his gaze locked intently with mine as he did so. "Even if you do happen to be a friend of Bonaparte's."

"It's interesting," Napoleon said, shifting his weight from one foot to the other, leaning toward me as he did so. "Here we are, a pair of warm-climate men, freezing our asses off in godforsaken Paris, and yet we find ourselves in the company of two southern women."

"Indeed?" Bernadotte raised an eyebrow, studying me just a bit closer.

"We come from Marseille, sir," I answered.

"That's where I met her . . . them," Napoleon said. "Years ago."

Bernadotte ignored Napoleon's remark, his eyes remaining on me. "A city I know well."

"Oh?" I cocked my head to the side. Napoleon was standing close, lean-ing in my direction, but I found my body angling toward Bernadotte's.

"On one of my first assignments," Bernadotte said, "I was sent to Marseille. The royal governor requested troops to keep the order, and so I was in charge of a squadron of men with the marines."

"Yes, he's an ocean man, you'll have to forgive him for it." Napoleon waved a footman over for refills of champagne.

"Clary, you say?" Bernadotte asked.

"Yes." I nodded.

"I knew of a Monsieur Francois Clary when I was stationed there. We all did."

"My father," I said eagerly.

Bernadotte offered half a smile, his face suddenly bearing a look of remembrance. "A well-respected merchant in the area."

I offered a small nod. "You are kind to say so."

"The truth." He fixed his eyes more intently on me, taking in the shape of my sapphire gown. I felt a slight tremble in my frame when he asked: "What do you say to a dance, Mademoiselle Clary? We've bested these Habsburgs on the battlefield, now how about we best them on the dance floor? What did you call this new Austrian thing, Bonaparte—a *waltz*?" I did not look toward my sister or Joseph, nor did I look toward Napoleon. I simply smiled, nodding my agreement and allowing Bernadotte to take my hand in his and lead me toward the dancing.

Bernadotte was tall, much taller than I was, and his strong hold guided me easily through the triple time of the strings, even though the steps of the waltz were foreign to me. Servants flitted around the space, refilling glasses and whisking away discarded plates. I caught sight of Josephine, who stood near the dancing, chatting between Talleyrand and her daughter, Hortense. Napoleon was nearby but not beside her, speaking to an attractive society hostess in rich aubergine silk and an elaborate headdress of peacock plumes. I thought again how odd it was that he was spending the evening heaping his attention on women other than his adored wife.

Bernadotte spoke first. "You are a longtime friend of Bonaparte's?"

I weighed my words a moment before answering; I did not know what Napoleon might have told this man. I decided to offer an account that was entirely truthful, even if perhaps a bit incomplete: "He was stationed in Marseille for a time, and his brother courted my sister. And then married her, so I've come to know the Bonaparte family well."

Bernadotte nodded, accepting my answer. "My first assignment with the marines was on Corsica. I got to know Letizia and all of them. Everyone on that island knew the fierce Mamma di Buonaparte. She was Mamma then, of course. Now she's Madame Mère, I hear. A good French name."

"Just as her son has changed his name from when I first knew him," I said.

"Ah, yes." Bernadotte guided us both through the dance steps with an easy grace in spite of his tall frame. "She's not here tonight. Letizia."

"I noticed."

"She cannot bear her son's wife, so she made a convenient excuse to be out of town with her girls. She is feuding with her son, you know," Bernadotte said.

"They are quarreling once more?" I asked, my interest piqued. "I thought they had reconciled."

Bernadotte shook his head. "Letizia accuses Josephine of wasting her son's money, while sharing other sorts of . . . gifts . . . with too many other men. And Napoleon knows of the accusations."

"She is openly spreading these rumors about her own son and his wife?" I asked. "He must be furious."

Bernadotte nodded.

"And . . . how do *you* know this?" I asked, cocking my head to the side.

Bernadotte laughed. "Come now. Soldiers gossip more than salon hostesses—you didn't know that?"

I knew Napoleon well enough to know that he would never stand for open slander from his own family members against his beloved. And yet, I knew he loved his mother fiercely as well. It must have been torturous for him to have the two women he loved most at odds. But clearly he had made his choice, for only one of them was here tonight.

I steered the conversation toward a more appropriate topic: "Were you and Napoleon friends, back when you were deployed to Corsica?"

Bernadotte nodded, chuckling to himself, perhaps recalling some distant memory. "He was nothing but a scrawny scrap of a boy when I met him. Always hanging around our barracks like some local stray, asking us all sorts of questions on how to use cannons and the different types of gunpowder. He left for the academy at Brienne shortly after that. Whenever he gets a bit too high on his own glory, I remind him that I was keeping the peace on his island as an officer of France before he had ever shit in a military school latrine." Bernadotte realized his mistake only after the words were out, and his dark eyes went wide in embarrassment. "You must pardon my vulgar language. My manners. I'm a louche southerner to begin with, and then put me out in the field with a bunch of coarse men for months and I forget my manners entirely. Will you forgive me?"

"I suppose I can forgive you, if only because you did not chide me for stepping on your toes a moment ago," I said, smirking. In truth, I was impressed at this Bernadotte fellow's candor, his casual self-assurance, and I was enjoying his company.

I was also slightly amazed at the confidence this man displayed opposite Napoleon—I'd never seen anyone stand up to him in such a way, not even his older brother. And certainly not Josephine, who seemed to handle him with both delicacy and reverence—a well-seasoned sailor harnessing the winds of a massive ship, doing what she could to direct the course in her favor but always recognizing and indeed deferring to the overriding strength of the much larger force.

But not Bernadotte. Not only did he tower over Napoleon physically, but he teased him as well. Both out of his presence but also in his presence. And, miraculously, Napoleon seemed to abide it with perfectly good humor.

I studied the man, this Bernadotte, a bit closer. I noted the warm tone of his skin, the thickness of his dark, wavy hair. I hoped then that this strange jaunty music, this waltz, might continue a while longer so that I might remain in his arms.

"I can assure you, Mademoiselle Clary, my toes did not feel a thing," Bernadotte said after a moment. "You're a perfectly graceful dancer."

I lowered my eyes, feeling my face flush. "And you?" I asked. "Did you join the military at a young age as well?"

He nodded. "I was little more than a boy when my father died. I had intended to study the law, open up a practice in our small southern town of Pau. Do you know Pau?"

"Not well." In fact, I'd never heard of it, but I did not say as much.

"It's just north of the Spanish border. A mountain town buried in the

Atlantic Pyrénées. Not much to do there, and Father left us with massive debt. Mother had so many children at home, and I became as burdensome a mouth to feed as my dreams of the law became implausible. So I left, joined up with the Royal Marines."

I listened intently, appreciative of how he confided in me after such a short acquaintance. "Humble beginnings," I remarked. "But this Revolution has made for the possibility of advancement—even for that of a poor, fatherless boy from the mountains of Pau."

"You're a Clary. If I remember clearly, your origins were not so humble?"

"You remember correctly," I said. "Though that, of course, made for some worrisome times for us during the Terror."

"Yes," Bernadotte said, his dark eyes narrowing in understanding. "But that's all behind us now. Hopefully we shall have peace and prosperity in France. And some good leadership." We both turned now, instinctively, toward the short figure in the center of the room.

Fresh from war and victory, our city's hero seemed intent that winter on making merry with his wife, and the rest of the capital's high society fell in line willingly. Hordes of officers newly returned from the front gathered each night in salons and supper clubs, mingling with ambitious civic leaders and charming heiresses, each vying for favor in the inner circle that had sprung up solidly around Napoleon. Joseph, being the closest of Napoleon's confidants and advisers, had a constant stream of guests and supplicants in his home that winter, and Julie and I grew accustomed to acting as impromptu hostesses.

A few nights after the ball given by the Bonapartes, we found ourselves at the center of one such spontaneous reception in Joseph's spacious townhouse, with Talleyrand and his clique of clerks and ministers stopping in to offer their respects. But another visitor arrived just shortly after them, his sudden appearance surprising us all.

"Sergeant Jean-Baptiste Bernadotte." The footman announced his entry into our salon, immediately causing my pulse to quicken. I plunged myself into conversation with Julie, attempting to appear diverted and carefree. Within moments, after offering his greetings to my brother-in-law and Talleyrand, Bernadotte made his long-legged stride over to my side of the room, where I greeted him with a curtsy and a checked smile. "Sergeant Belle-Jambe, good evening," I said. He kissed my hand, then Julie's.

"Some champagne, sir?" Julie asked.

"Delightful, thank you, Madame Bonaparte," Bernadotte replied, and Julie disappeared without another word, leaving me alone with this tall, dark newcomer. We stood beside the mantel and its blazing fire, and I hoped Bernadotte would credit its heat for the sudden rush of color to my cheeks.

"Mademoiselle Clary, it is good to see you," he said. He wore his officer's uniform, and his hair fell in unruly waves around his handsome face.

"Please, you may call me Desiree, sir."

Bernadotte nodded as a footman appeared, proffering two flutes of champagne on a silver tray. I accepted my drink and noted that Julie had not rejoined our small group but rather had woven herself into conversation across the room between her husband and Talleyrand. They were leaning close and speaking in low voices, and I sensed that Bernadotte and I were their topic of conversation, even as they made sure to give us a wide berth. My sister, of course, would be intrigued by my interactions with this man, and Talleyrand and Joseph, well, as rising stars in our new government, wasn't it their business to know everyone else's business? Suddenly the fire beside us felt unbearably hot, and I felt my cheeks smoldering from red to an even deeper scarlet. "Say," I said, looking up at my companion. "What do you think of taking a quick step outside?" I gestured toward the glass doors that gave out onto the terrace and the darkness of the back garden.

"Lead the way," Bernadotte said, nodding gamely.

Once outside, I breathed deeply in the cool air, feeling myself relax in the darkness and the distance from my sister and her co-conspirators. The night was chilly and clear, though not bitter cold, and the stars overhead pierced the sky with just enough light to offer a pleasant glow over the terrace. I took a slow sip of my champagne.

"I miss our southern skies," Bernadotte said, slipping his officer's jacket over my shoulders without my asking him to do so. I accepted this gesture, enjoying the warmth from his body even as the cool air felt nice on my face.

"The stars in Marseille," I said, my voice wistful. "I could never decide whether I liked them more in the sky or the way they shimmered in the sea."

"In Pau," Bernadotte said, "in the mountains, I felt sometimes as if all I had to do was reach up and I'd be close enough to graze them with my fingertips."

I nodded, taking another sip of my drink. The bubbles fluttered down my throat and into my belly, filling me with a pleasant softness.

"Warm nights," he continued, "after Papa died, when Maman would have half a dozen crying babies in the house, I'd slip out as often as I could. I didn't know where, exactly, Papa had gone, but I had some vague understanding that he was there...." He gestured skyward. "Somewhere up there. As the priest in our village had told me, he was looking down."

I sighed a slow exhale. "Was it very hard on you when he died?" I asked, thinking back to my own father's death, noting how our twinned losses wove Bernadotte and me together with a common understanding of young grief.

He considered his words a moment before answering: "It was, mostly because of how it changed our family. How it changed Maman. She seemed lost to me, too, after Papa was gone. Without hope, somehow. For any of us."

These words hit me in the stomach with a familiarity and a pained sense of knowing all too well what he meant, as I recalled my own maman, her constant fears and ailments in the wake of Papa's death.

"I'd look up and I'd pick which star I thought was my papa," Bernadotte said. "And then I'd name the members of my family, giving each of us a star."

I smiled in the darkness. I liked that, imagining this tall man as a young boy, tucked in the grass under a southern sky, staring up at a vast realm of stars and seeking out his comfort with his own mind and dreams.

"And of course," he said, stepping closer beside me, "I always gave myself a star."

"Of course," I said, angling my face sideways to look at him. "Which one is your star?" I asked, turning my gaze skyward.

"Well, now," Bernadotte said, following my eyes upward. "It would change, depending on the season. Let's see. Perhaps I could be that one," he said, pointing toward a determined light that I saw as the bright tip of a ladle. "Polaris," Bernadotte said.

"Polaris," I said, repeating the name. And then, before I knew what he was doing, Bernadotte took my hand in his own and lifted it. My heart thrilled at the press of his warm skin on mine, at the way his fingers gripped my own. He continued, his lips now so close to my ear that I felt his words at the same time I heard them: "But you, you must have a star as well, Desiree."

"Oh?" My voice was faint, but my heart was thunderous; I could feel it clamoring against my ribs and my corset.

"Yes," he said, sweeping the heavens, my hand in his, eventually settling our pointing on the brightest light. It had an unapologetic glow, almost amber and rose in its hue. "Venus," he said, his voice decisive. "There she is. The loveliest of all the heavenly lights. That's yours, Desiree."

Before I knew what was happening, my mind flew back to another night, with another man, standing beneath another clear sky strewn with stars. *You see that flame that flies past, spreading light across its path? Come with me, Desiree, and you see how that star flies? You shall have the chance to do the same.*

How different these two men were, I thought, even if the pull I felt toward each of them was oddly similar. Napoleon had declared himself a shooting star, a bright and unstoppable light scorching its way across the sky; if I was lucky, I might join him by clinging to his comet's tail in order to be pulled along behind his glory. Bernadotte, on the other hand, was telling me that I shone bright and beautiful on my own. He saw me, Desiree. *How different indeed,* I thought, not for the first time. And not for the last time, either.

# Chapter 15

*Paris*
*Spring 1798*

T HE FIRST HINT OF SPRING CAME TO PARIS IN THE SOUND
of birdsong, in the welcome sight of new buds brightening the bare
branches of the city's chestnut and plane trees. The evenings grew longer,
the mornings began to arrive earlier, and the air was gradually warmed by
a gentle, strengthening sun.

Julie and I walked the leafy lanes of the Parc Monceau one afternoon in
late April. It was a lovely space, once a nobleman's private grounds but
now the property of the people. The neighborhood remained affluent
even after the Revolution had made its mark, with private mansions lining
its border. The park itself was filled with flower beds and stone benches,
narrow allées framed by shrubbery and a gracious fountain, but the heart
of the grounds was a small classical temple, with columns and a rotunda
built on the site of what used to be one of the dreaded royal tollbooths.
From here, His Majesty's customs workers had collected fees from the
long-suffering subjects as they passed. That hated structure, like so much
else once belonging to the crown, had been razed in the Revolution and
was replaced by this temple to the republican ideals of antiquity.

But as we strolled that day, neither Julie nor I was thinking of the
violence of the Revolution. Nor were we thinking of any sort of politics.

That day, our conversation was of quite a different nature. We were discussing the tall, dark-eyed person of Jean-Baptiste Bernadotte.

He had handed me a letter just that morning in the sunny salon of our home, and I clutched the paper as we walked, relishing his private words. *You have turned this officer into a young soldier again, no more sure of himself than one who has never faced the battle lines. I find myself suddenly without defenses, as they fall willingly before your smile.*

"With Napoleon, it came to an end because of Josephine," Julie said, her arm woven through mine as we strolled side by side.

"Yes," I said.

"And with Duphot . . . poor Duphot . . . it came to an end because, well, let's not return to the horrors of Rome."

"Indeed," I agreed, shaking my head. "Poor Duphot." I made a cross over myself, an instinctive gesture from childhood and one that no longer put me at risk of a death sentence, given the more tolerant government of the Directory.

"Bernadotte is a good man," Julie said. "And a well-loved general. Some say he's better in the field even than . . . well, never mind that. I don't care what others say. I care only what *you* say." Julie paused, turning toward me. "Do you see any reason why it might come to an end between you and Bernadotte?"

I thought about my sister's question, feeling my cheeks grow warm even as I knew it was useless to try to hide anything from her. I cared deeply for Bernadotte and she knew it. Ever since dancing with him at that winter ball in honor of Napoleon, and then welcoming him into Joseph and Julie's home a few nights later, my thoughts had been consumed with Sergeant Belle-Jambe. And that was, in large part, because he had proven determined in his regular visits and letters of courtship.

Bernadotte had just recently leased a large estate, replete with servants and acres of land, several miles past the southern barrier of Paris. He wasn't in the city at all times, but whenever he did come in, his first stop was to pay a call at Joseph's home. Bernadotte had proven reliable and unwavering in his attentions. We chatted in the parlor with my sister and Joseph. We enjoyed card games and laughter late into the night. Once, when he played his knave of hearts to vanquish me in a round of whist, I asked him, my eyebrow arching upward: "And how about you, Sergeant Bernadotte? Is it common for you to play the knave with hearts?"

He looked at me, eyes earnest, as he responded: "Once, perhaps, I fancied myself a knave. But these days, when the suit is hearts, I find myself willing to yield to a queen."

Julie and Joseph barely concealed their meaningful looks, as I turned my attention back to the cards in my lap, biting my lip to bridle a full and beaming smile.

On nice afternoons, Bernadotte and I would stroll through the city, ambling the riverside quays or winding our way along the paths of the Tuileries gardens while one of Joseph's manservants followed behind with the coach at a discreet distance. Julie and Joseph had imposed on me all the strictures of a traditional courtship, and with Maman back in Marseille with Nicolas, they saw fit to monitor us like watchful parents.

Bernadotte had, apparently, been perfectly content to pursue such a proper courtship; perhaps a bit *too* proper for my liking—he had not yet kissed me. As pleased as I was with his steady attention, that fact did trouble me. In truth, I longed for his kiss. I thought about it, both when I was with him and when I was not. Did I not stir the necessary passion in him? I wondered.

When I voiced this concern to Julie that afternoon as we strolled the pebbled allées of Parc Monceau, she offered only a sly smirk in reply. "What?" I asked, my interest immediately roused. "What are you withholding from me?"

Julie looked straight ahead at the pathway before us, apparently deliberating how to answer. Eventually, she yielded to my insistence, saying: "I do not believe you shall have to wait too much longer for that kiss, my dear sister."

I paused mid-step, staring at her. "What do you mean?"

Julie beamed as she finally let it gush out of her: just that morning, following his visit to our home, Bernadotte had asked Joseph if they might speak in private. The two men had retreated to my brother-in-law's study while I had gone out on an errand to the florist's shop, none the wiser that such a meeting was taking place. Following his conversation with Bernadotte, Joseph had pulled Julie into his study. And here I was, a few hours later, walking in Parc Monceau with my sister. "He's asked for your hand, Desi," Julie said, guiding me to the nearest stone bench.

I felt my heart leap in my chest. Bernadotte wished to marry me. Did I wish to be Bernadotte's wife? Julie asked.

I sat beside her on the bench, considering my response. It was odd—with Napoleon, I had known him better. I had spent more time with him, and I had been madly in love with him, recklessly so, infatuated in the way that only a young girl can be before she's ever known heartbreak or betrayal. And yet, look at how he had treated me, how he had behaved once he'd secured my affections.

Bernadotte I knew less intimately, to be sure. After all, he'd never even kissed me. And yet, somehow, I trusted that Bernadotte would not hurt me in the way that my previous fiancé had. I felt, perhaps naïvely, that Bernadotte would prove to be the good man I had seen him to be so far. The sort of man with whom I could trust my wary heart. The sort of gentleman I would want for my husband.

Now I did not try to suppress the smile that burst across my face; I *did* want to marry Bernadotte. I knew that. I wanted to marry him more than I'd wanted anything since Napoleon's abandonment.

Julie read my face, and she took my hands in hers. "And so, I ask you again: is there any reason why Joseph ought to refuse our dear Bernadotte's request?"

"No reason," I said, beaming at my sister. "No reason at all."

On the day when spring finally and fully took possession of the city, when the crocuses burst forth with petals and the leaves of the plane trees unfurled fat and green, Jean-Baptiste Bernadotte asked for my hand, and I happily gave it.

"Desiree Clary, you've made this soldier see that there is more to life than warfare." He held my hands in his as we stood alone in Julie's salon. "*Mon Dieu*, I thought I was immune to nervousness, having stared down enemy muskets, but I find myself lacking . . ." He swallowed, taking in a fortifying breath before he tried again: "I find myself lacking the words to tell you how deeply I care for you now, Desiree. How . . . happy you would make me if . . . well, if you'd . . ." I saw how he trembled, how his guileless features flushed as he forced himself to keep my eye contact.

"Yes," I said, hoping to encourage him with my smile.

He raised a dark eyebrow, the hope apparent on his face.

"Yes, Sergeant Belle-Jambe," I continued, "I will marry you."

With that, he pulled me toward him, letting loose a loud whoop as he twirled me around the room. Julie and Joseph, upon hearing this celebratory exclamation, took that as their invitation to burst into the salon, the champagne already poured. There were hugs and handshakes; Julie wiped tears as she whispered to me: "I am so happy for you both." Handing each of us a flute, Joseph offered a toast: "To the Bernadottes, and many happy years for them."

*The Bernadottes.* As I gulped the cold, bubbly drink, I felt my entire body ripple with a giddy sort of exhilaration. I stared at the man beside me, taking in his handsome features, his bright and earnest smile, his strong figure, and I marveled at all that had led me to that moment.

While Napoleon's intentions had been whispered in the darkness, his affections hastily given and even more hastily withdrawn, Bernadotte had done everything properly. He'd written to Marseille to request my mother's and my brother's blessings. Having secured those, he'd spoken to Joseph, just as Julie had told me. And now, on that glorious spring day, he became my fiancé.

Bernadotte didn't promise me a comet. He did not promise to pull me, blazing, across the sky. He only promised to give me himself, wholly and faithfully. And that, I decided, would be quite enough.

# Chapter 16

*Paris*
*Spring 1798*

I T WAS THE BIGGEST NEWS EVER TO COME TO FRANCE. THE newspapers teemed with daily reports, as the gossip spread down streets and through cafés. It was to be the largest, most ambitious, most far-flung military campaign ever attempted by any French army. A campaign to be carried out across sea and desert sand. A quest to capture the storied and ancient kingdom of Egypt.

And yet, what does any of that mean to a young lady, newly twenty, suddenly and unexpectedly in love and planning to be married?

Very little, I'll confess, once I found out that my Bernadotte would not have to take part in the massive force. In fact, Bernadotte had put in a request for several months' leave, ostensibly for rest after the grueling campaigns with the armies of the Rhine and Italy, but, he confessed to me, that wasn't the real reason. "I need to take a break from soldiering and play the part of lover for a time," he admitted, grinning as we ended an evening of supper and cards at Julie's home. I felt my face grow warm, my features spreading into a smile, and I allowed Bernadotte to steal a quick kiss before he hopped into his waiting carriage.

We were planning for a late-summer wedding. Though Bernadotte had taken the lease on a handsome estate to the south of the city, I'd admitted to him that I didn't wish to live in the countryside, so far from my sister.

Being the dear he was, Bernadotte took out another lease on a grand townhouse in Paris on the Rue de Monceau, just a few blocks from Julie and Joseph, and a short walk from my beloved Parc Monceau.

The Egyptian war that Napoleon was planning mattered little to me compared with the concerns of assembling my trousseau and furnishing the home in which Bernadotte and I would live as newlyweds. And yet, I couldn't help but hear the rumors and gossip that trickled into Julie's household through Joseph and his brother.

France's ruling body in Paris, the five-person Directory, had fallen from favor due to widespread corruption and ineptitude. Napoleon, more interested in marching armies abroad than squabbling over politics at home, shrugged off the mounting cries of the people that he seek office and wrangle the nation's politicians as effectively as he had wrangled our troops and foreign heads of state. Outwardly, he had no interest; his focus was turned entirely toward capturing Egypt and ending the British dominance of the Far Eastern trade routes.

Josephine was beside herself—I knew this because it was the Bonaparte sisters' favorite topic to discuss whenever they visited Julie and me. Pauline, particularly, was gloating, as puffed up as a peacock. "She's positively begging him to take her with him on campaign. Weeping every night. She claims that the thought of their separation torments her, but we all know the real reason: she is in debt, and she knows the creditors will cut her off as soon as Napoleon is gone and no longer paying her bills."

Word of Josephine's profligate spending had become common knowledge throughout Paris. Shopkeepers and bankers delighted in the appearance of her gilded coach, the alighting of her narrow frame, her eager smile, amber eyes scanning always for the latest wares. She deployed francs with the same unmitigated verve with which her husband deployed troops. Only there was a recklessness to her expenditures—some hunger for luxury and acquisition that seemed impossible to sate. "Her wardrobe alone for a single season costs more than what most families will ever earn," Julie told me. "Joseph cannot believe it."

Though Napoleon had returned from his Italian campaigns with veritable trunks full of plundered jewels—diamonds, rubies, sapphires, amethysts—she still spent on jewelry with an appetite that rivaled Marie-

Antoinette's. She spent on each jar of rouge what our soldiers' widows were allotted to spend in an entire year. Her gowns, hundreds of them ordered custom from the exclusive Parisian dressmaker Rose Bertin, set the trends each season for fashion. And the renovations she had undertaken for their home on the Rue de la Victoire had exceeded even her mother-in-law's disapproving predictions; she'd enlisted our famed national painter Jacques-Louis David to create a sprawling masterpiece of friezes and murals on the walls. The final price of this project—millions—now fueled public outrage, even from a populace inclined to adore her husband and see his consort as faultless.

Napoleon was the only person, it seemed, who dared to tell her no. Though he never denied her requests for material comforts (in fact, he'd just recently acquiesced to her request to buy a sprawling estate, the Château de Malmaison, on the western outskirts of the capital), he would not allow her to join him on his campaign to Egypt. She wept at this. He'd told her that France would colonize that kingdom and he could be gone for as long as six years, but her presence would prove too much of a distraction. He would take her son, Eugene, a young officer who had recently completed his training at the military academy, but not Josephine. While in Egypt, he would need to play general, not husband. She could travel with him to his embarkation at the port of Toulon, but he'd bid her farewell on French soil.

Those of us who saw them together in intimate moments—family dinners or outings to the theater—knew that their relationship was as volatile and erratic as ever, with frequent outbursts and tears smearing her rouged cheeks. When we went to *Macbeth* as a family in the week before Napoleon's departure, Josephine spent the entire first act in the carriage, crying, refusing to come out.

"It's because she wanted him to wait with her, to sit there and soothe her, rather than see how Lady Macbeth resembles his own scheming wife," Pauline said, whispering to Julie and Joseph loud enough that I overheard.

I was overjoyed to have my Bernadotte as a refuge from the Bonaparte family's histrionics. Though I'd never consider giving up my intimacy with my sister, I relished the thought of an escape from the daily interactions with the rest of the clan. Joseph's home, just like Napoleon's, had become a hive of constant and chaotic activity as they prepared for the departure to Egypt. Napoleon would be taking not only tens of thousands of soldiers and sailors with him, but also the elite minds of French academia. He'd be transporting botanists, zoologists, astronomers, surgeons, writers, and painters as part of his floating force. Joseph would not go, but would remain behind to safeguard Napoleon's interests in Paris, both with the ruling authorities and within the Bonaparte family.

And when Josephine and Napoleon left for Toulon before dawn on an early May morning—early enough that the English spies who trailed them would not notice their exit from the capital—I welcomed the thought of turning my focus from Napoleon and Josephine to my own romance, one with decidedly fewer quarrels.

The Hôtel de Ville at Sceaux was an old lemon-yellow building in the center of the rural town, just a short carriage ride from the country estate Bernadotte had recently considered home. Joseph and Julie gave me away with Maman's full blessing.

We retired to Bernadotte's nearby estate after the ceremony for the wedding luncheon. There in the garden under the shade of the leafy plane and chestnut trees, my sister made a toast to my bridegroom. Joseph wished us happiness and then honored his absent brother Napoleon, whose fleet was at that time fighting the desert tribes of Egypt against the backdrop of the grand pyramids.

Josephine, who was ensconced at Malmaison overseeing the renovations to the sprawling château, had declined my invitation with effusive regrets. I knew that she dreaded the thought of facing the unified Bonaparte clan without her husband present. It was just as well—and no small relief to know that the day would pass with far less tension.

We feasted on a spread of champagne and oysters and roasted pheasant stuffed with sage and apples. After our guests had eaten their fill, I stood beside my new husband in our large forecourt and saw them off, waving happily at the line of departing coaches.

When the last guests—Julie and Joseph—had receded from our view,

Bernadotte turned to me, taking my hand in his. "Alone with my wife. At last."

I smiled. *At last.* He was correct; how many times had I lamented the fact that marriage seemed like a doorway through which I had been barred entry? I squeezed his hand in return. "My husband."

Bernadotte carried me to our bedchamber and made a grand gesture of bearing me over the threshold. His arms were so unlike Napoleon's—indeed his entire frame was. Napoleon had been sinewy, narrow, nearly my height, while Bernadotte towered over me. I felt nubile and supple in his arms as he lowered me to the bed. "Well, then, Madame Bernadotte."

"Yes, Monsieur Bernadotte?"

My husband looked down at me, his dark eyes alight. "You make a seasoned soldier feel a bit shy."

I tugged on his shirt, pulling it over his head. My mind swam in a heady whirl of champagne and giddy feelings—nervousness, eagerness, even a bit of bashful modesty—but I gasped when I saw his bare skin for the first time: *Death to Kings* had been tattooed across his broad chest. I looked from his body to his face, my shock surely apparent on my features.

Bernadotte lifted his hands, a protective gesture, as he looked down at the words. "Yes. This is . . . I gather you've never seen a tattoo before?"

I shook my head.

"I had it done in one of my . . . younger moments. That's the thing about engraving your skin in ink—it's permanent."

I studied the letters. "I . . . I wasn't expecting it."

"No," he said, reaching for my hand. "I'm sure you weren't. I'm sorry if I startled you." He paused a moment. "But . . . but I don't regret the sentiment."

I didn't say anything. The bedchamber was quiet; the rural countryside beyond our windows was so very still compared to the foot traffic and coach clatter din of the capital. I blinked, staring once more at the words on my new husband's chest. *Death to Kings.*

"Do you find it . . . terribly off-putting?" he asked, his voice timorous.

I studied the rest of his body, taking in the carved ridges of his flesh and muscle. His thick arms, expansive chest, strong shoulders. His skin fairly hummed with desire, and so, I realized, did mine. "Not at all," I answered honestly, leaning forward to meet his lips with mine.

Bernadotte accepted my body's invitation and proved my fears wrong with that first, long kiss as man and wife—there was certainly no lack of passion between us. He took me in his arms with a strong, determined embrace, pulling me ever closer until there was no more fabric or modesty to separate us, and there was no more conversation that evening, at least not of the spoken kind.

We gave the servants very little work those first few days, barely emerging from our bedchamber and our newlywed joy. Meals were brought in on trays and enjoyed in bed. I cared very little for exploring the grounds or the large rooms of the home, so consumed was I in acquainting myself with my new husband's body and the previously unknown pleasures he seemed so intent to pull forth from my own.

After our brief stay as man and wife in Sceaux, we relocated to our new townhome in Paris. As was so often the case with my Bernadotte, he did not look at new places as we approached, but rather watched me as I saw them. It was as if his reaction could only be formed once he saw that I was happy.

"Here we are, Madame Bernadotte," he said as the coach pulled up to our new property. An iron gate led to a broad forecourt, with the mansion tucked back away from the street. The front of the home was brightened by tall windows with balconies and flanked by two gracious wings, or *pa-villons*. The home was large, much more than we needed for just the two of us, but it would be perfectly suited for both entertaining and . . . I thought with a blush . . . a growing family.

"Does it please you?" he asked, his focus still fixed on me as the coach slowed to a halt. "Oh, Bernadotte, it's lovely." My excited smile was met now by his own happy expression.

Inside, the home was bright and the décor was tastefully elegant. Per-haps not as lavish as our family villa in Marseille, or the Bonapartes' *palais* here in Paris, but I knew that we could be very comfortable—indeed, happy—here. I had overseen the decorations and had selected the furnishings myself, with Julie's help of course, and I was delighted to see how it had all come together. Sèvres porcelain covered the long mahogany table of the dining room. Just across from that, our salon was appointed with marble-topped end tables accented with porcelain vases and delicate dishes painted in pastoral scenes. On the mantelpiece ticked a gilt clock fashioned in the elaborate style of Louis XIV. A row of tall gold mirrors reflected the flickering light of the candelabras and would make this the perfect room for gatherings lasting late into the night. One room over, a long gallery filled with oil paintings led to a conservatory with a high ceiling, the airy space awash in natural light. In that sunny room, overlooking our lovely gardens, I intended to take up my girlhood passion for drawing once more. My husband heartily supported my plan.

A broad, curving staircase in the center of the front hall led to the second floor. It was toward that stairway that my husband now carried me, and he made quick work of the steps. "Where are we going?" I asked as he whisked me upstairs, making me feel light in his arms.

"Where do you think, madame?" he asked, his eyes lit with a rakish twinkle. "To our bedroom, of course. That drive was far too long."

I couldn't help but giggle. "Oh, you need a rest?"

"I did not say anything about resting," he answered, picking up his pace. At the end of the hallway the master suite loomed, and Bernadotte kicked the double doors open. In the center of the room was a massive mahogany bed with a silk canopy and heavy damask bedcovers. Upholstered armchairs and a sofa formed a small seating area. There was a tall mirror and a silk dressing screen. From the mantel came the soft click of an ormolu boudoir clock. My husband turned us toward the bed. "Time to christen our marital chamber, *ma chérie*."

Bernadotte lay me down, the plush pillows absorbing our bodies as we laughed and struggled with my husband's boots and heavy uniform. "I might need your help, Madame Bernadotte, in shedding all of these trappings. Unless you want me to call my valet in."

"I am here to serve you, monsieur."

We spent a delicious afternoon together, oblivious of all else that happened in the house or the outside world. Afterward, I lay in his arms, Bernadotte's thick, rough finger tracing a gentle line up and down my bare, goose-pimpled back. "The servants must think we are mad," I said, chuckling. "We arrive and yet they barely catch a glimpse of us."

"We *are* mad," he said, rolling me toward him. "At least, I am. I am mad for you, Desiree."

I was overcome for a moment. By the fact that he said it, and more so by the fact that I knew I could believe him. But then, collecting myself, I voiced the question that had been weighing on my mind in recent days: "Why me?"

He looked at me askance. I could tell that the question had surprised him.

"Why are you so kind to me?" I asked, clarifying. "Why have you chosen me for such a love?" My hair tumbled around my bare shoulders and pale, exposed breasts, and I noticed how distracted he was. But then he looked back to my face, answering: "I could just as easily ask you the same thing."

He reached for me but I swatted his hand away. "That night at the ball, there were so many women. You could have had any of them. Why choose a naïve younger sister with no friends in Paris?"

He lay back, resting his head against a plush pillow. Eventually, looking up at the silk canopy of the bed, he asked: "If I tell you something, will you promise not to get angry?"

I felt my body stiffen. Such questions rarely boded well. "Will you?" he repeated.

I nodded. "All right."

"Well . . ." His exhale was audible.

"Yes?" I asked. "What is it?"

"He . . . told me that he wanted to see you married. I don't take my orders from him, but I told him I would at least consider it. Allow the introduction. That was, of course, before I met you."

The words hit me like a blow, and had I not already been lying flat, I'm certain my legs would have given out. *He wanted to see me married?* There could be little question as to the identity of this *he*. My stomach clenched harder than stone. Could this really be true? Napoleon had arranged this match? Just as he'd attempted to arrange the match with Duphot? My body instinctively slid away from Bernadotte's. I pulled the bedcovers over my breasts as I felt my veins swell with rapid and furious blood. So Bernadotte had not pursued me on his own interest, but rather as a favor—or in obedience—to Napoleon? I was going to be sick.

"Now, there, there. You promised." He pulled for me, but I resisted his embrace.

"Must that man control absolutely everything?" I snapped, shifting away from him. "From our governmental affairs down to the father of his ex-fiancée's children?"

"I regret telling you because I think it gives you the wrong idea," Bernadotte said, his tone conciliatory, even as I felt myself grow more enraged. My face burned hot with shame. He continued: "Desiree, I fear that now you might believe that perhaps I wasn't interested in you of my own accord. I can assure you, I was."

"Only because he had told you of me. What else did he say? Did he share the private moments of our intimate encounters, too?" My voice was a sharp hiss. I was mortified. Was that all Bernadotte wanted from me? He knew Napoleon had had me and had given his approval?

"Hardly, Desiree." Bernadotte's face blanched. "It mattered little what he said to me. I made up my own mind. I introduced myself because of his suggestion, I'll admit that. But the conversation never would have continued past that if the interest on my part had not been genuine. Believe me, it was."

I felt tears sting my eyes, but I refused to let him see them. I would let neither him nor Napoleon make me cry. Fool! I had allowed myself to trust. To love. To believe that this man could be different and to believe that I could finally be free of Napoleon Bonaparte and his autocracy. What was next—for the two of them to compare boudoir notes?

Bernadotte tugged on my shoulder. "Please, Desiree."

"Do not touch me." I jerked away, trying to writhe from his grasp and out of bed, but he was stronger, and he did not let me go. Instead, with a strong but gentle grip, Bernadotte turned me toward him. "Hear this," he said. I protested, shouting, "Let me go!"

"Hear this and then I will let you go. Napoleon did love you once, and you loved him in return. And he did tell me of your charms and that I'd be fortunate to court you." He paused, his dark eyes suddenly full of feeling, pleading with me. My breath quivered. Bernadotte continued, "We can't change that, Desiree. But we can allow ourselves to be happy together. Desiree, my wife, please, allow me to make you happy, because I do love you. More than I had imagined possible. And that has nothing to do with Napoleon Bonaparte."

# Chapter 17

*Paris*
*Fall 1798*

A ND SO I DID JUST THAT: I TRUSTED, AND I ALLOWED MY
Bernadotte, my husband, to love me. His actions more than his
words coaxed me back into faith once more. As with the courtship, he
proved dependable and consistent, and I came to relish the small, inconsequential moments of our marriage, the moments both unplanned and
routine, made possible only through intimacy and comfort with another
individual—my cold foot finding the warm, bare crook of his leg under the
bedcovers in the dark of night; the first kiss of the morning, both of us still
hazy with slumber; breakfast together at the table, his hand reaching
across to pour cream into my coffee. I came to know his smile and what
would prompt it; I learned to delight in the gentle squeeze he would place
on my waist as he passed me in the corridor of our home—our little secret,
an exchange in which the servants buzzing around us were not included.

The overpowering presence of Napoleon and Josephine—their violent
tempests that had loomed so large over nearly every aspect of my life before Bernadotte—had receded, allowing me to settle happily into this new
family of mine. We were a good match, Bernadotte and I, and we were
relishing our joy, the simple pleasures of our small domestic sphere.

Though I was a married woman and therefore entitled to savor my
breakfast and coffee on a tray in bed, in the languid comfort of my dressing

gown, I often rose early to join my husband at the table. I savored that time with him preceding his morning departure for his offices. My husband was busy, and his days away from me were long, for Bernadotte had just recently been named Minister of War. He was good at his job; within months he had rooted out much of the corruption and incompetence in the army bureaucracy. The people read the journal reports of how Bernadotte worked diligently to make sure our troops across the Continent were well-supplied and well-fed. That salaries were paid in full and on time. How Bernadotte was an honest man, a patriotic man, a capable man, a good man.

All of this served to give my husband a satisfying sense of purpose, and I could tell that the people's approval warmed his soldier's blood; when Parisians called out to our passing coach such praises as "Vive Bernadotte!" he smiled like a giddy young man—and I beamed at his side.

Not only did the War Ministry appointment come with a reliable, generous salary, but the position was more likely to keep my husband at home in the capital, rather than on some assignment abroad to the Rhine or the Alps. And as the summer heat gave way to the cooler, shorter days of autumn, I certainly wanted my husband home with me, more than ever—for I found out that we were expecting a baby.

Our marriage was only several months old, but we'd grown close as man and wife, and we'd conceived quickly. Only Julie knew my news; I'd dreaded telling her, given the many years through which she'd struggled, so far unsuccessfully, to have a baby of her own. But, as she was my darling sister, she'd reacted in the only way she knew how—with kindness, with joy for my joy, masking whatever pain or envy she might have so naturally felt.

I had chosen that morning to tell my husband. I waited until the servants left us alone in the small, sunny breakfast room. Bernadotte was making his way through a stack of newspapers, both French and British, but here was my opening. "My darling, I realize that you must read each morning, to keep abreast of events within France and abroad."

"Indeed." He offered his distracted agreement and kept reading, sipping his coffee as he did so.

"It might become a bit harder for you to read in the mornings," I ventured.

He still did not look my way. I continued: "It will be louder at the table. You'll soon have new distractions."

Finally he glanced up from the journal, eyeing me, unsure of my meaning. An arch of his eyebrow indicated his confusion. "When the baby arrives, that is," I said.

He blinked a moment, lowering the paper. And then understanding broke across his features, giving way to a wide, hopeful smile. "Is that so?"

I nodded, donning my own bashful grin. "A baby?" he asked, his tone tenuous.

Again I nodded.

At that, my Bernadotte let out a whoop, a buoyant exclamation, and he leapt from his chair. "What excellent news! A baby!" He looked down at my body, where beneath layers of silk brocade and petticoats my stomach betrayed very little change. Perhaps I was a bit thicker, but anyone might presume that to be merely the result of a happy marriage and an indulgent husband who paid for a good cook.

"How do you know?" he asked, his features alight. "I can't see anything."

I smiled sheepishly. "A woman knows these things. When for several months her body does not do what it ordinarily ought to do."

"But . . . have you felt sick?"

I shook my head. "I've been fortunate, I feel no sickness." In fact, I felt even stronger than before. Tired, yes, but possessed by some mysterious new vigor as my body performed its work to create and nourish a life within.

Bernadotte allowed himself to celebrate more, and he clapped his hands before landing a strong kiss on my lips. Just then a servant entered the room, carrying a refill of fresh coffee, and we separated, sitting back down in our chairs, a pair of chastened cut-ups caught in their indiscretion. But we giggled as we did so.

"I'm so happy," he said, taking my hand under the table.

"As am I."

"But you must take care of yourself. You must rest. And eat. And you must let me know what I can do—anything—to bring you comfort."

I nodded, feeling my cheeks grow warm.

"Oh, it's . . . it's wonderful!" He beamed, his dark eyes brimming with delight.

"It is," I agreed and turned back to my breakfast, suddenly hungrier than before.

We ate opposite each other in contented silence, relishing the tender glow of our happiness. My husband picked up the newspapers, putting the top one aside to turn to a British journal. I leaned forward to serve myself another slice of baguette, but I paused when Bernadotte gasped. I looked at him in alarm, noting how his ruddy cheeks had gone white, how the smile from a moment earlier had faded. "Impossible!" he groaned, running a hand through his hair. "She's really done it."

"What is it?" I felt my heart flip, and I looked down, scanning the newspaper that lay spread before him.

"How could she have been such a fool?" he asked, and I realized to what he referred. There, on the front page of the London newspaper *The Morning Chronicle*, was an article featuring the names of Napoleon and Josephine. Though I couldn't read much English, I could tell that much. "What does it say?" I asked, desperate to know.

Bernadotte translated for me as he read the column. "A British warship has intercepted a French mail ship traveling from Egypt back toward France. On board were Napoleon's personal letters, which have been seized and printed in this British newspaper."

I sighed aloud. "What a horror for him. He'll be mortified."

Bernadotte read on: "This letter, one from Napoleon to his brother Joseph, discusses the most, well, the most personal situation imaginable."

"What?" I asked.

"Josephine has . . ." Bernadotte stammered, shifting in his seat. "Well, it appears as though her husband has discovered ongoing infidelity on her part."

I propped my elbows on the table, my mind suddenly burdened by a rush of thoughts and questions. Of course the Bonaparte women had whispered rumors such as these among themselves for years; I was not deaf to their accusations. But I'd never actually imagined them to be true; I'd never believed that Josephine would, in fact, be devious—or foolish— enough to do such a thing. At least, not after they had been married.

"In his own words," Bernadotte continued reading, "Napoleon wrote to Joseph of his heartbreak and anger: *That she should have deceived me like this! . . . Woe to her and to them!—I will exterminate them all, fops and puppies. I have no wish to be the laughingstock. I will divorce her. Divorce—I want a public and sensational divorce. The veil is torn, the illusion is shattered, and there is no way to repair it."*

Knowing him as I did, I could feel the rage gushing from his quill, all the way from Egypt. And how dreadful, perhaps worst of all, that these most intimate of wounds and words were now laid bare before the entire world, made public by his most hated enemies, the British, who openly laughed at his heartache. How would he respond?

But then, Bernadotte continued: "It goes on. Here's a letter from Napoleon just a day later: *I would give anything for it to be untrue. Or even for it to be true, but for my ears to unhear it. I love her so much. I can't live without her. I may conquer nations, but Josephine, she has conquered my heart."*

"What a frightful turn of events," I said, pushing away my breakfast plate. "It's certain to become a scandal."

Bernadotte's frown deepened. "And it grows worse."

"How can it possibly?"

"Here, he's explaining more of what he's learned from his generals. Not only was Josephine engaging in amorous liaisons with these other men, she was also profiting financially from them."

"How?"

"She was asking for money, outrageous sums of money, in exchange for access to Napoleon or his generals."

The Bonaparte women had accused her of as much.

Bernadotte continued: "And she's been dabbling in some seedy business deals, it appears. Well, this is worst of all. Black-market trading in army supplies." Bernadotte's frown deepened as he scanned the news and distilled it for me. "In effect, she's been acting as a profiteer on arms sales and weapons contracts, compromising the well-being of our troops in the process. Even if Napoleon could forgive her for sacrificing the sanctity of their marriage, how could he possibly forgive her for compromising the safety of his men?"

I dressed quickly and left for Julie's home as soon as my husband departed for the office. I found Julie still in her dressing gown, her household in utter disarray. Letizia was there, covered in black crepe as if attending a funeral. Pauline stood over her mother as Joseph paced the room; there was much screaming and swatting of hands. *"La puttana! Che serpente!"* Letizia railed in her native Italian.

"How could she do this to him?" Pauline added, plopping herself beside Julie on the sofa. "And while he's so far away, fighting for his life in the desert!"

"I always knew he should have married you," Letizia said, reaching for my hand. I accepted the grip of her strong, bony fingers, and lowered my eyes. I would never say it, but I was blissfully happy with my Bernadotte and so grateful that I had been spared the fate that Josephine had grabbed from me.

Joseph, who had been quiet until now, paused in his pacing to rest his elbow on the mantel. The rest of us turned to him. He spoke after a pause, his tone decisive: "She shall be cut off. Not another cent of his money."

"*Our* money!" Letizia moaned. "Think of all that he gave her!"

"And she shall not set foot in my home again," Joseph added, ignoring his mother. "Not until he's returned. He can decide for himself how to handle her, but I shall not receive her." Joseph looked to Julie, who nodded her agreement. "Our first priority," Joseph said, "our *only* priority now, is to protect him. However we can. That is the primary task of every Bonaparte."

As the news of the scandal broke across Paris, a crowd began to build around Josephine's mansion—and Joseph's as well. I could see the mob gathering through the windows from my sister's bedchamber, and I could hear the angry shouts. Guessing that she would indeed be cut off from the Bonaparte wealth, bankers and merchants approached the front gates to demand the payments Josephine owed. "Draw the drapes," Julie ordered. "I've seen enough of angry crowds for several lifetimes."

A day later we received word that Josephine had fled in the middle of the night to her country estate at Malmaison, barricading herself behind the château walls with her daughter, Hortense, and her large fleet of servants. How she was paying their salaries, I did not know.

I received a letter from her the following day. I stared at the seal in shock, tearing through the hardened wax to find her handwriting, elegant and slanted, her words as soft and gracious as ever. The paper smelled of her floral perfume. Josephine didn't mention the news outright, but she wrote:

> *My darling Desiree,*
>
> *My sister, my friend, would you be willing to come with your cherished Julie to visit my estate in Malmaison? I do long to speak with you both, to unburden my heart and savor the comforts of fair-minded and faithful friends. My daughter is with me, but my son is with my husband, serving as his aide-de-camp in Egypt. I miss my Eugene terribly and worry for his well-being daily.*
>
> *Will you come to me? I believe that you shall be delighted by the greenhouses and flowers I have out here. We girls from southern climes do not get enough of the lush greenery of our childhoods while in Paris.*
>
> *Please know that my husband and I cherish you so, Desiree, and hold you in a special place in our hearts.*
>
> *Believe that I am and shall remain,*
>
> *Your faithful,*
> *Josephine*

Bernadotte was out, so I marched the letter straight to Julie's. Unfortunately, Joseph was at home, so I had no choice but to show him as well.

"*Faithful?*" Joseph spat in tight-lipped rage. "How dare she! She invites my own wife, as if she'd whisper her honeyed words into your ears and conspire to win your allegiance against our family!" He paced the room, his flesh a dark, mottled red. "Or worse—she'd seek to corrupt you as well! Inviting you to partake in her drunken orgies with her seedy men out there, and whatever else she gets into in that sinful palace!" Joseph read the letter once more, crumpling it upon completion. "I have a mind to march out to Malmaison myself and bring her back to Paris in irons. *Faithful?* Faithful as a jezebel, besmirching our family name. If only the Bastille still stood, she could rot in there!"

"Joseph, please," Julie said, walking to her husband's side and putting a hand on his shoulder. "She is simply seeking an ally because she knows she's been entirely cut off."

"And she suspects she'd have a better chance with either of us than with your sisters," I added. "Or your mother, for that matter."

"Bonaparte women are loyal, she's right to suppose that! And she won't have the chance to make a try for the two of you, that's for damned sure. You are to decline," Joseph insisted. "Or better yet—you are not to reply at all."

But I did reply. I felt it too harsh not to. I was grateful to have the pregnancy in order to plead my excuses and indisposition. I told Josephine as much, and several days later, a cartload of baby gifts arrived from her—Chantilly lace and cashmere blankets and a hand-painted wooden bassinet—along with a warm note professing her joy on my behalf.

If only she'd had a child of her own by Napoleon, Josephine's situation might have been less precarious. Napoleon would have been less inclined to leave the mother of his heir. But their marriage had never produced any children, so none of us knew what Napoleon might do to her upon his return.

As the months passed, the lenders continued to lurk around her home on the Rue de la Victoire, but Josephine remained ensconced out at Malmaison with Hortense and her household, and she didn't invite me again. It seemed that even as she fell from grace, her husband's stock only continued to soar ever higher.

The mode in fashion and décor that winter and spring was all things Egyptian because of Napoleon's victories in the east. As my belly grew rounder, I indulged in a bit of the loose, flowing style, grateful for a break from the corseted silhouette of constricting layers and unyielding boning.

People were voracious to read about how Napoleon had vanquished thousands of tribal warriors before the imposing backdrop of the ancient pyramids and the Sphinx. How he had brought the glory of France to the land of ancient wealth and knowledge. Newspapers now regularly compared Napoleon to the great conquerors of antiquity, his idols Julius Caesar and Alexander the Great. I knew all too well how delighted he'd be to read such comparisons, and I didn't doubt that he'd had some part in inviting them.

And, like those legendary conquerors of old, Napoleon had taken it upon himself to become an insatiable lover in the exotic east, as well. In addition to the news of his military victories, the papers spilled over with accounts of his romantic conquests—stories that, I suspected, he had also invited and abetted. As I grew bigger, approaching the time of the baby's arrival, I read almost daily a new salacious report. Though he was encamped in remote desert outposts, Napoleon did not suffer in the least for lack of pleasure, or so the papers reported with their giddy and gushing descriptions. He diverted himself, it seemed, with a different woman every night—there were the dark-eyed Egyptian women who danced, nearly nude, for our general and his top officers; there were the "camp girls" who traveled with the French army, doling out their favors in exchange for monetary rewards; and there were the French society ladies, too, the powdered wives of Napoleon's officers and staff. It seemed Napoleon had begun a rather ongoing and ardent affair with a twenty-year-old beauty by the name of Pauline Fourès, the wife of one of his lieutenants. I saw the portrait of the young Madame Fourès when it was printed in the newspaper and couldn't help but shudder—the lady could have been my twin sister, we were so alike in appearance.

The labor pains began in the middle of the night, waking me as I discovered that I lay in a tangle of damp sheets. "Wake up." I shook Bernadotte, pulling him from deep sleep beside me.

"What is it?"

Just then a fresh pain gripped me around my middle, a ruthless vise, and I winced. "It's time," I whispered in the quiet of our bedchamber. "The baby is coming."

Bernadotte leapt from bed, dashing out of the room to rouse the sleeping servants. In less than an hour I had our doctor at my side, along with a midwife, my sister, and a small cluster of our female servants. Bernadotte left the house to go to Joseph's, along with his closest aide, a man named Antoine Maurin.

I clung to Julie's hands as the hours stretched on, crying out in agony. My bed was wet, and I was not sure if it was the blood or the fluids from labor, perhaps both. "I'm here, Desiree," my sister whispered, remaining at my side as daylight once more gave way to darkness.

The room was a blur as the servants hurried in and out with fresh linens and pots of water, the midwife swabbing my face with a cool cloth as she urged me to breathe. Finally, when I feared the pain would rip me in half, I shut my eyes and a strange noise filled the room: a thin but hearty yelp.

I opened my eyes, looking to the foot of the bed in slow, exhausted astonishment. He had arrived, at last, a crying boy with dimpled, rosy flesh and a shock of dark hair. The midwife wrapped him in fresh linen and placed him in my arms as my sister looked on, weeping. The midwife then showed me how to latch him to my breast. He ate lustily, his small fists pounding my breast as I squirmed, feeling ticklish at the odd new sensation.

My husband returned home an hour later, bursting into my chamber. He ran to the side of the bed as the others excused themselves from the room, and we sat together, staring in shock and wonder at the babe in my arms, amazed by the sudden reality and permanence of his small physical presence in our lives. "What shall we call him?" I asked my husband, speaking quietly so as not to disturb the baby's dozing. Just then his small lips let out a whimper and we both laughed, overtaken, giddy with our primal adoration.

"What do you wish to call him?" Bernadotte asked me, leaning forward to pass a finger through our son's thick hair. "Have you any ideas?"

Of course I'd thought about it. Francois had been my father's name. But then there was the man who had been beside me nearly every day since my father's death—the man who, I knew, longed for a son more than anything. The man who longed to give my sister a son. "I was thinking Joseph Francois," I said. My sister would be deeply moved, I knew that.

"I love the idea," Bernadotte said, his eyes still affixed to his son.

"Really?" I asked.

He nodded. But then he frowned.

"What is it?" I asked. The baby opened his lips, as if seeking out his next meal, and I adjusted him in my arms, guiding him once more to my breast.

"There is one other opinion," Bernadotte said, his tone tenuous.

"Oh?" I looked from my son back toward my husband. "Who else would have an opinion on what we should name our own son?"

Bernadotte leaned his head to the side, looking down at the nursing baby. "You might guess. Who always has an opinion?"

"You can't be serious," I said, my tone dropping low. "Napoleon?"

"He did write to say that, if it was a boy, he thinks I should name him after his favorite poem, 'The Legend of Ossian.'"

I crinkled my nose in irritation—I knew that Napoleon was a voracious reader and that he loved the classics, but I'd never heard of the poem. "What's the name?"

"Oscar," Bernadotte said.

"Oscar," I repeated. It was an unusual name, not typically French. A strong name, but certainly a bit funny sounding. My first instinct was to reject it. To tell Napoleon he had no right to interfere. If he longed to pick a boy's name, then he should have a son of his own. Or sway some other couple who sought his approval, because the Bernadottes most certainly did not.

But then I paused a moment, thinking. Napoleon *was* the most powerful man in France. If he flattered himself in thinking that our son's name was in some way a credit to him, well, perhaps that could benefit our son. I felt the world shift beneath me in that moment, a pivot both subtle yet permanent; I knew, suddenly, that my own pride and self-interested vanity mattered little compared to my son's future and well-being.

And what did it matter, really, if we slipped one more name in there? "All right then," I agreed. "But only after the others. Joseph Francois Oscar Bernadotte."

"One more thing, my darling," Bernadotte said, taking my hand. "You shall be allowed to choose the godmother. And I have no doubt whom you shall name." He stroked my palm. "But I shall choose the godfather."

I shifted my body in the bed. "I had wished to name Joseph along with my sister. But I suppose it is fair this way. Whom shall you choose? Maurin?"

Bernadotte shook his head, suddenly avoiding my eye contact. "I think there is only one natural answer."

"Indeed?"

"He made our introduction possible. He gave me the post that allowed me to be here by your side right now. Our son's godfather could be no one other than Napoleon."

# Chapter 18

*Paris*
*Fall 1799*

I T BEGAN AS A WHISPER, AS IT ALWAYS DOES. HUSHED VOICES in the darkness, more quiet by far than the shouting mob that railed outside—more quiet, and yet far more dangerous. A veiled insinuation, a raised eyebrow. An invitation to a candlelit midnight rendezvous. A slow and cautious dance toward the topic of treason.

Even though I was entirely consumed by my new son, immersed in his constant demands for milk and soft caresses, I couldn't help but hear the words.

Coup.
Quiet.
Overthrow the fools.
We make it quick, before they have the chance for resistance.

I couldn't help but notice the men who gathered in my home, seeking my husband's counsel, whispering behind gloved hands when they noticed that Madame Bernadotte and her new baby sat nearby. There was the political leader Abbé Sieyès. My husband's military ally, Antoine Maurin. Minister Talleyrand became a regular visitor. And Joseph, too, sometimes accompanied by Napoleon's other brothers, Lucien, Louis, and Jerome.

Though they were always friendly to me, inquiring after my well-being and the health of my new babe, these men never truly waited to hear an answer, instead ushering my husband to the other room and shutting the door.

As Minister of War, my husband seemed to be the only popular leader in our nation's government these days. He'd become a national hero of sorts in recent months. He'd taken to writing popular bulletins in *Le Moniteur* calling for patriotism and service to the nation. The recruits and enlisted men loved him and trusted him; the generals saw him as knowledgeable, steady, and pragmatic.

All I had to do was read the newspapers to know that a growing unrest was stirring. Our political leaders were reviled, our government all but defunct. Not since before the storming of the Bastille had there been such widespread misery in the streets. People were starving as bread lines wrapped around the filthy street corners, and winter would only make the fuel and food shortages worse. Royalists and Jacobins were now regularly fighting in the boulevards. Our Directory, the five quarreling and incompetent politicians at the head of our republican government, had lost all respect. Years earlier, when the times were less patient, they would have ensured their own trips to the guillotine.

Without his leadership, our army had lost nearly all of Napoleon's gains across Europe, suffering catastrophic defeats throughout Italy to the Austrians and Russians. In France, the people cried out for Napoleon, all but holding their breath as they awaited his return from Egypt after nearly two years away.

Because our little Oscar—yes, Napoleon's choice of name had won out—woke me so often in the night, I noticed the gathering of men who spoke over candlelight on that particular September evening, just a few months shy of the new year and the new century. They were not aware of my presence; they did not detect me as I positioned myself outside the study door, Oscar suckling noiselessly at my breast. Thus was I able to hear their open and honest conversation with my husband.

"The army's confidence is entirely ravaged." It was Barras, Napoleon's former mentor—and Josephine's former lover. He was now a member of the unpopular Directory. "It's been nothing but financial waste and fraudulent army contractors. Morale is abysmal, and defections are at an all-time high."

Talleyrand interjected, "We need someone whom they can trust."

"I understand that." My husband's voice. My spine stiffened, my arms instinctively clutching my baby tighter as Bernadotte continued: "But would it not then be an abuse of that same trust?"

"Come, Bernadotte, you must see: you would be doing your nation a service," Talleyrand said.

"I serve the constitution," Bernadotte retorted.

"The military would stand behind you." That came from Sieyès, also a member of the Directory and a man known throughout France—and indeed the Continent—for his cunning. I could detect his haughty tone and clipped cadence as he went on: "And we would form a government to quickly legitimize your claim. Make it a sanctioned administration. Draft a new constitution."

My husband sighed. "Why do you come to me with this? Why not one of you, if you're so decided upon a coup d'état?"

Barras answered: "It must be you, Bernadotte, can't you see? You're the Minister of War—the most popular leader in the government. The common people love you, and you have hundreds of thousands of troops under you, spread across Europe. The generals admire you; the soldiers adore you. And the people of France are fed up with incompetent civil servants. They want strength. They want a champion to unite and then lead."

I braced against the wall, going dizzy as I heard all of this. These men, Sieyès and Barras and Talleyrand, already had their hands on the reins of the country's power, but now they were urging my husband to help them arrange an overthrow. To oust the discredited Directory and the incompetent legislature. To form yet another new government, and one in which they could hold an even larger portion of the authority. But they needed a general to provide the military strength and legitimize their claims, to be their partner—a respected general, a good man. They wanted my husband to be that man.

Oscar fidgeted at my breast, perhaps feeling the hastening of my heart, and I quickly rocked him. On the other side of the doorway there was silence in the room as my husband considered these words, wrestled with the enormity of their proposition. They wanted a coup, and they wanted my husband to do it for them. I was certain they would hear the rapid pounding of my pulse as I stood there.

"There is no one to stand in our way." Talleyrand pierced the silence with an urgent whisper. "You have the army. The power can be ours. And yours, Bernadotte, if only you'll reach forward and seize it."

But these words would not move my husband, and I knew that; I understood that without even hearing his answer. Did they not know of my husband's unwavering character? His loyalty to law and reason? Did they not know of the words he had branded on his own chest? *Death to Kings.*

# Chapter 19

*Paris*
*Fall 1799*

"I CAN'T BELIEVE HE WOULD DO IT." MY HUSBAND'S FURY was quiet, restrained, and all the more terrifying as a result. I had never before seen him like this. Though I was in the room rocking Oscar, who slept in the bassinet beside me, blissfully unaware, my husband and his companions spoke openly and freely. Discretion was no longer necessary, as the situation was unraveling out of their control and across the city.

"Let's wait and see. Give him time to prove the claims false," Barras said, his tone more slack than my husband's.

"But they aren't false claims, and we know it." My husband paced the room, a newspaper rolled up like a club in his hands, and he used it now to smack the mantel. I winced, looking to my son, but he slept on with that newborn peace afforded only to the most innocent.

It was Napoleon whom they discussed, of course. Napoleon, following a crushing loss to the British at the Battle of the Nile, had left Egypt quickly and secretly, abandoning his men to make his own hasty return to France.

"He's heard of the instability here in Paris," Bernadotte said. "He sees his opening. And he's coming back to seize it. All of his talk of 'glory for France' and 'camaraderie with the men' goes to pot. He hasn't kept quarantine, though members of his regiments are quite clearly carrying the bubonic plague. Now he abandons his men in Egypt in defeat, leaving them stranded. He returns to his own safety and to snatch his own moment of glory and risks bringing a plague of biblical proportions into our nation. The man could be court-martialed for such selfish, reckless behavior. Service to the nation and the army indeed! He is thinking of one thing only, and that is the insatiable ambition of Napoleon Bonaparte."

The *Messager du Soir* newspaper had told us all of this, the same newspaper that my husband was now hammering against the mantel. At the top of the article, the headline read: EVERYONE WAITS IMPATIENTLY FOR BONAPARTE, BECAUSE FOR EVERYONE HE BRINGS FRESH HOPE!

"Patience, Bernadotte, patience," Barras urged once more. "Bonaparte is ambitious, that I grant you. That I know better than anyone, as it was I who launched his career. But he's no fool. If he plans to return to Paris, it's for some sound reason. We will learn soon enough."

The next morning, the news grew more troubling for us. My husband kissed me and Oscar farewell and arrived as normal to his offices at the Palais du Luxembourg, only to be met at the door by half a dozen of his fellow officers—all of those men lower than him in rank. The impromptu leader of this assemblage told my Bernadotte that he was being removed from his position as Minister of War.

"On what grounds?" my husband demanded. "On whose orders?" But they were stone-faced and unified in their silence. Any opposition or refusal to vacate the office, they declared, would result in his imprisonment. A carriage waited to take him home, and a full company of armed guards stood ready to make sure my husband got in it. Bernadotte was ashen by the time he returned to the Rue de Monceau and told me of the morning's events. We were incredulous—and terribly confused. "This government goes from bad to worse," he said. And though I did not say it aloud, I was deeply troubled as I tried to understand what it all meant.

Napoleon arrived back in Paris at the end of that week to a hero's welcome, and Bernadotte and I awoke to the news that he was once again at home on the Rue de la Victoire. Julie appeared, breathless, at my breakfast table that same morning. She told me over hastily gulped coffee that the entire Bonaparte clan was gathering that evening, and my family was expected as well. Napoleon, she told me, wished to meet his godson. I had a footman fetch my husband and told him the news in front of Julie.

"I'm not going," Bernadotte said, flatly refusing. "And I do not think you should, either. Unless you fancy exposure to the bubonic plague."

I shifted in my seat, glancing from my husband to my sister.

"Respectfully, I must disagree," Julie interjected, crossing her hands before her waist. "Napoleon issued these invitations himself, and for his reasons, he wishes you to be there."

My sister left, and my husband and I quarreled for the remainder of the morning. Eventually, we reached a compromise: I would leave Oscar at home with Bernadotte, but *I* would go with Julie and Joseph, simply so that our family would have some representation. I was desperate to know what Napoleon was planning now that he was back in Paris, where our government was teetering on collapse. But mostly I needed to know what it might mean for my family.

"Who else will be there?" I asked, as we rode the short distance in the coach from my sister's home to Napoleon's. Outside, the night was wet, with rain falling in slanted sheets over eerily quiet streets. I pulled my cloak tighter around my arms.

"The whole family," Julie answered.

"The ... *whole* ... family?" I asked, and Julie understood my meaning. She nodded, but before she could answer, Joseph said: "I went to my brother first thing this morning to welcome him home. But I was told by a servant that Napoleon was still abed. And Josephine was in there with him."

I shook my head, finding the news incredible. "How did she ... ?"

Julie shrugged. "Perhaps he can only fight his wars on so many fronts."

The crowds swarmed outside the gates at No. 6 Rue de la Victoire, and they applauded even at the sight of Joseph. "*Vive* Bonaparte!" they cried out, waving the tricolor as our coach pulled through the gate and into the forecourt. "Hurrah for Bonaparte—he shall save the country!"

In spite of the rain, the entire neighborhood roiled in an atmosphere like that of a national holiday. Several in the crowd waved the newspapers calling for Napoleon's installation as king. I pulled my hood over my head and hurried from the coach into the mansion, grateful that my boy was safe and dry at home. And that my husband did not have to witness this scene.

Inside, Napoleon already appeared as one enthroned. He sat at the head of his grand dining room table, Josephine perched on his legs. Perhaps my sister was correct, that Napoleon was less interested in waging a domestic war when he was so clearly poised for some political maneuvers. Perhaps it was politically expedient to remain married—divorce would mean a scandal, and Josephine was a colorful and well-established Parisian favorite in her own right. Perhaps she had wept and convinced him of her innocence. Or perhaps he simply loved her so much that all had been forgiven. I did not know; but then, hadn't I been perplexed and aghast at the love affair between Napoleon and Josephine from the beginning?

Whatever Napoleon's reasoning, I supposed it didn't matter now, because there Josephine was, dressed in white, her perfumed curls framing her relaxed, cheerful face. Napoleon's sisters sat beside them on each side, scowling, infuriated at the couple's reunion but present nevertheless. I did not see Mamma Letizia, and Julie told me that she had taken to her bed with a headache.

Napoleon looked directly at me as I entered the room. His skin was bronzed from the Egyptian sun, his hair slightly lighter. He wore a saber around his waist like some desert warlord. The cloying smell of his cologne filled the room, as did his self-assured voice: "Ah! Welcome to the radiant new mother. Congratulations are in order, Madame Bernadotte."

"Thank you." I curtsied. "And welcome back to Paris," I replied.

"I return home as a godfather."

I nodded. "And we are grateful that you've accepted the role."

Napoleon looked around the room, then back toward me. "But it was my pleasure. I only wish I could have met the little lad this evening. And seen his proud father. Where is Bernadotte?"

"Yes. Bernadotte is . . . so busy these days."

Napoleon cocked his head to the side, and I noticed the surplus flesh around his neck. It appeared he'd eaten well in the desert. "Surely not with work? I've heard the Gascon's been removed from his post at the Ministry of War."

"Yes," I stammered. Had Napoleon had something to do with that? I wondered, my blood heating. Did he view my husband as a rival, an obstacle even? I felt all of the Bonapartes in that room looking at me and decided to steer the conversation back toward safer ground: "And the baby..."

"Yes?" Napoleon leaned forward in his chair.

"The baby took ill this evening, and so we wished for him to remain home. This rain hardly seemed good for his health."

Now Napoleon narrowed his eyes, offering me a wry smile. "Ah, yes. Bernadotte always did make such a splendid nursemaid. I'm sure that's it."

The next day, Napoleon invited my husband to his home once more. And once more, to my mounting frustration, my husband declined.

"I feel very strongly that you should see him," I said, no longer even trying to curb the agitation in my voice.

My husband merely shrugged off my protestations. "I don't care to sit down to dinner with someone carrying the plague."

"But... you know he's up to something, Bernadotte. You know how shaky our government is. That members within the Directory itself are hungry for a coup. They merely need a general to join them. Should the crisis that you expect... arise, won't it be bad to have resisted the man who... well... what if he makes himself a king?"

"He will not become king." My husband waved his hand in dismissal. "The people don't want another king. Not after everything we've been through for this Revolution. They'd just as soon send a man to the guillotine as to the throne."

I shuddered at this, but I did not share my husband's convictions. Did the people even know what they wanted, further than wheat and wine, safety and a nation not in tatters? And what if *Napoleon* wanted it? Didn't

I know better than anyone that Napoleon found a way to get what he wanted?

The next day was my birthday. I turned twenty-two years old, and my sister paid a call that morning with her husband to wish me well. "Thank you," I said, though I hardly felt like celebrating. All of Paris was on edge with rumors of riots. National guardsmen stood on alert outside of the Tuileries and along the bridges.

"Have you . . . agreed to see him yet?" Joseph asked Bernadotte as we sat in our salon. Julie bounced a fussy Oscar on her knees while I sat beside her, twisting my hands in my lap, trying to conceal the depths of my agitation in front of our guests.

"No." My husband shook his head. He wore the navy blue officer's uniform—a soldier awaiting an assignment—even though he'd been sacked from his post at the War Ministry.

Joseph looked to me, then back toward Bernadotte. "I strongly urge you to see him. And sooner rather than later."

I could have kissed Joseph with gratitude for these words, but my husband rose from the sofa, crossing to the far side of the room and the row of windows that opened out over our walled gardens. Eventually, all he offered was: "Joseph, please."

But my brother-in-law's face was one of fixed resolve. "Bernadotte," he said, his tone hard as granite, "I advise you as a friend. And a brother."

Julie's eyes met my own. Bernadotte crossed his arms, and I could feel the effort he put into remaining calm. Eventually, he nearly whispered, "Don't ask this of me—"

"I ask it of you because I care for your well-being, and I wish for Desiree, and for my nephew—"

"Enough!" My husband interrupted, his face inflamed. "I won't speak ill of your brother to you! Don't force me to do it. Please."

We all fell silent, the tension clawing at the room and each of us in it. A log on the fire burst with a pop, showering a spray of ash across the hearth. The baby let out a plaintive squeal, but none of us spoke. After several moments I stood, taking Oscar from my sister and walking cautiously toward my husband. "Bernadotte, please."

He turned toward me as I put my hand softly on his shoulder. "Darling," I said, "do it for me. And for your boy." My husband looked at me, incredulous, deeply offended that I would hold our family over him like this. But I forced myself to continue, feeling quite certain that we were running out of time. "It is my birthday. You shall ruin not only my day but quite possibly our entire lives if you continue with this stubborn refusal. Why must you insult him? You know he never forgets a grudge."

I waited up for my Bernadotte's return, knowing that sleep would be futile until he was home, safe, with me once more. It was late when he finally burst through the bedroom door, tearing his cap from his head and throwing it across the room. "Insufferable, shameless, delusional man."

I sat upright in bed, my hopes pierced, my voice faint as I asked: "What did he say?"

Bernadotte sighed, kicking his boots off each foot. "Only implications and insinuations. He asked me which posts I desired in our government. He implied that he had the power to instate me in any of them. If I would openly declare my support for him."

"Your support for him . . . in what?"

"He clearly wants power," Bernadotte said, sitting down on the bed. His entire frame looked heavy.

"Well." I sighed. "We can see which way the winds are blowing."

Bernadotte turned to me now, his face registering shock. Perhaps even disappointment. And then I saw it, the defiance gripping his features, taking root. "Never," he said, his voice no more than a whisper, and yet girded with stone.

At this I grew frustrated. "Why would you risk your safety, that of our entire family?"

"I cannot give my support to any man who would use his sway over the army to steal the power from the people. Not for Napoleon. Not even for myself! We are a republic of laws—we have a constitution!"

"You've seen how shifty the laws of this nation have proven in recent years," I said, my voice toneless.

"But I have integrity," he insisted. "I have principles. I thought you did, too."

"What good will our principles do, Bernadotte, if we are arrested—or dead?"

The servant woke us in the middle of the night. I blinked, my eyes not yet adjusted to the darkness of our bedchamber. "Is it Oscar?"

"No, madame, your son sleeps," the woman said.

"Then what is it?" I asked. I heard my husband stir beside me.

"It's a visitor, madame. It's, er, Monsieur Bonaparte to see you and the general."

Bernadotte and I both bolted upright. "Bonaparte?" my husband repeated the name. He hopped from bed, bumping his leg against the side table in the dark and releasing a string of curses.

"Aye, sir," said the servant as she lit a candelabra.

"What does he want?" I asked, sliding from bed, my pulse galloping as the servant handed me my slippers.

"He awaits you both downstairs, madame."

To our great relief, it was Joseph, not Napoleon, who sat in our salon. A servant had lit several candles, and I could see through the skittering shadows that Joseph's features were taut and pale. He stood when we entered the room.

"Oh, Joseph, thank goodness," I said, collapsing into a hug in my brother-in-law's arms. "I'm so happy to see you."

Joseph quickly returned my hug and then stepped away, turning toward my husband. His expression was grim, and I felt the dread thicken in my gut as he spoke: "Bernadotte," he said, "it is done. And we hope you shall remain a friend."

"What is done?" my husband asked, his tall frame going rigid. In our haste, we hadn't dressed, and both Bernadotte and I stood in our dressing gowns over our nightshirts, my husband holding a quivering candelabra.

Joseph, on the other hand, was fully dressed and appeared as though he had no plans to sleep that night. "My brother, er, General Bonaparte . . . has heard the desperate pleas of the French people. In seeing their pain, he has agreed that our disgraced government was nothing more than a den of vipers. And he has humbly accepted the reins of power that the people of France have seen fit to bestow on him."

"Enough of the lofty rhetoric, Joseph. It's me. Speak plainly, man," my husband growled, his voice raspy and impatient. He leaned closer to Joseph, towering over him with his great height. "When?"

Joseph lowered his eyes and answered: "This night."

"How?" I asked.

"He has removed the legislature from the Tuileries Palace and is holding them out in Saint-Cloud."

"*Holding* them? Under arrest?" my husband asked, his voice thick with disapproval.

Joseph shrugged. "Not . . . not in theory."

"But in practice," my husband said, and I saw how the candelabra trembled in his grip.

Joseph continued: "You know they had lost all credibility . . . with the people. He will disband the Directory and establish a new government. He has the regiments with him."

"A coup, using the military as his own arm," my husband spat. "He saw his opportunity and, where other men, *better* men would have—"

"Please, Bernadotte, stop," Joseph raised his hands. "I do not wish to hear anything that . . ." Joseph sighed, pressing his palms together as if in prayer, his tone beseeching when he continued: "He wishes you to join him. To take your place beside him as a partner. A brother in arms and a brother in his family." Joseph looked to me, then turned back to my husband. "You know that he returns from Egypt an incredibly popular man. He has the generals on his side. Barras is his ally. Sieyès and Talleyrand have been brought into the fold. Now he needs only you."

We'd heard all about this plan. We'd heard the scheming words of these men—the same men who had first asked my husband to seize power as their general. The very men to whom my husband had said a resolute no.

Bernadotte turned away from Joseph, crossing the room with his long-legged stride. When he reached the far side, he raised his hands and pressed them to the wall, leaning like a storm-battered tree. Joseph looked to me, and I only shook my head; I awaited Bernadotte's word with as much concern and trepidation as he did. We both remained quiet.

Eventually, after what felt like an eternity, my husband turned. Looking at Joseph, he declared: "I cannot do it. I'm sorry."

I groaned, lowering myself into a chair. Joseph dropped his head, shaking it. "Bernadotte," was all he said, as if mourning the death of a friend. He looked at me a moment, then returned his gaze to my husband. "If you will not make yourself a friend, then he will have no choice but to see you as . . . a rival."

I began to weep. Bernadotte crossed his arms, avoiding my gaze. His voice remained unyielding as he said, "I have no desire to overthrow the lawful constitution, nor to support any man who would. And you must tell him that."

Joseph turned to me, his features careworn and suddenly tired. "Desiree, please. Can't you . . . is there not something you might say?"

I shrugged my shoulders, my hopelessness surely apparent on my face. "I have tried, Joseph. Countless times. There is nothing I can do to change his mind."

Joseph nodded slowly, gazing back toward my husband. "Then you must leave Paris." The words hit me like a clenched fist. Joseph went on: "Both of you. It might not be safe for you if events . . . well . . ."

Bernadotte crossed the room and stood beside me now. He put his hand on my shoulder, but I shrugged him off. I had no interest in his touch; I could not even bring myself to look at him. I was to be forced from my home like a criminal because of his stubborn willfulness, his refusal to see that the events unfolding around us were larger than his damned principles.

"Leave Paris," Bernadotte exhaled, agreeing with Joseph. "Yes. Then that is what we shall do."

"Where will we go?" I asked, my words sounding choked.

"We will be all right, my darling. I promise you," Bernadotte said, his expression suddenly soft. I broke from his gaze, unwilling to meet his eyes.

Joseph lifted a hand. "But . . . there's something else."

"What?" I asked.

"I should keep Oscar," Joseph said.

Now it felt as if my heart might drop out of my chest. "No," was all I could say, a pleading sound.

"Only for a time," Joseph said, trying to reassure me with a gentle tone.

Bernadotte's cheeks blazed an angry red. "You're mad if you think I would leave my son."

"Never," I said, agreeing with my husband for the first time in days.

"Only until things have calmed down," Joseph answered. "This will all be resolved soon enough."

"I won't leave my son while I flee for my own safety," I hissed, ready to fly up the stairs and take my baby in my arms.

Joseph stood motionless before me. He was resolute now as he said: "Oscar will be safer with me. I will protect him as if he were my own, you have my word. On the life of your sister."

I blinked, feeling as if I might faint. I shook my head, fighting back against that sensation, and I stared into Joseph's eyes, seeing his brother's eyes as I asked: "Well, if you have that power, then why should we not all three stay with you?"

Joseph nodded, considering my question. "My influence . . . can only extend so far. A babe. An innocent. His godson, no less. But . . ."

"But you cannot guarantee our protection," Bernadotte completed the thought.

Joseph shook his head. "Not with the same certainty as I can Oscar's. But you both have my word, my solemn vow: no harm shall come to your son. You two will be safer out of Paris. But Oscar, he will be safe in my home, as safe as my beloved wife, whose blood he shares."

I nodded, and then the hot, silent tears began to stream from my eyes, any resistance against them futile as I reckoned with the idea of leaving my son, not yet a year old, behind. I had never been angrier with my husband, nor indeed anyone. I had loved Bernadotte for his strength—his willingness to stand up to Napoleon even when I saw no one else doing so. But now that same strength stoked a white-hot ire in me, a rage perhaps stronger and more powerful than any love I might have felt for him. He had put us all in danger with his damned principles and stubbornness, and now we had no choice but to flee. To flee from Paris, from our home, from our own child. "Please," I said, gasping out the words in between my sobs. "Julie. Tell her I love her. And my child . . ."

Joseph, too, looked shattered. "And she returns that love to you and to your baby, of course. We will write, when . . . if we can."

"Joseph." I took his hand, allowing myself to think, to wonder—for only a moment—how different it all might have been had I accepted and reciprocated his early attentions. "My baby?"

"Will be safe."

"Thank you." I nodded, my body going hollow, my heart beating uselessly as I accepted defeat.

# Chapter 20

*Paris*
*Fall 1799*

I DONNED A MANSERVANT'S BREECHES AND OVERCOAT, WITH a cap to cover my long hair, and we rode in a simple coach toward the barrier. The guard at the city wall barely looked at me, figuring me to be a young male attendant. He saluted my husband, dressed as a gentleman farmer, and we were permitted to quit the city with just a cursory review of our forged papers.

We rode in silence away from the capital, out to the wooded village of Villeneuve-Saint-Georges, each forward step feeling as though I pulled further away from my heart, which had been yanked out and left behind in Paris. *Oscar,* I thought, more frantic each time I saw his round face in my mind, *will you think your maman has abandoned you?* We arrived in the early morning, as dawn was just beginning to purple the thick forests, revealing a modestly handsome home tucked back off the river amid a copse of linden trees. I slipped out of my cap, but there was nothing to do about the breeches and overcoat, especially on such a chilly morning.

"This is the home of Dumas. General Thomas-Alexandre Dumas," Bernadotte explained to me. I was furious with my husband, but I listened with interest now. "Who is Dumas?" I asked. My voice was hoarse with fear and sleeplessness, a cold night of travel on a rutted forest road, and my arms ached for my baby.

"He's an old, trusted friend. An army man, an officer who cares little for political intrigue and rivalry. He's an outsider, like me. He will not betray our presence here." Bernadotte put a hand on my arm, saying in a low, quiet voice: "Desiree, just . . . don't . . . act surprised. His father was of the French nobility, but his mother was from the islands."

I didn't understand what Bernadotte meant, but I didn't have time to ask, because just then a shadowed figure emerged at the door of the home. The man held a candelabra in the early-dawn light, a sleeping gown covering his tall frame. "Bernadotte?" His deep voice called into the dim morning as our coach slowed to a halt. "You are welcome here. Come, come." He waved us toward the threshold of his home, and I guessed that our arrival had drawn him from bed.

I looked a bit closer at our host now that the man stood before us, suddenly understanding what my husband's warning had meant: the man's skin was a shade darker than any I'd ever seen. He appeared like one of the Caraïbes I had heard about, the enslaved islanders whom Josephine had described on her Caribbean plantation. He had side-whiskers and a muscular build—nearly as thick from front to back as he was from shoulder to shoulder. And yet Bernadotte had described this Dumas as an old friend and a fellow officer in the French army. What was this man's story? I wondered.

"We are sorry to arrive at this hour," my husband said as we entered a comfortable kitchen, the gray ash on the hearth showing that the cooking fires had not yet been lit for the day.

"What does the hour matter, in times such as these?" our host said, shrugging his broad shoulders. He looked at me, his dark eyes taking in my curious clothing, but he said nothing of it. "Ah, Manon, good." The man gestured toward an old woman who entered the kitchen just then. She shuffled in on threadbare slippers as she tucked her gray hair under her linen cap. A maid or housekeeper, I presumed, thinking it unusual that an old Frenchwoman waited on a man such as this Dumas.

"Manon will show you to your room, Madame Bernadotte," Dumas said, his face holding mine with a warm and hospitable smile. He was not unattractive, I conceded. Not at all.

"I'm sure that you would like to . . . change your clothes. And take some rest," Dumas said, directing the old woman to lift my hastily packed trunk. I was just about to reply, saying that there was no way I could possibly sleep, but then our host turned to my husband, saying: "Bernadotte, I think you and I will have a chat."

*The season of fog and mist.*

Brumaire.

We'd always known it as November, but since the Revolution and the advent of our new calendar, "Brumaire" had been the label for this time of the year. And it was a time of mist and fog, of obscured darkness and confusion, indeed.

We remained in the countryside at General Dumas's home for three days. Our host was a kind man, courteous toward me—even if from an aloof distance. I guessed that he sensed my agitated nerves, my frustration with my husband, and my desperation for my son. I thought of Oscar constantly: What was happening in Paris? Was my baby safe? Was he frightened, wondering where his maman had gone? The longer we stayed, the more I became convinced that I'd made a terrible mistake in leaving him.

I kept to myself mostly, cloistered in the small upper bedroom that Dumas had offered me. I dared not step outside during the daytime hours, even to walk through the small thicket of trees toward the Seine, for fear that someone might see me. Were Napoleon's agents roving these woods? Were they searching for my husband, and therefore me? Would Napoleon reinstate the guillotine?

My husband, on the other hand, took long walks during the day, sometimes with Dumas and sometimes on his own, leaving me behind with nothing but my agonized thoughts. He'd return, his brow creased in his solitary thoughts, but I could not speak to him. I could not even look at him. His own stubbornness had put us all in this present danger, had forced us to flee to the countryside and hide like thieves. Away from our son and at odds with our family members. It was a state of waiting, and nothing made the hours pass slower than the thick and clinging fear.

Finally, on the third day, we received word from Paris. Two letters arrived during breakfast—one from Julie to me, the other from Joseph to my husband. I tore through the red wax seal on Julie's note, ravenous for her news. It was a short letter, stating only:

*Come home, my dear sister. You shall be safe. Oscar is safe. There is nothing more to fear.*

It was Julie's seal and handwriting, of that I could be certain. Joseph's note gave more explanation but contained the same message: we were safe to return to Paris.

Much had happened in the capital since our midnight departure, Joseph wrote. Napoleon had been named First Consul of France, leader of a small council of men who were now ostensibly sharing the reins of power, though we knew enough of Napoleon to suspect that the First Consul was the true authority. Alongside the First Consul would preside the Senate, its members appointed directly by the First Consul.

*My brother counts you among his friends,* Joseph wrote. *And indeed, your wife and son are his family. I can vouchsafe that no harm shall befall you should you return to your rightful home and your place in our family—and government.*

Bernadotte looked at me, relief breaking across his features like sunshine after the dark clouds glide past. For the first time in days, he smiled, a faint flicker, but there it was nonetheless. I, too, allowed myself to exhale, but my tone was cold as I reached across the table and pointed at the letter, saying: "There. You made your stand. You said what you believed. But the events have unfolded as they have unfolded. We have a new government, and we shall have a new constitution."

Bernadotte heaved a heavy sigh. "And so it has come to this."

I rose from my chair, declaring, "You can do as you wish, but I am going back to Paris."

My husband's frame sagged as he nodded and tucked Joseph's letter into his pocket. "If you return to Paris, Desiree, then I shall go with you."

# PART THREE

# Chapter 21

*Paris*
*November 1799*

NAPOLEON SAT ACROSS FROM ME, HIS INTENSE EYES belying the friendly smile that he'd affixed to his features. "I finally had the chance to meet your son, though you were not there for the occasion," he said. Bernadotte was at my side on the silk settee, and Josephine sat beside Napoleon. She wore the red kerchief in her hair, and even though it was the afternoon, it looked as though our visit had roused her from bed. She was barefoot, her legs crossed and tilted toward her husband. "Try as I might, I could not find the two of you," Napoleon added.

We sat with our hosts in a large salon on the ground floor of their new home, the palace they'd taken for themselves on the night of the coup. They now occupied the largest apartments of Paris's Luxembourg Palace, the sprawling building that had once served as the château of Queen Marie de Medici before turning into government offices during the Revolution. "Coffee? Or wine?" Josephine asked, her harpist's fingers languidly stroking her husband's bare hand.

"No, thank you," I answered.

Napoleon kept his attention fixed on my husband, sitting quietly for a moment before he asked: "Did you have a nice sojourn in the woods?"

My husband stiffened beside me—I could feel it. He weighed his words before leaning forward, speaking in a calm tone. "Come, Napoleon, we are old friends. You know where I stood. It was nothing personal."

Napoleon's face was an inscrutable mask. He looked from my husband to me before speaking, his lips tight as he said only, "Indeed."

"But I serve France before all else," Bernadotte said. "And France has declared you to be its new leader. And so I shall serve you. With my life, if necessary."

Napoleon did not answer. I could hear the ormolu clock where it ticked on the marble mantel, but otherwise the room swelled with silence. Outside on the street, someone shouted, "*Vive* Napoleon!"

"It is noisy from dawn 'til midnight," Napoleon said, smiling now. "But what do you think of our new accommodations?" he asked, raising a hand as he looked around the massive, high-ceilinged room.

"Beautiful parks and gardens surrounding the place. Marie de Medici certainly took to the Bourbon way of luxury," Napoleon said. "And if you look out that window, you see Rue de Vaugirard." Napoleon pointed toward one of the large floor-to-ceiling windows. "And just up the street stands Les Carmes."

Josephine shuddered, and he put a protective hand on her thigh. "The prison where my little Creole was held during the Terror. Before her scheduled trip to the guillotine."

I swallowed, my eyes turning instinctively toward Josephine. Her amber eyes, rimmed in dark kohl, were fixed downward toward the ornate Aubusson carpet.

Napoleon arched an eyebrow, tilting his head as he glanced toward my husband. "I believe I heard, Bernadotte, that you predicted I'd end up at the guillotine, if I remember correctly. You said that my coup would lead to it. Did you not?"

"I . . . I misjudged . . . the will and desires of the people." I could feel the blood roiling in my husband's veins, but I resisted the urge to put a calming hand on his. Napoleon would notice such a gesture, I was sure of it. Instead, Bernadotte remained calm of his own accord; he knew the importance of this meeting. Of smoothing over relations with Napoleon once more.

"Ah." Napoleon considered my husband's defense for a moment, eventually nodding. "A dangerous thing to do—misjudging the will of the people."

"I see that now," Bernadotte said.

"It's something I'm certain never to do." Napoleon leaned to his side and wrapped his hand around Josephine's waist, whispering something in her ear—prompting her low, throaty laugh—before turning back toward us.

"You hurt my feelings, Bernadotte. I'll admit, when all my friends came to my side, offering their loyalty and support . . . and you weren't there, I was cross with you. Quite cross. I told Joseph as much. But he . . . and then there's my godson . . ." Napoleon's words trailed off, but my heart clenched. "Well." Napoleon looked directly at me now, and the sharpness of his features seemed to soften, ever so slightly. "Desiree is an old friend. And my little Creole here told me that she's grown quite fond of your wife. You've been kind to her, Desiree. Even when my own flesh and blood were not. And she has seen it."

Napoleon held me with his intense gaze, even as my eyes slid toward Josephine. She nodded her agreement, shifting her lithe frame on the sofa as she continued to stroke her husband's hand. A soothing gesture, slow and rhythmic.

My husband uncrossed and then recrossed his legs beside me; I could hear the groaning of his leather boots.

"You idealize our Revolution, Bernadotte," Napoleon said. "But have you so quickly forgotten the fear? The chaos? The anarchy?"

My husband made to answer, but before he could, Napoleon cut him off with a wave of his hand, declaring: "The Revolution was worthy in that it ended the inefficacy of the Bourbons. It allowed the people to rise up and choose for themselves a new leader. To choose a leader who is one of them, a leader who shall serve for them. And choose they have. But now they want order. They want peace. They want prosperity. The Revolution is over. I am the Revolution."

# Chapter 22

*Tuileries Palace, Paris*
*Spring 1800*

"I WAS NOT MADE FOR SUCH GRANDEUR," JOSEPHINE SAID, sighing. "I can feel the queen's ghost asking me what I am doing in her bed." With that, she took my hand in her own and gave it a conspiratorial squeeze. "As a girl, I ran barefoot through the sands of the Caribbean. And Napoleon? He ran barefoot through the dust of the Corsican olive groves. And yet"—she looked around, as if unsure how she had arrived to this room—"here we are. The people have spoken."

I did not say so, but I was not entirely certain it was *the people* who had insisted that Josephine and her husband—our country's undisputed, if not exactly official, sole regent—make their home in the Tuileries Palace, the ancient residence of French princes in the heart of Paris. Nor had the people insisted that they take the apartments formerly occupied by Louis XVI and Marie-Antoinette, or sleep in Marie-Antoinette's mahogany bed, only recently restored after the havoc of the Revolution. But to have said any of that would have been madness. Not when we were so newly reinstated in Napoleon's good favor.

"This way." Josephine gave my hand a tug, and Julie followed beside me. We were there on a mild day in early spring, and the windows were opened to allow the soft, wet air into the musty palace halls. Josephine had invited us for tea, and though Joseph remained skeptical of his sister-in-law, even he had known that it was not an invitation to be refused.

"We'll have our tea upstairs, in my apartments," she said as she sailed toward the broad stairway before us. "It's too loud down here, with all of the work they are doing."

The sprawling palace was indeed a hive of activity. It was a labyrinthine building, added to and altered by so many ambitious and rich monarchs hoping to leave their own marks, satisfy their own whims—and now more than four hundred massive rooms comprised the complex. Servants clad in tidy uniforms of embroidered gold—a livery more fine than even that which the Bourbon servants had worn—darted about, adjusting the wall hangings, dusting the drapes, unfurling the ornate Moroccan and Aubusson carpets, arranging Napoleon's new furniture of blue and white silk. Blue and white—the colors of the former royalty, I noted. Elsewhere throughout the palace, the servants polished silver and arranged fine porcelain vases from Sèvres and hung the artwork from Napoleon's Italian conquests.

Though the new trappings were fine, even lavish, the building itself was in complete disrepair, and I saw that firsthand as we navigated the ground-floor halls and salons to climb the colossal stairway once ascended by the Bourbon kings and their noble ministers. Outside, the gardens were still open to the masses, swarming with urchins begging for *sous*, lemonade sellers peddling juice, streetwalkers peddling goods of another sort.

"You'll have to excuse . . . we are still working." Josephine waved a hand dismissively toward the near wall, where black, sooty grime darkened the tapestries that hung there, scars of the cook fires that had been lit by the miserable rabble who had set up camp in the palace after the royal family had been run out. More of the mirrors were cracked or smashed than intact. And much of the furniture was stripped or damaged, pieces of it having been used for firewood.

We walked across the grand hall toward the legendary king's staircase, and I felt my stomach clench when I saw the stains. Dark, wine-colored smears—the spilled blood of the dead king's Swiss Guards, the small and outnumbered force that had attempted to fight back the murderous mob as they'd entered this palace wielding pitchforks, their intention being to rape the queen and murder the king.

Josephine noticed my horrified intake of breath, and her eyes followed mine. "Yes, I know." She sighed, beginning her ascent up the stairs. "I've asked Napoleon so many times to have these walls scrubbed. We have thousands of servants working on this place, but they're all scared of this stairway. I'm so tired of living amid the blood of ghosts."

At the top, she led us down the long hall and toward a series of fine, spacious rooms. Their private apartments. If the ground floor of this palace remained shabby and in a state of war-torn disrepair, these rooms were quite the opposite. Josephine had personally overseen the redecoration of their living quarters and, with her husband's blessing, had set about to outdo even the grandeur of the Bourbons.

"Napoleon told me to make it better than Versailles," she whispered mischievously, as she led us through the first doorway.

We entered a sitting room lined with ornate and colorful tapestries, the furniture upholstered in a cheerful pattern of yellow silk. Sèvres porcelain birds decorated the marble mantel, and bright sunshine filtered in through the floor-to-ceiling windows to reflect off the large mirrors and the burnished chandeliers. Josephine paused to let us take it all in, and I was aware of my own gape. The room was tasteful and elegant, with Josephine's hand evident in every detail.

"Now, this way." Josephine breezed past the guards and we did so in her wake to enter the next room, grand and filled with statues. These were Napoleon's prized treasures, I guessed. "Caesar and Alexander and Hannibal and George Washington," Josephine explained, sailing past the rows of tall statues without looking at them. "You know how my husband feels about his heroes."

Without knocking, she led us into the next room, a salon draped with lilac silk upholstery. "This is *my* favorite room," she said. "I insist on fresh lilacs from the greenhouses every day to match the silk." The chairs were gilded in shiny gold to complement the large ormolu clock and elaborate marble-topped tables. "Nearly there," she said, gliding past treasure after treasure, these rooms indeed more splendid than I'd imagined Versailles's salons to be.

"Ah, here we are." Josephine opened the door to a massive bedchamber, and the three of us entered. I heard Julie's quick intake of breath behind me. I looked around, stunned, deciding that this room was even grander than the others.

"I wanted it to appear as if it were decorated by sprites and fairies," Josephine cooed. "Our peaceful retreat in a chaotic world. What do you think?"

My eyes roved admiringly over the details of the large chamber. Pale blue satin covered the walls. Sèvres porcelain vases stuffed with fresh-cut flowers adorned the mantel and the marble-topped end tables. Oil paintings lined the walls, their rich tones flickering beneath the candlelight of an immense chandelier. But the most striking feature of the bedchamber was the massive canopied bed in the center—the bed once occupied by our murdered queen.

So when Josephine had said she lived amid the ghosts of France's past, she had not been exaggerating; she slept alongside them. I remained transfixed for a moment, staring at the mahogany bed as I wondered: was all the splendor of the silk and the porcelain enough to make one forget that the dead queen had slept in that very spot? So distracted was I by that thought that I did not immediately notice the figure standing in the far corner.

"Oh! Darling!" It was Josephine who drew my attention to his presence. "We didn't realize you were in here."

Napoleon smiled at his wife, raising his arms and walking toward us. "Hello, my darling."

She ran to him and folded herself into his arms. He really had grown incredibly round. "I'm having our dear sisters for tea," she said, placing a kiss on his cheek. "I wanted them to see the fine rooms you gave me. And what were you doing?" she asked. She used the informal *tu* in addressing him, I noticed. She was the only person I'd ever seen do that. Not even Joseph or Letizia had been granted that level of familiarity.

"This balcony," Napoleon said, turning back toward the window. "I was just thinking."

She turned to us now. "This balcony . . . it's where my husband saw Louis standing in his shame. During the Revolution."

"Indeed." Napoleon put a hand up, silencing her, and took over his own story. "He was marched out here, they put the red cap on his head, and he waved, like some dancing bear. Fool. Unable to see that he could not appease the rabble with gestures or promises. They wanted only his royal blood."

Julie and I nodded, listening in silence. Napoleon then fixed his green-eyed gaze on me. "How is your husband? My old Gascon friend."

"He does very well," I answered. It was true, for the most part; much to my relief, Bernadotte seemed to have made his peace with our new government and its ratified constitution. He was back in the employ of the army here in Paris and, like the rest of us, waited to see what our new Consulate leadership intended for France. "He enjoys fatherhood," I added.

"Yes, I imagine he does. Isn't that nice," Napoleon said. His eyes roved over my body, lingering on my breasts; they were still full from nursing my baby. I resisted the urge to fidget, to draw my shawl closer around my shoulders and over my décolletage.

"I shall leave you ladies." He turned and put a kiss squarely on Josephine's lips. As he did so, he raised his hand proprietarily to her throat, a gesture as remarkable for its affection as for the latent brutishness beneath it. "This . . . I haven't seen it." He fingered the thick cluster of grape-sized emeralds that lined her neck as he pulled away from her kiss.

Her hand flew to the choker. "Oh, this? Oh, it's ancient. I've had it for years."

"Hmm. I know the emeralds you have from the Sforza estate. But I've not seen these."

She shrugged, grinning, glancing from her husband toward Julie and me. "Our tea will get cold."

"Well, we would not want that." Napoleon flashed a look that was more sneer than smile. And then, turning toward us, he said with a nod, "Ladies, enjoy." He kept his hand on his wife's backside a few moments before releasing her and walking from the room, shutting the door behind him.

Josephine exhaled audibly once he was gone. "He's so assiduous." She still touched the emerald choker, her trembling fingers outlining each massive jewel. "His mind—he never forgets a thing. I have to fib sometimes about my new jewelry or he scolds me for overspending."

I had had some idea of this. Joseph had told us, through gritted teeth, about how Napoleon had agreed to pay off all of Josephine's debts shortly after his return from Egypt. And of course I'd read that Napoleon had allocated for himself the exorbitant salary of half a million francs a year—this on top of the private money he'd made from his military haul collecting treasure across Europe. And yet, with the rate at which Josephine spent, she made quick work of even that astronomical sum.

*I was not made for such grandeur,* she had just told us. My mind reeled.

"But alas," Josephine said, "my apologies for the unexpected encounter. He insists we share a bedroom. He cannot stand to be away from me, even for a night." At this, she flashed a flimsy smile. "Plus, he feels that he's safer with me beside him. I'm such a light sleeper, should any attempt be made against him in his sleep, I would awake and call for help."

A servant entered just then, bearing a tea service with a whimsical pastel-colored pattern. We took our seats as Josephine poured for us, and I noticed how her smooth hands still trembled as she did so. For as much as she was the lady of the house amid unspeakable splendor, there was a certain restless, even nervous, quality that I had never before noticed in her. Her eyes seemed listless as she glanced around the room. Her conversation was less focused. "Thank you for coming to visit me. I quite missed you both. Desiree, how is your darling boy?"

Now I couldn't help but smile; Oscar was the joy of our lives, and I could happily speak about him with anyone.

"You will have to bring him out to see me at Malmaison." Josephine waved a hand. "This is all fine and good, but that, that is our home. I tell Napoleon not to grow too accustomed to living here. When I finish decorating Malmaison . . ." It had been an ongoing project, one that had taken years and millions so far, and from what I heard, it was not yet near completion.

"Your little boy will love our zoo. I have arranged to have an orangutan, and a llama from Peru, and black swans from Australia. Oh, and the plants! I have so many hothouses. My garden shall be the most beautiful little thing in the world. Er, not so little, I suppose. We will have tropical plants from as far as the Nile and the Orient! Orchids from Siam, mimosas from Tasmania, hibiscus from the Caribbean. My darling Bonaparte said he's always had a soft spot for exotic flowers from tropical climates. Like me."

*And me as well,* I thought, though I did not say it.

For as much as her husband loved her and spoiled her in the private domain of their lavish homes, he put forth quite a different image in public. Our First Consul passed a series of laws shortly after taking the reins of power, titled the Napoleonic Code. One of the most striking things about it was the harsh treatment of women.

*A wife must promise obedience and fidelity to her husband.*

The edicts were punishing: Any wife accused of committing adultery would be imprisoned, while for husbands a similar transgression meant only a nominal fine. Any man who caught his wife in the arms of another man could murder her without fear of being charged with a crime. It became nearly impossible for a woman to divorce, but the process was simplified for a man. Women were forbidden from politics, the law, and public debate, from business and managing money. The women of France, who had played such a central role in the Revolution, were now urged to adopt a quiet and modest virtue within the confines of their husbands' homes. A woman would do society its highest service, our First Consul declared, by marrying and birthing many babies and by molding France's children into loyal patriots.

Meanwhile, Bernadotte told me that it was common knowledge that Napoleon was engaging in all sorts of indiscreet love affairs—sleeping with Parisian actresses, courtesans, the aristocratic wives of his generals and advisers. Josephine, for her part, was no fool. After she had nearly lost her husband with the public exposure of her own dalliances, I suspected that she was now faithful and uncomplaining, even in the face of these recent humiliations.

Elsewhere across France, life changed for us, too. Napoleon did away with the salutary titles of Citizen and Citizeness that had arisen during the Revolution, returning to the traditional forms of Madame and Monsieur. France welcomed the Catholic faith once more; long-silenced bells began to peal across Paris as Napoleon officially restored the Church to its ancient place of reverence, reopening houses of worship and granting amnesty to deported priests, encouraging the populace to embrace piety once more.

Place de la Guillotine was now Place de la Concorde, and the dreaded blade was packed up and put away. All of Paris, it seemed, let forth a long-held sigh of weary relief.

Easter would be the first holiday celebrated in Paris since the formal reconciliation with the Church, and so the Bonaparte family gathered at the Tuileries Palace that spring day to celebrate after Mass. We Bernadottes were invited.

Throughout the city, we heard the bells as our carriage pulled us toward the Tuileries. The air was damp, but nevertheless it held the hint of the coming warmth. Oscar was precious in his Easter clothes, white silk and linen starched to crispness, and he delighted with fresh squeals at each clanging of the massive bells.

We sat down to luncheon attended by the Bonapartes' liveried footmen, a lavish feast of lamb with potatoes and eggs and haricots verts. Josephine was not in her preferred muslin but a gown of rose-colored silk. Napoleon, stuffed into his officer's uniform, spoke to us as we ate. "Ladies, there is something that Josephine and I wish to discuss with you."

I fidgeted in my chair, taking a sip of wine. Napoleon continued: "A newly born government must dazzle and astonish. If it fails to do that, it fails."

Julie and I exchanged curious glances.

"You are the ladies of the roy—er, first household. As such, all of the nation looks to you. You must set the example." He eyed Josephine, who nodded her wordless accord. "All of Europe once looked to France as the leader in fashion. I wish to return to that."

"Indeed," Josephine agreed as her husband went on: "Josephine knows the importance of every decision she makes, how it will be scrutinized by the public and reported by the journals. For instance, she will not wear muslin anymore. Muslin is made in India—which is a British colony. Why would we enrich our enemies and deny work to our own countrymen? From now on, she will wear silk and satin made only in France. Velvet from Lyon, lace made in Chantilly or Alençon, linen made in Saint-Quentin. You know this, right, my wife?"

"Of course I know, darling," Josephine said. "Why, you remind me each morning, sitting there, watching as I dress." The comment was said with an unmistakable barb, and all eyes flew to Napoleon's face, awaiting the reaction to such defiance. I noted the quick flush of his cheeks, the scarlet tinting of his neck. But he checked himself, said nothing. Merely turned back to his plate. The row would come later, this I knew.

My dressmaker arrived at our home a week later, a seasonal appointment arranged months earlier. But she had fresh news: "Madame Bernadotte, I come with all sorts of new guidelines."

"Oh?" I asked, welcoming the smartly dressed Madame Bertin into my boudoir. "Of what sort?"

"From the First Lady herself," the dressmaker said, wielding a handful of papers in her gloved hands. Sketches, I saw. Madame Bertin unfurled them across the marble-topped table, spectacles perched across the bridge of her narrow nose. "This season, dresses will be cut in a new silhouette, the style requested by Josephine. All French fabric, of course."

"Of course," I agreed.

"And you see this outline? A higher waist and a loose, flowing skirt."

*Interesting,* I thought to myself—the perfect style to wear when one was pregnant. Had Josephine finally conceived?

As broad and sweeping as Napoleon's vision for our nation was, he made one decision that had a much deeper impact within our household. With the return of the warm weather, Napoleon began preparing to ride back toward the Alps and Italy, and he decided to make my husband the Commander of the Army of the West. This meant that my Bernadotte would have to leave Paris. He'd be stationed in remote, sea-swept Brittany, headquartered at Rennes.

I did not wish to go, any more than I wished for my husband to go. It was far from Paris, our home, my sister. I put it off as long as I could, remaining behind in Paris with Oscar and our household staff. Spring was a busy time of soirees and dances, walks through the parks and day excursions along the Seine, and I flitted around the capital—the lone representative of the Bernadotte family—along with Julie and her husband. But by late summer, my husband's letters had grown so lonely and miserable that I took pity and knew I had to join him, at least for a time.

We were reunited in Saint-Malo, that ancient fortified city of stone buildings and craggy hills along the windswept Atlantic coast. My husband had made his home and headquarters in an old château within the city's walls, the home of the former Bourbon governor for the region. Though it was still summer, a damp ocean breeze clung to the city all day, and the nights were quite chilly, causing me to fear that Oscar might catch cold. The château was drafty and steeped with the permanent odors of saltwater and musty linen. As I shivered in bed at night, I would weave my feet under Bernadotte's legs, seeking some additional warmth but instead only eliciting his scolding.

My husband's mood had been less than cheerful since my arrival in Saint-Malo.

Napoleon had earned a fresh string of victories across Italy that summer, most recently in Marengo. When word reached our Atlantic outpost, the cannons went off across the city in celebration. People gathered outside our château, drinking and singing, shouting "Vive Napoleon!" But my husband lay beside me in an ill humor.

"It is a great honor to be in charge of such a large portion of the military, is it not, my dear?" I said, trying to lift my Bernadotte from his gloom. The west had long been the most pro-Bourbon and problematic region; the threat of open revolt or naval assault remained possible at any moment out here, even I knew that. Strong military leadership was essential.

But this seemed to prove no consolation to my husband, who growled in response: "I'm basically a police officer out here, thumping my chest to keep the royalists quiet. He has pushed me as far away as possible, so as never to see glory. And never to threaten his own."

# Chapter 23

*Paris*
*Christmas Eve, 1800*

W E ARRIVED LATE TO THE TUILERIES PALACE ON CHRIST-
mas Eve, and there was nothing Napoleon despised more than tar-
diness. Well, there was *one* thing that gave him greater displeasure:
quarreling with Josephine. And it appeared as though he faced both woes
that evening.

I did not know what had initially caused that night's disagreement, but
by the time we arrived to join them in their carriages to attend the opera,
Napoleon was berating her. "You are a liar!" he roared. We stood in the
grand front hall of the palace, the space filled with liveried servants and the
Bonaparte sisters, Julie and Joseph and I keeping to ourselves in the corner
as the attendants readied the coaches. Josephine turned away from us now,
her face pale, her eyes red-rimmed as Napoleon continued: "I know the
Red Sea came. You think I am a fool?"

"But that doesn't matter!" Josephine replied, wringing her fur muff in
her hands. The Bonaparte sisters sniggered among themselves, but Josephine ignored them, speaking only to her husband: "It just means that I am
healthy! It shall happen, my darling. Please, just be patient."

"*Patient?* Have I not been patient? For years?" His chest heaved as he
pointed his index finger, holding it just inches from her face. "You tried to
hide it from me! You thought I wouldn't find out!" The high collar of Na-

poleon's officer's uniform appeared too tight around his red, bulging neck.

Suddenly I understood. Another month had passed, and still Josephine had not become pregnant with Napoleon's heir. She must have just begun her monthly courses, and one of her servants had surely been tasked with reporting that to her watchful husband.

Josephine, in hysterics now, ignored us all and knelt at his feet, pleading with him to forgive her. Just then, the clock in the grand hall struck eight. Napoleon frowned, glancing toward the door. "We will discuss this later."

And then he gave his orders for those of us gathered to exit the palace and load into the two waiting coaches. "You'll go behind me, in the second coach," Napoleon ordered his wife. "Joseph, come with me."

Bernadotte was already at the theater, awaiting us with other generals and ministers, so I was to ride with my sister. Julie and I chose the second coach as well, along with Napoleon's very pregnant sister Caroline, who was so round that it appeared the child might arrive at any moment. As she was helped into the carriage, I surmised from Caroline that the joy of her coming motherhood was nothing compared to the exultation she felt in knowing that her swollen belly infuriated her brother and agonized her sister-in-law. "If only the baby will wait a few more hours and allow me to see the whole performance," Caroline said, smiling broadly as we took our seats in the coach.

It was to be Haydn's *The Creation* that Christmas Eve, and Napoleon peeked his head into our carriage one last time to ensure we were all present. His eyes landed on his wife, and he glowered. "What did I tell you, Josephine?"

She returned his stare in confused silence. He went on, "Did I not tell you they'd all be there? Talleyrand, Bernadotte—" He caught sight of me looking on and changed tracks. "You were to dress your best."

Josephine glanced down at her narrow frame, clad in a sleek silver gown and a colorful scarf with an elaborate design of swirling vines. "But . . . but I have," she stammered. "Does my clothing displease you?"

Napoleon leaned forward into the coach and yanked at the shawl around her thin shoulders. "This scarf comes from Constantinople! I should know, after all, seeing as I paid for it! You dress in some heathen pattern on Christmas Eve, in open defiance of my orders? You wish to make me look a fool, as always? Inside now, and change quickly. I want a *French* shawl!"

We waited in silence as Josephine ran from the coach, back into the palace and up into her suite to hastily select a replacement. I could feel Napoleon's rage mounting, even from our separate coach, and I pitied Josephine. She finally emerged from the palace, this time wrapped in a shawl of pale blue Lyonnaise silk. She did not say a word as she rejoined us in the coach and the horses set off through the courtyard. We would most certainly be late arriving to the theater.

Caroline rubbed her belly as we rode. "He's just so large in there," she said. "I've run out of space. Do you remember feeling this way with your son, Desiree?"

"Yes," I answered, avoiding Josephine's eyes. Julie's, too.

After several minutes, we turned onto the Rue Saint-Nicaise, at the corner of Place du Carrousel. "My brother has so many questions for me," Caroline said, her hand resting on the dome of her belly. "He approaches everything with such an exacting, inquisitive mind. Oh, how he longs to know everything there is about childbearing! He's desperate to experience parenthood for himself."

"I remember, with my first, my son," Josephine said, interjecting. If she was pained by Caroline's words, she did not reveal it, but instead fixed a calm smile on her features. "He was positively frantic inside my belly; he moved from dawn until dusk. A fiendish little creature inside of me. And yet, when he came out, my Eugene was the most placid, most serene little baby. A sweetheart, even if I had worried that I carried a rascal in my womb."

"Oh, but that was so long ago," Caroline gasped. "How can you even remember that far back?"

"Well," Josephine wavered now, searching for words, but before she could find them, we were all rocked by a horrifying jolt, a ground-shaking blast. The horses screeched. It felt like a row of cannons firing over an earthquake. I cried out as we all tumbled to the floor, the windows of the coach shattering into a million shards. I could hear the coachman's frantic shouts, his useless attempts to calm the horses. I blinked, stunned, my ears ringing in momentary deafness. Julie lay beside me on the floor of the coach, rubbing her own ears as she screamed. Caroline was crouched forward, as if protecting her stomach as she wailed. Josephine fainted. Outwardly, on the surface of our flesh, we appeared unharmed, even if horribly shaken. But what had happened? I scrambled to my knees and glanced out the shattered windows, where several of the nearest houses had been reduced to rubble. Their roofs and doorways were ripped entirely apart, replaced by gaping maws of splintered timber and cracked stonework.

A bomb—I knew it in an instant. An attempt on the life of our First Consul. The horses in front of our coach still bucked and kicked as the coachman and several servants struggled to calm them. The people in the street screamed, darting about in front of our coach, a mass of bloodied limbs and chaos.

Darkness thickened around us as my hearing came back. I blinked. We were in a clinging fog, no doubt caused by the explosion, but I heard his voice. "My wife, my wife!" It was Napoleon, frantic. "Where is my wife?" He hopped into our coach, spotting Josephine's inanimate frame and taking her in his arms. "Josephine, my darling!" He did his best to rouse her, kissing and patting her face. Slowly she began to stir, disoriented, blinking as she looked around our demolished coach. "You've fainted!" he said, cradling her like a child. "But do you realize that you've saved my life?" She didn't understand his meaning. Nor did I. Napoleon, meanwhile, was as alert as I had ever seen him. Even a bit giddy. "I was saved because of your scarf, my darling girl! Because of the delay we had while waiting on your silly outfit change. Can you believe it? All because of you! I've always known that you were my angel, and now you've really done it, you've saved us from the bomb blast!"

I could not believe it, but Napoleon then announced that we would still go forward with his plans to attend the performance. "To the opera, this very instant."

"Are you . . . certain?" Joseph asked, his arms wrapped around a trembling Julie.

"Yes." Napoleon nodded, his face pale but resolute. "People must not think me dead."

We were all, miraculously, unhurt, though of course very badly shaken.

I wanted nothing more than to return to my own home, where I would have a tall glass of brandy and a warm bath before climbing into bed, with Oscar sleeping peacefully at my side. And yet, Napoleon declared that we would not allow his would-be assassins to intimidate us, to intimidate France, and so, with our carriages ruined and our horses petrified, we walked the short distance remaining to the theater.

We entered the Consul's opera box to whispers and applause, though no one in the hall could have heard yet what had just happened. The performance had begun, and the players continued on in spite of the excitement that our entrance elicited. I needed to sit. I lowered myself into a seat toward the back of the box, seeking out my husband, but I couldn't find him. Napoleon, too, noticed this. "Where is Bernadotte?" he asked me, not bothering to whisper in spite of the music.

"I . . . I do not know," I answered, trying to conceal the way my hands trembled in my lap.

Finally, several minutes later, the tall figure of my husband appeared in the box; he had a harried look, his dark hair somewhat disheveled. Napoleon watched him enter.

Bernadotte's breath was uneven as he leaned over to place a kiss on my cheek. "Hello, my darling."

Bernadotte bowed toward Napoleon and then took his seat beside me. I stared sideways at him. "Do you have any idea what just happened to us?"

He shook his head. "No. Why were you late?"

Napoleon was watching our exchange, so I kept my account brief, my face composed as I explained about the bomb, our coach, the streets in deathly disarray. "*Mon Dieu*," my husband said, taking my hand in his. "Thank God you are safe."

"Yes," I agreed. But then, agitated by my husband's loud breathing, I grumbled, "Why are *you* so out of breath?"

Bernadotte shifted in his seat, his body leaning away from me, looking out toward the opera stage. "I . . . I just ran . . . up the stairs."

*Curious,* I thought, my mind entirely unable to focus on the musical performance before us. My husband had wondered why *I* was late, but now I wondered the same thing about him.

After the opera, we returned to the Tuileries for a late Christmas Eve feast, just as planned. Napoleon insisted that nothing about our night be disrupted, even if we were a quiet, sober group gathering around the feast laid out before us. I had no appetite, and it did not appear that my husband did, either. As the bells of the nearby Notre Dame heralded midnight and the arrival of Christmas, even Napoleon succumbed to the somber, ruminative mood. In spite of his steely resolve from earlier in the evening, he now appeared visibly shaken, his wineglass trembling in his hands, his fork pushing the food around his plate but barely lifting it to his lips.

He leaned toward Joseph at the end of dinner, speaking in a quiet voice: "I have no heir. Who would have carried it on? Had they . . . succeeded in . . ."

Josephine turned a shade paler. Joseph nodded, stating: "My dear brother, do not worry about such questions, for the happy truth is that they did not."

Napoleon frowned at this. "But Joseph, I must consider it. I must wonder, who would step in, since it would not be a son?"

Joseph propped his elbows on the table, pushing his plate away. "One of your family, we would have stepped in, gladly. The good work of the Bonapartes . . . of, er, France, would be carried on in your name."

"No," Napoleon said, shaking his head, his voice toneless. And then he lifted his face, looking around the table before resting his attentive eyes on my husband. I noticed with a jolt that my husband returned Napoleon's gaze, his expression steady, even a bit defiant. Where had my husband been? I wondered again. Why had he arrived late to the theater, disheveled and out of breath? I had noticed, I had wondered; surely Napoleon had as well.

Napoleon's focus remained on Bernadotte as he pronounced, a joyless smile tightening his features: "It would have been General Bernadotte to whom the people would have turned in their grief. Like Antony, he would have hoisted the bloodstained robe of Caesar. And then he would have stepped into the place vacated by my death."

# Chapter 24

*Paris*
*Spring 1802*

ONCE MORE THERE WAS SCREAMING IN THE STREETS OF Paris, but this time it was a celebration. A clamor of revelry and bells. Peace had come, at last, to France—and Napoleon had brought it.

That was what our First Consul told the people, proclaiming it in the newspapers and pronouncing it through messengers on the streets and bridges and in the cafés of Paris; Napoleon, after more than a decade of Revolution and chaos and bloodshed, had delivered a victory for France abroad and a new era of lasting peace and prosperity at home.

Joseph had, in fact, been the primary architect of the peace treaty, traveling with Talleyrand that spring to the ancient French city of Amiens, where he joined the ministers of Great Britain, Spain, and Holland to carve out a new treaty for the nations of a blood-soaked Europe. The news was declared throughout France with state-sponsored feasting and the roar of cannons across each city's square. France was victorious; not only would we retain our borders and the lands we had won under Napoleon's conquests, but we would also regain free and open access to the seas, no longer haunted by powerful British warships. Our colonial territories were to be preserved across our empire, and thousands of French prisoners of war would be set free.

France reveled, but Paris was positively euphoric. Throughout the streets, people hoisted the tricolor and engravings of Napoleon's image, the "Great Angel of Peace," his likeness wreathed in laurel like the august emperors of antiquity. Newspapers named him the "Great Pacificator" and the "God of Peace," and printing presses churned out new songs and poems written in his honor.

When we attended the opera with the Bonaparte family that spring evening, his arrival in the consular box was greeted with thunderous shouts and standing ovations that stretched on, with no end in sight, until he finally raised a hand and offered an appreciative nod.

If the Parisians wished to deify him, Napoleon appeared ready to let them do so. I noticed, that spring, that he began to dress differently. Ever since I'd first known him, he'd worn the military jacket and breeches of an officer in the French army. Now that he had brought peace, however, he put aside his military uniform. That season, he began to wear a high-necked jacket of red velvet. The rest of his appearance showed more care as well: breeches trimmed in gold embroidery, high leather boots, a jeweled sword, a sash across his ample torso. When we would sit, *en famille*, for the Bonaparte dinners or evenings of cards or music, he'd have Josephine buff his fingernails with a cambric handkerchief, pausing every few minutes to scrutinize her work.

For the first time since I had been living in Paris, Napoleon did not ride out that warm season for battlefields in Italy or Austria but rather remained with Josephine and the rest of his family in residence at the Tuileries. Napoleon the soldier had given way to Napoleon the great statesman.

And he brought peace to more than just the battlefields. That spring, church bells pealed across Paris, celebrating the official reconciliation of France with Rome and the Pope. "We now have peace not only with the powers of the earth, but with the powers of the heavens as well!" Napoleon declared, triumphant, to the nation's newspapers. It was a reversal of one of the first and central tenets of our Revolution, but the common people of France rejoiced at the news. As with our revolutionary calendar, the nation had never truly taken to the mandated godlessness of the Republic, had never fully pushed aside Jesus Christ and the Virgin Mary for the Supreme

Being and the Goddess of Reason. The reconciliation with Rome was good politics, and Napoleon knew it.

We rode from the Tuileries to Notre Dame, a long procession of gilded carriages carrying the members of Bonaparte's family and government, to kneel and pray before the newly reinstated Archbishop of Paris. Bernadotte and I sat with Joseph and Julie in the carriage immediately following Napoleon, who traveled in front with his wife and her two children, Eugene and Hortense. "You see how busy our streets are?" Joseph pointed out the windows. He was right: the return of the warm weather always meant the return of the vendors and flower stalls, a fresh surge in foot traffic, and yet, that day, the capital was positively swarming.

Napoleon was determined to make the capital a thriving center that would attract not only the French but hordes of international tourists as well. The Brits and other Europeans flocked en masse after so many years during which our city had been out of reach, and Napoleon welcomed their arrival. He wished to make his seat at the Tuileries a vibrant and fashionable court, and he issued an order to his wife that they would host grand soirees every week. Soon these Tuileries nights gained a reputation across Paris for their gaiety and lavishness—banquets fueled with music and dancing, witty conversation and champagne-soaked flirting—and an invitation from Josephine, who sat on a throne during these gatherings, became the most sought-after ticket in town.

Following these festive nights of exclusive guest lists and excessive feasting, in the mornings, the public was invited to watch Napoleon and Josephine awake and dress, a public levée ceremony the likes of which the French had not seen since the same rituals of Louis XVI and Marie-Antoinette. The etiquette now governing daily life in the Tuileries was so exact and the ritual so precisely observed that one might have blinked and presumed oneself back in the Versailles court of a century earlier.

There was more good news for the Bonaparte family as that peaceful spring warmed into summer. After years of longing and disappointment, my sister was finally *enceinte*, her belly growing rounder by the day with Joseph's baby. Napoleon smiled when he learned of his brother's good news, but I noticed the small, barely perceptible tightening of his jaw, the minuscule twitch of his eyebrow as he glanced sideways at his own wife, her waist as slender as ever beneath her suitably patriotic French silk.

That evening, Napoleon pulled Joseph aside. As I stood with Julie beside her husband, we could hear their exchange. "Congratulations, brother."

"Thank you. We are happy." Joseph shifted from one foot to the other. "With any luck, it shall be you next."

"Indeed," Napoleon said, nodding. "But . . . how? After so long?"

Joseph leaned closer to his brother, speaking in a low voice that I could barely hear. "It was the waters. I truly believe it. Julie traveled to Plombières this winter, to the spas, where she took the healing waters. She fed on spinach dowsed in oil and eggs and drank from the curative fountains. She became pregnant shortly after her return."

The following week, Josephine was packed up, along with her daughter, Hortense, and sent in her coach to the spa town of Plombières.

Napoleon had studied the ancients, and he knew well enough the importance of both bread and circus; fortune provided him with the perfect opportunity for both when he turned thirty-three that August.

It was declared a public holiday across France. Previously, that same day had belonged to the Virgin Mary, as it was the holy day of her assumption to heaven. But even though we had reconciled with the Church, Napoleon had decided that the day would be in his honor instead, and he proclaimed it to be "St. Napoleon's Day."

The whole nation joined in wishing our popular First Consul, simply "Napoleon" now, a joyful birthday, but only a few hundred were fortunate enough to receive invitations to his private fête. He arrived, following a parade through Paris, with his brown hair wreathed in laurels, looking like his heroes of ancient Rome and Greece. Josephine entered beside him wearing a stunning gown of pink crêpe overlaid with fresh-clipped rose petals, her own dark hair ornamented with a diadem of brilliant diamonds.

Napoleon found Bernadotte and me several hours into the lavish party.

My husband was on his best behavior—I had begged him earlier that day to keep a subdued profile and offer only pleasant words of well-wishing. And that was what he did when Napoleon approached, I noted with great relief. "A toast to you, First Consul," Bernadotte said, lifting his champagne glass. "Peace reigns and the people are happy." My husband smiled, even though I knew, as his wife, how bitter those words tasted on his lips.

But, indeed, however much my husband had disagreed with the establishment of this new government, it appeared that Napoleon's leadership had been good for the nation in recent months. Our countryside appeared poised for a fine fall harvest, and Napoleon had been busy with orders to build new granaries to store the surpluses as a preventive measure against future bread shortages or price inflation. Through his treasury, he was in close communication with every regional governor, receiving regular reports on the price of bread. Far from the scarcity of the previous administrations, his own government had amassed reserves of grain, and he planned to meticulously monitor the deployment of those surpluses when and where they were needed, so that no French housewife might ever complain that her family went hungry under Napoleonic leadership. Business owners and merchants relished the promise of peace, tourists from across the Continent marveled at the artwork he had amassed and made public in the Louvre Palace, and trade boomed as it had not in years. We were a wealthy nation once more, our gold mints churning out new coins emblazoned with the profile of "Napoleon: First Consul."

And just recently, in thanks for these improvements, the French people had gifted Napoleon with the best birthday gift imaginable when they elected him, by a stunning majority, First Consul for Life. They wanted him as their sole and undisputed leader.

Nothing stood between him and complete power.

Napoleon received my husband's compliment now with a curt nod, his ever-alert eyes roving the crowd of his party. Perhaps he was seeking out Josephine. Or perhaps he was looking to see whether anyone had snubbed his invitation. Eventually, he answered, saying only: "Ambition is never content, even at the summit of greatness."

It was a curious statement, particularly since we were all gathered at a celebration of his life. But I understood; I knew how deeply unhappy Napoleon was in his personal life. The greatest single source of his discontent was his lack of a son. Julie was growing ever rounder with his brother's baby. Josephine had returned from Plombières, but as far as I could tell from her still-slender waist, she was not carrying his child.

Ever since the attempt on his life, Napoleon had displayed a singular obsession with begetting an heir. With the flood of British tourists into Paris had come British gossip—and newspaper reports as well. Unlike all French papers, these publications were not censored by Napoleon's government. "They infuriate him, these British writers," my husband said to me that morning. "They call him impotent. They call him short. They laugh at his lack of an heir. But more than that, they scare him. See here?" My husband pointed to that morning's cartoon in an English journal. A stout Napoleon stood wreathed in a crown of laurels, looking like a hero of ancient Rome, as behind him, toga-clad senators wielded sharpened blades. Underneath the image the caption said: *How did Caesar end?*

The threat was so thinly veiled that even I had quickly understood the meaning: the British newspapers were calling for assassination.

"Do you see Hortense?" Napoleon's question pulled me back to the present and his birthday ball, and my eyes followed to where his step-daughter stood nearby. "At least she gives me cause for celebration, even if my own wife does not," Napoleon said. I could see to what he referred—the soft swell of Hortense's midsection under a loose ivory gown. Hortense, now nineteen years old, had just married Napoleon's younger brother Louis only a few months prior. And already Hortense was pregnant.

"The child will be one half Bonaparte and one half Josephine, just as ours would be. And Louis assures me that if it's a boy, he shall be called Napoleon. So, it's something. But, alas, it's unfortunate to be made an uncle twice in one year, and a step-grandfather as well, but not yet a father."

# Chapter 25

*Paris*
*Spring 1803*

IT WAS INDEED A BOY BORN TO HORTENSE AND LOUIS, AND he was called Napoleon Bonaparte. But our First Consul did not grow any less impatient with his own childlessness. The fights at the Tuileries continued. The weekly Bonaparte family dinners were often delayed or disrupted, with Josephine arriving late, if at all. The Bonaparte siblings whispered the hateful lie—loud enough for not only Josephine to hear but the French newspapers as well—that Napoleon was, in fact, the father to Hortense's son. That the barren mother had pushed her own daughter into Napoleon's arms in the hopes of getting him a son and keeping him happy. It seemed there was no end to the vile malice that churned throughout the First Consul's family.

I came to dread my own visits to the Tuileries for fear of Napoleon's increasingly regular and violent outbursts, made all the more horrifying because of their shamelessly public nature. Julie, besotted as she was as a new mother to a baby girl, confided to her husband that both she and I dreaded the company of his brother, and so Joseph allowed us to excuse ourselves from many of the family gatherings. Instead we gathered regularly as just two sisters, with Oscar relishing his new role as big boy, petting and admiring his darling new cousin.

But the invitation that came to me that morning was unlike any of the others—it felt more like a summons than a request. It bore Napoleon's consular seal, even though it was written in Josephine's long, elegant hand. I was to go to the Tuileries alone—without my husband or my sister. Even without my son, who enjoyed his visits to his godfather for the *bonbons* and toys offered at the palace, unaware in his childish innocence of the darker undertones of the adult interactions.

As Bernadotte was back at his headquarters in Brittany with the Army of the West, he wouldn't have come anyway, but I would have liked the chance to speak with him before going. Nevertheless, when the morning of the appointed rendezvous arrived, I dressed with care, making sure that I selected a gown of French brocade and a fine brooch of sapphire and ruby stones—a color palette paying dutiful homage to our tricolor.

The Tuileries grounds were always bustling, especially the public gardens, but I was ushered quickly past the crowds and toward the grand stairway by a palace attendant clad in gold cloth. Inside, as I marched dutifully toward the staircase, I noted that the bloodstains across the wall were fainter, but not entirely gone. I shivered as I climbed.

I had no idea what Josephine wanted with me—I had long ago stopped trying to predict her moves. But if I had to guess, my suspicion was that perhaps she was finally pregnant and she wanted to somehow control how the news seeped out. Maybe she had use for me as some sort of advance messenger. Whatever my purpose to her, I was sure I wouldn't understand it until after I had unwittingly performed whatever duty she had in mind for me.

I was admitted into her yellow salon, but it was not Josephine who awaited me there. Napoleon stood, alone, before the row of tall windows. "Ah, Desiree." He turned upon my entrance. "My dear sister." He crossed the room to me, taking my gloved hand in his and kissing the top of it. I was immediately on edge as his green eyes held mine. When was the last time we had been alone in a room together? I wondered. Had it been in Marseille? No, Italy? Surely that had to be it.

"It's so good of you to come. Now, I'm just a rude soldier, but because my wife has taught me well, I know what my first question as host ought to be: What can I offer you? Something to eat? Drink?"

My throat was dry, but I answered: "Nothing, sir. I am . . . thank you."

"'Sir'?" He cocked his head, and I could see that he was in a mood to charm. "You are one of my oldest . . . friends." But he didn't tell me what I should call him instead of sir. He released my hand and gestured toward the nearest chair, upholstered in Josephine's merry yellow silk. "Well, then, sit. Please."

I did as he ordered.

"Josephine may join us eventually. She's bathing. You know how she loves to languish in her baths, my lazy little Creole. I realize that it's an outlandish luxury—these daily rosewater and jasmine baths of hers, when the Bourbon princes themselves set the tone at court for bathing only several times a year. But we certainly have the servants to haul the water. And she does love her perfumes and her oils. . . ." He shrugged, flashing an indulgent smile.

I did not care to hear more, but I nodded.

His eyes held me in their narrowed gaze. "It is good to see you, Desi." *Desi?* I forced my face to remain expressionless, saying: "You as well."

"How is my godson Oscar?"

I felt my body clench at hearing my son's name spoken by Napoleon's lips, but I managed an even tone as I answered: "He thrives, thank you."

"I am glad to hear it. And your husband?"

"He is in Brittany," was all the reply I offered.

"Yes, that's right." Napoleon crossed his legs and folded his hands on top of his knees. He didn't wear gloves, and I was momentarily dazzled by the pale, soft smoothness of his hands. A soldier's hands, a horseman's hands, yet they were as pristine as those of a lady who never lifted anything heavier than a porcelain teacup. I knew that Josephine gave him regular manicures—filing down his nails and massaging his palms with fragrant oils—and yet the sight still distracted me.

"I know," he said, flickering his fingers, easily perceiving my thoughts. "I tell my wife that she pampers me more than a woman." He shook his head. "But she is such a doting companion. She takes such pleasure in spoiling and nurturing me, I can't very well tell her no."

"Then you are lucky in your choice of a wife," I said.

"What about you, Desiree?"

I stiffened, sitting up a bit taller in my chair. "Pardon?"

He arched a lone dark eyebrow as he leaned forward, his voice low and confidential as he asked: "What sort of a wife are you?"

I tilted back in my chair, hoping to put as many inches between us as possible as I weighed my words. He had become such an unapologetic seducer, sleeping with all variety of women, married or not. Perhaps he had cycled through all the ladies of Paris and now sought to revisit old paramours? I cringed at the thought. "I am a faithful wife," I said, my tone decisive, without a drop of flirtation. "My husband and my son are, well, everything. As such, I try always to be an attentive wife and loving mother."

Napoleon studied me, and I couldn't help but notice the full, fleshy softness of his face. And not just his face—without the constant exertion of battle, with all of his feasts and parties and the celebrated chefs now in his employ, Napoleon was downright plump.

"Would you ever . . . stand up to your husband? If he needed . . . if the situation warranted it?"

I tried to mask the confusion that his question elicited. Was he asking me not to become his lover but instead act as his spy? To go against my own husband? "I'm not sure of the question, sir, and thus I fear I cannot provide you with the answer for which you hope."

He waved his hand, swatting the thought away. "Never mind." He looked around the room. "What do you think of the artwork?"

I tried to follow the thread of his thoughts, but I couldn't see any connection, so I answered as truthfully as I could: "I think the artwork adorning your palace is second to none. I think that here in this palace of the Tuileries and in the Louvre, you have collected a body of art that will be the envy of nations for many ages to come."

"Do you see that bust over there?" He pointed toward a marble piece in the corner of the salon. "It's done by an Italian sculptor, a man by the name of Ceracchi."

"Ah, Giuseppe Ceracchi, I admire his work," I said, glancing at the bust, relieved to find the conversation drifting toward something as benign as art. I was eager to keep it there. But Napoleon's green eyes careened toward mine, an unmistakable flicker setting them aflame.

"Yes, Giuseppe Ceracchi. So you know him?" The sudden intensity of his tone, and indeed his expression, unnerved me.

"Not . . . not well." I shifted in my seat, rearranging the folds of my skirt. "Bernadotte and I, we have met him once or twice. Most likely at parties given by you and the First Consuless."

Napoleon nodded, still studying me intently. "Is that so?"

"Sir?"

Now, his eyes narrowed, he said: "The same man, this Ceracchi, has recently been found guilty of plotting against my life."

I gasped. I knew that Napoleon lived in constant fear of dying without an heir. I knew that he had agents all over the city, and indeed all over Europe, constantly digging around for word of any potential attempt on his life. And yet, I didn't understand what any of this had to do with my husband or myself. I still did not know why I had been called here. All I could manage to answer was: "How horrifying. I am very troubled to hear that."

Napoleon uncrossed his thick legs and pressed his palms onto them, the tips of his manicured fingers going white from the pressure he exerted. "He followed me to the theater. He was covered in explosive material. He planned to blow me up."

I shuddered, my eyes flying to the door. All I wanted was to leave and return home. Or, at the very least, for Josephine to walk through that door and join us. Her presence would at least defuse the discomfort of this exchange.

Napoleon continued, oblivious of—or perhaps indifferent to—my uneasiness: "I know how to interrogate a man, Desiree."

"Oh?" I shifted in my seat.

"And a woman, for that matter," he said. "I know how to . . . pull . . . the truth out of someone."

I swallowed, noting that my mouth was parched. Even my words sounded dry as I said, "I'm sure you have had much experience."

"Yes. I have. You know, it's always interesting, when you are breaking a man. The three-hundred-pound German warrior cries out for his mama, while the scrawny thirteen-year-old might prove tough as sword steel. You never get what you expect." He paused, his eyes fixed squarely on mine. The room was silent; all I could hear was the steady ticking of the clock, and the blood thrashing between my ears.

"With Ceracchi . . . you know what I found out that I didn't expect?" he asked me.

I resisted the urge to fidget, forcing myself to return Napoleon's stare. "What is that?"

His voice was toneless as he declared: "Your husband owes him money."

The air fled my lungs. "What . . . what for?"

"Now, *that* I have not yet been able to extract." Napoleon crossed his legs.

"Surely I don't know. My husband is . . . as I said . . . he's not in Paris."

Napoleon looked away now, back toward the Ceracchi bust. When he spoke next, his tone was suddenly light. "Desiree, you know that I care for you, don't you?"

"Of . . . of course."

"And I feel as though I may be candid with you. Speak plainly. Is that the case?"

*Where was your candid speech when you were breaking my heart?* I wondered. *Evading and avoiding, while I ached for the truth. Only a girl waiting for the man she trusted.* But of course I said none of this; what purpose would it have served to dredge up the history buried so deeply in our shared past? And what did it matter now? Instead, I merely nodded my assent.

"Good," he said. "Yes, I am glad of it. Your sister is married to my brother. We are family. Corsicans value family above all else. Even when we should throw them all out to sea." A mirthless laugh, and then he went on. "I have been very forgiving of my family. You know that, right?"

I nodded.

"And now you're going to do something for me, in return for my loyalty."

*I was?* I said nothing, allowing him to continue. "Your husband is on his way back to Paris, even at this very moment. He's done leading a third of my army. He's done flinging muck at my government. He puts on a nice enough smile at my parties, but I know it's because you tell him to. I know his true feelings. I'm going to offer him a post, and you're going to tell him to accept it."

"I . . . what is this post?"

"Governor."

It hardly seemed a punishment. "That's most gracious of you," I said.

"Governor of our colony Louisiana. I'm sending you and that hot-headed Gascon to the Americas."

# Chapter 26

*Southwest France*
*Summer 1803*

O UR CAVALCADE MOVED SLOWLY, LABORIOUSLY, SOUTH-
west along the Loire River toward the western coast and the Atlantic.
We passed fertile countryside and farmland, swaths of green, fields
warmed and ripened by the long days of sun. Endless rows of vines, plum-
red and green bunches swelling ahead of the grape harvest. Oscar squealed
in delight at the sights of the stately châteaux and their bustling villages.
*France, you are glorious! How can I leave you?* My soul cried as my eyes stared
listlessly out the coach windows, hungry to record and remember every
last detail of my native land.

We spent nights in Orléans and Blois and Tours, during which my husband and I took our own rooms and barely spoke to each other save to bid
good night. During the long days on the road, I did my best to put on an
agreeable smile, if only for Oscar's sake, but in truth, I was terribly distraught. I had no interest in a long sea voyage and some barbaric swamp
posting in this colonial region of New France. I ached for Paris. I felt Julie's
absence like a missing bone, and we hadn't even left French soil.

Each night as we stopped at the modest *auberges*—the country inns—
the soldiers in the area went to very little trouble to mask their presence.
"Napoleon's agents," Bernadotte explained, when he saw me looking curi-
ously at the armed men who lurked outside our first inn. "We are under

surveillance, and we will continue to be until our anchors lift and we are adrift on the Atlantic."

I didn't know how to speak to my husband about the concerns that had arisen within me. On the one hand, I resented that his obstinacy had once more put him at odds with our nation's leader. But on the other hand, I did not suspect that he could ever be involved in a plot to assassinate Napoleon, particularly not with the seedy sculptor Ceracchi as some hired murderer. I felt that Bernadotte was being treated unfairly. I suspected that the latent hostility between my husband and Napoleon had more to do with pride and principle than any real malice.

But then I would remember back to the night at the opera, the night of the Christmas Eve bomb explosion on the Rue Saint-Nicaise. How my husband, who was to have been awaiting us at the theater, hadn't been there when we'd arrived. I recalled his sudden appearance, his face tight with tension. But no. Surely not. He never would have sanctioned a plot when his own wife would be riding in the carriage behind Napoleon's. Even if the words on his chest did say *Death to Kings*.

No. I couldn't believe it. And yet, I knew I would never have peace until I put my nagging doubts before my husband for him to address. For him to renounce them one and all. But not here, not on the road when we were under constant surveillance and spending our nights in cramped, foreign quarters. There could be no way of knowing just who was listening on the other side of the thin walls. But later. When we were alone. Perhaps once the vast Atlantic stretched between Napoleon and us.

Sometimes I tried to be positive, if only because my worry grew to be too heavy a burden to carry all day long. "I wonder what the governor's palace in Louisiana will look like?" I posed the question to my husband in the coach as Oscar looked out the window at a passing herd of cows.

My husband crumpled his brow as he answered: "Hope that it has plenty of windows, because I hear that New Orleans is a swamp."

Other times, when the crowds gathered along the route to cheer our passing carriages—we were, after all, traveling in Napoleon's service as proxies of his popular administration—my husband would clench his jaw and grumble, "All for the glory of France? This is not some promotion. This is exile gilded with laurels."

If it was exile, I only wished it would not be permanent. Julie and Joseph had promised that they would make our case and never relent. We would be called back after my husband served his duty—or rather, his sentence?—as Governor of Louisiana. I did not wish to raise my son away from France and my sister, nor did I wish for my niece to grow into a stranger whom I did not recognize. My sister assured me that her husband would intercede for us. I trusted Julie. Even Joseph, I knew, could be trusted. And so as Paris receded ever farther behind us, I clung to that hope as my lone solace and refuge.

"I wonder how different France will be when we return," I said one afternoon toward the end of our journey. The quality of the air was changing—the breeze was growing stronger and crisper, now with the faintest hint of salt; I guessed that we were nearing the Atlantic and our waiting ship.

"What does it matter?" my husband replied, looking at me, his black eyes devoid of the love and *joie de vivre* they had once carried. Now I saw only anger in them—or perhaps pain. "Everything is just as it was before—we have a king and we are once more a nation of superstitions and subjugation. The only thing that is different is that we have two million fewer Frenchmen, all of whom died for what they believed was liberty."

Our land journey brought us, at last, to the Atlantic port city of La Rochelle, from where we would take to the sea. La Rochelle, an ancient fortified city first built by the Romans and the one-time stronghold of French Huguenot resistance, was now the center of a thriving maritime trade with all of New France. Ships anchored and restocked in this city before sailing anywhere from Quebec in the north to Saint-Domingue in the Caribbean.

Fitting, I thought, that my husband's last glimpse of French soil would be the city known for its valiant resistance against the kings of old.

La Rochelle was a noisy city of seagulls and sailors, merchants and housewives hawking everything from salt to hand-painted porcelain. Our ship, the *Sibella*, awaited us in the harbor. We were to spend our final night in a cramped, crowded seaside *auberge*. We sat down to supper in the inn shortly before nine o'clock, the hostess placing bowls of a flavorful fish stew before us. My stomach grumbled after the long day, and the stew smelled fragrant, as did the warm, freshly baked bread. I was just about to begin my meal when my husband's aide knocked.

"What is it?" my husband growled, glancing toward the door as Maurin entered.

"Word for you, General, from Paris."

"Paris?" Bernadotte reached for the letter and ripped through the wax seal. Out fell a folded newspaper clipping from *Le Moniteur*. Bernadotte's features were inscrutable as he read first the letter, then the clipping.

I did not touch my stew, but rather kept my eyes fixed on my husband, eager for this news Maurin had brought. Eventually, Bernadotte lowered the papers, heaving an audible sigh before turning to me. His dark eyes had a new light in them, one that I had not seen in weeks, perhaps months. "Well, my darling," he said. "It is good that you have not yet loaded your trunks onto the frigate."

"What is it?" I asked, my voice faint.

"Your fears have all been for naught. You will return to Paris, to your comfortable villa on the Boulevard Monceau, right near your sister."

I stared at my husband, unsure of his meaning. My words were toneless as I said, "I will not leave Oscar. I wish to be with you two."

"*We* will be returning with you. My appointment has been retracted."

"But—" I lowered my spoon, my supper forgotten. "Why?"

Bernadotte pushed the papers across the table toward me as he answered: "It seems our much-loved First Consul intends to sell Louisiana to the Americans, to their new president, Monsieur Thomas Jefferson."

I glanced over the papers, confused. "Why would Napoleon do such a thing?"

"There's only one reason why any ruler would sell a parcel of land as vast and lucrative as the Louisiana Territory. Napoleon needs money," Bernadotte said, his tone sober. "And *that* must mean he plans to go to war."

"With whom?" I asked. "We've signed a peace treaty with all of the European powers."

Bernadotte sighed, his fingers absentmindedly kneading his brow. "England would be my guess."

"But what of the peace? There's no reason for war with England."

"Certainly there is," he answered. "Napoleon wishes to go to war so that the people will be so distracted, they won't mind when he crowns himself Emperor."

# Chapter 27

*Paris*
*December 1804*

"THE WITCH TOLD ME I WOULD BE GREATER THAN A queen," Josephine said, her voice a low warble, her hands gently stroking the waterfall of white satin that rippled across her lap, awaiting her scrutiny and approval.

I looked at her, confused by her statement. At first I wondered if this *witch* to whom she referred was her mother-in-law, or perhaps Pauline or one of the other Bonaparte women. But then I realized that she might have been referring to some actual sorceress. My skin prickled.

"Yes, this will do." Josephine nodded, handing the delicate fabric to her head dressmaker with an approving nod. She turned back toward me. "Do you know what my first husband said to me when I told him this story? 'There's no such thing as "greater than a queen." ' But it all makes sense now, does it not?"

I looked around her busy salon, the large space teeming with harried attendants and hairdressers and seamstresses and artists, all preparing the final details for the next day's coronation.

"Empress *is* greater than queen, yes, madame," I said.

"I confess I did not know what she meant, the blind old crone." Josephine shrugged her narrow shoulders. "She was an odd woman; she lived alone in the hills of Martinique, a long walk from my family's plantation. I had to sneak out to visit her in the middle of the night, accompanied only by my slave girl."

A flurry of chills rippled my flesh, my body's instinctive response to such talk; I knew that tales of witchcraft were the devil's work and I should listen to none of it. And yet, I did not tell her to stop.

Josephine sensed my curiosity, and she flashed a conspiratorial grin as she continued, her voice low, only for the two of us: "The old sorceress took my hand in her wrinkled palm, and she squeezed it hard. She stared straight into my eyes, though her own gaze was vacant, glazed as if by some sort of coating. She said—and I still remember it vividly, as if all of these years had not passed in between—'You shall marry a dark man of little fortune. But he shall cover the world with glory, and he shall make you greater than a queen.'"

I stiffened in my seat, deaf to the noise of the attendants all around us as Josephine carried on. "My slave girl laughed beside me. She thought the blind old hag had to be speaking in jest. But I knew." Josephine sat back in her chair, crossing her bare legs and tilting them languidly to one side. "Do you know how often I've repeated those words to myself? In the dark. In the cold. All of those nights in that dreadful basement of Les Carmes prison, when they told me that death would greet me at dawn's first light. I knew they were wrong . . . even then. All of them. I knew what awaited me. I never lost my faith." With that, she reached for her glass of wine and took a long, slow sip.

I breathed out, my exhale audible as I considered all that I had just heard. Whether it had been faith or something else, Josephine's unwavering belief in her own eventual and inevitable elevation had in fact proven correct. For the next morning, she, Josephine de Beauharnais, the barefoot daughter of an impoverished Caribbean slaveholder, the condemned widow of a brutal nobleman, would stand beside her husband at the front of Notre Dame Cathedral, covered in diamonds and satin and ermine, and be crowned Empress of all of France.

Her husband had moved with speed and with stealth, but most of all with his unrivaled shrewdness, and the day was upon us already, even while those of us who had been privy to all of it were still scratching our heads, wondering how we had arrived at such a moment.

Napoleon, sensing the mood of the people, had rightly guessed that they were tired of warfare and hunger. They were weary of foreign threats. They wanted clear, competent, and decisive leadership, even if they had to forfeit their republican ideals in order to get it.

Just this past spring, after several more victories against the alliance led by the Habsburgs, Napoleon made his move. Newspaper articles and pamphlets started to appear across Paris. They were never written by Napoleon—at least, not overtly—but they always lauded him as our nation's hero and savior. While public opinion of him climbed, he put forth a demeanor of self-effacement and humility, all the while predicting openly that assassins from Britain to Russia were trying to murder him and plunge France back into anarchy. "Daggers hang in the air. The foreign tyrants seek to destroy the Revolution by attacking my person. I will defend it, for I am the Revolution," he told the adoring crowds who gathered everywhere he went.

The French newspapers, censored as they were by Napoleon's government, began to extol the virtues of a monarchy. Napoleon outwardly reacted to this with hearty reluctance at first, insisting that his government did not wish to change the structure from a Consul. "The people do not want another king," he declared publicly.

If not a king, then perhaps something else? The senate—that body appointed and controlled by Napoleon—then proposed a change in his title. Consul for Life was not decisive enough; it did not go far enough to ensure the stability of France. If Napoleon would not be king because of his deep reverence for the Revolution, then there would have to be another title. What about looking to the genius of antiquity? Rome and Greece—how had they handled such a question? The senate proposed, then, to make Napoleon's title Emperor.

"Only if it is what the people want," was Napoleon's answer, his modesty recorded for the public by his newspapers.

Using the great senate plebiscites of ancient Rome as his guide and precedent, Napoleon declared that it must be put to a vote, a popular referendum decided only by the people. And so, the people of France voted. They voted by the millions. And they decided that Napoleon's title would be changed from Consul for Life to Emperor.

I knew from my husband that the vote had been arranged in such a way that there was no possible outcome other than decisive victory for Napoleon. What with his pamphlets and press corps directing the public conversation, his ministers manning the polling locales, and his brothers counting the results, what could we expect? But still, the French experiment in republican government had left many of our citizens sorely disillusioned, their families no better off than during the hard times of the Bourbons, and so the will of the people was clearly behind the idea of this one strong leader.

And how did my husband—the man who wore *Death to Kings* emblazoned across his chest—feel about all of this? For him, it had simply been the final step in a process he had long understood to be taking place. He knew the heart of Napoleon Bonaparte. My Bernadotte had seen the man's ambition laid bare on occasions enough to understand what he had wanted for himself. Now it was simply a title to make official and permanent what had already been set in motion. And Bernadotte had watched with misgivings.

And yet, in spite of that—or perhaps directly because of that—Napoleon had worked harder to win over my husband than he had to win over the millions of France. He'd called both of us, my husband and me, to another private meeting at the Tuileries before the results of the plebiscite vote were announced.

We'd accepted the invitation—or perhaps, more accurately, we'd obeyed the summons. Upon our arrival, Josephine had swept me into her arms. "Desiree, my darling! I must show you something. Come with me to the greenhouses. Orchids! Vines and vines of orchids! Pink and white and yellow and even purple. I want you to pick one to take home. To remind you of your beloved south." With that, she'd ushered me out toward the Tuileries greenhouses, leaving my husband alone with Napoleon.

Bernadotte and I did not speak until we returned home from the Tuileries to the Rue de Monceau. There, assured of our privacy, even from servants and aides who surely were being courted by the Bonapartes, my husband told me of his conversation. "It will be fine, my darling. We have struck an alliance."

I crossed my arms, confused. "An alliance? But how? What did he say?"

"He told me that the nation has clearly desired and invited his leadership, that France needs the goodwill and support of all of her children now, and that it would be damaging if I were to hold myself apart. He asked me to march forward with him and with all of France."

"What did you say?"

"I was honest," my husband answered. "I told him that I had long hoped, and believed, that France might flourish under a republican government. He pointed out that that was not to be, and I said that I believed he was correct. He then asked me if I could be trusted, given my republican leanings, and I answered in the affirmative. I did not promise him affection. But I promised him my loyalty. For France. And I shall keep my word."

"So then, he intends to make a new government?" I asked.

"Yes. And if it's a new government he desires, then that is what he shall have."

I nodded, absorbing this. Wondering what it meant for us.

"Desiree." Now my husband's voice betrayed an excited edge. "My darling, he has asked me to join him in the new imperial government."

My stomach tightened. Did this mean more war—a posting higher in the army? Or perhaps an assignment similar to the one for which we'd been bound for Louisiana? "What will that be?" I asked, fearful of the reply.

"He will be returning to the ancient tradition, going all the way back to Charlemagne, when the great men of the nation were called the Marshals of France. He will create eighteen such Marshals, chosen from his best and most loyal generals, and he would like me to be one."

Even as my husband spoke breathlessly, my mind raced to absorb all of this. Bernadotte was popular in the army. He had proven himself a skilled general in battle. He had been an outspoken patriot of the Republic, resistant to Napoleon's efforts to grab power. And, perhaps most significantly, Bernadotte, in marrying me, had forever linked his fate to that of the Bonaparte family. Joseph, Napoleon's favorite brother, was married to my sister. That meant that for Napoleon, there was no escaping the Bernadottes, since Napoleon and Joseph would never be anything but the closest of brothers, and Julie and I would never be anything but the closest of sisters.

Did Napoleon, ever tactical and self-serving, wish for my husband to join his side because he truly respected him? Or, as I more strongly suspected, because he loathed the idea of having my husband as a critic at large? Was Napoleon, in offering these generous gifts and titles, attempting to neutralize Jean-Baptiste Bernadotte and bolster his own position?

Whatever Napoleon's reasoning, his outreach seemed to have worked, because my husband was flushed and excited now as he spoke to me: "Can you imagine? Jean-Baptiste Bernadotte, penniless, fatherless Gascon. Too poor even to study the law. Marshal of the French Empire."

I laughed at this. "I most certainly can imagine it. There is no man more deserving," I answered. And then I thought to myself: *Napoleone di Buonaparte, penniless, fatherless Corsican. Too poor even to afford dinner. Emperor of the French.* These were strange times indeed. "Did . . . did you accept the appointment?" I asked.

"I did." My husband nodded, reaching for my hands, which he swept up now as he pulled me closer. "He had me swear an oath of loyalty. I vowed to serve France, and so that is what I shall do, even if it means also serving that rascal Bonaparte."

And just like that, I had a crown of my own. I was named the Princess of Pontecorvo alongside my husband, who was henceforth its Serene Highness the Prince. Along with the Marshal's baton, Napoleon was gifting his family members and favorites with the many kingdoms he'd snatched in his victories. He'd seized so much property and wealth from the enemies of France—men who were now either dead or imprisoned—and what he did not bestow on Josephine or Madame Mère or his brothers and sisters, he dispersed among his Marshals.

Pontecorvo was a small Italian kingdom, its population less than that of my hometown of Marseille. We had never set foot in Pontecorvo; I didn't even know where it was located, other than the fact that it was south of Rome and near the Tyrrhenian Sea, but that didn't matter, as we would not have to relocate there. My husband would only have to visit our kingdom from time to time, but we would henceforth be the recipients of all its wealth. Imagine this, compared to governorship of Louisiana.

Bernadotte and I were also gifted with a sprawling mansion on the posh Parisian street of the Rue d'Anjou, a *palais* seized when its owner, a French general, was exiled on the First Consul's orders. Josephine had already plundered most of the household wares for her refurbishing of Malmaison, so Napoleon presented us with two hundred thousand francs to decorate the home, this on top of the three hundred thousand francs he had already bestowed on us simply for becoming Marshal and Marshaless of France.

And now, here I sat in Josephine's busy salon amid the harried preparations for the coming coronation ceremony. "Of course, the witch *did* say . . . well, she did warn—" But Josephine cut herself off. "Oh, never mind." I noticed how her cheeks went pale, how her eyes lowered.

"What?" I asked, an uneasy tremor agitating my voice. "What else did that fortune-teller say to you?"

Josephine shook her head, blinking her long lashes, refusing to look at me. "Nothing. I wasn't even certain that I heard her correctly. The ramblings of an old blind woman. Anyhow." She shrugged, forcing a smile to her features, raising her hands to gesture around the room. "Doesn't it make you think of a dream? As if we've landed in the fables of the Arabian Nights? How splendid to see such luxury all around us." Josephine looked at the servants who hurried past her, their gloved hands laden with priceless fabric and jewelry. "The only difficulty is that my husband doesn't know what to do about the matter of the virgins."

"The matter of the . . . virgins?" I repeated, unsure of her meaning.

"You know my Bonaparte has such a mind for details—he doesn't let a single fact slip his notice. Well, at the coronations of antiquity, there were always the pure temple virgins looking on, standing at the altar, blessing the emperors."

"Oh," I said, watching as Josephine wove a wisp of satin between her slim fingers.

"But Talleyrand and Sièyes, who have been tasked with finding these virgins for my husband, well . . ." Josephine shrugged her lean, bare shoulders. "Seems they can't find a pair of virgins in the entire city of Paris. Unless they want a nun for the role."

"Ah, I see the problem." I nodded, shifting my weight in my seat.

Josephine continued to stroke her satin, savoring the soft feeling between her fingers. "Of course, I told them: 'Don't look at me, gents! I can't even remember what the word means—and I certainly don't know any!'" And with that she began to laugh, twirling the satin in small circles through the air. "But enough of that, we'd better get you fitted, Desiree, my dear one. And then it's on to the next lady."

I obeyed, rising from my chair and walking toward the wall of tall mirrors. A team of seamstresses held out my dress for inspection and I nodded my approval, stepping into the soft layers of the magnificent gown. Josephine watched intently as I was adjusted and poked and prodded. Our dresses, as attendants to the Empress, were to be slightly less splendid versions of Josephine's white satin and gold tulle masterpiece.

"Look at mine," Josephine breathed, her tone reverent as she gestured toward the massive mound sprawled across the salon, its layers in the hands of a dozen gloved attendants. "Just as he wanted it," she said.

Napoleon had given his wife specific and exacting orders as to how he wished her to look on his coronation day, and she knew better than anyone the importance of executing his orders with flawless precision. On this evening, with only hours remaining before the next day's ceremony, the imperial dressmakers were frantically finishing the last stitches of this most important artwork: pearl-colored satin embroidered and embellished with golden tulle. Josephine would wear a whimsical ruffled collar above the gown's low neckline. Massive diamonds would drape her throat, her ears, her wrists, and the belt that cinched her famously narrow waist. Napoleon had suggested a wide hoopskirt, the silhouette preferred by Marie-Antoinette, but Josephine had talked him out of that. "We must be new. Better even than the Bourbons." She'd persuaded him to settle instead on a sleek skirt that flattered her still-slender physique, and a lavish train of red velvet and gold stitching, its sprawling length worthy of the central aisle of Notre Dame.

"It is quite grand," she said. "Oh, but you'll look lovely, too, Desiree dear. Napoleon gave me strict orders to make sure that all of my darling sisters appear resplendent. 'Caesar's wife must be accompanied by only beautiful and good ladies,' is what he said to me. And you are both of those things, Desiree. Beautiful and good."

I nodded my thanks. We had each been gifted ten thousand francs when we were asked to attend Josephine at the coronation, to cover the costs of our custom robes and jewelry for the occasion. In truth, I had spent far more than that. So had Julie. We were wealthy, and Bernadotte knew what was expected of me, so it was no problem. But he did remind me that the typical French household had less than a fraction of that for the entire year.

Josephine now flitted around the room in her dressing gown of soft rose silk, giddily overseeing my fitting as well as the artists and seamstresses who were finishing her own gown.

"And to think . . . all of this for me." She glided toward where I stood, smiling, taking my hand in hers as she whispered: "Shall I tell you a secret?"

I shifted on my feet, eliciting a frustrated sigh from the seamstress inspecting my skirt. "Only you can answer that," I said in reply.

Josephine's hazel eyes sparkled, and I imagined the mischievous Creole girl stealing sugar from the *sucrerie*. She tossed her head back in a quick laugh. "Oh, I shall. I'll tell you. You've always been the nicest to me." She leaned closer, breathing the words into my ear so that no attendants might hear: "We shall be married tonight."

"Married?" I repeated the word, confused.

She nodded. "Napoleon and I. At midnight."

"But . . . you've already . . ." They had been married for years. I myself had seen it happen.

"By the *Pope!*" she said, her voice low and conspiratorial. "Our marriage is a civil arrangement only, but we have yet to be joined in the eyes of God. Tonight that shall change, right here, at home. Blessed by the Holy Father himself. Truly married, a sacred bond that no man can break—nor any woman. Not even Letizia."

Bernadotte and I had been married in a civil ceremony only, but that had always been sufficient for us. The same was true for Julie and Joseph, and nearly all of the couples united during the revolutionary years, when the secular law reigned supreme over any teachings of the outlawed Church. Though always respectful of the Church and the clergy in his military dealings, my husband was not an overly religious man, and so the approval of the Church would have done little to add legitimacy to our union in his eyes, just as the absence of the Church's sanctioning had done little to delegitimize it. Napoleon had reconciled France to Rome and to the papacy, but I had believed that to be a savvy move of political expediency; in all the years I'd known him, I'd never suspected him of having any deep or meaningful faith. Had Josephine suddenly become a religious woman? I looked at her now, seriously doubting it.

"I went to the Pope myself," she told me. "You know that he's here, in Paris, for the coronation."

"Of course," I said, nodding. "What business did you have with the Pope?"

"Well, the coronation is to be a Mass. A holy event sanctioned by God. When I met with the Pope, I wept and trembled, told him that I did not feel right participating in the coronation as Napoleon's Empress when I was not even Napoleon's true wife. At least, not according to the laws of heaven."

I was beginning to understand. But I let Josephine continue: "What did old Pius do? His Holiness went directly to my husband and said he could not officiate the coronation—he could not anoint a woman with holy oil who was only a concubine in the eyes of God. We must either be married by the Church or lose the Church's blessing altogether. My husband might have refused the request coming from me, but he wouldn't refuse when it was a direct order from Rome. And risk the entire coronation? Not at this late date. Not when he is this close."

"But . . . was he cross with you?" I knew Napoleon's temper, and I knew how he hated to be outfoxed, particularly as it so rarely happened.

Josephine lowered her eyes, thinking a moment before answering. "He was cross. I let him rail at me; I rode out the storm. But I simply cried. When he was done, I fell to my knees . . ." And she did so now as well, pressing her palms together in humble supplication, demonstrating with her body how she had performed for her husband. "I told him that I served him and no other man and I only wanted to do everything in my power to ensure that all of the various factions around us were united in their support for him, that there could never be any cause for any camp to claim there was even a drop of illegitimacy to his rule. And that meant reconciling even God himself to our—to *his*—cause. He eventually forgave me." She rose now, patting down her dressing gown, offering a quick, offhand shrug of her shoulders. "Besides, he can't bear to fight with me at the same time he's fighting with his sisters and mother."

I understood—I understood without Josephine having to say more. Behind the smiles, the giggles, the shrugs, Josephine hid a world of other emotions. Chief among them: fear. She, the Empress after tomorrow, was terrified. Just like so many others across France were scared, unsure of their own position or even safety.

Her recent trip to Charlemagne's holy pilgrimage site of Aix-la-Chapelle—her frantic attempt to present Napoleon with the one gift he wanted most ahead of his coronation, a baby—had proven a failure. In recent months, his calls for divorce had begun to shift from passing insinuations to outright threats. He no longer even attempted to deny the many lovers whom he bedded in his offices and dressing room. In fact, when Josephine recently walked in on him in the middle of an afternoon tryst with one of her own ladies-in-waiting, rather than being apologetic or shamed that he'd been caught, Napoleon had been furious with his wife for interrupting him, chasing her from the room and around the palace, trying to get his hands on her as he roared loud and violent threats. When he failed to snatch her up, as her lithe frame had outrun his, he'd turned instead to hurling chairs and yelling that she sought to ruin him. He'd vowed to throw her out of the palace—and then, he'd returned to his lover and resumed his liaison.

Of course Josephine didn't mention any of this now. But she didn't need to. I'd heard plenty from my husband and my sister. "There's a paper model of Notre Dame Cathedral in the palace," Bernadotte told me. "Napoleon reviews it each day, laying out his plans for every moment of the Mass and coronation. He's had thousands of small figurines made, each with a name to correspond to a guest of the Mass. He does not know where to put the tiny Josephine figurine."

And Joseph had said in front of both Julie and me: "I am urging him to seat her with the rest of the congregation, rather than crowning her beside him."

So Josephine had done what she'd needed to do for herself and for her children—she'd cornered him into a holy marriage, sanctioned by the Pope himself, a bond from which he could not escape. And now, on the eve of the Mass, it appeared that Napoleon had decided where his wife's paper figurine would be positioned in the model of the great cathedral; she was to be crowned alongside her husband.

It was true that Napoleon had wanted to keep his wife on his side because his family had erupted into open rebellion in recent weeks. Not Joseph or the rest of the brothers, but Letizia and her daughters; the Bonaparte women were furious that Josephine would be crowned Empress and thus officially elevated to a rank above their own. They reacted with unchecked hostility. They no longer stood when she entered a room. They did not look in her direction when she spoke to them. They called her barren and laughed in her presence about her husband's mistresses; they loved to recount the episode, now infamous throughout Paris, of Josephine storming in on Napoleon in bed with two of her household maids.

I saw the vicious hostility firsthand that evening at dinner, when Bernadotte and I joined the Bonaparte family at the Tuileries Palace. It was the night before the coronation. The next day, their golden son would be elevated to the highest position in all of France. It was a staggering feat for him, for all of them, rising as they had from penniless refugees of a dusty farm on the island of Corsica to their adopted nation's First Family. And yet, the Bonapartes were not in a celebratory mood as we sat down to the meal.

Elisa, Caroline, and Pauline presented a united front of dark scowls as they took their places at the long table. I knew of the sisters' fury—they were incensed not only over Josephine's position but my sister's as well. Julie, as wife to Joseph, was to be made a Princess of the Empire. While Napoleon had no son, his brother Joseph was his rightful heir and a Prince of the Empire, but the sisters remained out of the order of succession. They had only hours left to have their way, and they intended to use the dinner, apparently, to make their case to Napoleon. "Why should *we* not be named princesses?" Elisa demanded, with an angry wave of her ring-covered hands. "You would condemn your own blood to obscurity while elevating others over us?"

Napoleon heard this with a tightening of his jaw, his eyes fixing squarely on his dinner plate of roasted chicken. He seemed determined to finish his meal and be gone. "I would remind you, sister, that there are thousands of people in France who have given greater service to the State than you. And yet they receive far less. You would be wise to keep these selfish grievances silent."

"Is that any way to speak to your own flesh and blood?" Letizia leaned forward in her seat, her hawk-like features aflame. "Does he forget that we are his family? That we should come before all the others?" She posed the question to her daughters, who shook their heads with shared indignation.

Letizia was perhaps the unhappiest of all; her formal title was to be Her Imperial Majesty Madame Mère, when in fact she had wanted to be called the Imperial Mother. Though Napoleon had attempted to appease her by giving her a splendid château in Brienne, a large *palais* in Paris, and millions of francs, she was still dissatisfied. "I have a mind to skip it entirely," she said, a dismissive wave of her liver-spotted hand. "Nothing more than a circus."

"I tell you, Mamma, I would skip it with you," Pauline said in a low, flinty voice, her eyes darting toward her brother before landing back on her mother. "The idea of bowing before a common Creole *horizontale* . . . I can't stomach it."

My eyes flew toward Josephine, who sat pale and quiet at her place at the table. Surely she heard these remarks, but she said nothing to oppose them. Nothing to defend herself. I guessed at Josephine's reasoning: she knew from her own vast experience that Napoleon hated nothing more than the disrespect of others—whether the slights were in fact real or imagined. In this instance, she knew, his family's open opposition would likely not bring him around to their own side but instead rouse him to fight back.

She would not interfere and thus deny him that chance. Not at this late hour, when her own hopes were so close to being realized. She knew that her husband was fed up with his family's constant carping, and perhaps she thought it best to let them bring about their own undoing.

And that, it seemed, was precisely what they planned on doing, for Caroline now asked aloud to the entire table: "Do you know the last time France actually crowned a queen?"

When no one answered, she went on: "The year was 1610. Marie de Medici. Pity—her husband was butchered a day later. I know how my brother loves history . . . let us now hope that history does not repeat."

"Is your gown ready, Josephine?" my sister asked, looking at each of the sisters in turn.

"It is," Josephine said, leaning forward, her face brightening with a grateful smile. "It is ready, and it is just . . . even better than I had imagined. Why, the train—"

"She has lost her head if she thinks I will carry her train," Elisa said to Pauline and Caroline. The sisters sniggered.

"I wouldn't think of it," Pauline agreed.

Now Napoleon lowered his fork, his face reddening as he eyed each sister. "You *will* carry her train."

Pauline snorted, an indignant laugh as she raised her wine to her lips. After a moment, she spoke, her tone one of open defiance: "On what grounds should we, sisters of the Emperor, be made to carry her train?"

"On the grounds that she is the wife of the Emperor," he replied, his voice low and gravelly.

"But you are our brother," Elisa said. "You should want better for us, for the family, than to make us grovel before anyone. Especially—"

"I did not hear you dispute my rights as Emperor, Elisa, when I made you the Princess of Lucca, giving you that principality. Nor you, Pauline, when I made you the Duchess of Guastalla. Nor you, Caroline, Duchess of Berg. And thus you shall not begrudge my wife what is her due as Empress." He stabbed at his chicken, forking himself a huge bite that he began to chew at a furious rate. I watched as Josephine sipped her wine, barely touching her food.

"I find it rather cruel, Mamma, that he would have us bow before such an unvirtuous woman," Pauline said, her face crumpling with the threat of tears.

Letizia heaved a heavy sigh, her voice hard as she answered: "Especially since I don't even believe that she honors *him* with any of the loyalty expected of a wife."

"Enough!" Napoleon slammed his fork down, causing me to jump in my seat as he pushed away from the table and rose to his feet. "I've lost my appetite entirely. Josephine?"

"Yes, *mon cher*?" She eyed him, her voice soft.

"Bed. Now," was all he replied. She rose from her chair as Napoleon turned his gaze on the rest of us still seated at the table. "Tomorrow, I put on the imperial purple. Those among you who do not wish to accept my gifts need not attend. But those of you who do attend will see to it that my commands are followed. I will not have this! I am Emperor!"

"Let's hope it lasts." Madame Mère sighed under her breath.

"*Basta!* That's enough!" he roared in Italian, staring at his mother, his eyes bulging out of a darkly flushed face. "I govern the entire nation. And yet you pack of ingrates give me more sleepless nights than all the rest of France."

# Chapter 28

*Paris*
*December 2, 1804*

I AWOKE WELL BEFORE DAWN TO SEE SNOW FALLING OVER
Paris, coating the cobblestone streets in a slick and inhospitable cover.
It was cold in our bedchamber; both Bernadotte and I saw the fog of our
breath as we dressed. It would be even colder outside, but still, we knew
that they would come—by the millions, they would come. Before dawn,
huddled in the dark and the freezing wind, they would stand and watch,
waiting for a glimpse of Napoleon, the man they had made Emperor.

The date for the coronation had been a compromise—the Pope had
wanted Christmas; Napoleon had wanted the ninth of November, the anniversary of his coup. And so they'd settled on a date between the two.

But the pageantry was all Napoleon's. In everything, one could see his
avid devotion to history, a celebration incorporating the influences of
French history and its founder King Charlemagne, mixed with the dignity
of ancient Greece and the majesty of Imperial Rome. He chose the eagle of
Caesar as his imperial symbol. The bee would be his own personal herald,
the symbol of the ancient kings of the Franks.

We ladies gathered in the predawn darkness in Josephine's Tuileries
apartments, surrounded by hairdressers and seamstresses and artists putting the final touches on our elaborate ensembles. Due to a shortage of
time that morning, my hair had been done the night before, and I had

barely slept for fear of ruining it. Josephine confessed to me that she had not slept much, either, for nerves and excitement, but that did nothing to diminish her energy that morning. She was exquisite, her face covered in rouge and kohl, her hair woven into buoyant chestnut curls, every bare surface of her warm skin doused in perfume and shimmering with diamonds and pearls.

"I am grateful that we do not have to go to Rome," she said as she stood before the mirror, scrutinizing her long, lean figure. "We think it is exhausting here in our own home. Imagine doing all this in a foreign place."

Napoleon had refused to go to Rome, insisting instead that Pope Pius come to him over ice-slicked roads. The Pope was old, and aside from the weather and other discomforts of winter travel, he remembered France's savage treatment of the Catholic Church during the revolutionary years. The concordat between Paris and Rome was new and it was fragile. Nevertheless, Pius was made to understand, with gold and flattery and well-landed threats of military action, that it would be in the best interest for all that the Holy Father come to Paris and honor Napoleon's wishes for the coronation. But the Emperor would not bow—he had already declared that.

Once we were dressed, we met Napoleon and the men on the ground floor of the Tuileries. I took in his appearance, studying the burst of color and cloth around his thick figure. He would wear one outfit in the procession and change at the Archbishop's palace once we arrived at Notre Dame, that much I knew from Josephine. For the parade, his outfit was a nod to the Middle Ages and Charlemagne, so he wore a short coat and pants, a crown of laurels on his head, and a purple velvet cape. Diamonds and colorful precious stones covered his clothing, and rings covered his manicured fingers.

He took us all in as we swept into the grand hall, his eyes studying each of us before landing with exacting attention on Josephine. I held my breath a moment as I saw him scrutinize her. Then I, and I believe all of us, exhaled aloud when he offered an appreciative nod, his green eyes alight as he said, "Beautiful."

Next, I looked through the small crowd and found my husband's tall figure, waving him toward me. "Well, hello, Marshaless Bernadotte." My husband's outfit was less elaborate than Napoleon's, but I thought he looked far more dashing. His velvet coat, silk stockings, and culotte breeches fit well on his tall, strong physique. He wore a high cravat of white satin and a crimson sash draped across his broad shoulders, and I nodded approvingly. "Sergeant Belle-Jambe, you are every bit the strapping general of France."

"And you, the worthy and beautiful companion of the Imperial Consort, though I was made to understand from our Emperor that no lady was to outshine his own?"

I lowered my eyes, flattered by the remark, feeling giddy in a way I had not in years. All of France felt giddy that day, I was sure of it. A veritable ripple of excitement was gliding across the cold air we breathed.

"It is time," Napoleon announced to our group, ever devoted to punctuality, and my husband gave me a quick kiss on the cheek before returning to his place among the gentlemen attendants.

The coaches had been rolling across Paris toward the cathedral since dawn, and now it was our turn to join the procession. I took my place with Julie and the Bonaparte sisters as Napoleon and Josephine were ushered toward their private glass coach, pulled by a dozen white horses. I marveled as I watched her walk toward the conveyance: Josephine, covered in more than a thousand diamonds, glowed like a halo against the fresh white snow.

Cannon salvoes roared from Place de la Concorde as we departed with Napoleon and Josephine's cortege. "Look at all of them," I gasped, as our own coach rolled through the gates and toward the packed quay that would bear us along the river. Even though the air bit with snow and wind, millions of spectators lined the entire parade route, cheering and singing and waving the tricolor flag as we rode past.

It took us more than an hour to ride a distance that ordinarily would have taken minutes. When we finally entered the square, the flood of people who were gathered before the cathedral met our arrival with deafening shouts. The cannons fired a fresh round of earth-shaking volleys. I blinked, momentarily stunned by the scene. Eighty thousand armed soldiers stood at attention. The noise grew even louder as Napoleon and Josephine's coach arrived and rolled into the square right behind us.

Just then, the snow stopped and the sun pierced the clouds. "Look!" Julie gasped, pointing toward the shafts of striated light that filtered down, crystalline, through openings in the thick cloud cover. I gasped, saying: "God himself follows Napoleon's orders."

We alighted from our coach just as Napoleon helped Josephine down from theirs. The people roared with euphoric cheers, screaming her name, frantic to see her dress and jewels. She greeted them with a wave, curtsying before the crowd as Napoleon looked on, his face brightened by a proud smile.

We were ushered inside the Archbishop's palace adjoining the cathedral. It was just before noon when Napoleon changed into his second outfit, emerging into our small waiting room in a crimson cape of velvet and ermine. Bernadotte and Joseph had helped him into it, for it weighed almost one hundred pounds. Golden bees were embroidered along the trim, as were the laurel leaves of a Roman emperor. He carried a scepter in his gloved hands. "Magnificent," Josephine said, clapping and gliding to his side.

"Yes?" Napoleon tilted his chin toward her, eager for her approval; she nodded, her amber eyes full of it. "If only my papa could see me today," he said, his voice more wistful than I had ever heard it.

Papa, and Mamma, too. Letizia had refused to attend following the arguments of the previous evening. She had thought her son would relent in the final hour, as he often had, and grant her daughters higher status than his Caribbean bride, but Napoleon had stood firmly beside Josephine and insisted that his sisters stand behind her. If it shook Napoleon that his mother had decided to boycott the most important day of his life, he did not show it now. Instead, he gave a nod to the cluster of servants and attendants gathered by the large doors, and the next phase of this most important day began rolling into action.

With the command from her husband, Josephine strode forward, head held high, a canopy hoisted over her imperial head as was previously done for the pure-blooded queens of France. I stepped into my place behind her and Julie and the glowering Bonaparte sisters, and we made our way to the rear of the cathedral, where our long march up the aisle would begin.

Music greeted our entry into Notre Dame. I trembled at the deafening sound, feeling the power of the song as it reverberated throughout my entire body. Nearly five hundred musicians packed the cathedral—every instrument imaginable, plus the choristers singing at their loudest volume to give words to the melody.

Hundreds of ministers, priests, governors, generals, and nobles had been filing into the cathedral since the early morning—even the vanquished Mameluke warriors whom Napoleon had brought back from Egypt were there, clad in feathers and turbans of emerald and sapphire. Now they all stood and turned, craning their necks, vying to gain a glimpse of us as we began our procession, their number making even the massive vaulted space of Notre Dame feel cramped.

The Archbishop splashed us with holy water as we made our way toward the front of the cathedral. I followed in my place in the procession, carrying Josephine's veil and handkerchief on a pillow of plush red velvet. Josephine's progress was slow, each step a struggle because the sisters were not holding the heavy train in the way they were supposed to. They were allowing it to drag, its weight impeding Josephine's steps up the interminable aisle, like an ox laboring under an unbearable yoke. I gritted my teeth, frustrated as I saw this, wishing that I myself could step in front of Pauline and take up the heavy train that she was allowing to fall.

I spotted a man toward the front, sketching frantically as he observed us. His black hair was disheveled, his eyes ravenous to observe every detail of the resplendent cathedral and the pageantry of our approach. Jacques-Louis David was the artist, the favorite painter of Napoleon's. I wondered how he could possibly capture it all—the crowd, the colors, the clamor of the choir and the murmurs of awe that pulsed around the packed sacred space.

Finally, we arrived at the front of the massive cathedral, and Josephine assumed her position before the Archbishop and the Pope. Now it was the moment for which all of France waited. Napoleon appeared at the top of the aisle to the roar of trumpets. His Marshals stood behind him, carrying his sword, necklace, crown, globe, and other accessories. Bernadotte was named Bearer of the Imperial Collar for the event, and I spotted his tall figure in the procession.

Napoleon had an easier time making his way to the front of the cathedral, and he joined Josephine in kneeling before the altar, where the Pope anointed them both with oil on their hands and foreheads. Previously, French kings had lain prostrate before God for this blessing, but Napoleon had refused this humbling piece of tradition.

Next, Pope Pius blessed the pair of imperial crowns and set them before the altar. Napoleon's crown was a replica of Charlemagne's, since the Austrians possessed the original and would not loan it to their enemy. Josephine's was a brilliant diadem encrusted with massive diamonds, grander and more expensive than any treasure her deceased predecessors had ever worn.

Napoleon rose, took the larger crown in his hands, and, while the Pope looked on, he placed it on his own head. The trumpets roared, as outside the cannon blasts ripped across Paris, their triumphant sound met with the jubilant voices of so many million cheering Frenchmen and women.

Napoleon turned to Josephine and, with a flick of his wrist, summoned her forward. She rose, made to walk toward him, but just then, the sisters dropped the heavy train of her gown from their hands. She wobbled, her slender frame pulled backward by the falling weight of the mantle. Napoleon saw it happen and flashed his sisters a severe look, but Josephine remained the picture of calm and composure, even as the sisters sniggered behind her. She regained her balance within a moment, and she glided gracefully toward him, her beautifully painted face unruffled. She bowed her head and knelt in front of her husband. Taking her crown in his hands, Napoleon leaned over her and tucked it into her dark hair. Then he patted her head approvingly, a proud father blessing a child. When she lifted her chin to meet his eyes, I saw that she was weeping.

The Pope approached them and pronounced a blessing in Latin, embracing our new Emperor. Then Napoleon turned and addressed the rest of us, loudly reciting his coronation oath to uphold the integrity of the Republic and respect the laws.

Jacques-Louis David still stood before the altar, sketching it all, his long hair flying away from his intensely focused face. I wondered: Would he paint the sisters with beneficent smiles, or would he capture the scowls I saw on their faces beside me?

The ceremony concluded with more rousing music, more cannon thunder outside. Napoleon was now Emperor of France, and Josephine, its Empress.

All of France was now ready to fête the imperial pair. We traveled back to the Tuileries along a circuitous route so that our new Emperor and Empress could wave to the millions who had traveled from across the nation to celebrate. Massive banners bearing the letter "N" were draped over doorways and balconies. Buildings throughout the capital were lit up— orders from the Emperor. It had been declared a national holiday, and the people of Paris were treated to red wine flowing from the public fountains, carts loaded with meat and bread, and a fireworks show set to color the Paris sky that night. In Place de la Guillotine, renamed Place de la Concorde by Napoleon, over the exact site where the French had killed their last monarch, there now gleamed a massive new statue of a star.

Inside, the Tuileries Palace was festooned with lilacs, lilies, orchids, and oleander, all clipped that morning from the imperial hothouses, their exquisite beauty and abundance standing in defiance of the frigid December snow. Platters of fragrant food filled the massive banquet tables when we arrived. Thousands of candles brightened the space and illuminated the newly restored splendor of the Emperor's home, as footmen wove among us, offering flutes of chilled champagne.

The guests streamed in, quickly filling the massive rooms. Those of us who had played roles in the coronation Mass were relieved and lighthearted—eager to celebrate after the nerves and preparations of recent months. Those who had not participated in the ceremony appeared with their congratulatory smiles and their lavish attire, eager to jostle and vie for a place near the imperial couple. Napoleon, eyeing the splendor of the surroundings, nodded approvingly. Then he lifted his gloved hand. We all fell silent, attention fixing on our new Emperor as he made his toast. Instead of toasting, however, he announced to all of us that he would eat privately in his own salon—with only his Empress at the table.

My gaze went immediately to the sisters. I saw Elisa, scowling, as she announced: "Mamma was right to skip this."

Napoleon ignored the insult, turning to his wife with perfect calm. "Come with me. And you will wear your crown throughout the evening, because no woman alive could wear a crown with more grace."

Josephine smiled at this, then turned to her husband's sisters. "Enjoy your dinner," she said, her voice silky and low. And then they were gone.

# Chapter 29

*Paris*
*Winter 1805*

"MAMAN, WHAT IS A . . . *FEBRUARY*?"
I smiled at my son's confused frown. He studied the front of the morning newspaper, and I leaned over to read it with him. "It is a month, my darling boy. It is the month in which we find ourselves."

"But I thought it was Pluviôse," Oscar said.

"That was the revolutionary calendar," I explained. "Napoleon . . . the Emperor . . . has returned us to the calendar we always followed, before the Revolution."

"So then what comes next, if not Ventôse?"

"Next it shall be March."

"March," Oscar repeated, considering the new word. "But, Maman, how do you know all of this?"

I sat down beside him, smiling. "It was the calendar we had when I was a young girl. It was always the way we divided the year, until they changed it during the Revolution."

Napoleon had done away with the revolutionary calendar within a month of his coronation. In truth, I was glad to be back to the old manner of recording time, before the awkward and unwieldy month names had been introduced—words like "Thermidor" to describe the summer heat, or "Floréal" to describe the time of spring blooms.

And the calendar was not the only change that our new Emperor swiftly enacted. Gone, too, was the modest, egalitarian austerity of the Republic. Napoleon declared that France and its leaders would return to an opulence not seen since the Bourbons—indeed, not seen since the court of *Le Roi Soleil*, the Sun King, Louis XIV. Napoleon had made us a rich country, and he wanted all the world to see it. "What I want, above all, is grandeur," he proclaimed. "To throw golden dust into the French people's eyes."

The Tuileries Palace was too bare and simple, he declared, even with the artwork he'd hung and the new furniture he'd acquired. He wanted a more flagrant display of wealth and glory. He hired a new team of designers and ordered them to build a grand new banquet hall, where two thrones burnished with gilt would preside over the massive space. He ordered that the walls, some of them still stained by revolutionary battles, be covered in plush silk, tapestry, and brocade. His imperial eagle, the symbol he'd chosen for the nation, was carved into moldings on the walls and the new mahogany tables. Golden bees, the personal symbol of Napoleon's choosing, were now ubiquitous at the Tuileries—woven into the carpets and curtains and clothes, carved on the gold of his massive coaches, ever-present on the jewelry of his Empress and her ladies.

"And I shall choose the swan as my insignia," Josephine declared, announcing her decision to Julie and me during one of our weekly audiences with her. She invited us often, for tea or wine or games of whist, and we understood the foolishness of declining such invitations.

"The swan," I said, nodding, "a lovely choice." I thought this perfectly apropos: a figure of grace and elegance in the eyes of the world, and yet, no one knew how hard the creature worked beneath the smooth waters, kicking itself along. A picture of placid beauty, but a fierce and vicious fighter when called to defend itself.

My Bernadotte had left us once more, gone from Paris that winter to assume command of thousands of Frenchmen in Hanover, where Napoleon's Grande Armée was once again preparing for a great offensive. Our newly crowned Emperor had asked his senate to raise him an army, the grandest army France had ever mustered, to fight the coalition of Germans, Austrians, Russians, and British who opposed his coronation. Napoleon needed eighty thousand more men to stand up to such a force, and Frenchmen rushed to answer his call.

We attended a grand parade on the Champ de Mars to honor this force shortly before Napoleon and his men marched out of the capital to meet my husband and his troops to the east. There, on the vast green fields, the eagle standards loomed over neat squares of soldiers. Oscar stared on, clutching my hand as his mouth fell agape at the pageantry of it all. "Look, Maman! There is Godfather!"

"Yes, my dear," I said, forcing a bright tone as I followed my son's gaze. Napoleon stood before the soldiers, the ministers, the cheering crowds, exalted over all of us atop a raised dais. After years in the civilian clothing of his Parisian administration, Napoleon appeared apple-shaped in his new imperial military uniform, fidgeting as he inspected the troops, a jumpy, restless energy pulsating from him. "Soldiers!" he cried out, eventually bringing the ebullient mob to heel. "These eagles shall be your rallying point! Do you swear to lay down your lives in their defense?" The men in uniform shouted their hearty assent as, all around us, the crowds waved the tricolor. Napoleon continued: "Apparently, the Habsburgs and their friends wish to remind me that I'm a soldier. The imperial purple has not caused me to forget my first trade. If Austria wants war, then she will have it!"

Josephine carried on in her husband's absence, just as he had ordered her to. She frequented the state box of the opera house and listened to the petitions of the crowds who gathered in the gardens of the Tuileries. She hosted receptions and parties and ensured that her husband's court was a gathering place for elegant people of fashion, politics, and the arts. She invited me often to attend her state dinners and informal salons.

The strict court etiquette of the Bourbons, established by Louis XIV, governed formal and social gatherings once more. Josephine told me that Napoleon had ordered the old manuals and guidebooks of Louis's court brought out of storage and studied. Ritual and rules dictated every detail of palace life, from how people entered a room to how they were to sit at the table.

"We will out-etiquette even the Bourbons themselves," Napoleon had ordered his wife before his departure, and she carried this on in his absence.

And there were so many rules he had left *her* as well. He wished for her never to repeat an outfit, even though she was to change her gown at least three times each day. She was to have a full team of attendants dedicated entirely to her wardrobe and jewelry and its upkeep. She was never to ask the price when merchants and dressmakers presented their jewels and gowns and trinkets. Soon, the papers reported that Josephine had tossed out Marie-Antoinette's old jewelry case because it was not large enough for her collection.

All of Paris wished to dress like Josephine. Those who hadn't seen her in person saw her image every day in *Le Journal des Dames et des Modes,* the fashion publication. I recalled how she had bucked Napoleon in designing the svelte silhouette of the coronation gown, eschewing the Marie-Antoinette hoopskirt that he had originally wanted. Overnight, Josephine had given France—and Europe—a new trend. It was being called the empire style, with a high waist and loose, free-flowing skirt. I wondered if Josephine appreciated this style because it concealed her stomach, making it impossible for people to see whether a baby was growing within.

As summer turned to fall and the weather grew chilly, my thoughts traveled to the east, and I longed for my husband. It was the longest absence we'd faced since the start of our marriage, and my son asked after his father often.

Josephine had quit the capital that fall, traveling to meet Napoleon in Munich, so my sister and I were free of obligations at court for Christmastime, and I welcomed the idea of a small, intimate holiday, even if I would miss my Bernadotte. I hosted Julie and Joseph and my niece, Zénaïde. We laughed in delight as the children learned the carols and enjoyed the *bûche de noël,* the traditional Christmas cake made to look like a Yule log.

And yet, even the happy moments of that Christmas were tinged with sadness for me. As Joseph had recently been named King of Naples by his brother, he and my sister would have to travel there for a time. I dreaded her absence, growing sad whenever the thought returned to my mind that Julie would be leaving.

But then, several days later, some good news reached Paris. Napoleon, with my Bernadotte beside him, had crushed the alliance and had taken the Habsburg seat of power in Vienna. They had won a great battle near the Austrian capital at Austerlitz. Both Napoleon and Bernadotte, along with the other senior French officers, were installed in the Schönbrunn Palace as the Austrians fled toward safety in Russia.

Napoleon's letter soon arrived for Joseph, and I hurried to their home to hear the news. *"I must say how satisfied I am with the conduct of all those who had the good fortune to fight in this memorable battle. My soldiers! They are the finest warriors in the world. The recollection of this day, and of our deeds, shall be eternal! For thousands of ages hereafter, as long as the events of the universe continue to be related, it will be remembered."*

Joseph paused from reading the letter, wiping a tear from his eye. "Anything else?" Julie asked.

"Just a bit more," Joseph said. He read on, relaying Napoleon's words: *"Now, I have not changed my shirt for eight days. But I am wonderfully well. Austria's Emperor Franz begs me for peace. Can you imagine—an Emperor born of kings coming to humble himself by pleading for peace to the son of a modest Corsican family? Now I stand at the summit of power, arbiter of the destinies of Europe. We shall return to Paris."*

Napoleon had his victory over those who had insulted him. He had his glory. Now I simply hoped that, with the Habsburgs and their allies crushed, my husband would return safely to me.

# Chapter 30

*Mainz, the Confederation of the Rhine*
*October 1806*

"**D**O YOU TASTE THE EARTH? I DO. I TASTE IT—IT'S SWEET. Like flowers. But also heavy. Thick, like a syrup. Or honey?" Josephine raised the cup to her lips, breathing in the aroma of the wine before draining the contents in one gulp. As she lowered her cup, she smirked, offering an afterthought of a toast: "To pleasure! And the men who give it to us!"

Josephine was drunk. I turned away, raising my glass and taking a small sip of the sweet Riesling wine as my eyes roved over the view that unfurled before us. The German language struck me as severe and guttural, their food as overly rich and heavy, but their scenery was indeed breathtaking. I could admit that much.

We were lodged in the Rhineland, in a picturesque curve of the majestic river for which the region was named, where vineyards striated the beautiful rolling hills and river ships made their languid passage across a layered horizon. The men had left, moving east toward Poland, but Napoleon had ordered his wife and her ladies to remain behind. And so, here we were, in a region of German states annexed by Napoleon to his ever-growing French Empire.

I saw my time in the Rhineland as an assignment more than any pleasurable adventure or sojourn. Oscar, installed back in Paris with his tutor and his nanny, was safe at least, but without my son, my husband, or my sister—who was with Joseph in Naples—I felt unmoored.

And yet, even with this, I knew that Josephine suffered far worse than I did. Our Empress put forth her best attempt at cheeriness, but I could see how miserable she was to be left behind, marooned here as her husband moved on to conquer further lands—and lovers. I could see it in the restless, shiftless way she took my hand, raising it to her cheek as though in need of a mother's touch, the gesture of a lost girl. I noted the way she filled our days with manic activity—boat rides along the Rhine, horseback riding with some local German prince or count eager to curry favor with Napoleon through his infamous Empress. The way she had us drinking the sweet Riesling native to the area constantly, from breakfast until bedtime. "I'll bring this Riesling home with us to Paris," she said now, her lips loose and sluggish around her words. "Crates and crates of it. He'll love it. My Bonaparte is always saying it's up to me to make sure there is good taste at our court—that he doesn't know how he'd get by without me. God knows, my soldier, if it were up to him? We'd be eating roast chicken off of spits and drinking that awful vinegar that Corsicans call wine."

She had the hiccups now, and her narrow body jolted as she bent her legs and pulled her knees up to her chest like a young girl hugging herself tight. "I'm the one with noble blood," she said, hiccupping once more. The afternoon sun filtered in through the lead-paned windows, washing her in a small, bright puddle of autumn light. "Napoleon always tells me I have the best taste of any woman."

She smiled then, but her attempt was careworn, forced; she wished to be with her husband. Or, rather, she wished for *him* to wish for her. Gone were the days of the Italian campaigns, when he had pined daily for her, begging her to cross rough roads to join him at camp. Now he wouldn't allow her to join him. *I cannot have you here,* he wrote, when she begged to join Napoleon's army as it moved east. *An army camp is no place for a lady.* And yet, we knew the thinly veiled excuse for precisely what it was; we knew there were plenty of other ladies to fill his time.

On days when his letters did arrive—he no longer wrote her daily as he once had—Josephine would take to her bed for the remainder of the afternoon and weep. His words weren't enough. He was stingy with them. His letters served only to remind his wife of his distance—both physical and emotional. Josephine was starving for more news, more affection, more of an assurance that she still held the prime place in his heart. Oh, how I knew her agony. How I remembered being the recipient of those terse, withholding letters. But of course I could say nothing to her of that. Those memories were mine, and they would remain buried in the past where they belonged.

Somehow, Napoleon heard of Josephine's regular crying fits, and this fueled his annoyance, even at the great distance of his eastward camp. He wrote with censure in his words: *I hear that you cry all the time. Be worthy of me, show more strength of character. I don't like cowards.*

And so the days passed, all of us growing restless at our German camp, but no one more so than Josephine.

It was a chilly night in mid-October, and we ladies were gathered in Josephine's salon, huddling around the fire as a way to ward off the damp and dark. We weren't allowed to retire to our own beds until she wished to sleep, and that was often impossibly late, sometimes only as dawn approached. I guessed that she feared the dark, dreaded the troubled thoughts that hung heavy as sleep evaded her, because she always insisted on activities at night—charades, chess, whist, musical talent shows. Tonight, she had arranged a tarot card reader.

"You all know how the sorceress in Martinique foresaw my rise," Josephine said, seating herself opposite the visitor. The old woman wore a mauve turban on her head, making it impossible to see the color of her hair, but she had the appearance of a Roma, and she had a dark-eyed young girl beside her acting in a servant's capacity. The old woman summoned the girl forward now and took two piles of cards into her bare, weathered palms.

Josephine clapped her own hands excitedly. "Isn't this fun?"

I exchanged a look with Elise la Flotte, another lady in Josephine's party. Elise was about my age but widowed. In Julie's absence, I had grown somewhat close with Elise during my time in the Rhineland. She was, if nothing else, a far more pleasant companion than the three Bonaparte sisters in our midst.

"There is to be a child," said the old fortune-teller, pulling my attention back toward her table.

Josephine swallowed. We knew that she was now in her early forties. Her window to have Napoleon's heir was rapidly closing. "There is?" her voice was raspy with longing.

"But this child . . ." The old woman shut her eyes a moment, her voice low and trancelike as she continued. "I am not seeing it clearly beside you. It won't be yours."

Josephine leaned her head to the side. "I know!" she said, snapping her fingers after a moment. "You are seeing my darling daughter, Hortense. She is with child again. With Napoleon's nephew. And grandson."

"Hortense?" The soothsayer repeated the name. "Fair of hair?"

"Fair? Well, no. Dark hair. Like mine." Josephine ran her hands through the hair that poked out from under her red bandana.

The woman shook her head, disagreeing, but before she could continue, Josephine interrupted. "What else? Tell me something else." She leaned forward, hoisting her wineglass in the air toward me and saying, "More wine."

I exchanged a look with Elise as I turned to fetch the wine; we knew the rumors. Word came to us even in Mainz that one of Napoleon's mistresses back in Paris, a young beauty named Eléonore Denuelle, was pregnant. Was she fair of hair? I wondered.

Josephine hugged her legs in toward her chest now as she looked at the cards spread before her. I passed her the refilled wineglass and then retreated to the back of the shadowed room, where I could not see her cards, only her face, which had gone pale. I pulled my fur cloak tighter around my shoulders.

The old woman, droning on in her low voice, continued: "A beautiful home. More lavish than a palace."

"Malmaison," Josephine said, nodding. She looked relieved. "My greatest source of joy."

"There are many plants there," the woman said.

"My greenhouses. Napoleon gives me specimens from all over the world. Australia, Tasmania, Siam, Madagascar—"

"But in your life . . . there is one." The woman was rocking back and forth now, no longer looking at anyone as she spoke, her eyes rolling back as if what she saw was not in the same room we occupied. "This one grows so high that it threatens to choke all the others. It could choke you as well."

"What could you possibly mean?" Josephine demanded, her tone imperious as she sat back in her chair.

"I don't," the woman groaned, shaking her head. "I can't see it. All I see are these plants. But . . . take caution. That's all I can say. Be careful. Watch whatever it is that climbs too high."

"Weeds!" Josephine leaned forward and swept the cards from the table, reaching for her refilled wineglass. "I think that's enough. I didn't ask for a gardening lesson."

But the woman was not yet finished. "There will be a great victory. He will tell you—"

We all shrieked when a knock sounded on the door; we had all been fairly entranced ourselves by the woman's strange words. Josephine stared at the door as if she felt misgivings about answering, fearful of what might lurk on the other side. Finally, pulling herself straight with a fortifying breath, she said: "Come in. What is it?" She sat tall, the Empress once more, as a liveried page appeared. "Majesty." He bowed, eyes lowered. "We have word from His Imperial Majesty."

Josephine waved the man forward and took the letter. Her hands trembled; her face had gone paler than the parchment on which the note was written. But as she read the words, her features began to soften. And then, she giggled, reading aloud her husband's words: *"Never was an army more thoroughly beaten. I've executed some fine maneuvers against the Prussians at Jena and won a great victory."* Josephine lowered the paper and looked at the old fortune-teller, laughing as she said: "A great victory. Well, it looks like you did see one thing correctly this evening!" She turned back to the letter, reading aloud: *"The armies of my enemies continue to fall before me. My Grande Armée is the greatest force this continent has ever seen. Although it's no thanks to Bernadotte. I ought to have him shot—at the very least court-martialed."*

The words were out before Josephine realized what she read. She dropped the paper and looked at me in a flash, apologetic, as the women around me sneered. Only Elise, my new friend, frowned.

"Desiree," Josephine said, her face creasing with genuine remorse. "I am sorry. I . . . I didn't know before I read it."

"It's quite all right," I said, my tone steady, hiding the concern I truly felt. When I spoke again, I forced levity into my words: "You know how these men are, their emotions hot from the battlefield. They shall be friends again tomorrow."

But I heard from my husband the next day, and his letter confirmed the quarrel with Napoleon—an exchange of heated words following the French victory at Jena. *He was irrational,* Bernadotte wrote, his anger evident in his note. *He would not hear me speak. He kept fuming that he could have me shot. That he would have had me shot but for the anguish it would cause you. I had done nothing but follow the orders of my direct superior. Berthier ordered me to march my men to Dörnberg—I had no idea I was needed by Napoleon at Jena, nor did I know that that was to be the main site of engagement. None of us knew. Napoleon is simply seizing this moment to vent the feelings he has long held for me, namely rivalry. Jealousy. He tells me that he spares me because of you, when in fact, I suspect that perhaps it's the opposite: that he despises me because of you.*

I lowered the letter, my hands and the paper trembling.

There was no way for my husband to see my reaction to these words, and for that, I was thankful. I thought for a day before responding with great care—writing soothing words to try to calm him, while also indicating to him that I understood his sense of injustice and heard his frustrations. My husband was a good man, an honest man, but he would have been the first to admit that his hot Gascon blood made him no diplomat. That much I knew. My only hope was that, with time, both he and Napoleon might calm down and the cooling of tempers would bring about some sort of reconciliation in their friendship. Or at the very least, a détente in their relationship as officers.

More news streamed in. Within a few weeks, our French forces had taken the critical German city of Berlin, but Napoleon's letter announcing the victory sent Josephine to bed in hysterics. I wondered what he had written to her. I found out soon enough, when Pauline came into the drawing room that afternoon with a letter of her own. "A son!" she said, waving her note like a flag of victory.

We all looked up, curious for more news. We need not have worried: Pauline was happy to gush to us. Eléonore Denuelle had given Napoleon a son, and she'd named him Leon, in a clear honor to his father the Emperor. An illegitimate son, yes, but still, it proved that Napoleon was not sterile. A fertile wife would have given him a legitimate heir by now. I knew the sisters' hopes, that this would provide yet another argument for Napoleon to leave Josephine.

The Empress called me to her chamber that evening. I found her in bed, her hair tucked into the Creole bandana, her eyes red-rimmed and puffy. She appeared so small under a pile of covers, her dinner tray untouched on the bedside table. She asked me to join her in bed, so I obeyed.

"It is all simply to make me jealous," she said, her voice hoarse. I did not say anything but let her continue. "To be sure of my love. He has never forgiven me for taking my pleasure elsewhere early in our marriage. He is testing me. But I shall remain faithful. I shall pass this test, and our love shall soar to ever greater heights."

And it seemed that perhaps she might have been correct, for November brought with it news that our Emperor would be leaving Berlin to travel to the Polish front, and he had finally invited Josephine to join him. He wished for her to meet him in Warsaw. She read aloud from the letter at lunch the following day. "*The nights are long and cold without you. I long for you beside me on these frozen plains. You, my sole source of warmth and joy in this otherwise wearying life.*"

Josephine lowered the paper, a well-timed blush turning her rouged cheeks darker. These past few weeks had taken their toll, and her features had started to appear drawn, even a bit gaunt. Yet this most recent letter had done much to revive her spirit, and indeed her complexion. "I would read on," she said, glancing at her husband's note, "but I cannot possibly share the remainder of the letter. It would make you all too embarrassed."

Pauline rose from the table, frowning, and left the room, her sisters following after her. Josephine merely grinned, digging into her meal with a greater appetite than I had seen in weeks.

I would go to Warsaw along with my Empress, but also to see my Bernadotte, who would be marching there with the Grand Armée. I was glad of it—I longed to see him after so many months apart. If only Oscar could join us, and then we would be reunited as a family once more, but my son was still installed safely back in Paris with his nanny and tutor.

We ladies prepared for the hard, cold journey across the Polish plains. It would be December by the time we set out, and the road to Warsaw would be a bleak one; we were told to expect heavy rains, perhaps even early-winter snowstorms.

Josephine had arrived in Mainz with six coaches full of clothing and jewelry, and so we began packing her up weeks before the journey, for we knew the task was a daunting one. The first day of December brought with it snowfall and a new letter from Napoleon. I sat with her and Elise in her bedroom, sorting brooches, when the servant brought it in. The Bonaparte sisters had gone off to some other activity, which was just as well for the rest of us.

Josephine sprang up to grab the note off the golden mail dish and hopped into bed to read it. She was giddy with anticipation for their reunion. It seemed, however, that the letter did not bring good news. "Impossible," she groaned, leaning backward and curling into a heap on the bed. I walked slowly toward her. "Empress?"

Her eyes were shut, her back to me. A confused shrug from Elise.

"Madame, is everything all right?" I asked, though of course I guessed the answer.

"No!" she rasped, turning toward me. I saw, in that instant, how tired she looked. Her eyes—scrubbed clean of her customary makeup by the tears she cried—had a netting of fine lines encircling them. Age and worry and disappointment were closing in on her once-bright features, waging a battle of inevitability that she could not win. I had never thought she looked her age; I had never believed her beauty to have faded. Her body was still svelte and lithe, her personality still vivacious when she was in the mood to be so. But just then, in that moment, I could see the years on her. Hard years, most of them. And perhaps doomed to grow harder still.

"No, everything is *not* all right," she responded. "See for yourself." She pressed the crumpled paper into my hands and I looked down, reading Napoleon's familiar hand: *I am inclined to think you should go to Paris for the winter. The roads are bad and these plains are frozen. I cannot expose you to such fatigue, and it is hardly appropriate for an Empress to find herself in bivouacs and taverns—go back to Paris.*

It was an order, and one quickly and decisively issued. Napoleon was disinviting her from the front. But were his reasons in earnest—or merely an excuse? We did not know. I certainly had a guess.

Several days later, after our trip had been canceled, word came of Bernadotte. Terrible news, a letter that sent *me* into frantic tears, when I was so used to being the one to comfort Josephine. My husband's aide, Maurin, wrote to me that my husband had been struck in the neck with a Russian bullet, near a place called Spanden in Prussia. He had survived, but just barely, and he had fallen from his horse before being carried off the battlefield in a cart. The army field doctor who was treating him feared for his life.

I ran, hysterical, into Josephine's room, waving the letter in my hand. She listened, nodding gravely, as I read. "Of course you must go to him," she said after I had finished reading.

"Thank you" was all I could say, my breath uneven, my mind racing with the plans for my trip across the frozen winter roads.

"Think nothing of it," she said. "Why, I bet your trunks are still packed."

"Indeed, Empress, they are."

"Then go. Leave at once. And . . . if you see Napoleon . . . well. Tell him that I love him, and I long for him. I would gladly join him where he is, be it bivouac or tavern."

It was hardly a bivouac and hardly a tavern. I reunited with my husband—who had mercifully survived and was expected to make a steady, if slow, recovery—at Schlobitten Castle in East Prussia: a squat stone home once belonging to an ancient noble family. The weather was too cold for us to enjoy the grounds or the nearby lake, and, besides, my husband was up for little more than resting on the sofa before the fire, but I was happy simply to sit beside him, warm, grateful that his body was healing.

Napoleon and his attendants were nearby, my husband explained, at Finckenstein Castle to the south. "Has he visited you in your recovery?" I asked. We lay in bed that evening, burrowed under several heavy quilts, but my feet were still cold.

"No," Bernadotte answered. "He wrote. After the injury. But I haven't heard from him since."

In spite of this, my Bernadotte's spirits were high. He said nothing more to me of his feud with Napoleon, so I did not ask. Instead, he seemed eager to speak about his recent campaign against the Prussians, in an oddly named place called Lübeck.

"I had the most remarkable time there, Desiree. With some Swedish generals. My men had taken them captive. I was of the mind that, rather than treat them like prisoners, we stood to gain far more by treating the Swedes like gentlemen and thus learning their ways. I freed them of their braces; I treated them as my guests. I heard all about their country. Truly, it sounds like a fascinating place, this Sweden. We shall have to go sometime."

"Sweden? Yes, certainly," I said, trying to stifle a yawn, when really all I longed for was sleep. But then my husband said something that jolted me instantly awake. "And while I was falling in love with the Swedish generals, our Emperor was falling in love with a Polish noblewoman."

I sat upright in bed, leaning toward Bernadotte with a sudden, keen interest. "What?" *Falling in love?* We all knew that Napoleon had mistresses and lovers—many other women, too many to possibly count—but to fall in love with someone other than Josephine? I had never imagined it possible. But Bernadotte nodded his head. "Indeed, it's true. Our little general is quite enraptured."

I glanced at him sideways, incredulous. "Who is she?"

"A countess."

"She's Polish?" I asked.

"Yes." Bernadotte seemed significantly less surprised than I was. "They are holed up together in Finckenstein Castle. You know that is why he won't allow Josephine to join him?"

I absorbed these words. "I suspected there was some . . . reason."

"That reason is named Countess Marie Walewska."

I stared straight ahead, stunned.

"Come now." Bernadotte placed a hand on my arm. "You know he's no saint."

"Of course I know that. I just never imagined anything . . . serious."

"With him," Bernadotte said, sighing, "everything is serious."

"But . . . what is she like?"

Bernadotte considered my question a moment before cocking his head, answering: "She's the opposite of Josephine."

"How so?" I asked.

"She wanted nothing to do with him," Bernadotte said. "Which, as you might imagine, does not happen to him anymore. Napoleon picked her out of a crowd when we first marched into Poland. Thousands lined the streets. He saw her on the route, blond and unsmiling, wrapped in fur, and he immediately arranged for his men to bombard her with bouquets of flowers."

I couldn't help but see Josephine's face in my mind, even as I listened to the story. Josephine's parting embrace of me in Mainz, her final words: *Tell him that I love him, and I long for him.* I believed that to be true.

Bernadotte carried on, his Gascon flare for storytelling now at full tilt: "He invited the countess to dinner at his camp, but she declined. He thought her refusal was some ploy, so he sent her jewels, but still she re-fused him. She simply sent the jewels back, along with a short note stating that she was married. As you can imagine, this only delighted our general. There's nothing the man loves more than a conquest."

"So what did he do?" I asked.

"He kept inviting her to visit him. Finally, her *husband* insisted she accept his invitation. Can you imagine? He knew an opportunity too good to pass on, even if his wife didn't."

"You can't be serious," I said, pulling the bedcovers closer around my shoulders in our drafty room. "Well, what is she like, this Countess . . . Marie . . . Waska?"

"Countess Marie Walewska," Bernadotte corrected. "Well, she is rich and beautiful. She speaks flawless French. She is intelligent. . . ."

"Well!" I said, chortling. "I believe you may have fallen a bit in love as well, Sergeant Belle-Jambe."

He reached for me in bed, beginning to tussle with me, but then his injury gave him pain, and he released me, leaning back. "No, no. I admire her, that's all. She is a woman without any design, which is rare in the orbit of the Emperor these days. She truly had no interest in being Napoleon's latest quarry. She didn't care for the gifts, the attention, the power. Her husband is ancient and ill, and it was he who supported the liaison. Finally, she relented, and Napoleon happily took her to his bed. Since then, he has seen no other woman."

I thought about all of this a moment, contemplating something in my head: "But this can't have been going on that long, since Napoleon invited Josephine in November and only rescinded the following month. Perhaps it isn't *really* love? Perhaps it is simply some passing infatuation?"

Bernadotte shook his head. "The love is still young, but it is love indeed. He is mad for her. She shares his bedroom. He has never allowed that with anyone, well, other than Josephine. He lingers all day beside her like a sick puppy. I haven't seen him like this. Ever."

To our shock, Napoleon invited me the next day to Finckenstein Castle. Bernadotte was still on bed rest and far too weak to travel those frigid roads alongside me, even if it was only for the day. And yet, I noted, the summons had not mentioned him; Napoleon had expressly stated my name, and my name only.

I went. Of course I went. One did not refuse the Emperor such invitations. But even more, I longed to catch a glimpse of the beautiful Countess Marie Walewska; I wondered if she'd be beside Napoleon when I arrived.

He received me in a private study, alone. I almost frowned when my eyes swept the room and I saw no beautiful Polish countess, but only our Emperor, seated behind a desk on a raised chair that allowed him to look down on his company. He looked stout, rounder even than the last time I had seen him, but his face had a new, uncharacteristic aspect to it—he looked to be at peace. Even, I wondered, happy?

"Desiree Clary," he said, rising to greet me. I curtsied, and he showed me to a chair, dismissing the attendant who had admitted me. "Good to see a pretty French face out on these Polish plains."

So then, he was in the mood to charm. I sat up a bit taller, girding myself even as I kept a mask of carefree calm on my features. "Good to see you, sire. Congratulations on a stunning victory."

He nodded appreciatively. "Tell me, did your Marseillaise blood freeze on the roads here?"

I smiled, leaning my head to the side. "I have brought every fur I own."

He studied me with his intense green-eyed gaze, the hint of a smile touching his lips. "I can't imagine the young girl I once knew ever buying a fur."

My feet fidgeted under my skirt, but I crossed them at the ankles. Pulling my shoulders back, I answered: "I wouldn't have imagined many of the things that have come to pass, sire."

"Perhaps that is true." His jeweled fingers drummed the top of his desk. "Tell me: how does your husband do? Recovering over in that castle?"

"Indeed, sire. Thank you."

"He must be happy that you are out here to nurse him, eh?"

"He grows stronger every day."

"Good, good."

I wondered yet again why he had called me here. If it was to inquire about the status of Bernadotte's recovery, surely a letter would have sufficed. Pushing that confusion aside, I braced to deliver the message from Josephine, but just then, the door opened and a blond figure swept in, clearly not believing that a knock was necessary. The beautiful young lady smiled bashfully at Napoleon and then saw me seated opposite him. "Oh! I am sorry! I did not know . . ." Her words tapered off, but I had heard enough to detect the wiry tinge of the Polish accent. Countess Marie Walewska looked at me, her large blue eyes taking in my appearance with a quick, full-bodied appraisal, and then, sadness settled over her lovely features. A childlike disappointment, guileless, pure and forthright, with no attempt on her part to mask it; she presumed me to be a rival lover.

It was hardly an unreasonable supposition, given Napoleon's reputation. He lifted a hand toward her. "*Mon ange,* my angel, please, come here."

He had seen it, too, of course. He saw everything. "This is my family . . . this is Desiree Bernadotte. Julie's sister, the one married to my General Bernadotte. You remember?"

"Oh!" Countess Marie Walewska's face changed in an instant. Grief gave way as relief bloomed across her fresh, unlined features, and she glided toward her lover with a newly restored cheerfulness. "Desiree, of course! I've heard so much about you and your husband. It's so wonderful to meet you. How does Bernadotte fare? Better, I'm sure, now that you are at his side. Are you attending him with great love and care?" Indeed, her French was flawless, with just the hint of a Polish accent to add a charming touch.

"I am, madame," I answered. "You are kind in your concern."

"Well, we have been so worried about him," she said, pressing her hand over Napoleon's. He received the gesture with a beneficent smile, placing his other hand atop hers, as if they were exchanging vows. And then, rais-ing an eyebrow, he asked: "My darling, will you leave us for just one moment? I shall be finished shortly." His voice was softer than I had ever heard it.

The countess bobbed her head of thick golden ringlets. "Of course." She glanced once more toward me, her limpid eyes smiling with warmth. "It was wonderful to meet you, Desiree. I hope we see one another again. And, please, give our best to the dear general." At the door, Countess Marie Walewska glanced back one final time toward Napoleon, a perfect little smile on her lips, the faint hint of a parting giggle. With that, she shut the door, leaving a sprinkling of charm in her wake, as well as the lilac aroma of her perfume.

Napoleon continued to stare at the door after she had gone, still en-tranced by the mere memory of her. And then he remembered himself. "Yes," he said, focused and alert once more as he turned back toward me: "Desiree." He said nothing of the girl I'd just met. Nor did he ask after his wife, whose presence he knew I had only recently quit. He merely looked at me, and his face reverted back to an expression of matter-of-fact busi-ness as he rose from his chair. He crossed the room to where a massive trunk stood in the corner. Lifting the top, he explained, "I met the Tsar of Russia recently. When he surrendered to me. He presented me with these three fur coats, splendid pieces worthy of a Russian winter." Just then he hoisted a large pelisse from out of the trunk; it was thick, a plush dark brown. It looked heavier than Josephine's coronation gown. "I have been wondering to whom I shall give them."

"Oh?" I replied, confused.

"I have just the three. They are quite precious, as you can imagine. I shall keep one for myself," he said. "The other I must give to Mamma, of course. She has been so cross with me lately. But this third one . . . I've thought long and hard. I have decided that I shall give it to you, Desiree."

I stared at him, then the coat, speechless. *Why me?* I wondered.

Of course there was a reason. And Napoleon did not wait for me to ask. "In exchange," he said, his eyes traveling toward the door once more, where the beautiful countess awaited him on the other side, blue-eyed and fair-haired, with her floral-scented smiles and charming accent.

And then Napoleon turned back to me as he said: "I would appreciate your friendship when . . . if the time comes when I have need of it."

# Chapter 31

*Paris*
*July 1807*

BERNADOTTE AND I WERE PART OF THE CAVALCADE AS Napoleon and his army entered Paris in state, crossing the eastern barrier and slowly marching through the streets of the capital to the backdrop of a grand parade: flags waving, citizens cheering, windows opened as children leaned over the balconies, craning for a glimpse of their newly returned Emperor. Napoleon had commissioned a massive new arch to honor his victories, and both the soldiers and the crowds gaped as they beheld the work beginning on this Arc de Triomphe.

As splendid as it all was, my husband and I cared little for the fanfare, hastening to Rue d'Anjou for the reunion with Oscar that we so desperately craved. Our boy had just turned eight, and he ran outside on sturdy legs to embrace us as our carriage rolled into the forecourt.

"Maman! Papa!"

"Oscar, my darling!" I wept into his glossy dark curls as I pulled him close, breathing him in as though I would never get enough. He looked less like a baby and more like a boy, I noticed with a twinge of pain in my heart, but at least his body was still soft and sweet as I held him.

"Maman, I saw your carriage coming! I waited all morning, and I knew you would come!"

"There's my boy. Look how tall you've grown." My husband, I noted, still moved his neck gingerly, but the bandage was off and his doctors were confident he'd make a full recovery.

"What did you bring me?" our son asked, his big brown eyes lit with excitement as the servants hurried around us, unloading trunks and baggage.

"Wait until you see the toy soldiers I've brought," my husband said, chuckling. "A gift from a great Swedish general. You and I shall lay them out in my study so I can show you how we French have won a great battle."

"I wish to hold the figurine of you, Papa! The Great General Bernadotte." My husband beamed at this; though Napoleon seemed to have nothing but derision for my husband's military prowess of late, our son's praise brought a welcome smile to his travel-weary features.

But before our trunks could be unpacked, before Bernadotte could overtake his study with the battle scenes of his great Swedish toy soldiers, we saw the summons. Josephine's handwriting, I knew. We were expected at the Tuileries for dinner.

We arrived for the family gathering at the palace, Bernadotte and I, scheduled for a prompt six o'clock, as was the Emperor's wish. It was a pleasant evening in midsummer, and the windows of the ground floor were open, allowing in the balmy breeze from the fragrant gardens.

Josephine greeted us. She wore a lilac gown accented in peacock feathers, her fingers, wrists, ears, and hair sprinkled with diamonds, a massive choker strung tight around her perfumed neck. But behind her smile, I detected the telltale signs of tension: puffy eyes, a haggard pallor that even the most liberal application of her expensive rouge could not entirely conceal. "You are so good to join us, Desiree." She looped her delicate arm around my waist. "Even when you yourself must be overcome with joy and relief at being home once more with your Bernadotte and Oscar."

"A year was a long time to be apart," I said, agreeing with her.

"Too long," she agreed. "But they are back now. Even if we don't know for how long. Ah, Julie! Joseph, welcome. Bonaparte is just finishing up in his study; he shall be down directly."

My sister greeted Josephine with a smile, while her husband went directly to his mother and gave her a dutiful kiss. Josephine ignored Joseph's snub, walking after him to repeat her welcome and, I presumed, hear what he discussed with his mother.

I was delirious with joy to be reunited with my sister, and I pulled her into a giddy hug.

"Desiree!" She returned the embrace and then linked her arm in mine. "Come with me." She pulled me to the corner of the room, where we slipped through the glass doors and out onto the terrace.

"You look well," I said, taking in her appearance. She had a healthy color to her cheeks, and her green dress complimented her figure. "Naples suits you," I said. "Though I wish you would never leave France."

"We are here now for a while. But you are one to talk," she chided. "Only just freshly returned from your Prussian castle."

"Indeed, and so happy to be here," I answered. "What have I missed?"

"They are quarreling already, even though he's only just returned," Julie said, glancing around the terrace to ensure that we were free of eavesdroppers.

"Hardly a surprise there." I had long since grown accustomed to their tempestuous exchanges. I simply wished to speed through this dinner so that Bernadotte and I could return home to Oscar after so long apart.

"No." Julie shook her head. "It's different this time."

"Why?" I asked. It seemed that every time the Bonaparte family became confident in their ultimate triumph over Josephine, she somehow found a way to thwart them. "She is a cat with as many lives as she needs. Their saga will never be over."

"Because this time *she* might be the one to depart."

I looked at my sister askance, unsure of her meaning.

Julie continued, her voice low: "She found something this afternoon while helping him unpack."

"What did she find?" A portrait of Marie Walewska, perhaps?

"A list, drafted for him by his advisers. Of all the marriageable princesses of Europe. For his review, so that he may choose one as his bride. The Tsar has offered his sister."

I absorbed the words and, with them, the shock of their meaning.

"And of course we've all heard about his love affair with the Polish countess. That Marie Walewska."

"Yes," I said, nodding. "I met her."

"You did?" Julie's eyes widened. "Is she as lovely as everyone says she is?"

"Yes," I answered.

"Napoleon told Joseph he plans to bring her to Paris and set up a household for her. If she should conceive his child? It's only a matter of time before Josephine . . . well, her situation grows ever more precarious."

"To be sure," I said, sighing. That explained the Empress's red eyes, the mirthless smile. Perhaps it also explained Napoleon's acquisition of those three fine Russian coats, one of which he'd gifted to me, for some reason I still did not yet understand. *I met the Tsar of Russia recently. When he surrendered to me.* So then, the Tsar had offered him more than just priceless Russian fur—he'd offered him a Russian princess as well.

"Poor Josephine," I said. "All the world is against her."

Julie nodded, but offered a sideways tilt of her head as she replied: "Not so poor, covered in those diamonds."

Napoleon appeared from his study promptly at six, and we sat down to a supper of roasted chicken, rosemary potatoes, and Chambertin red wine. "You'll have to excuse the simple menu," he said, looking around the table, landing his eyes on me. "A soldier's tastes. I'm not yet reacclimated to the decadence of this place, the decadence with which my Empress eats and . . . so forth."

Josephine ignored the comment, smiling. "We are all simply happy to have you back; I think we would eat wet cornmeal just to have you at the table once more."

He grunted in reply, cutting into his chicken. Josephine, for her part, pushed away her plate, sitting upright, an expectant smile on her face. "But the timing is so perfect."

No one responded to her cryptic comment, but Josephine continued: "I really am so delighted to have all of our family gathered, because I do have joyous news to share." She beamed at Napoleon.

My pulse quickened. It could not be—had Josephine finally conceived a child? Just in time, and not a minute sooner? But no, it was not possible—not when they'd been apart for so many months.

"My darling son, Eugene, has had his baby, and it's a beautiful little girl!

He's named her Josephine Napoleone—after her grandfather and grand-mother. So, there you have a baby, my darling. And she bears your name."

A consolation, a desperate gift offered by a terrified supplicant. Napoleon loved his stepson, Eugene, and so Josephine was hoping he would feel that the child could be a suitable heir.

But Napoleon did not return his wife's smile from the far end of the table. Instead, he shrugged at the news, finishing his bite of chicken before he answered: "Ah, so she bears my first name. But not my surname. There is still no heir to bear my surname."

Napoleon vented his frustrations by taking ever more lovers and planning to seize ever more land through relentless war. He told my husband, who was once more in his good graces, to prepare for a march on Spain. If he could take that wealthy kingdom, he would control all the way from the Atlantic Ocean to the River Elbe, and from Germany in the north down to Italy in the south—more territory than any ruler of modern times.

My husband had grown into a rich man under Napoleon's imperial pa-tronage, but he became disillusioned as this talk of fresh war escalated. "It's an insatiable appetite for war. Almost a madness. As if he wishes to conquer the entire globe. And he doesn't care how many men he loses along the way," Bernadotte fumed to me in the private confines of our mansion on the Rue d'Anjou. "Do you know that in Prussia he made us fight having had no food in days? How are men to fight when their bodies are starved?"

Meanwhile, the Bonaparte family grew ever more frustrated by Napoleon's unwillingness to leave Josephine. When a madman escaped the asylum in Paris and attempted to attack Napoleon as he was leaving the theater, Napoleon asked his reason for doing so. "I am in love with the Empress Josephine!"

"So she'd bring about his death but leave him with no heir," Letizia said when she heard the story.

It seemed that with every quarrel, they presumed it to be Josephine's end, and yet, somehow, our Empress remained. When the imperial painter,

Jacques-Louis David, finally unveiled his masterpiece of Napoleon's coronation after years of unrelenting labor, we were all summoned to the Tuileries to admire it. Napoleon studied us as we studied his new tableau—but I did not need to feign any awe or approval. The work was overwhelming. It stood as tall as four men, and wider still. The rich colors of the oil and the artist's skill in capturing the glorious detail of the crowd inside Notre Dame Cathedral presented a stunning feast for the eyes. As I looked on, I imagined that I could study this scene for hours and still find new and magnificent details to admire.

Even with the artist's undeniable technical skill and classical techniques, the work was done not according to reality but according to Napoleon's specific wishes. In the painting of his coronation day, Napoleon stood lean and handsome. His sisters looked on with beneficent smiles, even though I remembered the scowls they had in fact worn for the entirety of the ceremony. Letizia was present, positioned as prominently as the Pope, a proud and approving mamma. But it was Josephine alone who shared the glory with David's rendering of the Emperor. The precise moment that David—and thus Napoleon—had chosen to highlight was the moment not of Napoleon's crowning, but of Napoleon crowning a humble, kneeling Josephine. To look at this exquisite portrait, hanging so prominently over Napoleon's staterooms, was to see just how deeply the Emperor still adored his wife. So she continued to share his bed and spend his money as the summer days cooled toward autumn. And yet the only thing she truly needed, the one thing she could not acquire for herself, continued to evade her.

"Do you know that they hatched a plan to fake her pregnancy?" My sister sat beside me in our coach on an afternoon in late summer. Her husband was on a diplomatic mission to the south, but Julie and I had been invited out to Malmaison, Josephine's beloved estate on the Seine to the west of the capital. My sister, my husband, and I were to spend the weekend with the Bonapartes.

"Who staged this?" my husband asked, interest piqued as we rattled west along the river. "This alleged plot to fake a pregnancy?"

"Napoleon and Josephine," Julie answered. "Apparently, it was his idea. He wanted her to pretend she was pregnant. He would arrange for one of his bastards by one of his dozen mistresses to be brought into the palace, a boy, and they would pass him off as Josephine's."

I looked away, glancing out the window as I heard this. I pitied her, truly. The indignity she must have felt—she'd been barren for the entirety of their marriage, and now here he was asking her to agree to such a lie, to claim another woman's child as her own or risk losing her husband. "How dreadful," I said.

"She was willing," Julie said. "Only, the imperial priest and doctor refused. They told the Emperor that they could not be complicit in such a plot. He was furious. At them. At her. It seems that it was his last desperate idea. She's too old now. Mid-forties? Trying for a decade? If it didn't happen years ago, it won't happen now."

I knew it wouldn't happen for her. What was worse, all sorts of rumors swirled—not just at court but publicly, in the papers and in the café gossip. Tales that she had been sterilized in the prison during the Terror or that all of her homemade efforts to ward off pregnancy during her years of bedding the French officer corps had led to a permanent infertility. Even worse, that her first husband, the sadistic and cruel Vicomte de Beauharnais, had maimed her after accusing her of infidelity. Who knew what was true? I certainly hoped that none of it was. All we knew was that Napoleon had married her with the assumption that she would give him sons, and even though she had not, he was perfectly capable of producing sons with other women, and his patience had all but expired.

"Ah, we are here," Bernadotte said, disrupting my troubled daydreaming. We pulled through the gates of Malmaison, and the coach made its way up a long, tree-lined boulevard. At the top of the lane was a lovely, sprawling château, with a central court and entrance flanked by two towers and long pavilion wings.

We'd heard so many tales of Malmaison, from Josephine and Napoleon and others. Tales that she dressed her orangutans in white gowns to dine with her at the banquet table; that she and Napoleon swam naked with their guests in the fountains and pools, alongside Josephine's black and white swans. But the house itself did not disappoint. Malmaison sat on three hundred lush acres, a riverside estate of vineyards, an aviary, hothouses, a menagerie of animals from all over the world, flower gardens, statue gardens, and acres of woodland parks for hunting, riding, and strolling. In addition to the château, I'd heard there was also a summer pavilion, several cottages, a grotto, and a Love Temple—whatever that may be.

"Look," Julie said, pointing toward a row of pools and fountains lining the castle's gracious façade.

"Is that . . . ?" I paused, staring.

"Yes, I believe it is. It's him," Bernadotte answered. From one of these man-made lakes, amid Josephine's black and white swans, emerged a giant stone statue of Napoleon at its center. "A bit taller than the real thing, but just as hard in the head," Bernadotte said, and my sister and I laughed.

Our hostess emerged from the wide front doorway as our carriage rolled to a halt. "You made it! Oh, I'm so delighted." The day was a pleasantly mild one, and Josephine looked casual in a simple dress of white lace, with purple ribbons woven through her hair. She appeared happy, at peace; whatever the state of relations with her husband these days, we would soon find out—of that I had little doubt. But her color was good and her mood seemed bright as Josephine leaned forward and kissed my cheek, then my sister's. "Napoleon arrives from Paris this afternoon; he'll be here shortly. What do you think of Malmaison?"

"It is lovely," I answered. From this close, I could see just how massive and labyrinthine the sprawling château was.

"The house is something," Josephine said. "I have over five hundred paintings and works of art that Napoleon seized—collected—during his foreign campaigns. We have art from every Italian master, every Russian Tsar, every Persian warlord. Everything but English art . . . Napoleon won't abide that. But my true pleasure is my garden! Come, you *must* see my hothouse."

She took off with a skip, and Julie and I followed as Bernadotte stayed back to oversee the unloading of our trunks. We accompanied her into a tall glass building with an elaborate iron frame. Inside, the air hung thick and loamy, dense with the exhales of the thousands of tropical plants that warmed beneath the sun-drenched glass. "We have all manner of plants that my Napoleon brought me from all across the globe: dahlias, roses, hibiscus, jasmine, amaryllis. Sometimes I close my eyes and I feel the moist air on my skin, I smell the plants, and I can imagine that I am back in the Caribbean."

We meandered down the plant-strewn paths, past trees laden with ripe oranges, vines bursting with bougainvillea. Josephine paused at the end of one row. "Ah! You know what they call this sharp one? Mother-in-Law's Tongue. Rightfully so." Next we followed her past a cluster of ferns and toward a small fountain, where a massive bust looked on. "And here is our philosopher, Rousseau. I've read all of his words at my husband's urging. 'Man is born free, and everywhere he is in chains.' Are you familiar with Rousseau?"

"Only a little," I said, shaking my head. I remembered back to the earliest days of my own ill-fated courtship, and Napoleon's fruitless insistence that I read his philosophers. He had done the same, apparently, with Josephine. But she had obeyed.

We exited the greenhouse back into the warm afternoon. Josephine inhaled, spreading her arms wide as she turned her face up toward the sun. "You know, we widened the lake so our view would be grander. Just like Louis XIV did at Versailles. Isn't it lovely?"

We strolled on, glancing back in the direction of the château. "Only here can I get Napoleon to forget about work, to forget about war, even just for a moment. I've designed every inch of the house, every blade of grass, so as to bring him ease and pleasure."

We walked along beside her. I had no idea what to say, other than to compliment the sprawling grounds, the peaceful fountains, the lovely castle. But Josephine frowned for a moment, saying to no one in particular: "At least, here, we can have some peace. What a horrible thing a crown is."

Just then I heard the sound of carriages on the far side of the house, a dog barking. And then a louder noise, a guttural grunting, pulled my attention toward a series of outbuildings farther down the river. "What on earth?" Julie asked, hearing the noise as well.

"My apes," Josephine explained, giggling as she pointed toward a massive cluster of nearby buildings. "Over there is my zoo. All of my little dears. Hardly a ship comes into a French port from a foreign voyage without bringing me some new creature. Napoleon and I love to give them all names. But he's such a naughty zookeeper, my husband. The last time we were here, he was giving my gazelles and kangaroos fistfuls from his snuffbox; he almost started a stampede."

Just then another noise tore across the languid afternoon: a loud crack, an explosion. "*Mon Dieu*," Josephine exclaimed, grabbing my hand.

Julie took my other hand. "It sounded like a gun!"

Could it be? Had the war come to the west of Paris? My heart lurched into my throat.

"Not to worry," Josephine said, glancing toward the house. "Napoleon is here," she explained, blinking rapidly, the soft ease with which she'd carried herself just moments earlier suddenly replaced by a taut uprightness.

"But it did sound like gunfire," I said, still confused.

"I'm sure it was," Josephine sighed. "He always takes target practice on my poor swans."

We sat down to dinner, my sister and I beside each other and across from my husband, while the Bonapartes sat at opposite heads of the low table. "Tonight we honor my husband's victories across North Africa," Josephine announced. We were dining out of doors, under a canvas tent on their sprawling lawn. Elaborately woven carpets covered the ground on which we sat, the table before us laden with platters and tagines of lamb and rice and hummus. The servants were dressed like Bedouin herders, and small flames flickered over jeweled candelabras. The setting may have been designed to conjure the desert, but Josephine was the figure of antiquity in a flowing gown of white, a tiara tucked into her dark, loose hair. Massive sapphires dripped from her ears and throat.

But in spite of the pleasant weather, the lovely, candlelit ambiance, the beauty of his wife, Napoleon appeared to be in a foul mood. "Your swans were pissing on my statue again today," he said to Josephine as he accepted a large serving of lamb. "I saw it when I arrived."

Josephine unfurled her white napkin, laying it across her lap with a subdued smile. "They are wild, my darling. The poor creatures don't know any better."

"Swans are hardly poor creatures," Napoleon answered, his jaw set in a tight line.

She ignored the comment, looking to my sister. "Do you know that the butter and the meat on this table come from our own grounds? And tomorrow, our eggs and bread and fruit shall all be from the estate as well. It is like we are real farmers out here! Oh, but breakfast is such an informal affair. Don't rise until you've slept to your heart's desire. We never serve breakfast before eleven, at the earliest. Our mornings out here are for—"

Napoleon interrupted her, asking: "Do you know what they do to their predators?"

Josephine looked to her husband, arching a thin eyebrow. "My dear?"

"Swans," he said, his tone brittle. "Do you know what they do when they are being hunted?"

Josephine shook her head. I could see, from the rise of her chest, that she took in a steady, calming inhale.

Napoleon's focus was fixed on her as he said, "They swim in circles until they exhaust their enemy, and then they approach, and—" He slammed the table with a balled fist, causing us all to jump. Wine sloshed out of my cup, spilling onto my plate, staining my lamb a dark red.

Now Napoleon lifted his hands, his fingers pointing toward his own face. "They peck their eyes out. And thus, the enemy drowns, a blinded fool."

Josephine's cheeks went pale as she looked down at her lap. Only the sapphires on her ears sparkled—all else of her appearance appeared diminished in the candlelight.

"And that's your beloved swan for you, Empress," Napoleon said, flattening his palm on the table before him. "I wonder, did you know that, when you made the swan your insignia? The cruel, cunning calculation of which the beast was capable?" She didn't answer, and he pushed back from the table. "I'm finished."

Josephine lowered her fork, looking to him. "Did the lamb not please you?"

I could only imagine the fortitude it required for her to turn her gaze on him with such a soft expression, the gentle tone in her voice as she posed the question.

He didn't answer but instead said: "A game!"

We looked toward him, confused. Napoleon clapped his hands and repeated himself: "We shall have a game!"

"Very well," Josephine said, smiling obligingly, nodding to the servants to clear the barely touched feast. She really looked terribly thin. "What game should we play, *mon cher?*"

"Prisoner's base," Napoleon said.

"I don't know that one," Bernadotte said, rising from the table.

"Ah! And you, Desiree?" Napoleon looked in my direction.

I shook my head. "I am not familiar with it, either."

Now he smiled—a strange, fiendish expression devoid of genuine cheer. "Ah, my darling, then we have the uninitiated in our midst!"

We gathered in the music salon, the heavy drapes drawn so that the room was plunged into total darkness. Napoleon alone held a candle, and his green eyes glowed with feverish intensity as he explained the rules to us. "Now, when I blow out this final candle, we shall be in complete blackness. My desk here"—he tapped the heavy oak behemoth—"is one safe base. And this sofa"—he crossed the room and kicked the upholstered sofa with his boot—"is the other." We nodded our understanding and he went on: "I shall be the first guard. You are to run back and forth from base to base. I shall have to catch you. Last person to escape my grasp wins."

"And what is the prize?" Josephine asked, her voice merry once more.

"How about the winner gets to keep his or her clothes on, while all the rest of us will be forced to strip naked?" Napoleon proposed.

"In that case, I volunteer to lose!" Josephine said, and Napoleon laughed.

"I'll keep my clothes on, thank you," my husband said.

"Of course you will, Sergeant Belle-Jambe. You're never one to obey my orders or follow my commands."

It was said with a smile, but the tone was biting. "Let's begin," Julie said.

Napoleon blew out the candle, and I blinked as my eyes adjusted to the total darkness. I stuck my hands forward and found the desk. I could hear Josephine's giggles, but I could see nothing but vague moving outlines. Josephine squealed. "I got you!" Napoleon shouted. "Who is this? Ah, this is Josephine. I know this arm."

"You're like a homing pigeon, my darling; you can always find my body, even in the dark."

"You're out," Napoleon said. "The rest of you, keep running."

I kept my arms before me as I plodded across the dark room, moving slowly to avoid bumping into furniture.

"Ah!" My husband's voice sounded next.

"Bernadotte, you bungler! You're out. Another commanding performance on your part."

I kept moving. My breath was growing uneven. I wanted this game to be over. "Ah!" I heard the familiar voice and knew that Julie had been caught.

"So now just my old friend Desiree remains," Napoleon said in the dark. "I should have known you'd be the best at this."

I kept moving. After a moment, I felt arms pushing me, but they weren't Napoleon's. They were thin. Josephine's. "What?" I squirmed. I could smell her wine-soaked breath, her syrupy perfume, as she giggled quietly beside me. But why was she grasping for me in the dark? And then, before I could make sense of anything, she nearly pushed me into another pair of arms. A man's hold, but not my husband's, that much I knew. Napoleon held me. I cried out, ready for him to announce that he'd found me, but the pressure with which he leaned into me caused me to lose my balance and fall backward. The couch broke my fall, thankfully, but Napoleon was on top of me now. I felt the press of his form as he held me pinned down. I could smell his breath. "Who do I have here?" he asked, as if he didn't know.

"It's me!" I cried out, trying to wiggle free even as he held me flat beneath his entire weight. "It's Desiree!" I declared, squirming, but his hands were roving all over me. It was so dark. I felt him cup my breasts, and I called out again: "You found me! It's over! The game is over."

But there was something warm and moist on my neck—his lips? At that, I went silent, so stunning was this sudden and unexpected development. A jab at my midsection, and I felt desire harden his lower body.

And then, a light—my Bernadotte had lit a candle. I blinked, my eyes careening for his face in the sudden glow. My gaze fell on him. Pure rage smoldered in his eyes when he beheld me, prone on the couch, the bodice of my gown askew, Napoleon on top of me. Josephine looked on as well, an odd, emotionless smile on her lips. She did not wince, did not react at all when she viewed the same scene, but only said: "Bravo, my darling, you've found us all! Desiree is the winner, it seems."

Napoleon cleared his throat and forced a laugh, pushing himself off of me and the couch. "I couldn't see a damned thing!" He laughed, shifting his weight as he adjusted his tight-fitting trousers. "You knocked me right over, Desiree!"

I blinked, my eyes moistening as they adapted to the sudden light. Or perhaps the tears were caused by something else. I met my husband's gaze again, and then I couldn't help but look away, my mind awhirl. Had I truly knocked Napoleon over, as he now claimed with such stout conviction? Was that all it had been—an innocent stumble in the dark? But surely I hadn't imagined it all, feeling as I did how his wife had pushed me into his outstretched and waiting arms?

# Chapter 32

*Vienna, Austria*
*Late summer 1809*

"NOW THAT HE'S AS RICH AS HE IS, HE THINKS EVEN THE Habsburg palaces are dull in comparison," Bernadotte told me. We stood a safe distance from the palace, where no one might hear us. "But look out over that view. There is nothing dull about these grounds," my husband added, his voice with a pensive, even melancholy aspect to it.

We were atop a hill on the vast grounds of Schönbrunn Palace, the summer estate that Napoleon was currently using as his headquarters, having displaced the Habsburgs from their capital. There, at Schönbrunn, I had been reunited with my husband after the most recent campaign across Central Europe. Napoleon had won yet another decisive victory for the French at Wagram, defeating the coalition forces of the enemy so badly that the allies had feuded among themselves, breaking their own treaties to separately surrender to the French.

And yet, in spite of these victories, my Bernadotte was furious. Once more on the battlefield, Napoleon had turned his ire on my husband, accusing him of not being where he needed him, calling him a bungler and threatening to have him shot.

We had been walking for hours, and I was trying to cool Bernadotte's temper before we were expected at dinner with the other generals and our Emperor. My husband was fed up with everything about Napoleon, both on the battlefield and off, where the two men seemed to be locked in a fight of their own. If Bernadotte needed to vent weeks' worth of frustrations, then let him do it here, where only my ears might hear it and where I might attempt to steer his troubled thoughts back toward calmer waters. The setting was lovely, the air mild and golden, and all of Vienna stretched out beneath us as we sat before Maria Theresa's Gloriette monument. Just below, the grotto fountain churned and gurgled, its stone figures frozen mid-frolic in the water, and beyond that, the vast maze of shrubbery and Habsburg tulips.

"Interesting to think," Bernadotte said, "that this is where Marie-Antoinette grew up. We beheaded her for being a queen. And yet, Napoleon has set his Empress up in a manner more lavish than anything Antoinette ever enjoyed. And him? He lives more wastefully than any Louis Bourbon ever did. The people are so easily manipulated. And he knows how to do it."

I nodded; of course it was true. And yet, I would never trade places with Josephine, not for all of the treasure in her massive jewelry box.

"Tell me, how is our Empress?" Bernadotte asked. "The embattled Josephine."

"Embattled is the correct choice of word," I answered. Even when my husband had invited me to join him in Vienna, and many other generals had done the same with their wives, Napoleon had insisted that his remain in Paris. "She is not happy. She cries often. Napoleon no longer writes to her. She senses how far he has strayed. And now that she's turned forty-six, there will be no hope for a child."

"Well, if you think she was unhappy when you last saw her in Paris, her sadness shall only grow."

"Why is that?" I asked.

"Countess Marie Walewska is pregnant."

I sighed, staring out over the view of green hedges and tightly clipped lawns. "His mistresses have fallen pregnant before. Josephine has weathered each announcement with calmness."

"No." Bernadotte shook his head, his arms crossed before his broad chest. "This is different. Countess Marie is not some Parisian actress or officer's wife. She is noble. But worse still—Napoleon loves her. She was by his side for the entirety of this past campaign, in his bed every night. So inseparable were they that people began to openly call her the 'Polish Wife.'"

I listened closely, my heart speeding up as I understood his point. Would Napoleon finally put Josephine aside?

"His advisers approve of her—she is young, beautiful, and pliable. If this child is a son . . . it shall be hard for Napoleon to resist making him legitimate."

"Through marriage to Countess Walewska?" I asked.

My husband nodded. "Perhaps. But, knowing him, he might have his eyes set on an even higher target. A princess from somewhere else in Europe. The man's hubris makes it difficult to guess."

I frowned, looking out over the glorious lands of the once-glorious Habsburg Empire. They had been humbled, these blue-blooded rulers of Austria—vanquished on the field of battle and then chased from their lands, chased from their kingdom, just like all the other crowned heads of Europe who had fallen before Napoleon.

Could I really imagine him cutting ties with Josephine? No, I couldn't; the two of them were so deeply and inextricably linked in my mind, two threads of the same rope, it was impossible to imagine one without the other.

A breeze rippled across the hilltop just then, sending a sprinkling of raised gooseflesh to the surface of my skin. I noticed, then, how the sun was dipping low toward the west. "We had better go in to dress for dinner," I said, glancing toward my husband.

"Yes," he agreed. "We know that our Emperor does not abide lateness. And I need not give him one more cause to berate me."

We walked down the hill slowly, each of us wrapped in our own thoughtful silence.

"Oh, hell," Bernadotte groaned. Though I startled at his profanity, my eyes followed his stare and saw the same thing he did: the small, round figure emerging into the back gardens, walking down the horseshoe stairway just as we were approaching the same door. "We have no choice," Bernadotte whispered to me, tightening his grip on my hand. "He's seen us already. We will greet him."

"Desiree!" Napoleon lifted a hand in our direction.

"Sire." My heart galloped as I curtsied in greeting—I hadn't seen him since the house party in Malmaison. That horrifying fumbling in the dark room.

He watched us approach, placing a hand on his thick waist. "You always seem to show up, Desiree, just as things are getting lively and fun. Good to see you, my dear girl. Now the party can really begin, eh, Bernadotte?"

My husband did not reply, because just then, all of our attention turned toward a servant racing toward us, a young man in plain clothes, his long hair disheveled and loose. His face struck me as bizarre—his features almost feral. I stepped an inch closer to my husband.

"What is it, man?" Napoleon stared at the approaching figure, but he clearly did not recognize the attendant, either, even though he never forgot a face.

"Please, sire, a petition." The man approached us with a harried, frantic stride, his pale eyes ablaze with a peculiar intensity. "A petition for you."

"What?" Napoleon asked, confused. Bernadotte pulled me back, closer to him, and I watched with misgivings as the man removed the petition from his pocket. "Halt right there!" Just then, two of Napoleon's nearby aides shouted, lunging toward the young man. Two more gendarmes stepped in front of Napoleon as the man raised his hand, brandishing the petition, and I noticed then that it was not a paper at all—but a massive carving knife. I screamed in surprise as it all unfolded right before us, fast as a blink. "Death to the tyrant!" the man yelled, his body writhing in protest as a swarm of guards descended on him, his eyes alight with murderous intent.

"Assassin! Seize this would-be assassin!" Napoleon's face was ashen as he understood, as he saw how close death had come. As the Emperor was whisked away indoors, I turned to my husband, who stood in mute shock beside me. We had nearly seen our Emperor murdered right in front of our eyes—and by a man screaming the very sentiment that was written on my husband's chest.

# Chapter 33

*Château de Fontainebleau*
*Winter 1809*

"I SN'T IT SOMETHING—AS THOUGH PLUCKED FROM A FAIRY tale?" Josephine's breath misted the air around us as the horses *clip-clopped* forward, pulling our gilded coach up the broad avenue toward the picturesque castle tucked back in the snow.

"It's enchanting," I agreed, examining the place as we approached. Indeed, it could have been plucked from a drawing in one of Oscar's storybooks.

"My husband said, 'Now, Fontainebleau, *there* is the true home of the kings of France.' It's over fifteen hundred rooms." Josephine sat a bit taller in the coach, adjusting the sable collar that draped over her shoulders, her svelte body encased in a snug travel cloak of purple velvet. "I think it will be a splendid little party."

Our Emperor had declared that he, like the grandest and most ancient ruling families of Europe, should have a winter court to which he and his government might decamp, and I could not disagree that he'd chosen one of France's most stunning spots. "Have you ever been here?" Josephine asked me, weaving her arm through mine.

I shook my head.

"That's right. I always forget that you're a southerner like me," Josephine said. "Accustomed to palm trees and ocean breezes, not these castle moats and snow-covered forests. But we will have fun nonetheless, won't we?"

Our retinue came to a halt before the sprawling palace and its grand front entrance, where a light sprinkling of snow dusted a massive stone staircase that unfurled in a wide horseshoe. Already, Napoleon had made his imperial imprint on the ancient castle, for I saw that, amid the tall windows and the fanciful turrets, the golden eagles of his reign kept guard over the entryway.

Josephine was helped out of the carriage, her ensemble of imperial purple presenting a stunning splash of color against the white snow. "Oh, I am so happy to stretch my legs," she said, as I stepped out behind her, and then she added: "And to see my husband."

Oscar, who had ridden with his tutor and his nanny in a coach farther behind, exited and quickly took off to explore the snow-covered grounds, impervious to the cold air and delighting in his freedom after so long a journey. I gave him a quick kiss but remained with Josephine, bracing for what might come during her reunion with her husband. But as we made our way up the broad, imposing stairway and into the castle's large front hall, we noticed, with surprise, that it was not our Emperor who awaited our arrival.

"Paulette," Josephine said, using the affectionate family nickname but barely masking her disappointment at seeing her sister-in-law. "How good of you to receive us."

Pauline said nothing but simply kept a tight, haughty smile fixed on her lips.

"Where is the Emperor?" Josephine asked, stuffing her hands farther into her fur muff.

"His Imperial Majesty, my brother, is occupied. He has asked that I receive you in his place," was all Pauline offered by way of an answer, and she looked only to me as she said it. "He has already been here for a day, and was surprised to have arrived ahead of your party. He was . . . less than pleased . . . that no one was here to receive him when he arrived, weary, after so many months of war."

Josephine didn't say anything to Pauline, but instead tugged on my arm and directed the waiting mob of footmen toward the second floor. "I wish to go to my suite," she said as we made our way up the grand staircase, its panels colored with tableaux of Alexander the Great's many lovers and romantic conquests.

There, at the top, Napoleon stood.

How long had he been watching?

Upon seeing his wife's ascent, he fixed a hand on his thick waist and tossed his chin back. He smiled, but no hint of good cheer reached his eyes, or his voice. "Ah, Josephine! Here at last? Good of you to join me."

Josephine took her flowing skirts into her hands and ran up the remaining stairs toward him. "But how did you beat us here? I came as soon as I received word that I was to meet you. I couldn't have been here any sooner." She raised her thin arms toward him in an embrace, but he shook his head, lifting his hands between them. She remained a step lower as he looked down on her, saying: "That was it? I guessed that perhaps you had other important business to attend to in Paris."

Josephine stiffened, her voice going quiet, the girlish ebullience of the carriage ride vanishing. "What could be of more importance to me than you? Of course not."

I glanced down the stairs and noticed how Pauline watched the whole exchange from below, her lips curled upward in a satisfied sneer.

Napoleon cleared his throat and turned from Josephine toward me. "The servants will show you both to your rooms. I trust you'll be comfortable. Dinner at six." And with that, he turned and made his way, alone, toward some room at the end of the dim corridor.

"Wait." Josephine trailed him, arms aloft as if begging for his benediction, or perhaps his mercy. "But . . . won't I stay with you? I wish to stay with you!"

I kept my eyes down and climbed the remaining stairs, following the servants who offered to direct me to my own bedchamber. Bernadotte was currently stationed with the army in the north, negotiating a treaty with the Swedes, and Julie and Joseph weren't scheduled to arrive from Naples until that evening, so I would be largely on my own for my first afternoon in Fontainebleau. Already I wished it would be over, my only joy coming at the thought of a brief reunion with my sister.

My desire for our stay to speed by was only heightened when, while settling into my suite, I began to hear shrieks and wailing. Horrified, I left my trunks with the servants and made my way back into the corridor. There, I found Josephine collapsed in a heap, her thin arms banging uselessly on a massive, unyielding door. She did not appear to care who might hear her as she cried out: "Let me in! Let me in! Please, can't you see how you are murdering me with this cold treatment?" But the door was impassive before her desperation, as was her husband on its other side. I pitied Josephine in a way that I never thought I would.

"Empress?" I grimaced, kneeling onto the floor beside her. "Can I help you?"

Josephine turned to me, her eyes glassy from weeping. "He's barred the doors! To his bedroom! Even the adjoining door between our bedrooms. Bad enough that he won't share my room, but to put me in a separate room and then refuse me entry at his door. . . ." She collapsed her head onto the door with a dull thud.

I turned and saw them there—Pauline, Elisa, and Caroline. They stood among the flickering shadows at the end of the long hallway, openly laughing as they looked on. If Napoleon loved the tragedies of antiquity, then they were his trio of Furies, dancing with glee at the bonfire of the damned.

I turned back to Josephine, my hands resting gently on her back, as I did when trying to comfort Oscar. "Come, Empress, you aren't well. You must rest."

"No!" she protested. "I won't sleep in that bed! I won't be stuck in there alone! He'll lock me in. I know it."

"Then you must come into my bedchamber."

"But . . ." She clung to me, her grip surprisingly strong as I tried to help her to standing. "Will you stay with me?" Her voice was desperate.

"If that is what you wish, then yes, I shall stay with you."

This seemed to give her some measure of comfort, and she allowed me to pull her upright. Her body was feather-light. "He means to throw me over, Desiree. I know it. He's wanted to for some time. They've all been telling him to, but he's unwilling. He hoped, instead, to make it so bad for me that I would leave him. But doesn't he see? I would never leave him. As God is my witness, I love him more than my own life. I would never break our sacred vow that we made to one another, even if it meant following him to hell. It would be no hell, so long as my Bonaparte was there with me."

But their vow was not sacred—at least not anymore. It was all over the news: Napoleon was feuding openly with the Pope, the same man who had attended his coronation and blessed his marriage to Josephine the night before. Fed up with Napoleon's flagrant disrespect and the constant war he was making across Europe, the Pope had excommunicated Napoleon. The Emperor reacted by putting the Holy Father under armed house arrest, showing how little he truly honored the Pope's authority, much less some hastily uttered midnight marriage vows.

"What am I to do?" Josephine asked me now, her tone plaintive. As I looked at her, scared, shivering in the shadowy, cold corridor, I thought of her as a girl in the Caribbean, her home in shambles after a hurricane destroyed the entire estate.

I sighed, unsure how else to answer: "Well, you shall do the one thing you can do in this moment. You shall dress and you shall join him for dinner at six."

Julie and Joseph arrived just before dinner, and I found great relief in the brief but happy reunion. Julie gushed over my Oscar and how much he'd grown, and I savored the sight of my two nieces and their girlish smiles. My sister and I saw our children happily settled with their nannies before making our way down to the meal. I did not have time to acquaint Julie with the events of the afternoon, for just then, Pauline appeared on the stairway and we made our way as a small, quiet group. Surely my sister sensed that something was amiss—misery crackled through the cold castle air.

Josephine appeared in the dining room just before the stroke of six, her narrow frame draped in white—her husband's favorite shade on her—a broad white hat and veil covering her haggard face. She trembled throughout the meal, her body wilting in her chair as she tried to suppress her tears, but we all heard her weeping beneath the thick veil.

No one spoke at the table. I couldn't eat, even as the servants brought out an endless procession of platters—duck and pork and filets of tender beef. No one touched their food, really, except for the three sisters, who ate with gusto. After the dishes were cleared, Napoleon looked up and spoke for the first time, his eyes fixing on his brother Joseph as he asked: "What time is it?"

Joseph glanced at the clock, but before he could answer, Napoleon pushed away from the table and stood from his chair. The page rushed toward the table, the Emperor's after-dinner coffee ready in his hands, and the young attendant made to walk toward Josephine so she might pour her husband's cream, as she did each night—and as only she was allowed to do. But Napoleon shook his head toward the man. "No. Bring it here."

The page, confused, obeyed his orders and brought the tray of coffee and cream to the Emperor, who poured his own coffee, swallowing it in one gulp, and, without glancing back at his wife, quit the room.

Josephine fainted.

He went to her bedroom that night, that we knew. Not because we could hear the sounds of their reconciliation, as we had on so many other nights, but because we could hear her hysterical shrieks, the low groans of her weeping.

I lay in bed with Julie, Joseph elsewhere in the house, probably conferring with his sisters or the aides and ministers who had been opposed to Josephine for so long. Perhaps they were dancing downstairs with bottles of champagne; I had no interest in gloating over the wreckage of Josephine's private and public disaster.

"He told Joseph that he still loves her," Julie said, slowly pulling the pins from her hair and placing them on the bedside table.

"He certainly has a curious way of showing it," I said.

"He said that he loves her and wishes to keep her, that the only happiness he has ever known is because of her, but he will not be controlled by his own wishes. He will do what is best for France. He tells Joseph that his dynasty is only a few years old; it cannot withstand a war of succession.

He *must* have an heir. A son born to his wife and no ambiguity. You know he is such a scholar of history."

I nodded.

Julie's hair was loose now, and she shook her head, allowing the graying waves to fall over her shoulders. "He says, 'Think of the civil wars that followed Julius Caesar and Alexander the Great'—neither of whom had surviving sons. Napoleon believes he comes from them, and so he won't repeat their mistakes. Not when he has studied them so faithfully."

Napoleon wanted it done quickly and decisively—it would be an annulment. But an annulment required credible reasons why the marriage could not stand. So he declared publicly that he had been forced into the union by Josephine and that their certificate was an invalid document because they had both lied about their birth dates. I remembered back to that night, the dark upper room with no chairs; I remembered noticing how they had each changed their dates of birth. Back then, it had been an act of love, an effort to bridge the chasm between their ages. Now, Josephine's age was once again to be used against her.

That took care of the legal side of things. In addition, Napoleon avowed that there had not been witnesses for their church ceremony because Josephine had insisted on doing it the night before the coronation—in secret, with only the Pope, so that no member of the Bonaparte family could present any impediment. The Pope, all the world knew, was a man whose authority Napoleon no longer recognized. That, then, took care of the religious side of things.

Over the next few weeks, as I watched all of this unfold alongside my sister and her husband and their family, I could not help but think: *Does anyone in this world know how Josephine feels so much as I?* A secret exchange of vows, promises made from heart to heart, put aside when *his* heart changed.

As was the case in my own life, Napoleon decided it was done, and so it was done. Now he just needed to sell it to the public. A public that had long loved its Empress.

Like the Caesars of his beloved antiquity, he turned to bread and circus to dazzle and distract: Napoleon announced that the official annulment ceremony would be carried out with a grand party, and the entire court would attend. It was to be in the throne room at the Tuileries. All of us who had participated in their glory at Notre Dame only a few years earlier were now required to come and watch this final unraveling.

Josephine arrived looking more regal than ever, composed even, in reams of purple satin that hugged her still-enviable figure, her jewels glittering in her upswept chestnut hair. Her son, Eugene, held one hand, her daughter, Hortense, the other.

Joseph told me that Napoleon had broken down just that morning, saying that he wished to cancel the annulment. Josephine had refused his tearful pleas, saying that now that he had made plain what his intention was, she could not go on living as his Empress. Then he begged her to continue to live with him at court as his mistress. She would not do that, either. She would take her refuge with Eugene and Hortense at her beloved Malmaison, where Napoleon would be welcome to visit at any time, as a dear and special friend.

The Bonapartes entered the throne room en masse, unlike the coronation just five years earlier. Letizia was in scarlet satin, her daughters trooping around in various shades of garish jewel tones.

Josephine smiled and curtsied before those who greeted her and ignored those who slighted her, not showing a crease of pain on her flawlessly made-up face. The food and champagne were set forth on the long, candlelit banquet tables. Musicians played, and our host implored us to dance. Napoleon sat beside Josephine on their two thrones, clutching her hand, visibly trembling. Weeping, even. Now that it was done, he appeared, by far, the more bereft of the two.

He had been generous to her—she'd keep not only Malmaison, which he would continue to pay for, but also the Élysée Palace, just a short walk from the Tuileries in the capital. He'd give her a yearly income of three million francs, and she'd retain both her imperial title and her mob of servants, hundreds of them, their salaries and households funded by her distraught former husband.

Shortly before dawn, as the musicians began to pack up their instruments and the servants entered to clear the debris from a night of uneasy feasting, Napoleon and Josephine rose from their thrones, hands still intertwined. We looked on in silence as he kissed her one final time, walking her toward the door, though it looked like it was Josephine who held him upright, and not the other way around.

An imperial coach waited in the forecourt of the Tuileries, where a drizzle of gray rain had begun to fall. We were not to join her there for any official farewell; we were not to see her off. Before gliding out the door, Josephine turned around one final time, her amber eyes sweeping the room before landing on Napoleon's, then Julie's, then mine. When my eyes locked with hers, my frame went rigid, a strange jolt shuddering through me, a serpent of sensation writhing from my belly up to my chest. I gasped in a quick breath as my vision began to swim. *This is not the end—for Josephine and me.* She, who had melded herself so firmly to my own fate when she'd usurped my fiancé and the position and the family that was to have been mine—she was destined to be in my life yet.

I knew not when or how.

And yet, somehow, I knew.

Eugene whispered something in his mother's ear and she nodded, standing taller. When she broke from my gaze, the thrum of curious energy coursing through me ruptured, a cord snapping, and I heaved a sigh. All I could do was stare at her slender figure as she held fast to her son beside her. And then she walked out, pale, visibly shaking, but her face a mask of resolved dignity, so different from the sniggers of Pauline and the other sisters, so different from the despondent weeping of Napoleon as he watched her go.

We heard the rattle of her coach as it rolled through the rain and out of the Tuileries. The room throbbed with a thick, unpleasant silence as we stood in her wake, and I wondered: Would it always feel this way, now that she was gone? Would the air henceforth hang this heavy and joyless without her, the gracious lady who had stood beside our charmless leader?

Though I never would have admitted it to our Emperor, I was sad to see her go. She, Josephine, my one-time rival and the woman who had been the cause of my first and harshest heartbreak, had nevertheless, somehow, become a woman I cared for, rooted for, even admired. Josephine had gone with as much grace and allure as she had entered. A lady, lost and broken, but a lady until the very end. When the weak sun rose over the drizzly winter morning in Paris, Josephine was gone, and we were in the capital city of an Empire without an Empress.

# Chapter 34

*Paris*
*March 1810*

H OW COULD NAPOLEON REPLACE JOSEPHINE? HE COULDN'T. But as it always happened with him, he acted swiftly and decisively, catching us all completely unaware.

We had suspected that he'd choose the Countess Walewska, the "Polish Wife," the pliable beauty for whom he clearly felt much affection; she'd already given him one son. But we knew, also, of his hopes for Grand Duchess Anna, sister to Russia's Tsar. Marriage to Anna would be a deft strategic move, a clever step to neutralize the vast behemoth to the east.

But a Habsburg princess? The eighteen-year-old daughter of France's greatest enemy? The child of Napoleon's unrelenting and most frequent foe? No one had seen that coming.

As a Habsburg princess, Marie Louise had been raised to expect a political marriage, one made to advance the dynastic interests of her father's empire, to be sure, and yet I could not help but wonder how she must have felt. How did Marie Louise react when her father's stern ministers told her the news, that she would be expected to wed the same man who had forced her and her family to flee their own palace? Had she not been taught since childhood to hate this man? Did she not think it supremely unfortunate?

Marie Louise was less than half Napoleon's age, and she'd no doubt been raised to loathe the French, the nation that had been at war with her own family for the entirety of her life. We were the same people, after all, who had beheaded her great-aunt Marie-Antoinette. Now she would travel here to be our Empress and to sleep in the former bed of her unfortunate ancestor.

"The rumors are that she looks just like Antoinette," my husband told me. It was the morning of the wedding, which had been put together in great haste, as Napoleon was as impatient on matters of the heart as with everything else. We sat together at breakfast, Bernadotte and I, in our home on the Rue d'Anjou. My husband was in a foul mood; he had been so for months, ever since the announcement of Marie Louise's betrothal. "Did so many millions of our countrymen die fighting the Habsburgs, only to now put another one of their princesses on our throne?"

Outside, the cold March rain slapped the windows, dousing the pebbled walkways of our walled gardens. "Some introduction to Paris she shall have—splashing in this rain," I said, steering the conversation toward the bland and, I hoped, safer territory of our unrelentingly wet spring. "And it doesn't appear as if it will let up."

"The parade route will be slicked," Bernadotte said, flipping through the news journals sprawled across our breakfast table, the familiar knit pulling tight on his brow. "And if the people were already unexcited, these storms will quench any festive spirits." Bernadotte coughed, scanning the next page of headlines. "Ah, here we are. More news of our *former* Empress . . ."

Napoleon had been ordering for months that the papers stop printing stories about Josephine, but still she dominated the pages. The people still loved her, still believed her to be their true Empress. She had been the First Lady of the greatest years of the Republic and the proudest years of the French Empire. She had been French in her blood, and hers was a tale of modest beginnings, a rise that followed the ascent of our very nation. What fondness could they feel for an Austrian princess from Europe's most blue-blooded monarchical dynasty?

Plus, the people knew that they were not alone in their nostalgia, their longing for their erstwhile Empress. The Emperor himself still loved Josephine. It was common knowledge that he visited her almost daily at the Élysée Palace, where she had been given residence, and that they escaped on weekends to stroll, hands entwined, through the gardens they'd designed together at Malmaison. Though the bonds of their marriage had been dissolved, theirs was a bond not easily broken, and they were still lovers, more intimate and close than were most husbands and wives whose official marital vows had not been put asunder.

Napoleon declared publicly that he was a man very much enchanted by his new Austrian fiancée, but he did himself no favors with the common people by planning his upcoming wedding to follow the exact marital rituals of the old Bourbon princes. A man who relished the oversight of all details, he'd ordered his secretaries and imperial historians and archivists to resurrect the records of Louis XVI's marriage to Marie-Antoinette, declaring that he'd wed his Habsburg bride in precisely the same manner.

"Jean-Baptiste Bernadotte, Marshal of France, Prince of Pontecorvo, and Desiree Bernadotte, Marshaless of France, Princess of Pontecorvo." We were announced into the wedding feast in the grand Salon d'Apollon, a sprawling hall inside the palace, where thousands of glistening candelabras sprinkled their light over long banquet tables heavy with platters of rich food, vases of fresh-clipped flowers, and crystal flutes of chilled champagne.

The couple was married by the cardinal before a jeweled altar at the front of the hall. My sister served as an attendant, as did the three frowning Bonaparte sisters. "They've realized their error," my sister had explained to me earlier that week. "At least with Josephine, they had no heirs as rivals. Now, they stand to lose so much more than they ever did under her. Marie Louise is young; she'll give him a dozen sons where Josephine would give him none. Fools, all of them, to direct their venom as they did." Nevertheless, they were there, as was Letizia.

As for the French people, equally withholding of their approval, Napoleon hoped to dazzle them into acceptance, if not sanguine support. At the moment the imperial union was blessed by the Almighty, fireworks burst across the Parisian sky, and red wine began to flow in the squares from the public fountains. Skewers of mutton legs and sausage links were delivered across the capital, and concerts and parades filled the streets with festive music and dancing. There was even, I noted with a bite of my tongue, a hot-air balloon display over the capital.

Inside the palace, we were among more than a thousand guests, and I stood beside my husband in the endless queue, dutifully awaiting our chance to congratulate our Emperor and meet his young bride. Bernadotte grumbled beside me, shifting in his starched uniform, clearing his throat with impatient coughs. He was eager to leave this feast and be home. "And you, my dear, shall have far more time on your hands," Bernadotte said to me.

I nodded. I was not to be in Marie Louise's household as I had been in Josephine's. The Austrian princess came to court with her own cadre of German-speaking attendants, and she would fill out the rest of her household with the allies she acquired in the Tuileries. I was a member of the old guard, a longtime confidante of her powerful predecessor, and thus of no use to our new Empress. "Whatever shall you do with all your free time?" he asked.

I looked around the palace, affecting an expression of indifference, even though I had pondered the same question myself. "I shall be delighted to have more time with Oscar," I answered. "Perhaps I shall teach him a bit about art, since his papa is so intent on teaching him about toy soldiers."

Finally, we reached the front of the interminable line, and I got my first close glimpse of our new Empress. She wasn't an exquisite beauty—she didn't have the innate allure that Josephine so powerfully exuded—but she wasn't unattractive; the freshness of her youth and the splendor of her rich attire gave her a pleasant enough appearance. I blinked as I studied her. She did look alarmingly similar to the portraits of her murdered great-aunt: strawberry blond hair, fair skin, a round face with the notable jut of the Habsburg chin.

Marie Louise had a good build—she was thicker than the willowy Josephine, her figure one that might well turn to plumpness with age and childbirth. Like Josephine, she was tall. Taller than Napoleon. But in spite of her solid frame, the poor girl looked as if she strained to keep her neck upright under the massive diamond crown that covered her head. I followed my husband, bowing before the pair of newlyweds.

"Ah, Bernadotte, you are welcome here. And my dear sister, Desiree."

Napoleon really did look quite round in his ermine cloak crusted with diamonds. He wore a satisfied smile—everything was going according to plan. He was pleased with his bride. He was pleased with the peace it had brought between France and Austria. But most important: he would have a son. At last, after all these years, his succession might finally be secure.

Following the feast, we were invited to dancing at the mansion of Austria's Prince Karl von Schwarzenberg—a family friend of Marie Louise's—whose diplomacy had been helpful in facilitating the marriage. My husband loathed the man as he did most Austrian ministers, but we knew that Napoleon would notice if we were not there. These days, my husband could not risk arousing our Emperor's temper.

"We will go, dance one dance in front of him, and then slip away," my husband grumbled. It sounded like a fine plan to me. I was just as happy to get home and under our warm covers. Outside, the rain still came down—inauspicious weather, though it didn't seem to dampen Napoleon's ebullient mood.

We took our places beside Julie and Joseph for the quadrille. I let my husband guide me, but I noted how his steps fell heavily, so unlike his usual grace on the dance floor. As the music progressed, I began to detect an odd smell and I crinkled my nose. My husband noticed as well. My eyes traveled toward the far side of the room, where a flurry of activity had broken out. I saw why, and I screamed: "Fire!" Bernadotte followed my gaze. There, against the far wall, the flames from the candles had traveled to the muslin drapes, setting them ablaze. The room was rapidly filling with an oppressive cloud of smoke. I began to cough.

"It's spreading. Come." Without hesitation, Bernadotte pulled me off the dance floor and we ran to the door. Julie and Joseph were beside us. I heard screams as we dashed out into the forecourt, gasping in the clean night air. All was chaos around us; there were so many hundreds of people inside the *palais* and only a few doorways. Through the windows, I looked with horror as the entire hall succumbed to a roiling blaze of orange and smoke. More shrieks, but I could not see Napoleon or our new Empress; I did not know whether they had made it out. All the while, the flames showed no signs of stopping. Soon, if it continued at this pace, the whole palace would be engulfed in fire, with hundreds of souls still trapped within.

# Chapter 35

*Paris*
*Spring 1810*

"HE BELIEVES IT TO BE A CURSE," BERNADOTTE EXPLAINED. "A curse on his marriage—indeed, on his succession."

We lay in bed, my legs interwoven with my husband's. I had felt unwell for days, the sickening smell of fire still clinging to my nose and skin and hair, and I held on to Bernadotte now, hoping to draw comfort from his tall, strong frame. My sleep had been troubled ever since the tragedy of Napoleon's wedding ball, pierced by the screams of all those poor souls trapped within the burning building. How easily it might have been us, had we simply stood on the other side of the hall, had Bernadotte not pulled me quickly to safety. How would Oscar possibly navigate such shifting and dangerous days as an orphan? I shuddered once more, forcing the thought from my mind.

The days immediately following the disaster were filled with waiting; all of Paris waited as firemen and gendarmes combed through the rubble for any possible survivors. Once it was all settled, it was counted that a handful of people had burned to death, including Prince Schwarzenberg's own sister, whose charred corpse had been identified by her massive family diamonds. The Emperor's sister Caroline narrowly survived, but she lost the baby she had been carrying in her womb.

Napoleon was so horrified by the catastrophe that he ordered the creation of a new fleet of public firefighters throughout Paris. But superstitious as he was, he believed his marriage already doomed, his dynasty once again in peril.

"Now he will be even more paranoid, even more restless. He will never stop making war," my husband said with a sigh. The night was dark, but neither of us could sleep.

"With whom will he make war?" I asked. "He's married into the Habsburgs."

"There will always be another enemy. England. Prussia. Perhaps even Russia?"

I turned to Bernadotte, ran my fingers through his dark hair, noting errant wisps of gray. My husband was aging, I noted to myself. "Perhaps she'll give him a son. And quickly," I ventured. "Perhaps he'll be content to stay put and play the role of papa, of husband. Even just for a bit."

Bernadotte grunted, a noise to indicate that he did not share my same hope. After a long pause, his words pierced the silence: "My darling?" His voice was tender in the dark, a bit tenuous.

"Yes?"

"I will die if we stay here."

I felt my frame stiffen in his arms—I was certain he felt it, too. What did he mean by such a horrific statement? Hadn't these past days been grisly enough? Bernadotte continued: "He will never stop fighting in Europe. Never. Because he will never be satiated. Each new victory, rather than bringing him closer to peace, draws him deeper into his paranoia. I am sure of it: I will die, either on his battlefield at the hands of the Prussians or Austrians or British or Russians. Or else . . . I will die by his orders."

Now I was genuinely distressed, because I sensed how earnestly my husband meant his words. "How can you say such a thing?"

"He's trying to get rid of me," Bernadotte said. "Has been for some time. He offered me Governor of Rome. You know what has happened to his generals in Rome—it's a city hostile to us. Even more so now that our Emperor is keeping the Pope under house arrest."

My heart clenched. In my mind, I was standing in a Roman palace, staring out a window: darkened streets, crowds gathering to curse France, screaming figures clambering over a fence that suddenly seemed ludicrous in its futility. "Duphot," I said, my voice sounding strangled as I uttered the name.

"That's right." Bernadotte glowered. "And the point is, Napoleon wants me out."

"I won't go back to Rome."

"You don't have to, my darling. I'd never accept the post."

"What did he say? When you turned it down?" I asked.

"He called me a hotheaded Gascon. Told me I don't know my place."

I grimaced, taking my fingers to my forehead and slowly rubbing my brow.

"He hates me," Bernadotte added. "Since Wagram. Or perhaps before that—the battles at Jena and Eylau as well. But really, I suspect it took root even earlier."

I turned and glanced sideways toward my husband. "Why?"

His eyes held my own in the dark. "You."

"Me?"

"You, and Oscar. He sees our happiness. He sees our son. He sees what he could have had—he hates that he chose to forgo it. And he hates me for getting what might have been his. My happiness stands in censure of his stupidity. He grows ever more hostile toward me with each passing month." Bernadotte exhaled slowly, emptying his breath completely. Eventually, he said, with a tone of finality: "We must go."

I was grateful for the bed beneath me, because my body felt weak. "Go?" My voice sounded hollow. "Go where?"

He slid out from under the covers now and hopped to standing. He began pacing before our large bed. "Bernadotte? You are frightening me. France is our home."

"But really, does it feel like a home, Desiree? With Julie gone quite often, Joseph as King of Naples. And with Josephine out, you can't tell me that you feel comfortable at court. You were a member of the old order . . . but surely you see that times have changed. He . . . has changed. Or perhaps he is precisely as he has always been, only he's changed everything around us."

That was true, and that served to silence me a moment. It was true that I had no real place at court these days. At least, certainly not near Napoleon and not anywhere near his new Empress. She was a girl who preferred to speak German and surround herself with the close friends of her Habsburg homeland. Of course Napoleon, well, he was always looking forward, ceaselessly so—to the children who would come, to the victories he could win.

Bernadotte and I, we were of the past. I, especially, was of his past. I turned to my husband now, asking, "But . . . where would we go?"

Bernadotte paused his pacing, turning to face me. He leaned forward and pressed his hands onto the bed before answering: "Sweden."

"Sweden?" I repeated the name of the foreign country, frowning in my bewilderment. I knew nothing of Sweden—I could not even see in my head where it was found on a map.

"It's a northern country," he explained, noting my surprise. "On the Baltic Sea."

"But . . . they aren't French."

"No. But they are enlightened. They are very pro-French and seeking to strengthen their ties with us."

This did little to clear up my confusion. "But . . . don't they have a king of their own? A Swede?"

"Their King Gustav was an imbecile—feeble in body and mind. They forced his abdication. They put his brother on the throne, King Charles XIII, but he is old and without children. This once again leaves them vulnerable. Then they chose the king's cousin, but he just recently fell dead. He suffered a fit, slid from his horse, and was gone. So . . . their situation remains precarious."

"I still don't understand why they would turn to . . . Paris . . . for an heir."

"Much less to me, common-born as I am," my husband added, seeing my point. "I was as startled as you are when I first heard. But it does make sense on further consideration. They've fought a bitter war with Russia and lost—to disastrous consequences. They lost much of their territory in that defeat, and now they're scared they could lose their Baltic ports as well. They want to align with Napoleon; they have signed on to his Continental System. They know me to be related to him through marriage—thanks to you—and they remember me fondly. I oversaw their captured officers and prisoners of war during our campaigns in Prussia."

"Yes, I remember. The Swedes." My mind spun.

He crossed his arms. "I was kind. And I was fair. They remember me in Sweden, in the military but also the government."

"But . . . do such things happen this way?" I asked. "The crown of Sweden is simply up for offering?"

"They have sent their minister and diplomat, a man I once held as my prisoner, a Count Mörner, to Paris to meet with Napoleon."

"Oh?" My fingers felt cold as I gripped the bedcovers. Why did I feel as though things were already in motion—that I was being pulled by a wheel much larger than anything I could steer?

"Desiree . . . it looks as though they mean to offer me the crown."

My pulse raced. Bernadotte was entirely serious. "Think of it," he said. "King and Queen of Sweden."

"But . . . Bernadotte."

"Yes? What do you think?"

"I . . . it's . . . I—"

"Please tell me."

*Now* he yearned for my thoughts? I swallowed, my voice toneless as I answered: "My home is in France."

I did not like Count Gustav Mörner. Not through any fault of his own—in fact, he was a pleasant enough man, well-dressed and well-mannered, polite, eager to offer smiles and a soft voice to Oscar when he visited our home on the Rue d'Anjou. But I disliked him because I knew what he wanted and I knew why he visited; I knew what he and Bernadotte discussed once they shut the heavy oak door to my husband's study, closing me out.

My husband would leave these meetings with his cheeks flushed, his hair flying away from his face as though the discourse of these private conversations with the Swedes involved some intense physical feat. He was excited—I could see that. More so than I had seen him in years. Filled, suddenly, with a glimmer in his dark eyes, a sense of purpose enlivening his steps around our home.

I learned from Bernadotte in those weeks more about the strange northern place that was trying so hard to lure him—to lure *us*—to accept its crown. Sweden was a constitutional monarchy, with both a parliament and a king, but they would have no one to sit on their throne when their current monarch, an elderly man with little spirit and even less popularity, died.

Their government supported Bernadotte's appointment as heir to the Swedish throne, and so they dispatched a small army of ministers and diplomats to negotiate with Napoleon's government. It seemed as though our own Emperor could be brought around to the idea, based on what my husband was hearing from his friends in the court. All that would remain then was for Bernadotte to accept the crown. Or, perhaps more accurately, for me to accept the crown.

I had no desire to leave France. To leave Paris. It was odd—as strange and foreign as the capital had once felt to me, a young girl newly arrived from Marseille, somehow, over these many years, it had come to feel like home in a way that I was sure no other place ever would. I could not imagine leaving, particularly for some place covered in snow where the sounds and sights would be alien. More alien than even Louisiana in New France would have been.

And yet, France had proven a fickle companion to both my husband and me, hadn't she? France was a changeling—constantly shifting on us, swerving just when we felt as though perhaps we might finally have a sure footing underneath. Last year, I was in the inner circle of one Empress; this year, I could not understand the German being spoken by the new Empress.

All that spring, the Swedish ministers and diplomats kept knocking on our door at the Rue d'Anjou. I began to soften to the idea, gradually, for two reasons. The first was that I saw my husband hopeful again, invigorated by the idea, eager as he hadn't been in quite some time.

The second reason was that I came to understand that, even if Bernadotte *was* made King of Sweden, it need not mean that I would move there. At least, not permanently. Napoleon, who fancied himself a glorious and flying star, plucked crowns from the constellations with apparent ease; my sister had been named Queen of both Spain and Naples, her husband recently gifted yet another throne by Napoleon—and she was often in Paris. And I was Princess of Pontecorvo, after all, yet I had never even been there. Napoleon put crowns on the heads of Frenchmen as though they were as changeable as the season's hats. Wouldn't this mean that we could simply stay in Paris, even if we were suddenly named King and Queen of Sweden?

And what's more, would it not be good for my son, my boy, to have such an illustrious title added to his inheritance? Oscar Bernadotte, Prince Royal of Sweden—someday to be named a king of an ancient European power? It was more than I had ever dared to imagine for any child of mine. The thought did fill me with a giddy excitement.

And yet, as I began to warm to the idea of my husband's new assignment, it seemed that Napoleon began to waver on whether to approve it. Word came to us through the Swedes that Napoleon was suddenly avoiding their envoys and ministers, frustrating their diplomats by canceling meetings and neglecting to reschedule. Our Emperor's support for the venture had cooled.

"He is toying with me," my husband would rail, when he would hear from his Swedish visitors that they had had no response from the Tuileries. "He shows me no respect. Can't you see why I must get away from that man?"

Weeks passed in this way, with no word from our French court. Then, to our surprise, Count Mörner informed us that Napoleon had instructed the Swedes to offer the throne to Eugene, his former stepson, the child of Josephine. Eugene had declined the offer immediately, but what move, we wondered, would Napoleon make next? My husband was infuriated as Count Mörner began speaking dolefully about a return trip to Stockholm.

And then, just as spring warmed and blossomed, the trees around us ripening into the lush fullness of summer, an unexpected invitation arrived at our home on the Rue d'Anjou. The Emperor and Empress— I thought of Josephine at first, and only remembered it was Marie Louise after Bernadotte reminded me—wished for us to join them for dinner at the Tuileries.

We arrived early, ten minutes before six. It was a pleasant June evening, and the Tuileries gardens were in the full throes of early summer, the doves in the trees warbling softly in the bright light of Paris's long evenings.

We were shown into the Salon d'Apollon, where Napoleon and his new bride received us with tight, forced smiles. As she greeted my husband, I took in the appearance of my hostess.

Marie Louise appeared to me as a girl playing dress-up in her mother's lavish gown. It was not as though her manners and her posture were not flawless—they were; she was, after all, a Habsburg bride, and she had been schooled in the ways of a princess since her earliest years. It was more that she did not yet appear entirely at ease in her role as wife—or, perhaps, as Napoleon's wife. If the two of them had grown comfortable with each other, acclimated and intimate in their new union, it did not yet show in their body language, which was unnaturally formal, even aloof. And yet, as my eyes quickly scanned her appearance, taking in the rich sweep of her yellow satin gown, I noticed the first telltale signs of a new pregnancy: the soft swell of her belly, fuller breasts, the hint of a flush on her otherwise pristine skin. Napoleon would finally get his heir.

"Well then, shall we eat?" Napoleon said, apparently in no mood for cordial chatter. We nodded our assent and he led us into dinner, his wife walking stiffly beside him.

The meal was served, but Napoleon did not speak and so neither did we. Marie Louise made no attempt at small talk, in stark contrast to how Josephine had once conducted her own lively dinner parties at this same table. The food was cleared, and the Empress poured her husband's coffee.

It was only then that Napoleon propped his elbows on the table and looked at us, something clearly on his mind. "Bernadotte. My old friend."

My husband nodded, waiting for more.

Napoleon's eyes were two green stones as he said, "Shall we speak about Sweden?"

My husband cleared his throat, folding his hands in his lap as he accepted a serving of black coffee. "Sire?"

"I know that is what you came here to discuss."

"I came here, sire, at your invitation," my husband answered.

Napoleon stirred the cream in his coffee slowly, staring only toward my husband. I hoped that perhaps the happy fact of his wife's pregnancy might have put him in a more charitable humor, but I was not entirely certain that Marie Louise had told him yet. Surely he would have said something, had he known. He would never have been able to resist an opportunity to boast—especially on the matter closest to his heart. Finally, after a long pause, Napoleon said: "Very well, Bernadotte. You may have your crown."

Silence hovered around the table. Inside my chest, my heart galloped.

Napoleon took a slow sip of coffee, his gaze remaining fixed on my Bernadotte. "A fatherless Gascon lad," Napoleon said, grinning after a moment. "Too poor even to be an attorney. Now offered a throne."

What about a Corsican boy too poor to buy an olive farm? But I did not say it aloud. Bernadotte swallowed a gulp of coffee, shifted in his seat. Napoleon continued: "It is good. It is a monument to my reign and an extension of my glory. You shall be yet one more point on my star."

Bernadotte cleared his throat, and I knew that as he did so, he was biting back words that would only hurt his cause with Napoleon. So then, he really wanted this crown—enough to mind Napoleon and bridle his own hot blood.

"There is only one matter on which I will have your agreement," Napoleon added. "Before I can send you off into the great white north with my blessing."

"Oh?" Bernadotte raised his cup.

"I must insist on a clause that you, and therefore Sweden, will never make war against the French."

Bernadotte sipped his coffee, and I sensed that he was using the time to form his response. When he lowered his cup, he spoke slowly: "I understand the sentiments of that, sire. And though of course I agree with it in my heart, and my head, you must see why I could not agree to it as a fixed principle. That would make Sweden a vassal state."

Napoleon shook his head, a quick, tight gesture. "I must insist, Bernadotte. How can I allow you to go there with the chance that you might someday fire on your fellow Frenchmen?"

"But how can I agree to something that binds my son—er, Sweden's future monarchs?"

Napoleon looked toward me, perhaps wondering whether he might count on me to help make his case; I lowered my eyes. Apparently deciding against that course, Napoleon turned his gaze back toward my husband, sighing. "Very well. I see that you are in an oppositional humor, Bernadotte. Something new, eh? How might . . . one million francs . . . help my case?"

"Sire." Bernadotte shook his head, a sad smile creasing his dark features. "It's not a question of money. It's the principle."

Napoleon grinned. "It always is with you, is it not, Bernadotte?" But it did not sound as though Napoleon meant it as a compliment, and his face showed no mirth.

"Sir." Bernadotte leaned forward, his voice quiet. "Would you make me a greater man than yourself by requiring me to refuse a crown?"

Napoleon jerked upright in his chair, his entire frame going rigid. I felt the breath constrict in my lungs, suspended. Napoleon opened his mouth as if to snap at my husband, but in the next instant he checked himself, cut his words short. When the Emperor spoke, after a long pause, his tone was steady but filled with steel: "Very well then, Bernadotte. Go. And let our destinies be fulfilled."

In the coach on the return home, Bernadotte was subdued, even a bit solemn. I studied him in the shadowy light that seeped in through the windows. "So then, it is settled," I said. When he offered no reply, I added: "I thought you would be happier."

He took a moment before answering. "I . . . I am. It is simply, well. It's a big thing. King. An entire nation looking to me."

I shrugged. "It can't be that terribly difficult. Joseph is rarely in Spain." My voice sounded casual, but then my husband leaned toward me, pressing a hand into my arm. "Desiree, do you understand?"

"Understand what?"

"What it means?"

"You've told me: it means you'll be Prince Royal of Sweden, the heir to the throne. Just like you are Crown Prince of Pontecorvo. You'll go sometimes to visit, and then—"

"No, Desiree." My husband shook his head, his brown curls falling around his darkened face. "No, I won't simply *visit* Sweden. I shall live there. We all will. Oscar will be King of Sweden one day as well. And you will be Queen beside me."

The magnitude of it all did not truly pierce me until Bernadotte left in September, dressed as a Swedish officer, with a smiling Count Mörner in the coach beside him. Standing in the forecourt of the Rue d'Anjou, clutching Oscar's hand as we waved our farewells to the receding carriage, I could not help but think of Marie-Antoinette and Marie Louise; what an odd thing it was to take up the crown of a foreign land. Those princesses were taken to an island in the Rhine River, a slip of earth between nations, where they were ordered to shed their Viennese gowns for new Parisian ones. The curious things we did in order to win and keep crowns, I thought, even those of us from a country that had claimed, only years earlier, to reject all crowns.

Though my husband had spent the past few months furiously studying Swedish under a tutor, I had refused to join in the lessons. A part of me still clung to the hope that I would be allowed to remain in France with Oscar. I did not wish to go. I was a bride wed in battle, accustomed to prolonged separations; I could accept the distance and the time apart from my husband, as long as we would be permitted visits. But Sweden? How could I make my home in Sweden? All I knew of the country was that it was a region far to the frozen north—a place of great white bears and bleak, sun-starved days.

And yet, even as I held firm to my hope, the time of our scheduled departure neared, and Bernadotte still insisted that my place, and Oscar's, was in Sweden with him. We were to join him in time for Christmas, so, in November, Oscar and I prepared to say farewell to our homeland.

My sister was in Spain for the holidays, and so I reached out to an old friend, someone I had traveled with before and knew I could trust: Josephine's former lady-in-waiting Elise la Flotte. Widowed at a young age, Elise had never remarried, and she had no place at court now that Marie

Louise was installed as Empress, and so, to my great relief, she accepted my invitation to travel north to Sweden.

With Elise, I finished my packing and finalized the plans for our departure. We would leave Paris in a cavalcade of three coaches, bound for the northern city of Hamburg. From there, we would travel farther than I had ever been from home, north into Denmark, before crossing by boat over the Öresund Sound into Sweden.

What my new homeland would look like, I had little idea. Indeed, what my new life would look like, I knew even less.

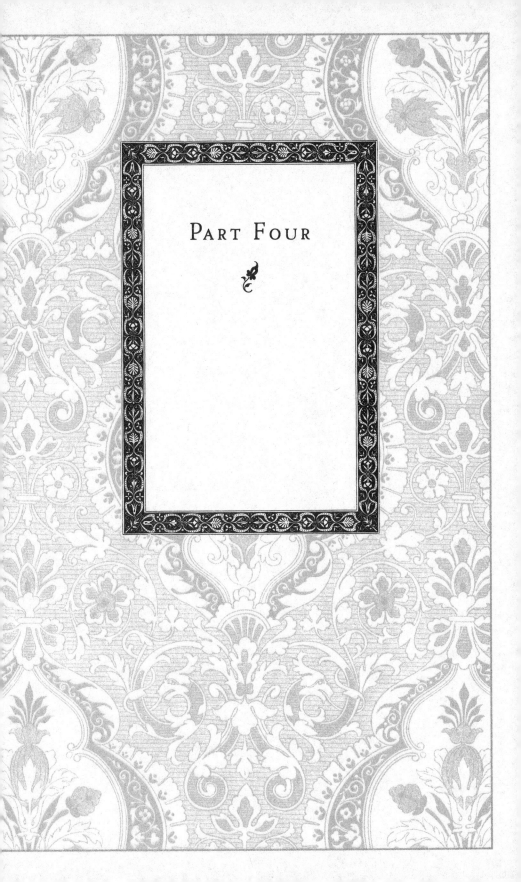

# PART FOUR

# Chapter 36

*Stockholm*
*Winter 1811*

"YOU SHALL HAVE TO CHANGE YOUR NAME." BERNA-
dotte said it to me as if it were the most mundane of statements.
And yet I knew that he understood my shock, because he was avoiding eye
contact as he inspected his Swedish military coat in the bedroom mirror.

I stared, openmouthed, toward my husband. Just behind him, on the
other side of the tall windows, the snow swirled, an erratic to and fro,
borne on a strong winter wind that seemed to blow relentlessly off the gray
water. I cleared my throat, winced at the soreness there, and looked back to
Bernadotte: "Change my name?"

He nodded. "It sounds too"—he grasped for his word, waving his broad
hand, still avoiding my eyes—"French."

I sat in bed under a thick comforter, propped up by half a dozen downy
pillows. In the next room, Elise oversaw the unpacking of my trunks while
Oscar sat with her, arranging his soldier figurines for some imaginary battle. I turned my focus back toward my husband. "Too . . . *French*," I said,
repeating his words.

"Indeed." Bernadotte swept his hands aloft, as if conducting instruments as he said: "Desiree."

"It's a French name," I replied, my tone wooden.

"Right."

"Because we are French."

"Yes, I know." He sighed.

I crossed my arms before my chest and leaned my head to the side, a posture of passive but stubborn resistance. "Presumably, the Swedish people understand this fact as well, seeing as they came to Paris to offer you their crown. They wanted you *because* you are French, Bernadotte. Connected to Napoleon."

"This is true, my dear," he said, exhaling loudly. An effort, I sensed, to remain patient. "But now we are *here*. In Sweden. Representing the Swedes. I believe . . . my ministers very much believe . . . that such a move would be received as a highly symbolic gesture. A token of goodwill to our new people, one they would very much appreciate."

"Well, Jean-Baptiste is as French a name as one could have," I said, my words now tinged with a childish petulance.

His dark eyes met mine as he answered, "Precisely. Which is why I've changed *my* name as well."

My mouth fell open. "You . . . have?"

He nodded. "Henceforth, in public, I shall be Carl Johan, Crown Prince of Sweden."

"Carl Johan," I said, repeating the odd-sounding name. I scrunched my face, unable—unwilling—to conceal my distaste.

"A good Swedish name," he said, turning back to the mirror, ignoring my expression.

I coughed before saying: "But not *your* name."

"I am to be their king. If I say that I've changed my name, it is changed."

So that was it? That was all it took to change one's name? One's nation, one's heritage? To wipe out an entire life? Was my husband so unfeeling, so unattached to our French lives, the lives we'd led together for so many years, to issue an edict and wipe away all that came before?

"I've asked them for some suggestions for you as well," he said.

I stared at him, felt the blood of my cheeks growing warm. "Have you?"

"They've suggested one."

I sat up taller in bed, twisting the handkerchief in my hands as I placed them primly in my lap. "Well? I would be interested to hear what they have proposed."

"Desideria."

I lifted an eyebrow; surely he was teasing me. But his face showed no signs of a jest. I looked away from him, back out the window. Gray. A vast vista of gray: iron-colored skies and stone buildings and choppy water, touched only by the white of snowfall. That's what it had been since we'd arrived. My first glimpse of Sweden had been one of chop and fog across the pewter gray Öresund Sound—a boat ride that I'd had to wait three days to take because of the inclement weather and the waves.

I'd arrived in Stockholm with Oscar and Elise in the middle of the night, our carriage bearing us through the snow-covered capital, a dark cold unlike anything I'd ever experienced. A gun salute heralded our entry into the city, where people lined the icy streets, cheering and waving their Swedish flags. How could they stand it, waiting as they did in the black and bitter wind? I myself had been wrapped in furs, encased in a covered coach, and yet I'd felt that I would never thaw.

I longed for color. Did the golden arms of the sun never reach this place? Even indoors, inside this unfamiliar and odd palace, I shivered. I remembered thinking that Paris had been cold, back when Julie and I had first arrived from Marseille. That had been nothing in comparison. Here, my nose was always red, my handkerchief always at the ready, and my throat burned with pain each time I coughed. Was I destined to never again live in the sun?

"The good news is that Oscar will not have to change his," my husband said, pulling my mind back to the present.

"What's that?" I asked, lifting my kerchief to my nose.

"His name, Oscar, it's a good Scandinavian name. No need to change it."

I shrugged my shoulders. "Well, I suppose we can thank Napoleon for that, then." Bernadotte frowned at me. "Why do you look at me like that? It *was* Napoleon, after all, who chose the name," I said, feeling no remorse for the barb against my husband in my current ornery mood.

"But he will convert to Lutheranism," Bernadotte said. Now I was certain he was joking. I laughed.

"Desiree, I am serious."

"Excuse me?"

"Oscar. He shall have to convert."

I grimaced. After a moment, I said: "But . . . but we are Catholic. France is a Catholic nation."

"Yes, but Sweden is a Lutheran nation, and we are the heads of Sweden. Oscar will be king someday. Sweden will only be ruled by Lutherans."

I made to say that I would never abandon my Catholic faith—not that I was particularly devout in my practice, but it was simply who I *was*. I was French. To be French meant to be Catholic. I'd been raised in the schooling of a convent. Even through the years of the Revolution, when all signs of a Catholic faith had been outlawed on fear of death, that strand of my identity had somehow continued, persisted. No pale Swedish minister would tell me that it could not be so. But before I could say all this, I began to cough. Oh, this cough; it had been terrible since Hamburg. My throat hurt, my head throbbed, even my gums ached.

"Your cough persists," Bernadotte said, a statement so obvious that it barely warranted a reply.

I made a grand show of my next cough to affirm his observation. He watched me, his frustration from a moment earlier turning to a look of genuine concern.

When I had recovered myself enough to speak, I said: "Of course my cough persists—how could it not, in this frozen place?"

He heaved a long, heavy exhale. "I shall order you a broth. And you must rest. You must get well."

"I *have* been resting," I answered. I would never be well. Not here. I pulled the blankets closer around my shoulders, eager to simply roll over and shut my eyes. To stop seeing, for just a few hours, this deadening view of gray. I yearned for color. Birdsong in a fragrant garden, tree branches heavy with blooms. The first bite of an orange slice, its juices like a burst of sunshine on my tongue. Perhaps my dreams could bring me some refuge, if only this soreness in my throat would allow me to drift off to sleep.

"I'll let you rest," Bernadotte said. He crossed the bedchamber, walking toward the door in several strides. I let him go without another word.

But he paused at the threshold, wavering, and turned back to me. "To-morrow . . ."

"Yes?" I opened my eyes and reached for my cashmere shawl, pulling it to my body, remembering as I did so the first time I'd bought myself cashmere—the colorful marketplace at Les Halles, with Julie, our first winter in Paris. I'd never needed it before, but now it seemed as if it was all I would wear.

Bernadotte looked away, out of the room toward the swirling snow, then back toward me. "Tomorrow will be your formal presentation to the court."

"You must tell us, my dear madame, what do you think of our palace?"

I stared into the oval face of Queen Hedwig; she was an unsmiling woman, with an unusually high forehead and bland, pale features. Her body, like her face, was long and narrow, and she wore an elaborate gown of golden damask, layers of lace cascading down her lengthy white arms. If she had once been a beauty, that bloom had faded along with her youth.

Elise, a far better gossip than I, told me that the queen had borne several princes, one-time heirs to the throne of Sweden, but all of her babies had died young; she had no hopes of producing more children. She was born a German duchess—I knew that from my husband—but she'd asked me the question in French. *Hedwig. What an odd name,* I thought. Hedwig Elisabeth Charlotte, now Queen of Sweden, wife to the sickly man beside her, King Charles. He fidgeted in his seat, appearing uncomfortable in his high-necked military coat and golden epaulets. A large, heavy-looking medal hung around his neck. His sparse white hair receded from a lined brow, and his narrow eyes darted nervously around the salon.

"Hedwig is in charge—everyone knows it," Elise had confided to me that evening as she helped me into my heavy dinner gown of dark purple brocade. "Though, outwardly, Hedwig declares herself more interested in sewing than in politics, I hear that, in fact, the opposite is true—she visits the king's private chambers every day to set the agenda, and she sits with him during the meetings of the council and helps him respond to his petitions and letters. So, have a care when speaking with her."

The king hadn't yet spoken to me this evening, other than a formal and cursory greeting upon my entry into the salon, but Queen Hedwig cleared her throat now, an expectant gesture on her features. "Well?" Hedwig prompted, lifting an eyebrow. She had asked me a question, but I had forgotten it. "Our palace?"

Ah, that was it—she wished to know what I thought of the palace. But how could I answer? To tell the truth would be to offend. How could I explain that I'd spent my days in the grandeur of the Tuileries and Fontainebleau? How could I describe for her the brilliance of Malmaison, with its massive, frescoed rooms? Endless galleries of priceless Italian art framed in gold. Gardens filled with swans and lilies of the Nile, unfurling with a splendor to shame Babylon. To think of those places, I found this residency to be as bland and unimpressive as any basic French army barracks.

"My wife, Your Highness, is a lady from the south," my husband said, stepping beside me, a broad smile turned toward Hedwig. "Marseille, if you are familiar with the city. She will be happier when spring comes." He, too, spoke in French. We were to begin our Swedish lessons soon, but for now, the court was obliging us by speaking in our native tongue.

"Ah, a delicate flower of the south." Hedwig nodded knowingly, as if to say that she had heard of my breed, though she herself most certainly did not identify with it. "And shall you be so sensitive in other aspects of life here at court as well, my dear girl?"

I turned from Hedwig toward my husband, unsure of how to answer.

The queen continued: "I hear you have the sort of constitution that renders you . . . shall we say, less adaptable?"

"I'm not . . . not certain what you mean, madame." I looked around the room, desperate for Elise to come to my rescue; perhaps she'd know how to handle this disagreeable woman.

"Your dear husband keeps requesting broth for you. And the servants tell me you ask for ever more blankets."

I stared blankly at my hostess for a moment, mouth agape. Josephine, born on a run-down plantation in the Caribbean, had presented a far more gracious and queenly bearing than this woman, groomed in her ducal castle since birth to wear a crown. I could not imagine Josephine ever making a new acquaintance feel so uncomfortable. Just then, dinner was announced, saving me from this dreadful conversation, and I gladly took my husband's arm as we made for the table.

It was my husband's forty-eighth birthday, and thus the banquet was in his honor. As the servants brought out the platters of food, I stifled the urge to draw my napkin to my nose and block the pungent odors of these dishes. "Madame?" A footman hovered beside me, his face expectant, gloved hands poised to serve from the platter he held.

"Oh . . . yes, please." I nodded. He leaned forward with a flourish of his silver fish spoons. As he placed a long, slimy, gray lump on my plate, my nose filled with the horrid scent of a salty, frigid ocean. I crinkled my face.

Before I could remember my manners and hide my scowl, Hedwig noticed. "Ah! She doesn't like our food, either?"

I looked up, away from the gray filet and toward my hostess. "No," I stammered, searching for the right words. "It's not that at all."

"It looks delicious," Bernadotte interjected. "What is this dish called?"

"*Inlagd sill*," King Charles said, joining the conversation for the first time. "Pickled herring is a national treasure of ours." He took a bite.

Hedwig's gaze was still fixed on me. "You poor thing. I suppose you long for a bouillabaisse, coming from Marseille."

"There, there, my dear, you must be nicer to our new arrivals." The dowager queen, the old woman named Queen Sophia Magdalena, tut-tutted beside her sister-in-law. "Why, I remember you yourself as a shy thing, if any of you can believe it." Sophia Magdalena, the widow of the former king, still resided at court even though her late husband's brother now ruled. I wondered whether that created an awkward tension between the two queens, one past and one present. I only knew that, as the queen of the future, I had no interest in joining any potential rivalry. I would happily keep to myself.

Hedwig ignored her dowager sister-in-law now, chewing her herring before posing another question toward me: "Will you join our faith, Desideria, as your husband and son have agreed to do?"

I glanced toward my husband—hoping to convey with my dark eyes that I had had quite enough of this woman's conversation and that he had better join in. But he was busy, speaking with Count Mörner and two other noblemen, brothers with the name of Löwenhielm, on the far end of the table. Ah, and there was Elise! I would have to make sure that she was seated beside me at future meals. But for now, both my husband and my lady were out of my reach.

And so, to save myself from further conversation, to avoid having to reply, *No, in fact, I intend to retain my faith, thank you very much,* instead, I lifted my napkin to my lips and began a horrid fit of chest-heaving coughs.

# Chapter 37

*Stockholm*
*Winter 1811*

"I BELIEVE THAT HER ROYAL HIGHNESS INTENDS TO SAY: 'I *have* a little boy.' Is that correct?"

"Yes," I said, nodding toward Oscar, unsure of my error.

Our royal tutor, a reserved Swede by the name of Herr Wallmark, eyed me with his earnest expression. "Well then, you might . . . that is, if it pleases Your Highness . . . instead say: *Jag har en liten pojke.*"

"*Jag har en liten pojke.*" I repeated the words, finding them guttural and odd.

"Very well done." The tutor nodded his approval.

"What had I said?" I asked.

"Your Highness had unintentionally said: 'I *am* a little boy.'"

Oscar and Bernadotte burst into laughter beside me, and I offered an apologetic smile as I answered the tutor: "It will come as no shock when I say that Swedish does not come easily to me."

"Nor will it come as a shock when we confess that we have not done our homework, my good man." Bernadotte pressed his palms together in a gesture of playful contrition. "We are terrible students. Only Oscar here has any hope."

"Your Highnesses simply need time," our tutor said, undaunted. "And practice does help."

But in truth, we were terrible, and I had little interest in practicing. We grew bored easily at our lessons, and why would I practice when the only people with whom I wished to speak were my son, my husband, and my lady—all of them French? As for the rest of the court, they were all fluent in French, slipping naturally into our tongue. It was the language of Europe, after all; Napoleon had seen to that.

Bernadotte, especially, relied on his French—particularly his Gascon flourishes—to tell the stories that entertained the whole court. It did shock me how at ease my Bernadotte was; it stood in sharp contrast to my own shyness—my slowness to make new friends or grow comfortable in the palace. At the dinners of state, he always ended up holding court, as if King Charles had already yielded the throne and the affection of his subjects. With his ministers, Bernadotte commanded a sort of casual respect and an easy camaraderie. He listened to everyone in silence, punctuating his observations with a well-placed joke or an appropriate question. He was absorbing the details of our new palace and learning the personalities of our new court much more easily, and willingly, than I was.

As late winter clung to the city, with its gray clouds hovering over our sky and the chilly air maintaining its hold over our palace rooms, I settled into a sort of reluctant rhythm. After his morning audience, Bernadotte would join Oscar and me for Swedish lessons with Herr Wallmark. Really, only Oscar showed any promise, but Bernadotte insisted that we all participate.

The tutor always turned to me first, knowing that my husband, or more probably my son, would need to sweep in to my rescue. "Your Royal Highness, would you be so kind as to describe the weather?"

There was a question I *could* answer. "*Snö!*" I declared, my cheeks flushing in my triumph. "That I know!" It was the word I'd heard every day since my arrival to this frigid city.

The tutor was delighted at my sudden enthusiasm, but Bernadotte frowned—he was growing tired of my complaining. I ignored my husband's stare, turning to my son. "Did you know, Oscar, that I did not see snow until I was nearly nineteen years old? You shall grow up covered in the stuff. Why, I don't believe I have seen sunshine in—"

But we were interrupted by a quick, unexpected knock on the door.

I looked to my husband. They knew we were occupied; I was shocked that anyone would dare to interrupt our private family time in this abrupt manner.

"Come in," Bernadotte answered. Count Mörner peeked his head around the doorway. Less surprising—the count had become my husband's constant companion and favorite confidant; he saw far more of Bernadotte than I did, even though I shared the man's bed. But the count's face looked grave now as he treaded slowly into the room. "Your Royal Highnesses." He was short of breath, as if he'd run the entire way here. He knelt. "It's the king, sir. King Charles. He's suffered a stroke. We are not sure whether he lives."

The king survived, but only to lie in bed, slipping in and out of sleep, a fragile husk of his former self. Not even Hedwig claimed that he was able to perform his duties as sovereign. Within days, Bernadotte was made Regent of Sweden, and thus he would be expected to rule in all but name. It was far sooner than anyone had expected—most of all our family. We had been in our new homeland only a matter of months.

As winter slowly thawed, the days began to stretch and the sun remained above the horizon for long enough to warm the earth. My husband spent long hours cloistered in his staterooms with Count Mörner, the Löwenhielm brothers, and his other ministers. He had petitions and reports flooding in from across his vast realm. In Stockholm, the various factions of the Swedish government were at odds, restless over the coming succession and shifts in power. But the hardest part of Bernadotte's new position came not from within the *Riksdag*, the Swedish parliament, nor from restless Norway or even hostile Russia. Our main troubles that spring were coming from France—from Napoleon himself.

The weather was warming across Europe, and thus Napoleon once more had war on his mind; he wanted my husband to join him in a renewed fight against England. The French Emperor wished, particularly, for my husband's ships to thwart British trading vessels in the Baltic Sea along our coast.

My husband's council balked; we were weakened after the devastating war with Russia and the loss of Finland. "Sweden has no direct grievance with England," my husband told me. What could we gain from beginning a conflict with the world's great naval power?

The news from Paris that I cared for was of quite a different nature. In March, I read with interest the reports that Napoleon had, at last, been given an heir. Marie Louise had safely delivered the boy, Napoleon Francois Charles Joseph Bonaparte, after just a year of marriage. *All of France is in a state of rapture,* Julie wrote. She described the parties across Paris— wine flowing from the fountains, fireworks, francs raining down over the ecstatic crowds who danced in the squares. Inside the Tuileries, there would be balls and champagne. I ached for Julie and yearned to stand beside her during those feasts and galas. It was horrible to be so torn; on the one hand, I knew that Napoleon and my husband were growing ever cooler in their already frayed relationship, and yet, I could not think of Sweden as my home. I longed only for France.

# Chapter 38

*Plombières, France*
*Summer 1811*

"IT'S NOT ONLY THE WATER," I SAID, SKIMMING MY BARE FEET along the surface of the warm pool. "It's the land. French land. That's my cure, more than any of these healing waters."

Julie laughed, plunging her palm beneath the surface and splashing a handful of warm water in my direction. "What? You mean to tell me that you enjoy waters where there aren't seals and polar bears swimming alongside you?"

"Do not speak to me of Sweden." I shivered, in spite of the summer air and the balmy water.

"The Countess of Gotland does not wish to refer to her vassal Goths?" Julie teased, referring to the alias name under which I was traveling.

"My cold will return just thinking about it. I've only just now thawed."

Julie and I were visiting the hot springs at Plombières, the spa resort nestled in the Vosges Mountains along the northeast of France. These waters had been considered curative since the Roman times, a popular destination for the ailing and weary. I remembered when both Julie and Josephine had come to these forested hills, desperate to become pregnant.

"How is she?" I asked, my eyes focused on the rippling waters even as my mind traveled elsewhere.

Julie sighed; she did not need to ask to whom I referred. "I haven't seen her in months; he keeps his visits to her secret. He doesn't want the newspapers to find out—or his court. Or, God forbid, his new Empress. But I hear that she weeps most days."

I nodded.

"She still loves him, you know," Julie said. "And he loves her, even if she isn't the one to have given him his son." Julie ran her damp fingers along her forehead, wetting her brow. The afternoon was a balmy one, but she would hear no complaint from me. "But she is . . . surviving."

"Of course she is surviving," I said. That was what Josephine did—she survived. That was what each of us did, in our own ways. That was our lot in life as women.

I had come to this spa town in the early summer on my doctor's orders, after my prolonged cold refused to depart with the waning Swedish winter. I'd traveled from Stockholm with Elise, who had been just as happy to return to France as I was. Julie had met me in these mountains, leaving her country estate at Mortefontaine to take the waters with me. We enjoyed languid days together—sleeping late, eating breakfast on the veranda of our suite at the Grand Hotel. In the afternoons, we took the waters and walked along the wooded paths, or took naps on the porch while the fresh air rustled through the trees.

My husband had been willing to grant me this trip, as it was prescribed for my health, but I had not been permitted to bring Oscar. Much as I lamented it, he was no longer my little boy, but was growing into a young man in line for the throne. He had turned twelve that summer and was now going through the paces of his formal Swedish education.

The summer days grew gradually shorter. Autumn approached; I felt it in the longer nights, the tinge of crisp, dry air in the mornings. The changing quality of the colors across the mountains, the light shifting into a sideways, golden glow.

"Stay here." Julie was the first one to put the idea into my head. "Stay in France," she said one evening at dinner. It was late August, and we both wore shawls around our shoulders, something we hadn't needed to do until recently; it was yet another unwelcome portent that summer was waning.

"I'm Queen of Spain, but you don't see me ensconced in the palace at

Madrid. Good lord, the thought of a Spanish summer!" Julie waved a dismissive hand. "If these men want to go around giving and taking crowns, let them. Why should we women have to suffer? Stay here. You still have your home on the Rue d'Anjou. Come to Paris with me for the winter. Oscar is content in Sweden. Bernadotte is busy with his duties. Why must you rush back, when it will compromise your health?"

It was true that the thought of the sea voyage back to Sweden terrified me—the idea of another winter in Stockholm, holed up in that palace with Hedwig, eating from platters of limp pickled herring. Barely seeing sunlight through the windows and certainly never feeling it on my skin. I began to weep and tremble just thinking of it.

The doctor, seeing my anxiety, hearing of the sleeplessness that my nerves brought on, forbade my return trip. "It would be counter to all of the progress Your Royal Highness has worked so hard all summer to make. What Your Highness needs is more rest, not an arduous journey along land and sea toward a frigid winter climate."

I wasn't certain that *hard work* was an entirely apt description of the summer I'd just passed, but I did not argue with the doctor's orders. It was true that Oscar was happy and Bernadotte was busy; what urgency was there for me to rush back to Sweden? I wrote my husband, telling him of the doctor's recommendation—no, *orders*—and hoped that Bernadotte would take the news well.

Bernadotte might take a mistress; it was a possibility with which I had to contend. No man could stand such a long absence from his wife—especially not a king who had the most beautiful women of his court constantly dangled before him. He would be presented with any number of willing lovers, but that was a reality I was willing to accept. If it kept him happy, if it maintained harmony between us and allowed me the liberty to remain in my beloved France, near Julie, well, it was the price of my freedom, and it was a price I was disposed to pay.

Julie and I greeted the New Year, 1812, with champagne and oysters in my home on the Rue d'Anjou. I was living in Paris as the Countess of Gotland, though of course members of the Bonaparte family knew my true identity. The Bonaparte sisters visited from time to time, probing for details of Sweden and my husband. I sensed the spy work in their questions; I knew they were reporting back to their brother, just as they suspected me of reporting back to my husband.

I missed my men, Oscar and Bernadotte, but little else of Stockholm. Paris was a city in the midst of a grand transformation. Napoleon was slowly and gradually changing the names of the streets and squares from their revolutionary and Bourbon origins to reflect the glory of his new empire. He was building a massive temple modeled on the buildings of ancient Greece—it would be called La Madeleine, and he would dedicate it to the men of his Grand Armée.

Aside from the ambitious building projects, the brilliant art collections, and the growing wealth of Napoleon's subjects, the city of Paris was uneasy that winter, a latent ripple of tension traveling on the cold wind. A great comet rested over us, hanging low in the winter sky; a bad omen, according to so many in our capital. *When will it move on?* the priests and scholars wondered aloud.

And where would it go—where would it take all of us?

Julie burst through my door. It was Bernadotte's forty-ninth birthday, and I was finishing up a small charcoal sketch of our beloved Parisian home that I planned to send him as a gift. "Desiree!" My sister had not waited for the footman to announce her entry before she found me in my sitting room.

"What is the matter?" I put my sketch down and turned toward her, my body stiffening.

"I had to tell you as soon as I heard," she said, panting. "Joseph does not wish me to say anything."

"Julie, please, sit."

She did, catching her breath a moment before explaining her frantic state. "Napoleon has invaded Swedish territory, the ports at Pomerania, and he's seized Swedish ships in the Baltic. I can't imagine that Bernadotte does not see this as an act of war."

It was Bernadotte's birthday; that was all I could think of as my mind struggled to make sense of Julie's news. Hadn't Napoleon, with his peculiar genius for details and dates, known it was his birthday? And yet he'd chosen this day for his attack on Sweden?

Julie went on: "You mustn't write anything. All your letters will now be read."

She leaned forward and took my hand in her own cold grip, looking down to see my palm smudged in black from my morning's sketching. And then I looked at my drawing—the unfinished outline of our home's façade. I had hoped to send this small piece of Paris, of our former life, to warm my husband's winter days in Stockholm. Now, I didn't know if that would even be allowed.

My husband declared a Swedish alliance with Britain and Russia within a matter of weeks—a move that could only make us the enemies of France. Shortly after that, I read in the newspapers that Sweden and France had broken off diplomatic relations. I thought of Napoleon's parting words to my husband, given on the same day as the Swedish crown: *Very well then, Bernadotte. Go. And let our destinies be fulfilled.* I had never imagined it would have come to this, and so quickly. But perhaps it hadn't been quick at all.

By spring, just as that feared comet moved on and out of France, so, too, did our Grand Armée. Napoleon had war on the mind once more, and he was marching east, toward the vast and untamed steppes of Russia.

Outside, the carriage traffic rattled up the street just as it did on any other day. Suddenly, though, the world beyond my window seemed a frightening and unknowable place.

As I was still living in Paris, I was in hostile territory. Correspondence with my husband would be considered letters into an enemy land, so I stopped writing. He did the same. All that reached me were Oscar's innocent letters, written in French, filled with news of his language lessons and his military studies, the Stockholm weather and the names of the new horses in the royal stables.

My life in Paris felt as if I might as well be on a separate continent, a place where uncertainty reigned and the threat of war lurked constantly, an immutable dark cloud hovering always on the horizon. I was protected because of Joseph's power in the family and in the court, but I was held at a safe and cautious distance. The only person who visited was Julie; otherwise, my home was considered the place of one hostile to France. The Bonaparte sisters stopped coming—they knew that my letters from Sweden carried absolutely nothing of political importance, since it was their brother's censors who read them, and so I was of no further use.

Despite not receiving letters from my Bernadotte, I knew in my heart how difficult it all was for him; he did not want to make war against his own countrymen any more than I wanted him to. But he was a man divided now, sworn to protect Sweden's interests, balancing the desires of new allies such as Russia and Britain and Prussia, all the while carrying the deep and abiding love in his heart that he would always feel for his native France. What he wanted, more than anything, was an end to this constant scourge of war across Europe.

But there was to be no end, it appeared. As the summer warmed, Napoleon was moving east, seizing Polish and Russian territory with apparent ease. He crossed the Neman River and marched into Russia with the largest invading army in human history, boasting, according to the triumphant French newspapers: "I will take Russia in twenty days." And it seemed that his boast was not exaggerated. We heard in Paris how the superstitious Russian peasants watched him crossing their land, believing him to be the coming of the Antichrist, the harbinger of the approaching apocalypse following the comet that we had all seen burning its way brilliantly across the sky.

The bells pealed from Notre Dame to Saint-Denis when the news arrived that Napoleon had taken Moscow. It was early autumn, and our cool Parisian night burst with the noise and color of massive fireworks. Napoleon declared victory. The Russians, unbelievably, had burned their own capital before abandoning it to the French.

And now, my husband was forced to honor his allegiance to Britain and

Russia, and he joined the army of nations against Napoleon. This meant that I, too, faced a harrowing decision of my own—attempt a winter journey across hostile roads and waters to return to my husband and our new home, or remain in the country that felt like home, but now viewed me as an enemy of the state.

# Chapter 39

*Paris*
*1812*

Perhaps even God himself had grown tired of the insults and had joined the alliance against Napoleon. That was what I came to believe, that's what people began to whisper all across Paris and France and then Europe, after the Russian snow and ice managed what all the armies of Europe had not. It was as Tsar Alexander had predicted: *A Frenchman is brave, but our winter will fight on our side.*

The Tsar had been correct; as conquering Frenchmen braced for the harshest winter in living memory, fear began to harden over the wind-swept steppes of Russia. More cold was yet to come, and thus, more disaster for the once-indomitable Grand Armée.

As winter rolled into Paris, so did news of a mounting disaster to the east. Napoleon had been speedy and successful on his march into Russia—but what of it? As Moscow burned, as the golden breezes of September turned into the biting winds of October, France's conquering army found itself in an untenable spot: their supply lines were fractured, food stores had run out, and the massive army was left stranded, trapped between a burned capital city and a wasteland of ice, snow, and angry Russian patriots.

I read in the journals that Napoleon ordered a retreat, but battering snowstorms made movement of such a large force nearly impossible.

Merciless winter temperatures sunk below zero degrees. I could see it all in my mind as it was described: horse corpses piling up beneath fresh piles of snowfall, soldiers' lips frozen together so they could not cry out in their agony. The men who did not freeze to death found themselves dying of slow and cruel starvation; desperate men resorted to eating their frozen horses and dogs. Rumors, even, of Frenchmen eating other fallen Frenchmen. Others who did not freeze or starve or go mad were stalked by Russian soldiers and angry peasants, eager to enact vengeance at long last.

Napoleon, seeing the utter uselessness of it all, fled on a horse-drawn sled, racing across the snow in his sable coat and fur-lined boots. I heard in Paris about how he had arrived back to the Tuileries in time for the court's Christmas balls, while his men, far from home and without food or boots, lost their limbs and their minds to ice and snow and frostbite. *Well*, I thought bitterly, *he always did know how to take care of himself.*

And now, the armies of Russia, Prussia, Britain, and, yes, Sweden were chasing Napoleon's ravaged army back across Europe. By spring, they looked ready to march into the French Empire. Julie and I sat together most afternoons reading the journals, or pacing my salon, wondering how it might all fall apart. All of Paris waited on the blade of a knife.

Napoleon, we realized, was not invincible, as we had all supposed him to be. In fact, these other nations might actually be able to defeat the man whom they saw as the scourge of Europe. But they could accept only complete and total surrender.

As the allies closed in on France, my husband was encamped with his army near Brussels, just outside our own French border. I wondered—my heart filling with longing for him, but also pain for Julie—if I would see him right here in Paris. I was grateful that Oscar was settled in Sweden, but I prayed for my husband's safe deliverance.

"The Russian troops are moving closer," Julie told me, in what had become her usual harried voice. "The Tsar's troops are already on French soil. Joseph tells me they are now an easy march from the capital. All of the Bonapartes are frantic."

Seeing the inevitable, Napoleon fled to Fontainebleau, the glorious castle I remembered as a place from a fairy tale; the place where he had shattered Josephine's heart. For her part, Josephine sped to Malmaison, her favorite jewels stitched into her undergarments. Marie Louise was staying in Paris with her son—no doubt excited at the idea of falling into Austrian hands.

I, too, saw the inevitable; my sister was married to Napoleon's closest ally. His favorite brother, his constant confidant. Joseph and Julie would have to flee, and so they made plans to travel to the west, where they would be near the Atlantic and a quick water escape.

We hugged farewell at my sister's mansion on the morning of her departure. No words could capture how I felt at saying farewell; no words could put any certainty on a departure that we little understood. For as long as I could remember, and even further back than that, Julie had been the one constant in my life. The defining relationship, more so than any relationship with my husband or son or even Napoleon. "The most dreadful thing about this," I said, swallowing back my tears, "what makes it harder than any farewell in our past, is that I don't know what comes next."

"None of us do, my dear," my sister said, her arms holding mine. "But then, when have we ever known, really? Certainty is not a luxury we have ever had, not in times such as ours."

With Julie gone, my body capitulated. I was carried to bed that afternoon, my chest racked with a cough, my limbs aching as rheumatism enflamed my joints. The physician came and mixed me a draught, which I swallowed in three eager gulps. I shut my eyes and burrowed into the downy plushness of my old bed, slipping into the welcome reprieve of a dark, thoughtless slumber.

The Russians were the first to reach Paris, marching in through the eastern barrier. From there it only grew—the Russians and Prussians and Austrians descended on the city, as the French remained indoors in a nervous and silent huddle. But where were the Swedes? I wondered.

I dared not go outside. I kept my gates locked and my doors barred, but through the sliver of my curtained windows, I could see bearded men—Russian Cossacks—in their braided wool tunics and blue pants. I could hear snippets of their odd, impenetrable language. To think, these were the same men who had burned their own capital rather than allow it to fall into enemy hands, and now, here they were, tying their horses at the front steps of our grand limestone buildings and peeing on our springtime shrubs. Tsar Alexander rode at the head of a grand parade down the Champs-Élysées. I heard from my servants that His Excellency was staying with Talleyrand in his magnificent mansion just off the Tuileries, a mansion that Talleyrand had been given by Napoleon. The Tsar was reportedly eager to meet Josephine.

I was afraid, but I didn't need to be. Ironically, I was safer now that the allied troops were in the city than I had been under Napoleon's reign. I was the Princess Royal of Sweden, married to one of the heads of the coalition, even if I did in my heart still identify as a Frenchwoman. I just wanted my Bernadotte to be here with me.

Week after week, I waited. Every clamor of footsteps below brought with it the fresh hope that I'd see my officer, Sergeant Belle-Jambe, riding up at the head of a Swedish force. But he didn't come.

On Easter morning, I awoke to a riot of church bells. I pulled on my silk dressing robe and descended the stairs, wondering if the servants had picked up any news on their morning errands. There, in the grand salon at the foot of the stairs, my eyes landed on a sight I had not been expecting—one that brought tears of relief and joy to my sleepy eyes.

"Happy Easter, my darling girl."

"Bernadotte!" I ran to my husband and flew into his arms. "At last! Oh, I have been waiting for you. Thank goodness you've come."

He pulled back to take me in his arms for an inspection. I also swept his entire figure with my appraising gaze and could not help but find him dashing, dressed in an officer's tunic of plum velvet with a high collar and gold epaulets. He wore white breeches and high boots. His hair was longer and his face ruddy from such a long march. He offered me a weathered smile as he said: "You look well, my dear."

"Oh, but I've been sick. Sick with worry." I pulled him to the nearest sofa and sat him down. "What took you so long?"

"War, my dear. Napoleon was not easily conquered."

We sat together for hours as Bernadotte told me of the fighting of recent months. The final battle had come at a decisive gathering known as the Battle of the Nations, near a German city called Leipzig. Napoleon had been defeated, but his government had been quick to make its own separate peace. "Talleyrand is already hosting the Russians," I told him.

Bernadotte nodded. "Yes, and we hear that Josephine has entertained the Tsar in her gardens in Malmaison. And who knows where else."

"Good for her," I said, clasping my hands in my lap. "She would have fled with him and remained by his side, even in defeat. But he put her aside, taking up with his Habsburg princess when it suited him better."

"And now that Habsburg wife has betrayed him," Bernadotte said, sighing. "He should be little surprised. She'll raise his boy in Vienna, and he'll grow up to think of his father as the enemy."

I blinked, my mind spinning to absorb this stunning turn of events. All in a matter of months.

"But what has it been like in Paris?" my husband asked.

"Quiet, at least among the French," I said. "Most retreated indoors. I haven't gone outside. The foreign troops have been here, of course. But I've been seeing the Bourbon fleur-de-lys on the lapels of those who walk about the city."

Bernadotte listened, nodding decisively. "Louis XVIII will be put on the throne—the dead king's brother. France's top generals have denounced Napoleon and taken an oath of loyalty to the Bourbons." Now his brow creased, and I noticed that his face bore new and deep lines as he frowned. After a long exhale, he said, "It was all for nothing, in the end."

"Why do you say that?" I asked.

"Because Napoleon ruined it."

I leaned forward, my hand reaching for his. "But you are safe, Bernadotte. And so am I. We will be all right, won't we?"

"Yes, we will be all right. Sweden is part of the alliance." But he looked neither happy nor relieved as he said it. "And even France shall be better off as a result of this defeat. He is gone, at last. The diplomacy is up to Metternich and the Tsar and Talleyrand now."

"What about you?"

My husband was on edge, I could see that as he fidgeted in his creaky seat, his tall frame suddenly appearing unwieldy and restless. "They show me little respect. I've tried to advise them throughout the campaign, but the audiences are always brief and inconsequential. Should they treat me as French or Swede? Foe or friend? They can't seem to make up their minds on that."

I reached for him, putting my hands on his rough, chapped skin. He let out a slow exhale. I knew how tortured he was by the fact that he had been forced to fight against the French. To put on the uniform of the same enemy against which he'd been willing to give his life on so many other occasions. What a mad time in which we lived. "Darling," I said, searching for the right words, words that might grant him some small measure of comfort. I wanted to remind him that he was a leader now; he was worthy of his place among kings, even if he felt like only a soldier without a country.

But before I could find the words to say this, to lift him from his anguish, Bernadotte's whole frame was suddenly racked by a sudden and violent shudder. "Oh, Desiree!" He began to weep, something I had seldom seen him do. "The pain I felt in crossing into these lands alongside a conquering army, lands I have so many times defended with my life. And then to hear of the devastation of the French. I gave money from my own purse to the captured French soldiers, do you know that? I wish I could have done more. But now, I feel like a traitor in my own lands."

"You are no traitor, Bernadotte."

"I was not fighting against France, I was fighting against *him*. You believe me, right?"

"Of course I do."

"He has ruined our nation for our countrymen. He has ruined the Revolution and everything for which we fought. And do you know what he did? He's attempted to poison himself at Fontainebleau."

I gasped. "Attempted? Then, he didn't succeed?"

Bernadotte shook his head. "No, he lives on to see the full scope of his defeat."

"What will become of him?" Even more pressingly, what would happen to my sister and Joseph? But that had not yet been decided.

"It will be exile for him," Bernadotte said. "He can sit on the isle of Elba and torture himself with memories of his failure. Thinking about the abandonment of his wife and son, and his own abandonment of his men."

# Chapter 40

*Rue d'Anjou, Paris*
*Spring 1815*

I AWOKE TO THE HEADLINE AND KNEW INSTANTLY WHAT it meant, though it was only a single word:

NAPOLEON!

He was back, according to *Le Moniteur*. He had returned to Paris, escaping his exile on the rocky island of Elba. Within minutes of seeing the journal, my entire household was in a state of disarray. Elise burst into my bedchamber clad in only a thin dressing gown, her loose hair tumbling around her flushed face. "Does he rule once more? Is Louis gone? Should we go to the Tuileries? Send a note?"

I ordered a servant to go out into the streets to gather more information, and by luncheon, we had some answers. Napoleon ruled France once more, the servant told me, breathless. He had escaped and sailed, in secret, from Elba with just a small force of loyal men.

"Why do I always feel as though Napoleon catches me completely unaware?" I asked Elise, who sat across the table; neither of us was eating much of the lunch.

"Because he *does*," she answered. "He catches us all unaware. All of

Europe. You can be sure that no one is more alarmed at the moment than Austria's emperor."

I shook my head, looking down at the fish on my plate, considering all that had happened as the rest of us slept, completely unsuspecting. Napoleon had made an arduous but stealthy trip back to Paris. He'd landed on French soil on the southern coast, camped out in the mountains near Cannes, and marched over the Maritime Alps and up through Provence in secret. For eighteen days, he had moved, undetected and entirely unopposed, toward Paris. Only the army knew, and excited whispers had spread in secret, the fires of a beacon seeping its light across the nation; officers and enlisted men rallied to his side, swelling his numbers until he had a veritable army. "Paris or death," they whispered as they marched toward the capital with their one-time Emperor.

They'd arrived in Paris several weeks later, under cover of darkness. Louis, our fat, gouty Bourbon king, had been hoisted from bed by frightened attendants, packed into a carriage, and whisked from the city. Unlike his dead brother, the unlucky Bourbon namesake who had ruled before him, Louis had made it successfully across the frontier and into Belgium before forces favorable to the Emperor caught him.

Napoleon marched into the Tuileries unopposed and declared himself Emperor of France once more, greeting the shouting crowds who had flocked there to welcome him home.

Paris erupted into a state of stunned celebration.

Europe's leaders scrambled, aghast, while in the Tuileries Napoleon ordered his men to rip the Bourbon fleur-de-lys off the walls. The rumor popped up that the Bonaparte bee insignia was still woven into the underlayer of the carpets and drapes of the palace, and David's imperial paintings were pulled from storage and hung back in their original places.

I considered all of this, wondering if ever a woman had felt so divided—in her mind, in her heart, indeed, in her very soul. While I was unsure how my Bernadotte was receiving this news from his Stockholm palace, I was certain of one fact: Julie would come back to Paris. And that filled me with a greater joy than I had allowed myself to imagine.

Several days later, my sister was back, she and Joseph installed with the rest of the Bonaparte family in the Tuileries Palace. She sent word for me to come to her.

"Will you go?" Elise asked, brushing my hair before the mirror in my dressing room. Errant strands of silver now laced the dark waves, but my eyes shone with the excitement of the recent days. Perhaps I still retained some of my girlish charms. "Of course I will go," I said.

"Would he . . . wish you to?"

I eyed her reflection in the mirror; to whom was she referring? Bonaparte or Bernadotte? "Your husband," Elise clarified.

I evaded the question, simply stating matter-of-factly: "She is my sister."

It was a chilly March morning, but the Tuileries courtyard was abuzz with activity, soldiers marching in tight formation, citizens gathered in ongoing celebrations of the Emperor's return. If I paused and looked around, I could almost imagine that nothing had changed, that it was simply another feast day and I had never heard anything but *Vive l'Empereur!* shouted across these grounds.

I entered the palace, stepping gingerly past the guards who were dressed once more in Napoleon's imperial livery. I found my sister on the ground floor, bending over to examine a roll of bound carpet. "Desiree!" She immediately paused her task and ran to me, taking fists of her skirt in her hands so she could cross the massive room quicker. I fell into her arms. I didn't know whether I'd ever enjoyed a happier reunion with a loved one.

"I'm so happy to see you," she said, her breath warming my neck.

"As am I."

"We have so much to discuss. You can help me. Come." Julie took my hand and we walked briskly down the long portrait gallery, entering the music salon. Louis had redecorated—I noted how he had reupholstered much of the furniture with his favored icy blue and white hues, but the room still hit me with a haunting familiarity. How many nights had we spent here, watching Josephine at her beloved harp, or listening to songs, playing cards, and trading gossip?

Julie did not have time for nostalgia as she said, "There's so much to do. He's asked me to lift the carpets, because the servants have told him that the Bonaparte bees are still underneath. Will you help me?"

We hoisted the nearby carpet and, as expected, the imperial carpet was still there. Josephine's carpets—the ones she'd had custom-ordered at such great expense. We knelt beside each other, looking them over in thoughtful silence. "It's his son's birthday, you know. He turns four," Julie said, her voice suddenly quiet. "Napoleon has declared it a state holiday."

I noted the date, March 20, in my head. "That's right," I said.

"He longs for her to come," Julie said, and I knew to whom she referred. Marie Louise. Titular Empress of France once more, but still a Habsburg princess in her heart; she had not been back to Paris since his defeat.

"Where is she now?" I asked.

"In Vienna. With her family. Word is that she has taken up with another lover, a one-eyed Austrian officer who fought Napoleon for years."

I gasped. "Does he hear these rumors?"

"Of course he hears the rumors. He hears everything. But he won't believe them. He can't."

"*She* would have come," I said, my tone heavy. "She would have flown to his arms. In fact, she would have been on Elba with him and probably would have sailed the ship back for him."

Julie and I both slowed our work for a moment, reflecting on the lady whose ghost still filled so many of these rooms, for Josephine was dead. It had been shocking to us when it had happened: she'd died within days of Napoleon's exile to Elba. One evening she was hosting the Tsar at Malmaison, the next morning she was gone. There were whispers that she had been poisoned by our new Bourbon king, that her popularity with the people had made her a threat to the new regime, but I knew better. She'd died of grief; she'd always said she did not wish to live without Napoleon, and she'd held to that vow, even if he'd put his aside.

"You know the first thing he did when he got back to Paris?" Julie said. "After greeting the soldiers and declaring the restoration of his reign?"

I thought, venturing a guess: "Checked on his military supplies?"

Julie shook her head. "He went out to Malmaison. He visited her grave. Joseph said he wept the entire time. He said: 'Only death could have broken the union we shared.'"

"So he still worships at the altar of Josephine," I said, staring at the other carpets around the salon that we had still to lift and replace. "I pray she is at peace, even if I know that he will never be."

We knew it would be war. It was inevitable. The rulers of Europe could not allow their order to be so unceremoniously disrupted. Paris was abuzz with activity, and our depots and recruiting stations swelled with enthusiastic volunteers from across the nation.

Marie Louise finally responded from Vienna, but it was not the message for which her husband had hoped; she petitioned for a formal divorce. She would not leave Vienna, nor would she allow her son to return to Paris and his father. He was without an heir after all. I could only guess how Napoleon, holed up in his private rooms, received this most grievous of news.

There was a parade that afternoon in front of the Tuileries, and thousands of Parisians turned out for it, for the chance to see the Emperor atop his horse once more. I stood beside Julie and Joseph as Napoleon passed by, reviewing his troops and nodding down at the cheering crowds. He wore his general's uniform once more: bicorn hat, dark jacket over a white waistcoat and breeches, his fleshy neck squeezed by his high black collar. His alert eyes darted about as intently as ever, and he kept a look of intense focus as he surveyed his men and the throngs crowded together. Joseph waved the tricolor while all around us people shouted the "Marseillaise" national anthem.

Julie looped her arm through mine, leaning close to speak over the deafening crowds. "It's as though he never left, isn't it?"

I blinked, staring at the back of the receding figure as Napoleon's horse carried him past us and into the ceaseless mass of bodies lining the route. All of Paris was celebrating. But for how long?

As spring ripened, glorious and inevitable across Paris, a frontier darkened by war loomed before us. Napoleon dismissed all the changes to the con-

stitution and legislature since the Bourbon restoration, but he vowed not
to punish those who had held positions in that government. He wished for
a unified empire once more.

But so, too, were our enemies united, and by late spring, they had declared war against France. Suddenly, all Frenchmen of the fighting age
were called into military service. From Vienna, Marie Louise declared herself officially aligned with the allies fighting against her husband. And my
husband, ruling from Stockholm, was once again at war with his—and
my—homeland.

The French army left a few weeks later to face the enemy assembling
across our border, and the forces met at a crossroads near a rural village in
Belgium. "It's an odd name for a place," I said to Julie, scanning the journal
before me. "Waterloo." The writer for *Le Moniteur* predicted that any upcoming battle could be decisive.

It was early summer, and Julie and Joseph were staying with me on the
Rue d'Anjou, for fear that the Tuileries could be unsafe if the French forces
were not victorious. I was grateful to have them, not only because it meant
that my sister and I were together, but also because I was with Joseph when
the updates came in from his brother.

The day after the Waterloo battle, Joseph received the letter. Julie and I
sat silent but impatient as he read. "We lost," he said, his face going white
as he quickly scanned Napoleon's note. "A decisive loss. A crushing one."

Julie looked as though she might faint. My mind flew to my husband,
who I knew wasn't fighting at Waterloo but was in support of the allied
forces from Stockholm.

"But he tells me that all is not hopeless," Joseph said, reading on. "He
believes that he might be able to reassemble his forces. He will come back
to Paris immediately. Rally the support of the government, rouse the patriotism of the people."

"And what are we to do?" Julie asked, staring at her husband with the
same fear and uncertainty that I myself felt.

"What can we do, *ma chère*?" Joseph asked. "We wait for Napoleon."

Napoleon was back in Paris within a week, but the rallying cry he had
hoped for did not greet him. In fact, following the blow at Waterloo, his
parliament turned on him, with our one-time national hero the Marquis

de Lafayette leading the ministers in a vote to oust our returned Emperor. Meanwhile, the British navy was blockading French ports as, once again, Prussian and Austrian forces were marching into France and toward Paris.

Seeing the inevitability encircling from all sides, Napoleon abdicated just days after his return to Paris, declaring his intention to move to America. "Will they really allow that?" I asked Joseph. We sat in a modest, nondescript coach, traveling incognito from the Rue d'Anjou to the Tuileries, invited there by Napoleon.

Joseph shrugged. A meaningful look passed between him and my sister, and my sister looked away. I could read the tension on her face, the tightening of her pale features, but I did not know what it meant. I would have to ask her later.

We rolled into the forecourt, where soldiers and footmen and other imperial staff were in a frenzy of activity. The allies would arrive any day, and the French forces that had not already fled were now preparing for surrender. We entered the palace with our heads tilted down, our eyes avoiding any contact.

"My dear, I need you for a moment." Joseph put his hand on Julie's back, guiding her toward the grand stairway. "We are packing up the bedrooms, and we must sort through some final items."

Julie looked from her husband toward me. "Will you be all right? On your own?"

"It will only be a few minutes," Joseph said. "We don't really have more time than that."

"I will be fine," I said. "Go."

They left me, and I made my way through the ground floor, hardly alone amid the hordes of household staff, but slipping silently into my own thoughts. Servants were hurrying to pull down all the artwork, which they no doubt wished to move to a safe place in case the allies burned the palace. I stared at the endless rows of priceless art—Italian, Dutch, Spanish, and German masterpieces. He had amassed it all—and now where would it go? The splendors befitting a glorious empire. The grandest kingdom on the globe. And such an empire would still have been his, but for his insatiable stretching and reaching and grasping.

I was so mesmerized in these musings, in studying the chaotic scene before me, that I did not notice anyone behind me until I heard my name spoken aloud. "Desiree?"

Napoleon's voice. I turned, startling as I met his face. "Oh, hello. I didn't see you."

"And I was beginning to think I had lost my knack for stealth," he said, his tone wry.

I offered a sad laugh, staring into his eyes, studying the man I had once loved. I had not seen him this close, in private, in years—since before his exile. The years had not been kind to him; his hair had thinned around the ears, and he was now completely bald on top. His skin, once a golden shade, was ashy pale, and his green eyes, usually so alert and all-knowing, now darted about the gallery with a listless, agitated quality. The servants continued their work around us as he leaned close and asked me: "How do you do?"

I shrugged. There was no way to answer such a question. "You?"

He ignored my question, his restless hands clasping and unclasping before the round paunch of his stomach as he said: "Your sister will be safe, always. I want you to know that."

I lowered my eyes. "That is a relief to hear. Thank you."

"She will have to leave France, of course. But she will not be harmed. And Joseph is a good man."

I nodded. "He is."

Napoleon watched me closely. "And he makes your sister happy?"

"He does," I said. "Theirs has always been a happy union. I am . . . glad for them."

"To think, you could have had him."

I looked away, down the long hall of the gallery. Such ancient history was better to remain buried in the past.

Napoleon spoke again: "Your sister is a lucky woman, to be married to my brother."

"Indeed," was all I said in reply.

He followed my gaze, staring out over the hundreds of pieces of art, the priceless collection that he would now have to decide how to handle. "You know . . . Joseph has offered to change places with me."

I turned toward Napoleon, my eyes widening in shock. Joseph, change places? Bear the punishment so that his brother might slip away, free? Ah, so that was the cause of the tension I had sensed between Julie and Joseph in the coach. Her husband had made this offer, and my sister was furious over it.

"I've refused him," Napoleon said, sensing the distress I felt on behalf of Julie. "He has already given so much of his life to me; I cannot expect him to forfeit it entirely."

I swallowed, nodding slowly, feeling the relief wash over my entire body. After a long pause, Napoleon leaned close, whispering: "What about you?" He cocked his head to the side, holding me in his green-eyed gaze for what I knew would be the final time in our lives. I blinked, seeing, for just a moment, those same green eyes holding me from within a young, narrow, golden face. Wavy dark hair, thick and uncombed. The backdrop a fragrant garden where the warm breeze carried on it the sound of birds, the distant horn blast of a ship pulling into the seaside harbor. I blinked, and it was gone. Napoleon stood before me once more with his pale, tired, bloated face. And he was awaiting my answer.

"What *about* me?" I asked, not sure of the meaning of his question.

He fidgeted his hands, as if unsure of where to put them, but his eyes he kept focused on me. "Are *you* lucky, Desiree? In your choice of spouse?"

I shifted my weight, avoided his appraising gaze. Before I could say anything, he added: "We know that you are better off . . . that you did better with Bernadotte than you would have done with me. But does he make you happy?"

I straightened my back, my voice quiet as I answered, "Yes. He does."

Napoleon nodded, his eyes still affixed to me as he said, "Good. Yes. I am glad then." And then he forced a smile—a worn, joyless expression as he sighed, saying: "I was luckiest of all. Josephine was the wife who would have come with me to St. Helena. But I threw it all away."

# Chapter 41

*Stockholm*
*January 1818*

"A TOAST TO HIS ROYAL HIGHNESS, THE PRINCE ROYAL."
Queen Hedwig raised her champagne flute, tilting it in my husband's direction as cordial murmurs of assent rose up throughout the large banquet hall. Outside the palace the night was frigid, with a steady curtain of snow falling over the city, but inside the hall, where hundreds of candles shimmered off the elaborate jewels and clothing of our guests, the space shone bright and warm. We were not yet in the somber period of Lent, and the court had gathered at a ball in order to celebrate my husband's fifty-fifth birthday.

"May you live in good health, sir," Hedwig added, as her husband the king nodded feebly beside her, giving his blessing to her toast, though of course we all knew that it was not necessary.

Now Hedwig turned her eyes on me, her taut smile no longer reaching her eyes as she said: "And to Her Royal Highness as well, who has finally returned to us, joining her husband and son, and her court, once more."

I offered a subdued nod of appreciation, lifting the cold champagne to my lips as I guessed that Hedwig intended an insult rather than a compliment.

I did not owe Hedwig an explanation; it had been my doctors, after all, who had urged me against returning to this northern climate, cold and unpleasant as it was to me in so many ways. They'd written my husband on numerous occasions to tell him that the sea journey alone would worsen my cough and put my fragile health in peril. I'd been more than willing to follow their orders, remaining in my mansion on the Rue d'Anjou and taking up an inconspicuous but somewhat regular place at the Parisian court of Louis XVIII, the Bourbons having been restored once more to the French throne.

And yet my husband's impatience had won out in the end. My prolonged absence was creating problems for him at the Swedish court: gossipers falsely accused me of having taken a French lover, and advisers openly urged my husband to petition me for divorce and remarry a fertile young Swedish noblewoman who would give him a brood of Stockholm-born princes.

Several women were openly vying for such a position. I would not have that; I would not have Oscar's birthright and future put in peril. Not after everything my husband and I had endured and survived in the madness of our world.

So I returned to Sweden, leaving France and the hope of an eventual reunion with Julie in exchange for the reunion with my husband and son. And here I was once more, in the throes of a northern winter, with the cold nights and even colder looks from Hedwig, the most powerful figure at court.

We expected that Bernadotte's ascendancy to the throne might come soon; King Charles hardly left his private rooms these days, and when he did, as on court occasions such as this, he appeared ever paler and weaker. And yet here was Hedwig, ensuring that he carry out his duties in public this evening of my husband's birthday banquet. "Well, then, shall we dance?" Hedwig posed it as a question, but she turned to her husband with an expectant look, urging him to rise. King Charles obeyed, and several attendants hovered as he slowly pushed himself up from his chair, his breath rattling in and out through ragged wheezes. He had to dance at least one, and then he would quit the hall to return to his bed.

"Bravo," my husband said beside me, nodding appreciatively toward the sickly king's great effort. Courtiers filled in around us to watch as Hedwig and Charles crossed the hall toward the musicians to open the dancing.

The violinists lifted their bows, the two dancers took their places, and just as the music started, King Charles collapsed in the center of the hall, falling to the parquet floor in a heap before his stunned wife. Gasps popped up from among our two hundred guests. The music stopped as Queen Hedwig screamed, her gloved hand flying to her mouth. Within a moment, she had regained her composure, summoning a fleet of servants to her side to lift her husband. She trailed behind as they left the hall in a hurry, the stunned courtiers' shouts of "Long live King Charles!" swirling in their wake.

*Stroke.* The next morning, the word spread like a contagion down the long, drafty halls of the palace. The enfeebled king had suffered a second stroke. The court waited for news as a team of physicians and priests remained huddled around the king, day and night. Stockholm was a city on edge as the gray, sunless month of January came to a close. My husband's ministers briefed him twice a day on the king's condition, once in the morning and once in the evening. Though not much changed in practice—my husband had already been acting in the role of regent—we sensed that a more official change would soon be taking place.

A week later, my husband and I sat in his private salon, playing bridge with Count Mörner and the Löwenhielm brothers. A small cluster of musicians gave us song, and with the day's official duties completed, we were in a relaxed mood, laughing over my husband's Gascon boastfulness. Suddenly, several royal advisers burst into the room, their faces flushed.

We looked up, startled. My husband lowered his cards, and I noted the tightening of his jaw, his slow, somber nod.

Next thing I knew, the newly arrived men were bowing before my husband, their eyes lowered to the carpet. Count Mörner appeared to understand their meaning, and he immediately rose from his chair to do the same, his face solemn.

The old king, I knew, was dead. The room filled with cheers of: "Long live King Carl Johan! Long live the House of Bernadotte!"

How many times had I participated in coronation events and other court ceremonies? Too many times to count. But never before had I been at their center; never had I imagined that I would be crowned a queen of one of Europe's ancient and great powers.

It was early May, when the days were nearing their longest, and the sun rose early that morning, greeted by a thunder of ceremonial cannon fire as the city of Stockholm prepared for our coronation. Soon after dawn, church bells began to clamor across the city—for this was a day of importance not only for the State, but for the Church as well.

My husband and his government had declared it a national holiday, and the crowds turned out to enjoy the festivities. Heralds marched through the streets proclaiming the news: my husband was to be crowned King of Sweden, Norway, the Goths, and the Vandals. From my rooms, I saw the bright Swedish flags paraded across the courtyard and beyond the grand gates of the palace. This was new, not a part of the traditional Swedish coronation pageantry, but Bernadotte wished to conjure a festive feel, to lend the weight of ceremony since his was not a long or even Swedish heritage. We were to be a new dynasty, and so, my husband said, it was all the more important that our day be marked by majesty and significance, even if we had to borrow that significance from traditions other than our own.

Elise helped me dress, and we took the entire morning. I had ordered a new robe of spun silver to match my husband's attire. Bernadotte would wear the ancient crown of Sweden's beloved King Eric, to which he had added several large diamonds that he'd brought from France, and he carried a sapphire orb. I wore a tiara of diamonds in my upswept hair, a diamond choker around my neck, and matching jewels on my ears and wrists.

As I exited the palace beside my husband and son, I looked out over the scene. The crowds stretched farther than my eyes could take in; people cheering, children waving the Swedish flag, round-cheeked babies perched atop their fathers' shoulders. The church bells clamored in a frenzied chorus to accompany our footsteps as we left the palace and processed along Slottsbacken Avenue. We arrived at Storkyrkan Cathedral, where my husband was to be made the official leader of the national Lutheran Church. A great canopy of gold cloth draped over our heads. Oscar, now my tall and handsome young man, watched with pride as his father was anointed by the Archbishop.

Back in the palace, we were whisked into the throne room, where my husband and I took our seats at the front of the hall while an endless stream of Swedish nobles, mayors, parliamentary members, government officials, diplomats, and clergymen bowed before us, congratulating us and swearing their loyalty to the House of Bernadotte.

The long, sunlit night outside our palace roiled with the lively sounds of feasting and fireworks. Inside, I sat, stiff and erect, doing my best to carry myself with a queenly bearing. Did I think of her—Josephine? Of course I thought of her, the entire day; she had been the most elegant queen I would ever know, and now we shared more than just the one-time love of the same man. Now we shared the knowledge of what it meant to wear a crown—one plucked from fortune rather than passed through blood. And to know that a crown was both a great gift and an onerous burden.

# Chapter 42

*Paris*
*Spring 1821*

"HE'S DEAD," I SAID TO ELISE, THE WORDS SOUNDING preposterous even as I voiced them. "Napoleon is dead."

Elise gasped, placing her coffee on the table and running to my side. "I cannot believe it," she said, reading the French newspaper over my shoulder. "I can't imagine him . . . dead."

Nor could I. "Some men . . ." I shook my head. "You don't believe them to be mortal. You can't imagine that the same inglorious fate will befall them as everybody else."

I was back on my beloved Rue d'Anjou, my doctors having urged me to take another respite from the frigid Swedish winter, and I had happily obeyed. Being in the French capital, I saw firsthand how Paris plunged itself into a state of deep mourning. The city, though ruled once more by a Bourbon king, celebrated its one-time Emperor as though he still reigned in glory. Residents and store owners shuttered their windows in heavy black drapes. Flags were lowered. The soldiers marched through the streets pale and glum, appearing as if they might weep at any moment.

I longed to know if the news had reached my husband. And if so, what must Bernadotte think of it? Napoleon, his one-time friend, comrade in arms, rival, and then foe. The man who had destroyed the Republic Bernadotte had loved and bled for. The man to whom Bernadotte owed his crown and kingdom, and even his wife.

I dashed off to my salon to write him a note, including clippings of the newspaper articles. Napoleon, dead at fifty-one. An overweight man with swollen jowls and thinning hair, felled by a cancer of the stomach. I found it hard to believe; I couldn't help but see him as the young Corsican soldier with long, brown hair, unrelenting eyes the color of the darkened sea, uncouth manners that failed to conceal the ferocity of his ambition.

He'd been on the remote island of St. Helena in the Atlantic since shortly after his defeat at Waterloo, a captive in the custody of the British army. There, he'd passed the long southern days by gardening and walking the hills and speaking of bygone times with the small band of servants who attended him. But mostly, he wrote; he wrote journals, he wrote memoirs—his overactive mind was as unwilling as ever to relent, to give way to the slower pace of an island exile and an ailing body.

In the days following his death, the French papers began printing excerpts of his memoir. He'd intended for them to be published—of course he had. Why else would he, a man obsessed with history and legend and the idea of legacy, have spent his final years writing his own story, if not to share it with all the world? If not to have his word be the final say? It had always been his goal—to shape the thoughts and actions of those around him according to his will and vision. Hadn't he been so successful in doing just that in life? And so that was what he would do in death, as well.

I wasn't surprised to see how much of his writing focused on Josephine. She had dominated his thoughts even when he'd had matters as large as conquering Egypt or building an empire on which to focus, so of course she ruled his thoughts when he had nothing else to do but stare at the sea and pace the rocky soil of St. Helena. *She was the wife who would have come with me. She would have gone with me to Hell itself.* He loved her still, even after the divorce and her sudden death—perhaps even more after the divorce and her sudden death. He regretted that he had left her for a younger princess.

That younger princess had no interest in joining him on St. Helena or even allowing her son to know his father. The boy was living in Vienna among his Habsburg relatives, his title now an Austrian one, the Duke of

Reichstätt. Napoleon wrote lovingly of his son, betraying his longing for a reunion that would never come.

I was also not surprised to see that Napoleon wrote many passages about each of his military campaigns and his staggering victories—Austerlitz, Jena, Rivoli, Cairo, and so many others. Or that he wrote rather transparently about his political achievements, outlining the legacy he hoped he would enjoy as a revolutionary and a reformer among the French people and, indeed, across Europe.

I was surprised, however—stunned, really—when I saw *my* name, when I saw how much of his time and attention Napoleon had allotted to writing about me. *Ah, Desiree Clary—for she will always be Clary to me. I took her maidenhead, so it was only right that I should see her married off. At first I tried with Duphot, but then there was that unfortunate business in Rome. So, Bernadotte got to be the lucky man. And wasn't he all too happy to lap up what I had left for him?*

I gasped aloud, mortified, thinking first of my husband, and then realizing, horrified, that all of France would see this. Friends and strangers alike would read about these intimate details of my life with the two men I had loved. And there was more: *Bernadotte needed no convincing, given her wealth and her connections, mostly her connections to me through the sister.*

The blood thrashed in my veins. I looked to Elise, my eyes wide and unblinking—I was too horrified for tears. And then Napoleon continued: *Bernadotte, to say he was a disappointment would not begin to state it. I was the author of his greatness. To think, what he did to France. What he did to me. He was nothing at the outset, not even wanted by his own Gascon mother, but France made him a general, and a Marshal. And a rich man. Bernadotte was the snake we nurtured in our bosom. It was he who gave the enemy the key to our policies and the tactics of our armies.*

I lowered the paper, unable to go on. *Oh God,* I thought, *please don't let my husband see this.* It would break him; it would shatter his heart to read this darkest possible utterance of his own deepest-held fears and self-doubts. And in such a public manner!

I knew Bernadotte was tortured by the fact that he'd fought against France. I knew it haunted his sleep, still, to think that he had acted in the interests of his new nation, Sweden, over those of his motherland. But he *had* been acting in France's best interests, as well—for he had no longer believed that Napoleon was good for the French. And that was how he had made his peace. And yet, here was Napoleon voicing a vicious indictment of those difficult decisions, and I suspected that these thoughts would deal a more piercing wound to my Bernadotte than any stab of the sword on a battlefield might have done.

I knew, in that moment, that my husband's conflicted feelings toward Napoleon would not pass with the death of the powerful man. Napoleon would continue to haunt my husband long after this death, perhaps for the remainder of Bernadotte's new life in Sweden. I understood, because I understood a bit of how my husband thought; even though my husband ruled a kingdom larger than France or England or Prussia, with millions of subjects, he would never forget the rival who had come before him to secure both my love and the love of his nation. The man who had raised him up while also tearing him down. The man who had given him this very crown, after all, or at least, had given the blessing and the connections that were required in its attainment. My husband was beholden to Napoleon for so many things—for his rise in the army, his appointment to Marshal, his reception of this crown, even the introduction to me. He was beholden to him, and so for that he felt both gratitude and deep resentment.

When I did finally hear from my husband, he wrote only of his sadness. He wrote of his admiration for Napoleon as a soldier and he wished him an abiding and eternal rest.

Perhaps there was someone else in my husband's life these days to whom he unburdened his soul, but it wouldn't be me, most certainly not through a letter that was sure to be read by multiple censors along its way. Bernadotte never confided in me of his agony—but I knew of it, just the same.

Not surprisingly, after all the talk of Napoleon's death, my husband became more preoccupied than ever with his own dynasty. *Oscar must marry,* he wrote to me. *It is time.* Our son was nearly twenty-two years old, the heir to the Swedish throne, and he needed a wife. More important, he needed sons.

I wrote back to my husband, agreeing with this. Why, by his age, I'd already had an engagement and a heartbreak at Napoleon's hands, an arranged betrothal to Duphot, then a marriage and a son with Bernadotte. It was time for Oscar to start his own family. I had long hoped that my boy might wish to marry one of my nieces, Julie's two daughters, Zénaïde or Charlotte. They were lovely girls, several years younger than he was, and they'd been raised as princesses. But my husband immediately rejected the idea, seeing it for what it was—a sentimental move motivated by my own desire to be reunited with my sister, rather than a smart diplomatic play. Besides, my Bonaparte nieces had the worst possible last name.

*She should be either German, Russian, or Austrian. The daughter of a king, preferably, and most certainly from an advantageous family. I rather like the idea of a Bavarian princess,* he wrote back to me.

It was decided: Oscar, based in Stockholm, would make a grand tour, during which time he'd visit the great courts of the Continent and meet the most powerful crowned heads of Europe and, of course, their marriageable daughters.

I followed it all with a mother's interest, even if I was in Paris. Oscar went first to Denmark, but there was little interest in King Frederick's daughters. Next he went to the Netherlands, but young Princess Marianne of Orange struck him as too timid. From there, he traveled to Bavaria, where King Maximilian was the current ruler from the ancient and prestigious Wittelsbach family. My husband wrote that he was particularly excited about this stop for Oscar; the Wittelsbachs were a respected and prosperous dynasty, and they would lend legitimacy to our new reign. In addition to all that, the ruling family in Bavaria was descended from the ancient Swedish ruling family of Vasa. Thus, any alliance with them would make Oscar's children even more secure on his new Swedish throne.

King Max's daughter had given him a granddaughter who was not yet sixteen. She was considered a desirable match—Catholic, but then, so was I. Beautiful, with intelligence and many charms, and a large dowry. Bernadotte was ecstatic, writing me that an alliance like this would *join the new interests with the old.*

The young lady was said to be a great admirer of her paternal grandmother, a dark-haired beauty who had earned herself a throne in spite of a lackluster pedigree. Like her grandmother, the potential bride was known to be witty and charismatic, with impeccable manners and a grace that seemed to come naturally.

And, like her grandmother, she was named Josephine.

# Chapter 43

*Aachen, Rhineland*
*Spring 1823*

I COULD NOT BELIEVE IT: MY SON HAD FALLEN IN LOVE WITH Josephine's granddaughter, the young girl also called Josephine. To hear her full name unleashed ripples of memory that I felt with my entire body: Josephine Napoleone de Beauharnais. Named after her grandmother—at Napoleon's insistence—when she was born in 1807, the girl's middle name had been added as an honorific to her step-grandfather, then Emperor of France.

*This is not the end for Josephine and me.* Hadn't I felt it, all those years ago? Hadn't I known that farewell did not mean forever on that night when Napoleon had banished her from his life and his love?

Now, Josephine and I might be joined once more, and forever; I found it dizzying simply to wrap my mind around this fact. Josephine's son, Eugene, had married into the Bavarian royal family at the height of his mother's power, taking as his bride the Princess Augusta, eldest daughter of King Maximilian of the House of Wittelsbach. Surely his skills at survival had come from his mother: through decades of war against his native country and his stepfather's multiple rises and downfalls, Eugene had remained well-liked at the Wittelsbach court and indeed in Bavaria. Though he'd come of age as a boy riding alongside his stepfather into military camps across Europe, when the time came, Eugene successfully distanced himself from the ill-fated politics of his French family and had taken the title of Duke of Leuchtenberg. He and Augusta had had seven children in Munich. Their eldest daughter, Josephine, was famous for her beauty; she was known to be as gracious as the paternal grandmother for whom she was named.

Our two families were to meet that spring in Eichstätt, where we might allow the young couple to court in the relaxed, picturesque setting of a mountain resort. I knew that my son desired to become engaged to Josephine, but I was nervous, for I knew nothing of the young girl's heart.

The figure who greeted me on the Aachen train platform was no little boy, but a man. Oscar stood tall and lean, with the dark eyes and thick hair of his father. He was handsome, even if a bit reserved as he submitted to my enthusiastic kisses and hugs. I knew he was considered standoffish by some at court, but that was simply because he did not have the animated flourishes of his Gascon father; he was shy like me.

And yet, in spite of his shyness, I knew instantly that Josephine would be thrilled to marry Oscar. Just as I had been thrilled as a young woman to marry his father. Even beside the dashing figure he cut in his Swedish military uniform, Oscar was kind and he was earnest—and, he was destined to be a king. Any girl would be a fool to reject his suit.

Oscar and I rested for a few days in Aachen before traveling on together to Eichstätt, arriving in the late afternoon on a mild summer day. It was a charming village, built around an ancient stone church and nestled in wooded hills that hugged the Altmühl River. We pulled up to a gracious château, an iron gate giving way to a large forecourt. Our carriage halted before the door, and a small assembly of people stood ready to welcome us.

I knew Eugene de Beauharnais instantly. I'd known him as a young man, and his face had not changed much. He had his mother's long-lashed, amber eyes. Beside Eugene stood a woman; I presumed her to be his wife, the Princess Augusta. To her side stood another lady—fine-featured with chestnut hair—whom I recognized immediately. "Hortense, what a delight!" Josephine's daughter. I blinked, seeing a flash of her as a girl, the quiet, well-mannered daughter who had often appeared more stoic than the mother at whose side she always stood.

And beside them, Princess Josephine Napoleone de Beauharnais. She glided forward, offering me a cheerful curtsy before launching into her greeting, the excitement coloring her cheeks a lovely pink: "Oh, Your Highness, I am *so* delighted to meet you at last!" Then she leaned close and whispered in my ear, as if we were the oldest of friends and familiar co-conspirators; I found the gesture, forward as it was, to be surprisingly endearing. "I've been hearing about all of you for my entire life. Papa has *such* stories! I cannot wait to get to know you for myself. Oh, I'm sorry, I have yet to even introduce myself. I'm Josephine."

I smiled at this girl, trying to stealthily study her as she and Eugene greeted Oscar. At sixteen years old, she was fresh and bursting with a youthful vivacity. Beside my shy Oscar she appeared self-assured, even at ease. Goodness, but she was alike to Josephine: tall, slender, disarmingly warm in her temperament. The only difference came in her golden blond hair, where Josephine's had been famously dark.

"Thank you ever so much for coming," Josephine said to me, looping her thin arm through mine. It was a gesture so alike to those of her grandmother that I laughed aloud. "What is so funny?" she asked, her head tilting sideways as her amber eyes held my own.

"Oh, nothing," I said, falling in step beside her. I was back on the wintry street in Paris, a perfect stranger—the woman who had just stolen my fiancé—looping her arm through mine as if we were the oldest of friends. "Just memories."

"Ah, yes," Josephine said, nodding meaningfully, as if to say she understood perfectly. "I bet you have many of those."

We kept a pleasantly busy schedule for our two weeks in Eichstätt, filling the days with carriage rides and picnics and walks through the low mountains. The evenings were filled with family dinners and outings to the theater, a few nights of dancing and music. My son was attentive to Josephine, and I could tell by the constant tilt of her face toward his, the way her eyes sought him out in any room, that she welcomed his courtship. She was admirably poised, like her grandmother, but she was still a young girl, and thus it was not too difficult to guess at the hopeful longings of her unguarded heart.

Oscar was smitten. At the end of the two weeks, he knocked tentatively on my bedchamber door. "Come in, dear," I called. I sat before the mirror in my nightgown, rubbing a thick ointment into my sore, aching hands. My rheumatism only seemed to worsen with each passing year.

Oscar entered and plopped down on my bed, resting his head on my pillows as he had not done since his boyhood. I dismissed my last few remaining servants with a quick "good night" before turning to ask my son: "What is it, dear?"

Oscar sighed, trying to speak but then pausing a moment. Eventually, he managed to say: "Maman, I do love her so."

I placed the ointment down on the table, turning to my son. Smiling, I said, "Of course you do."

His face flushed as he stared at me. "Do you think . . . she loves me?"

"Yes," I said, certain of it.

Oscar chewed on his lower lip, his thoughts so apparent on his face. "How can you know?"

"Because," I said, "she is like her grandmother. And like her grandmother, she is no fool."

# Chapter 44

*Munich, Bavaria*
*June 1823*

"IS IT TRULY SO VERY…COLD?" MY SON'S NEW BRIDE looked across the carriage at me, and even though she tried to mask it, I saw how her brow creased with worry. I bit my lip, stifling the urge to laugh at the question, at the way she appeared to shiver, even though it was a sunny day in June; it had been my preoccupation as a younger woman and a first-time visitor to Sweden as well.

I reached across the coach and patted her hand. "Not in June, dear. In fact, in June, it's really quite lovely. Plenty of sunshine."

Josephine nodded, somewhat reassured, and then remembered to smile. "Thank you, madame." She turned away to glance out the window, watching as the fields surrounding Hamburg unfurled in a rolling tapestry of bright green.

I studied her profile, guessing that she was thinking of the home she had left behind. How could she not miss it? I myself was more than twice her age, traveling to a reunion with my husband and son, and even I still missed my homeland. I felt a pang in my heart for her; she was gaining a kind and handsome groom, yes, and the throne of a vast kingdom, and yet, our lot as women in this world was never an easy one. Even for those of us who, in the eyes of the world, were the fortunate ones.

"Oscar shall be so happy to welcome you," I said, hoping that my buoyant tone would give her joy. Josephine turned to me and smiled. "Yes." She nodded. "And I will be delighted to see him." She really was making a valiant effort to be agreeable.

It would be Josephine's first time in Sweden, and my first time back in years. My son had returned ahead of us to prepare for the arrival of his princess. He had left the important role of Josephine's companion and escort to me. I had fetched her in Munich, at the palace in which she'd grown up. There, we had spent a few final days with Eugene, Augusta, Hortense, and Josephine's many siblings and cousins. Hers had been a happy upbringing, that much was evident. Eugene had raised his large family in the royal household of his father-in-law—winters in Munich, carefree summers at the countryside villa in Eichstätt. Though they were royals, there was something comfortably domestic, even bourgeois, about the way they shared their meals and read stories together in the evenings. Upon her farewell, Josephine had been tearful but resolute, gracious even in her sadness, just as I imagined her grandmother would have carried herself.

I was now bringing her by carriage through northern Germany before our boat ride across the Baltic Sea. My son was fortunate in his bride; the many long hours in such cramped quarters revealed a person's true nature, and my own journey might have been significantly less enjoyable but for the fact that the girl was an entirely pleasant traveling companion. She was lovely—smart and well-mannered, self-assured while also appropriately deferential as both my junior and my daughter-in-law. She spoke fluent French, with just the subtlest trace of a charming German lilt, as well as Italian and German; she also knew some English and a bit of Russian. In addition to the basic tenets of a young noblewoman's education—dancing, needlepoint, music, and etiquette—she'd also studied literature, geography, history, mathematics, botany, and astronomy. She made easy conversation, asking me about Paris and Stockholm. But there was one topic to which she returned often. "Did you really know my grandmother and grandfather well?"

It was an early summer morning and I fanned myself in the coach, the air already close and a bit sticky; I could tell it would be a hot day. I considered Josephine's question. I saw how, as she'd asked it, she'd been careful not to appear overeager—it was risky, even years later, to raise the topic of

Napoleon in much of Europe, and she did not know how I felt about him. My husband had, after all, fought the final battles against him. Still, I could see the flame of interest hiding in her amber eyes.

"I did," I answered.

She folded her hands in her lap, looking down at her narrow fingers. After a pause, she asked: "What were they like?"

"What have you heard of them?"

She pursed her lips, thinking a moment before answering my question: "Papa loved his maman so much . . . though, of course, in front of Grandfather, he did not speak of her."

I nodded. That made sense; her grandfather was King of Bavaria, after all, and many of the German principalities had been the sworn enemies of Napoleon for decades.

"But I've read . . ." Josephine said, a coy smile tugging on her lips, and her expression reminded me so much of another Josephine in that moment that I felt my pulse gallop. Had her hair been dark like her grandmother's, I could have been looking at the face of the woman I'd known so many years ago. "I've read so much," Josephine said after a moment, her voice a conspiratorial whisper even though we sat alone in the coach.

I nodded, leaning my head back against the seat. Eventually, I said: "Everything you could ever read about Napoleon and Josephine is true, because they were all of that, and then even more."

Josephine breathed a slow inhale. "I do know that he . . . Napoleon . . . called her a witch."

I grimaced. "Well, *that*, that was not true."

"Then why did he say it?"

I considered the question. "For two reasons, I believe. The first was that he could not understand, even he who understood everything and everyone, how it was that he could love her as deeply and fiercely as he did. She held some power over him that was undeniable; she *did* enchant him. But I can assure you that she was no witch."

Josephine nodded, accepting this. "And the second?"

"Pardon?"

"You told me he accused her of being a witch for two reasons. What was the second?"

"Ah, yes. Well, he did it for the same reason that so many other men have accused their wives of witchcraft—he wanted a divorce, and he needed a reason to put the blame on her. If she had used witchcraft to ensnare him into marriage, then the union was invalid, and he was nothing more than a hapless victim."

Josephine's brow assumed a becoming furrow as she considered all of this. After a moment, she spoke again: "I know that his final words, on St. Helena, were about her. About how he would be with her again."

"Indeed," I said. I had read that as well. "He loved her until the very end."

The girl's eyes narrowed, her features thoughtful, her face hungry for more. "What *was* she like, then?"

"Your namesake," I said.

"Yes."

I fanned myself, searching my jumbled thoughts for the right words. "He once described her as 'a lady to the very tips of her fingers.' And in that, he spoke the truth."

Josephine's hands rested in her lap, and now she twisted the fabric of her skirts. Her face was heavy with thought. And then, after a while, she said: "I hope to be such a lady."

I smiled, nodding at her, lowering my fan. "You shall be, my dear."

We sat in silence a few moments, both of us looking out the windows toward the expanse of gentle green. The grasses were changing, growing thicker, an indication that we were approaching the sea. When I inhaled, I caught just the faintest hint of salt in the air, and my heartbeat quickened, my body's instinctive response to the familiar scents of my seaside childhood.

Josephine broke into my solitary thoughts. "I heard that . . . that he loved you. Before Josephine. That you and Napoleon were once engaged to be married."

I met her eyes, and nodded after a moment.

She gasped, a sharp intake of breath. "So then . . . it's true?"

"It is."

Her face flushed with the excitement of the news. She leaned toward me, asking: "Then why didn't you marry him?"

"Because he met her."

She flopped back against the coach seat, accepting my answer, but then her brow creased again, a guileless expression of curiosity. "But . . ." She prepared to ask another question, then thought better of it. "Never mind." She shook her head, sending her tight curls into a small flutter.

"Go on, dear," I said. "What is it?"

"I . . . I don't wish to be . . . forward."

I grinned. "It is all right. I give you my permission to ask your question."

"I suppose I'm just confused. If you . . . if you loved him, and you were engaged, but then *she* became his bride . . . how was it that you and she were so close? How could you be close if you both loved the same man?"

I sighed, looking out the window, resuming my rapid fanning. Now it was my turn to blush.

"I'm sorry. I've been too bold."

I shook my head. "No, no. It's fine."

"No, it's not. I've offended you," she replied.

"Not at all, my dear. It is a fair question, the reasonable one to ask. Only, I am not even certain how to answer it. All I can say is that ours were not ordinary times in which to live. Nor were they ordinary times in which to love, being the young and beautiful girls that we were, living in a world gone mad."

Josephine's face softened, her lovely features creasing with genuine feeling. Did she understand all that I said, all that I meant? I doubted it. How could she? But she leaned forward as she asked: "Were you *very* heartbroken?"

I lowered my eyes, stunned at the fact that questions such as these elicited such a powerful response in me, even after all that I had lived through, even after all these years. And yet, in that moment, I realized that she was the first person ever to ask me about my feelings with such a frank and earnest curiosity. To reach so deeply into my heart in order to pull out these long-buried memories, moments both beautiful and painful in their potency. Why, not even Julie had ever asked me this many questions.

"Heartbroken?" I repeated the phrase she had used. "I suppose I was, yes. At the time."

Josephine's posture wilted in an expression of empathy; I could tell that she longed to lean forward and place her hand on mine, but was unsure of the appropriateness of such a gesture. I didn't encourage it; I didn't invite any further intimacy. Already this was more than I'd ever said on the topic, and I felt a bit exposed.

I inhaled, pulling my shoulders back, rearranging my features into an expression of cool composure. When I spoke, my tone was upbeat: "But then I went on to meet Bernadotte, er, King Carl Johan. And I'm so very happy I did."

Josephine considered this a moment before nodding, mirroring my determination to be cheerful. "I'm so glad you did as well."

"Indeed," I said, folding my hands in my lap.

"Otherwise," she added, "Oscar would not be here. And you and I both love him so very much." It was the perfect response—flattering, after perhaps a bit too much prying. I liked this girl quite a bit. I made to smile at her, but just then it happened—my vision swam as a ripple of thought skittered across my mind, causing my skin to prick with shivers in spite of the warm air. What we French call *un éclair*—a bolt of lightning. It was only a fleeting feeling, call it a woman's intuition, but I knew it with certainty: she was as lovely as the grandmother for whom she was named, and, just like that grandmother, tragedy would befall her.

"What is it, madame?" she asked, her face going pale, reflecting my own unease back to me. "You look as though you've seen a ghost."

"Nothing, dear," I said.

But perhaps I had.

The sea voyage made me ill, even sicker than previous boat crossings, so I kept to my cabins below deck. I had no idea if Josephine felt similarly unwell, but the captain told me she did not appear to suffer, for she roamed the decks freely, smiling at the crew and chatting with the servants.

I emerged above deck only when the captain informed me that we had reached the bay of Saltsjön, where the waters were expected to calm. It was a glorious June day—unclouded sunshine in a vast blue sky. We sailed along the craggy coast, the banks covered in thick, sappy pine and shimmering spruce. I breathed in, a deep inhale that carried the earthy aromas of the northern woods, a mix of scents so different from those of the southern seaside ports of my youth.

We made landfall just a few miles outside Stockholm in mid-June, when the days were at their longest. I wobbled off the gangplank, assisted by several servants and happy to be on terra firma once more. As the attendants buzzed about us, hauling our trunks and coordinating with porters and coachmen, Josephine trotted up beside me, her own eyes clear and bright, her complexion a vibrant hue of perfect health.

"Is that for us?" she asked, staring at the coach and eight that waited. Clearly my husband—or perhaps my son—had hoped to make a good impression for Josephine, because it was one of our grandest coaches, burnished gold with purple ornamentation. A crowd surrounded it, cheering our arrival onto Swedish soil.

That crowd did not thin as we made our journey overland, but rather the people lined our entire route, growing in number as we approached the summer palace in Haga Park, just north of the capital. We finally pulled into the courtyard, where even more people were gathered, waving the Swedish flag and crying out for a glimpse of their new Crown Princess Josephine.

I hardly looked at the crowds, for there, ahead, was my husband, on whom I had not laid eyes since my departure for France. Bernadotte stood in his full uniform, a man of entirely gray hair but a tall, imposing figure still. Beside him, Oscar, my dear boy, looked a bit bashful, but happy. They were surrounded on both sides by soldiers and officers, and a military band played our Swedish national anthem, though we could barely hear it over the roar of the crowds gathered outside the palace gates.

Our carriage halted, and the footmen helped us down. Bernadotte kissed my cheek with checked affection, a public gesture befitting his royal status. It was a joyous reunion for the young pair: Oscar took Josephine's gloved hand in his and placed a kiss atop it, his cheeks flushing to a boyish tint. Then, eyes still fixed on her with evident adoration, he guided her toward the large front doors, outside of which they paused together to look out over the crowds once more, waving.

Though no formal ceremony had been planned, Josephine held her hand out toward the people. I was confused for a moment until I realized that she was asking for quiet. The crowd obeyed. *But what does she mean by this?* I wondered. To my great surprise, she began to speak. I could not understand what she said; Josephine was speaking in *Swedish*.

Oscar looked on at his bride, beaming with pride. Bernadotte's eyebrows shot up, and he glanced at me, startled. I shrugged my shoulders as if to say that I was as baffled as he was—Josephine and I had only ever conversed in French.

After her brief remarks were over, the crowd erupted in fresh cheers, even louder than before. They were elated, for not only was their new princess beautiful and young, but she was happy to be there, and she had told them so in their native tongue. In a capital that I still found to be cold and unwelcoming, even after years of being queen, Josephine was an instant success.

I sidled over to my daughter-in-law, my tone a bit wry as I walked beside her up the final steps toward the palace. "Josephine, that was well done."

"Thank you." She smiled, turning to me, her demure eyes lilting downward—a look her grandmother had given me so many times.

I still studied her as I said, "I had no idea you spoke Swedish."

And then she shrugged, gliding through the grand double doors and into the cool front hall of the palace as if she'd lived there her entire life. "I didn't. I practiced on the boat."

# Chapter 45

*Stockholm*
*Summer 1823*

T HEY HAD BEEN MARRIED BY PROXY—EACH IN THEIR
respective realm, as was the tradition among European royalty—but
we celebrated the official Swedish wedding a fortnight after Josephine's arrival.

The day of the service dawned clear and mild, and I dressed in my own
suite before going to hers. The servants stepped aside for me, and I found
her seated in her bedchamber before a grand mirror, attendants crisscrossing the room on last-minute preparations for her gown and jewelry.

"Good morning, Maman," she said, smiling at me in the mirror's reflection as she rose to greet me. "You look splendid," she cooed, admiring my
appearance. I didn't feel splendid—not beside her willowy frame, her
youthful smiles—but I had done my best, squeezing my ample curves into
a gown of taupe silk and topaz jewels. Oh well, no one would be looking at
me today, after all.

I stepped forward and allowed her to place a kiss on my cheek. She
smelled fresh—rosewater on her neck, some floral cream on her soft skin.
"Good morning, dear. How did you sleep?"

She took my hands in her own and gave them an excited squeeze, her
eyes brightening. "Barely at all; I was too excited. And of course tonight

I doubt I shall get a moment's . . ." But she raised her hand to her lips, a blush darkening her cheeks as she giggled.

I looked away, flustered. Hanging near her bed was the wedding gown, a sumptuous confection of pale blue and cream-colored silk embellished with diamonds and pearls. "That's it, then?"

"Isn't it lovely?" She glided toward her dress, just barely grazing the silk with her fingertips, fearful of dirtying the pristine fabric. "And of course you know these pieces," she said, reaching toward the bed. There, she picked up a stunning cluster of grape-sized diamonds, each jewel staggering in its brilliance. It was a necklace, and beside it, matching earrings and bracelets.

I swallowed. "Yes," I said, my voice quiet, "I . . . I believe I do."

"They were hers. In Paris. He had them made for her." Josephine crossed toward the mirror, holding up her grandmother's necklace so that it gleamed against the ivory of her neck. "I've had them cleaned so they will sparkle as they once did. When she wore them."

I studied her reflection, blinking, seeing for just a moment a dark-haired beauty gliding across a Parisian dance floor. Quick laughter, a smitten Emperor staring on, transfixed by the siren who had captivated him and the entire capital. "They will be exquisite on you," I said. Josephine didn't look to me, but rather kept her eyes focused on her own reflection. She cocked her head to the side as she asked: "Do I *really* look so much like her?"

"Indeed, I believe that you do. Your hair is lighter, of course."

"Yes, I've heard of her chestnut curls." Now she turned and faced me. "But how can I look so much like her, if our coloring is so different?"

I considered the question. "It's something intangible . . . the manner of your bearing. Your gestures. They are so like hers."

She considered this a moment before nodding, satisfied. "I am proud of that."

"As you should be."

"Do you think . . . ?" she asked, but then she paused. Outside, the bells began to toll. The city would be rising, the eager crowds flocking to the cathedral for the day's ceremony.

She glanced sideways at the gown. "Do you think Oscar will like it?"

"He will love it, my dear. You are a lady to the very tips of your fingers."

I looked on, slightly stunned, at how effortlessly Josephine glided through the Lutheran ceremony, more at ease, it seemed, than even my son, who had been schooled under the guidance and care of our stern Archbishop since his boyhood. In the moment they were pronounced married before God, when the cannons fired off their salvo and the city erupted in euphoric cheers, Josephine summoned the perfect blush to her cheeks. A happy bride, a lovely bride, yet a savvy girl who knew just how to perform as thousands of eyes watched in keen appraisal.

Bernadotte stood beside me at the feast afterward, content to watch the younger couples of the court as they swirled around the dance floor. My gaze remained fixed on my son and his wife. I watched, impressed, as they whispered and laughed, carving out a private sphere for themselves amid the music and the crowds and the prying eyes; a true warmth and intimacy were evident between them even in these first hours of their union.

"It was well done, to be sure," my husband said, his tone one of fatherly approval. "Now, let's hope for sons. And quickly."

"Come now, Bernadotte. You can't be in too great a rush? You're still young and strong."

"Neither young nor strong, I fear," he said.

"Well, if you long to be a grandfather, I don't expect a problem on that score," I said, chuckling at the obvious language of their tilted bodies, the clear attraction between my son and his new wife. Even as I laughed, my corset felt tight against my abdomen; I'd eaten too much at the feast. And my knuckles nagged me with their familiar ache. I sighed; perhaps my husband was right. Perhaps we were getting old. I turned back to the newlyweds, who were laughing now at something that Josephine had just whispered to my son. "They shall be happy," I said.

We exchanged a smile, a satisfied smile, the sort of look that can only come from knowing one's child is content.

"Bravo, my dear," my husband said to me, handing off his champagne to a nearby footman and taking my hand.

"I didn't do it," I said, shrugging off his praise. "Oscar did it for himself."

"You were there for the courtship. And you brought her to us. You've given her a proper and warm introduction into our family. I'm glad she has you here."

I grinned, accepting his approving words, basking in the attention of my king and husband. And then, ignoring protocol, ignoring the stares that I knew fell on me from across the crowded hall, I leaned toward Bernadotte and planted a kiss on his lips.

He looked at me with wide eyes, a bit stunned, but then he erupted in laughter, happy to shrug off the rules alongside me, his bourgeois-born wife. "What do you say, Madame Bernadotte? Shall we join the young bucks in a dance?"

I squeezed his hand and allowed him to guide me to the floor, the crowds parting as we passed. He was older and somewhat diminished by age, with a persistent cough that often bothered him, but his frame was still tall and broad, and I felt light in his arms, yielding to his steps, to the languid swell of the music, and the comforting familiarity of a dance opposite my longtime partner.

My husband still had a power over me, I noted—the ability to make me feel like the girl at the dance whose heart beat a bit faster under his dark-eyed gaze. And I knew that, for him, he still loved to turn that dark-eyed gaze on me. We had never lost that, even after all of these years and the other losses we had known.

We enjoyed a lovely and relatively peaceful summer as a family at Haga Palace, just a short ride from the center of the capital, but a world of difference from the court. Josephine adored flowers and loved gardening, and rather than turn up my nose at such a quaint interest—as the previous queens might have done—I encouraged her to study with the gardeners in the hothouses and the herb gardens. I could not help but think of her grandmother spending so many happy hours outdoors amid the sprawling grounds of Malmaison, and I encouraged her to dirty her hands and skirts with digging in the soil.

My husband, who was overjoyed to have a daughter-in-law, made a national holiday honoring the name day of Josephine, and so we had fireworks and feasting to commemorate both the anniversary of his election to the crown and the feast of Josephine Day. Crowds cheered, demanding not their king but his beautiful new daughter-in-law, and she happily greeted them from our royal balcony, smiling and waving.

The gossips at court loved to harp on Josephine's popularity and my resultant jealousy, painting a tableau of our royal family with a brush of discord and rivalry, claiming that I resented the attention that my husband and son lavished on our newcomer. Journalists wrote that I had been up-staged and replaced, once more, by a charismatic beauty named Josephine, and that I saw her as a loathed adversary, both at court and within our small family circle.

I didn't care about all that; the reality was that we were not at knives, nor did I view her as a rival. In truth, I was so very happy to see my son infatuated with his young bride, and to see the affection reciprocated by her. They were warm and kind to each other, and they shared so many in-terests and hobbies: they loved to paint in the garden; she would sing while Oscar played the piano; he would listen attentively as she spoke to him of her plants and flowers. My son was a good husband. He was courteous and solicitous with Josephine, offering the steady sort of care that her name-sake had never enjoyed at the hands of her own husband. At least, not that I had ever seen.

How long, I wondered, could their happiness—*her* happiness—last?

I missed Paris, and I missed the French summer, but indeed I was also so happy to be with my husband once more. He still suffered from fits of coughing, occasionally even spitting blood into his handkerchief. I took great care in doting on him and insisting he take his rest in the afternoons. The days were long and the sun remained high in the northern sky well past supper, and so we enjoyed leisurely walks through the gardens to-gether at dusk, once the rest of the court had retired to the salons for cards and music and gossip.

Quite wickedly, I was also relieved beyond measure to be rid of Queen Hedwig Charlotte and her dominant presence at the court. That formida-ble woman had passed away while I was in Paris, and I noticed a shift among the ladies at court toward Josephine as their new leader.

I made my peace with my Swedish life. My son was, after all, more

Swedish now than French; he spoke the language fluently, and he hardly remembered a time when he had not practiced in the Lutheran Church. Bernadotte and I never became Swedish in the same way Oscar did—we never lost the French in us. Nor did we conduct ourselves in the way that previous Swedish monarchs had. We insisted on French wine at our dinners, and my husband drank his Gascon brandy rather than the Swedish *brännvin*, the potato liquor that I found intolerably thick.

As the summer heat receded and the chill of autumn set in, we ordered our rooms to be kept warm, stoves blazing at all times, a heat that made the servants sweat, but we were southerners, the pair of us, and I loathed the cold.

We still shared a bed, however unusual the nobles of our court found that to be. As far as I knew, my husband's days of taking mistresses were behind him. We had grown old, the pair of us. I had gone from round to outright plump, and my husband's thick, once-dark hair now shone more silver than black. But ours was a warm and agreeable companionship, perhaps warmer in our advanced age than it had been even in our youth.

My husband still conducted his affairs of state entirely in French, partly because he'd never managed to become fluent in Swedish, and partly so I could participate as a trusted adviser and confidante. He was efficient as a monarch, even if a bit untraditional; we didn't rise from bed most mornings for the levée, the ceremonial dressing and breakfast, but instead my husband preferred to execute the matters of his government from under the bedcovers, particularly on cold winter mornings. There, knees propped up like a table, sipping good, strong French coffee, he would dictate letters or answer queries in bed with me beside him. I would doze or read my French novels or write to Julie or my nieces, chiming in when my husband sought my opinion on some matter. Often, we wouldn't dress until midday luncheon, which we always took together, with Oscar and Josephine, too, when they were available.

Sweden was at peace, and my husband was a popular king, particularly now that his heir was married. Though we knew that his ministers and servants occasionally raised their eyebrows at our peculiar style of conducting our business, Bernadotte never neglected his duty; he would answer and draft thousands of letters and state documents each month.

He was a good king, even if he never stopped referring to himself as a "crowned republican."

As the months passed and the long Swedish winter showed the first promising signs of the coming thaw, we hoped only for one piece of news: an announcement that Josephine was with child. So I was delighted when my husband told me that a blushing Oscar had whispered the news to his father over a night of port and cigars.

I decided that perhaps now was my chance to make a trip across the Baltic to see Julie, before the arrival of my first grandchild. I longed to see my sister, who was living a quiet life in Florence, removed from public life with her ailing husband. I'd invited her to join me in Stockholm on numerous occasions, but Joseph would not allow even a brief visit, so terrified was he at the thought of something happening to her on the journey—or worse, of his own death occurring without my sister at his side.

I proposed the idea of a journey to Florence one morning in bed, before the servants had come to deliver our trays of coffee and warm, fresh bread. I was hopeful that Bernadotte would quickly approve it, as he had so many other trips I'd undertaken, until I saw my husband's frown.

"Absolutely not," Bernadotte said, barely considering it for a moment.

"Why not?" I asked, bristling at the quick decisiveness of his answer.

"We are far too busy here," was all he offered in reply.

I sat up straighter in the bed, still convinced that I'd find a way to have my wish. "You need not come with me. I would go alone. I'm hardly too busy."

"We are coming into spring—there will be the move to the summer palace, and the anniversary celebrations, and Josephine's name day feast, and the preparations for the birth of the prince."

"Precisely why I feel that I should go *now*, so that I can return in time for the birth."

But my husband was unmoved. "No more of your solitary wandering, Desiree. You don't understand how difficult those years were for me." He shook his head one more time, silver waves of hair falling around his face, his expression one of decided finality. "No."

These words struck me with a surprising weight. Never before had my husband confessed to me how trying my absences had been for him.

He continued, saying: "There are too many reports and gossips as it is. We must be perceived as a unified family living happily together, joined in our common service to our kingdom." He pursed his lips as if to say *that is that*. "And besides," he added, "God forbid something should happen to you on the journey—can you imagine what that would do to Oscar and Josephine in their time of need? And to me? Can you imagine not knowing your grandson?"

I frowned, crossing my arms over the bedcovers, frustrated to have had my plans thwarted, and yet, touched by my husband's concern—by his very evident desire to keep me at his side.

Indeed, when the baby did come that summer, it was a boy—a plump, healthy boy, and they named him Charles after my Bernadotte's Swedish name. We were instantly in love with him, and the nation vaulted into days of state celebrations and feasting that filled the many golden hours of northern sunlight, as well as the few hours of purple nightfall.

A brother arrived just a year later, Gustaf, followed soon after by yet another boy named Oscar. My husband had wanted grandsons—and Josephine, as usual, played her part perfectly.

"Charles, Gustaf, Oscar, come here. Which of you shall sit upon my lap for the fireworks display?"

"I will! I will, Grandmère!"

I spread my arms and smiled as Charles toddled toward me. My first grandson, the little prince of my heart, with his dark curls that reminded me so much of both my son and my husband, reached for me with his chubby hands. "Then here you go, my little darling," I said, placing a kiss atop the boy's head as he settled into my lap. My husband took the baby, Oscar, from Josephine's arms.

It was a mild evening in late August, and our family was gathered at the summer palace. Oscar and Josephine were with us, along with our three little grandsons, all of them still babies, really. Josephine was already expecting their fourth, and the pregnancy had been a difficult one so far. I could see the toll that these years had taken on her young body—how her once-willowy frame had grown alarmingly thin, even brittle looking. I noted how her body seemed to be shrinking everywhere but for the round bulge of her constantly swollen belly. I could see the fatigue in her pale face, in her drawn expression, in her forced smiles and sunken eyes.

And it wasn't only her body that suffered; I could detect the signs of fraying in her marriage to my son, too. Tenderness had given way to tension—short, clipped remarks, a halt in the affectionate touches and easy whispers they had once shared. Eyes that barely met, even when they were forced to speak to each other about the boys or some official business. Oscar no longer turned when his wife entered a room, entranced by her beauty, remarking on her gown, or admiring the style of her hair. And she did not seem to care, did not seek his approval, did not glance toward him when she made conversation.

Oscar had taken a mistress, that was well known at court. A wealthy beauty named Jaquette Löwenhielm. With his wife constantly exhausted by pregnancy or in confinement or tending to a newborn, he hadn't had to look far amid the well-connected noblewomen who surrounded him each day.

The liaison was not entirely surprising—it was standard custom for the men of our court to have at least one mistress. Why, Jaquette was the protégé at court of one of my husband's rumored former mistresses, that I knew. And yet, I had nurtured a foolish hope that perhaps my son's marriage would be different. That my son would be different.

I did worry about Josephine, should she hear the persistent whispers about her husband's betrayal. I worried for the little boys, for the health of the baby she carried. She was not from this court, and based on all that I'd heard about her own upbringing, her parents had enjoyed a harmonious, devoted marriage. I did not know that she would easily accept the way things were done here. In spite of the difficulty of these recent years, she loved Oscar so, and she had entered into the marriage enjoying so much of his love in return. I would need to talk to my son, to urge him toward discretion and consideration for his exhausted wife.

But tonight, in spite of these concerns and the tension that lurked beneath the surface, we were all doing our best to be cheerful, as it was the anniversary of my husband's election to the throne and also Josephine's name day. It helped that the little boys scampered about, oblivious as all little ones are to the concerns of the adults who surround them. And it also helped that the palace was enveloped in a festive air of celebrations: we'd been out each night to balls across the capital, plays, parades in honor of the House of Bernadotte.

That evening we sat outdoors in the gardens that looked out over the park, waiting for the sun to dip just a bit lower before the fireworks could begin. All was lush and fragrant, and little Charles was giddy in my lap, elated at the fact that he was being permitted to stay awake past his bedtime.

"Grandmother?" He looked up at me from my lap, his almond eyes fixated on the massive cluster of rubies around my neck. "Why must we wait so long?"

"Because it is not yet dark, my little one," I said. "It must be dark in order to see the fireworks."

Beside us, Gustaf was screaming, his patience giving way at this late hour, and Josephine was wondering aloud whether he should be sent to the nursery. My son dismissed the idea, telling her that the boy should be allowed to remain for the special occasion. "He does not care much for any special occasion; he's a baby," Josephine answered back, her tone clipped.

I resolved to stay out of their quarrel, turning my focus to my eldest grandchild, who was posing a follow-up question: "But, in winter, it is dark all the time. Why don't we have fireworks then?"

"It's a wonderful idea," I said. "I think we should speak to the king about it. Only then, we cannot sit outdoors to see them."

"Why not?" Charles asked.

"Why, because it is frightfully cold in the winter."

Charles bobbed his head, considering my answer. Then, he asked: "When does winter begin?"

"After autumn," I said.

"When is autumn?"

"Soon," I said. "It is late August now. Very soon we shall be through with summer, and autumn shall begin." *Very soon*, I thought, *the days will turn bitter and the nights will grow long.* I shivered in spite of the pleasant summer air enveloping us. This time of year did carry with it a twinge of sadness for me, as I knew what was coming. Summer was my favorite season, but its only flaw was that it did not last forever. I knew that this was the last month that would leave on a mild note, its final day as pleasant as its first. I squeezed my grandson, pulling him closer to me, relishing the warmth of his little embrace as I fought back the rush of dread that suddenly filled my gut.

Tonight, we were doing our best to be joyful. Tonight, we sat together amid the green and the warmth, as all around us people celebrated. Our nation was free from war; my husband and I presided over a healthy family and a court and a kingdom at peace. *But how long*, I wondered, *until this happy and fragile season ends?*

# Chapter 46

*Stockholm*
*January 1844*

ONCE MORE, THE COURT WAS GATHERING TO FILL THE long darkness of a winter night with candlelight and music. A ball, in honor of my Bernadotte's eighty-first birthday—I could hardly believe the number.

I watched my husband as he scrutinized his own figure in the mirror, putting the finishing touches on his military uniform, wholly unaware that I looked on. He was still tall, yet his shoulders slouched forward, as if his soldier's frame were now engaged in a losing battle against either gravity or time, perhaps both. He adjusted the row of shiny medals across his breast, squinting to gain a better look at their reflection, and I noted how his movements bore a certain, well, creakiness. When had we grown so old? I asked myself, noting the brittleness of my own tired joints.

The ball would be a happy occasion; Josephine had overseen the preparations. Having done her duty of providing royal offspring for Oscar five times over, she had happily put the work of childbearing behind her and had jumped gracefully into her position as leading lady at court. Still a relatively young woman of great beauty and even greater talent, she was far more popular and influential than I had ever been in Stockholm. Just as well. I had never enjoyed being in the center of things, had I? At least the newspaper writers had stopped looking for a feud where there wasn't one, finally accepting the unexciting truth that my daughter-in-law and I got along just fine.

"Well then, I don't feel very much like a soldier this evening, but the jacket does a bit of the trickery for me." My husband dragged his fingers over the thin sprinkling of white hair that lined his temples.

I crossed the room to his side. "You look as dashing as the day I met you, Sergeant Belle-Jambe."

"You've always been a terrible liar, Desiree. One of the many things I admire about you."

I laughed, looking up at him. "Shall we go down?"

"Just a moment." My husband blinked, putting out his hand. I took it.

"No need for nerves," I said. "They love you more with each year." My tone was reassuring, as I guessed that perhaps he was experiencing a bit of apprehension, as uncharacteristic as that was for him. I had always been the shy one, while not a strain of timidity had ever run through his bold Gascon blood.

But he shook his head now, his gaze tilting downward. "I . . . I think . . ." His face had gone ashy.

"What is it?" I squeezed his hand, slightly alarmed at my husband's blank expression, at the trouble he was clearly having in speaking. "Do you need to sit for a moment?"

He nodded. "Yes, I . . . believe I do."

"Here." I guided him toward the nearby chair, calling for the servants as I helped him off his feet. "His Majesty is not feeling well; fetch the royal physician at once."

The nearest footman nodded, hurrying from the room to dispatch my order. It was getting to be a more regular request these days than I liked to admit—my husband often coughed up blood, often had difficulty breathing or sudden palpitations of the heart. "It's nothing, dear," I said now, turning back to him, forcing my voice to remain level. "Perhaps we shall just get you a sip of brandy and a moment's rest. You'll be ready to dance in no time."

But my husband, who usually proved unflappable, even in his physical discomfort, was staring blankly at the floor. "I'm having the hardest time . . . it's as if . . ." and then he closed his eyes.

"Yes, yes. Just shut your eyes. Rest. The physician will—" But before I could finish my thought, my husband slumped forward, collapsing in a massive heap onto the floor. I screamed. Several servants burst unbidden into the room. I turned to them, gasping: "His Majesty has fainted! Where is the doctor?" I rose from my chair to kneel beside my husband's inanimate frame, and I took his hand in mine. It was warm, but he did not rouse to my touch or my voice. "Bernadotte! Bernadotte, wake up! Oh, please wake up," I begged, pressing my hand to his shoulder. "The doctor's coming, you must wake up!" But still he did not move, did not stir. This was no simple slumber claiming my husband—I feared it was something far worse. "No, you cannot leave me! Bernadotte? Wake up, Bernadotte!" I grew louder, more frantic in my exhortations, but that only seemed to make my husband's nonresponsive silence all the more cruel, all the more terrifying.

It was all so eerily familiar: the dark time of year, the occasion of his birthday, the word—*stroke*—whispered on the lips of the nervous courtiers.

*Le roi a eu un coup.*

The king has had a stroke.

I did not need to hear it, did not need to mingle in the halls to know what was being said; I'd lived it once before, with old King Charles. Except this time, it was *my* king, my husband.

For a week, I barely left his bedside. Oscar and Josephine took turns beside me, bringing the grandchildren in for brief visits one by one. He stirred occasionally, awaking from time to time, but it was not Bernadotte who opened his eyes to that bedchamber—it was a blank face, a mind that seemed to have been scraped clean of both understanding and memory.

Hours of nothing, pierced by sudden, agonized stirrings. I'd hover at his side, taking his hand in my own whenever he opened his eyes, but I was not certain that he was seeing me, even when he looked upon me. "We must defend ourselves!" he would groan, his dark eyes wide and haunted.

"You are safe, dear," I would say to him, laboring to keep my tone calm, even as I longed to fall apart with tears. The physicians had told me to speak calmly to him, to reassure him and remind him where he was, so that was what I did, even as he thrashed about. "There, there. No one seeks to do you any harm, Bernadotte. You are safe in your palace. In Stockholm. We are at peace. You are a good king, and your people love you. And I am your wife, your Desiree."

"Don't!" He gasped, pulling his hand from my grip as if it burned him to touch it. "Don't!"

"What is it, my dear?" I asked, alarmed. I reached once more for his hand, but he recoiled. "Don't talk of 1813!" he groaned.

I leaned back, away from the bed. Now *my* eyes went wide. My husband could not tell me the current year, but he could speak of one so many decades prior. 1813. The year in which he, as King of Sweden, had waged war against France. The year after Napoleon ravaged the entire French army in his mad attempt to conquer Russia. My husband had joined the allied forces against Napoleon, fighting opposite the same army that had been his for so many years. Marching toward Paris. Toward me.

Bernadotte shut his eyes then, shaking his head violently, and I saw the tears that slid down his pallid cheeks. "My heart aches when I think of it," he said, crying like a small, frightened boy, wincing as though he suffered bodily pain. "Had I a thousand kingdoms to give to France, I could not repay her."

"Hush now, there, there." In moments such as these, I wished for the oblivion of his long periods of motionless slumber. Frightening as it was to watch him slip from consciousness, at least when he was deep asleep his mind seemed to be at ease. Anything was better than watching him wrestle like this, tortured, consumed by the ravings of one gone mad.

"Maman, you should take a break." Josephine had appeared by my side without my noticing. "You've been here too long. You'll collapse, yourself. Please, take a rest. We'll call you if he . . . well, if anything changes."

I obeyed, only because I was so terrified by these periods of his haunted ramblings; I did not wish to be pulled back into those memories myself. I would let Josephine carry a bit of it—she who had never had to live through it the first time. I rose and walked from the bedchamber, unfurling the black veil down from my cap so that I could hide my mottled face, so that my tired eyes would not meet the strained, curious looks that filled the palace hallways.

It was to be expected, I told myself. Tortured memories, deathbed agonies and regrets. When one has lived through times such as we have, one can never truly expect peace. The need to survive—once it has been so sorely tried—can never truly move far from one's thoughts.

He put up a valiant fight, my Gascon, my soldier, my Bernadotte. But in the end, we lost him—his aged body finally yielding after several months in bed. Oscar, Josephine, and I were by his side. Death came almost as a relief, as odd as that may sound—a gentler state than some of the agonized musings of his final weeks.

We buried him that spring, just as the first spears of light and warmth began to touch our northern climate. There was a state funeral as the entire nation plunged into official mourning, a Lutheran Mass, and the burial in the capital's Riddarholmskyrkan.

I looked on, my face concealed, my tired frame enshrouded in black, as my husband was laid to rest among Sweden's ancient rulers, entombed under the name given to him by his adopted nation: Carl Johan. Nowhere did it mention the name by which I had known and loved him, my Bernadotte. *Just as well*, I thought. *That remains for me alone.*

He was gone, and that meant I was no longer Queen of Sweden. My son was crowned that fall, Oscar I, with Josephine beside him as Queen Consort, of course. She'd been acting as queen in so many ways for years already; now it was merely official. She and my son seemed to have worked out some peace of their own, some tacit understanding to keep their union in harmony, even if the ardor of their earlier romance had cooled. I urged my son to respect his wife, to treat her with the kindness she deserved. She would play a central role in Oscar's government, that I knew. And well she should; she'd have made the best ruler of us all, if only that had been a possibility.

I had worn so many titles in my life up to that point: daughter, sister, fiancée, wife, mother, subject, queen. Now I stepped willingly into what would be my final roles: dowager queen and grandmother. The Swedes had long thought me unconventional, a bit bizarre, you might even say, a bit too *French;* now, that mattered little. Now, I could slip into relative obscurity, with age and widowhood as my veils to conduct myself entirely as I wished. Josephine was lovely and vibrant and fashionable—the eyes of the court were on her, and I tasted the sweet fruits of freedom. I slept when I wanted, I took my breakfast in the afternoon and my dinner after midnight. I relished my time with my grandchildren and declined any invitation that I did not wish to accept.

But I did have one task left—one final purpose that still required the energy and attention of my waning years. And if I was going to be successful in my mission, if I hoped for any peace or repose at the end of it all, I knew that I would have to put up the fight that I had been putting off my entire life. The fight that I had dreaded since my girlhood, really. The only fight that remained. The fight that I *had* to win.

I would finally fight Napoleon.

# Chapter 47

*Stockholm*
*December 1860*

ORDS, WORDS, WORDS—IT ALWAYS COMES DOWN TO
words, does it not? The words of a denunciation, sending my
brother to prison. The words of an influential revolutionary, sparing
my family before the guillotine. The tender vows of a courting lover, the
treasonous whispers of a plotted coup. Words withheld, and in that, heartbreak. A marriage proposal, a birth announcement, an invitation to wear
a crown. A declaration of war, a suit for peace. Words familiar and foreign.
Words on a tomb alongside so many other kings.

Conquering hero or maniacal tyrant.

Cunning witch or enchanting seductress.

Patriot or traitor.

Principled or opportunistic.

Loyal subject or reluctant queen.

We had risen higher, my loved ones and I, than a fatherless girl of sixteen would ever have dared to imagine, but what did that matter, any of it,
if we did not now safeguard ourselves for the ages? If we did not act
shrewdly to curate the words that would guide our passage through time?

Napoleon had known all along the power of his words, the fact that his
pen could do more for good or to strike down his foes than one thousand

swords or a hillside of cannons. And he'd done his best to flood the world with his own words, to offer his own telling of his life and legacy. Not only with the newspapers, the censors of his administration, the gossips of his court—but also from his island exile, where he had written furiously, using his final years to bombard a war-weary world with his words. And he'd used those words to condemn my husband. To expose and steal some of my most sacred and private memories.

But the Emperor was not the only one who could use words.

You see, I remain, even now, even after he is gone. Long after he is gone—I've outlived Napoleon by forty years next year. And I've outlived her, his Josephine, by forty-six years.

And so I am using my time, I am using my words, to put forth my story, as well. My Bernadotte is gone—he left me sixteen years ago—but I have used the last bit of my time and my energy to tell the world of our extraordinary life and love.

I laugh, even now, to think of the girl so many years ago. How Napoleon—but of course back then he was Napoleone—sent me so many books and instructions. How he urged me to *apply* myself. To exercise some discipline in my work and through my words. I hadn't then. At least, not to his satisfaction. Nor had I cared one bit for my Swedish lessons or learning the rituals of a new court. But in these recent years, I have applied myself.

I have overseen the handling of all of my Bernadotte's letters and journals, as well as all of *his* letters—Napoleon's—to both my husband and me. Far older than the St. Helena letters or memoirs, far older than his attempts to forge our legacies without our permission, these words go back to a girl of sixteen and the rough Corsican soldier who was courting her on the southern coast of France. These are the words of lovers and soldiers, of suitors and rivals, ordinary people thrust into extraordinary moments—on battlefields, in ballrooms, in the halls of power. It is all here in my possession, and I've kept it all this time, safeguarded this story; words, words, words, the original words that seem to grow more astonishing with each passing year.

I've worked with the writer Georges Touchard-Lafosse to set it all down.

A Frenchman, of course, and now a trusted ally and friend. Together, we shall deliver my husband's and my story to the ages. We shall ensure that Napoleon's shall not be the final word on our lives.

It has been tiring and laborious work. Exhausting, really. But it was the only way that I could earn myself any true and lasting peace. And now, we are done. The biographies are complete. Oscar and Josephine assure me that my grandchildren shall read them and hear my telling of my own story, just as their children after them. I may rest.

Words, words, words—I sit here at the opera, in my royal box, but I cannot understand the words, because they are not in French. I never bothered to learn any other language. But it's no matter—I can feel the music. And regardless, I arrived so late to the opera this evening that I am only now going to catch the final act. I saw how the audience noted my late arrival into the box; I heard the titters and whispers that popped up across the great opera house. *She is never on time. Always late, our old dowager queen. Does she ever know what time it is?*

I boarded a ship for France a few years ago, just before my eightieth birthday. I longed to see my homeland, even though nobody remained there to welcome me home. Maman and Nicolas are long gone, Joseph and Julie died years ago. And yet, I yearned to touch French soil one more time. But the roiling seas filled me with such dread that I lost my stomach for the trip before I'd even lost sight of the receding coast, ordering the captain to turn around and return me to the port. Abandon France, return me to Sweden—words I'd never imagined myself uttering.

The new arch in Paris, the Arc de Triomphe, lists my husband's name as one of the great heroes of France. His image adorns the hall at Versailles, that Bourbon palace resplendent once more. *Would he feel better?* I wondered. *Would it give him some measure of peace to know that France has forgiven him, even if he never forgave himself?*

Another man named Napoleon ascended to the French throne. He worked to make an empire in his image. The son of Hortense, I noted with a chuckle—the grandson of Josephine. I remember when the child was born. This Napoleon, he called himself Napoleon III, was pulled from power in due time, followed by the establishment of yet another French republic. And men claim that women are fickle?

In 1844, in the same year my husband's death filled every newspaper, the son of an old soldier friend of Bernadotte's, Alexandre Dumas, found fame and glory by writing a tale titled *The Three Musketeers*. His hero is a tall, dark, fiery Gascon. A poor outsider who finds a family only in serving among soldiers. A principled patriot who rises from nothing to make his own fortune in the nation's service and earns his way to the highest ranks.

Of course I remember Dumas's father, the friend who sheltered us for those harrowing nights as Napoleon seized power back in Paris. Of course the elder Dumas would have told his son of the valiant Gascon alongside whom he'd fought—a strong, dark-haired soldier who rose from nothing to make his own fortune in the nation's service. A friend, a fellow critic of Napoleon. A patriot, a leader, and yet, always a bit of an outsider. I know, as I read Dumas, that D'Artagnan is my Bernadotte. Words, words, words.

All my life, I've been told that I need the protection of others. The nuns. My father. My brother. Napoleon. Josephine. Julie and Joseph and Bernadotte. At times, our greatest challenge was merely to survive. And survive we did. Only now, they've all fallen away. And yet, here I am. I've outlived them all.

I laugh at this; I laugh too loudly. From my place in the opera box, I attract the stares of the people nearby. But their stern, condemnatory looks only prompt me to laugh even louder. Now people on the lower level are turning to stare up at me as well. It is all so hilarious—their prim disdain, their censure. Once I would have cared.

I learned this lesson too late; what a shame, how late in life we realize that we simply ought not to have cared! That all along, it turns out, we have been free, endowed with the power to tell our own tales. To fulfill our own fortunes.

I know that my own tale will soon come to an end. I've seen enough of death in this life to know when it approaches. I am old, so very old. My aching joints rail against me, the blood has grown weary in my veins. I am tired. I am at peace.

My final journey did not take me to France, and I never had the chance to bid farewell to those places that made me Desiree. *You shall have to change your name. Desiree. It sounds too French.* I am known here as Desideria, just as my Bernadotte was known as Carl Johan.

I sigh. None of that matters, not anymore. I smile and nod at the people who still look at me with their proud, half-pitying scowls. And then, I rise. Even though the opera performance is not over, I shall quit this box. I'll wave my hand and a cluster of attendants will see to it that my coach pulls up to the front, ready to convey me through the snow-covered streets, bearing me wherever I wish to go. *Kring kring,* round and round she goes.

When the snow falls at midnight, blanketing the empty cobbled streets, sugaring the gothic bell tower of Storkyrkan Cathedral, it becomes easy to imagine. To imagine and to remember—the two go hand in hand. The memories swirl and shift now, more dizzying than the erratic flakes of winter snow, more percussive than the pounding of the horses' hooves on the cobblestones. A girl, a beautiful girl, pulled into the center of a nation's turmoil. Heartbreak, and then hope. A lover, and then a wife. A mother, an attendant. A queen with a crown plucked from the stars that guide our fortune. I've been so many things, called so many different lands my home, and I've survived them all. I've found my way and I've ruled, even as those around me have fallen.

And now, at last, I am going home.

# Epilogue

DESIREE CLARY BERNADOTTE DIED IN STOCKHOLM ON December 17, 1860, at the impressive age of eighty-three. She left as her legacy a kingdom at peace and a popular ruling family that included her son, her four living grandchildren, and a growing brood of great-grandchildren.

The dynasty of the House of Bernadotte, begun by Desiree and Bernadotte and then solidified by Oscar and Josephine, still rules Sweden today. The descendants of Desiree and Bernadotte still sit on the thrones of many countries—more than the descendants of the Houses of Bourbon and Bonaparte combined.

Desiree is buried in Stockholm's Riddarholmen Church beside her Bernadotte. Together, through their multitudinous offspring and their forever-interwoven destinies, Desiree and Josephine not only survive, but also continue to rule.

# Author's Note

It started with a question posed by my father, one of the greatest history geeks I know: "Allison, what do you know about Desiree Clary? Desiree Bernadotte? The Frenchwoman, Desiree?"

"Desiree?" I considered the name a minute. "Honestly? Nothing."

"You should look into her. Her life—you cannot believe it's true. But it *is*."

That was how the conversation unfolded, years ago, when my father gave me the precious tip that would lead to my fascination with Desiree Clary Bernadotte and the constellation of larger-than-life characters around her, and the process of writing this book.

As a writer of historical fiction with a passion for telling the stories of women whose lives and legacies have been overshadowed in the forward march of time, I am often presented with such tips. Just the smallest grain of a story, dangled before me by fellow lovers of history and fiction; the teaser that a great tale lurks in the shadows of the historical record, waiting to be told.

In order for me to take up such a lead, in order for me to commit years of my life to researching, thinking about, writing about, editing, and then speaking about a proposed historical figure or time or place, several key things need to happen.

I have to feel that I'm looking at a way into history—through this historic individual (or moment in time)—that has not yet been sufficiently explored, particularly via fiction, but sometimes through nonfiction as well.

I have to feel that this story will be juicy and dramatic and compelling—both for me and for the reader.

I have to feel that this historic figure—usually a woman, in my experience—is calling to be pulled from a supporting role in the lives of others to a leading role at center stage, offering us an opportunity not only to learn the *facts* of her life, but also to imagine and explore the emotional truths located therein, to consider how the important events of her story might have *felt*.

And finally, I have to become utterly, madly, and inexorably obsessed.

And that is precisely what happened when I encountered Desiree Clary Bernadotte.

All of the above, many times over.

When I told my dad that I knew nothing of Desiree, that was indeed the case. I had never even heard the name. Desiree Clary? Desiree Bernadotte? A quick Internet search unearthed just the most basic of facts: Desiree was Napoleon's first fiancée. She's standing right there, in plain sight, in the iconic Jacques-Louis David coronation painting of Notre Dame, attending to the very woman who had displaced her from Napoleon's heart. And so is her husband, who was a power player in the French army and government before becoming King of Sweden. The exiled Napoleon wrote and spoke about Desiree and her husband until the end of his life, and she kept his love letters until the end of hers. Her descendants still sit on many of the thrones of Europe today—descendants whom she shares with Josephine, her one-time rival and then unlikely friend. And yet, her name is not a household one, nor is it nearly as well known as so many of her contemporaries, the people she called family, friends, and foes—sometimes all of the above. Desiree's story had its hooks in me, and there would be no letting go. As my dad said: history is often too good to be true. Especially when it *is* true.

What especially stunned me was Desiree and Bernadotte's prominence in *The Coronation of Napoleon* by David, which hangs in the Louvre. There they stand at the front of Notre Dame Cathedral, dressed in their finery alongside Julie and Joseph, the Bonaparte sisters, the Pope, Mamma Letizia, and the rest of the colorful imperial inner circle. As I stared at that masterpiece, I couldn't help but wonder: How was Desiree there? *Why* was she there? What must she have felt, looking on, attending to the man who had broken her heart and the woman who had replaced her as they made themselves Emperor and Empress of France?

And those questions kept coming up as I researched Desiree's life. Over and over again—she was there for *that moment*? And *that moment*? And *that*? How? Why? What must that have felt like for her? But there was one resounding question that clamored the loudest as I learned about Desiree, this ordinary woman who was thrust into the most extraordinary of times, and that was: how do I not know about her?

How is it that we have allowed Desiree's name to become obscured in history?

In many ways, the life of Desiree Clary Bernadotte was a historical fiction writer's dream. Though she lived through so many of modern Europe's most well-known moments, though she coexisted with larger-than-life figures who have since come to assume almost mythical proportions, Desiree herself has not had much opportunity to serve as the leading lady of her own story. While there are scores of biographies in existence about Napoleon, Josephine, Bernadotte, and so many of the Bourbons and Bonapartes and Habsburgs, I could not find an English-language biography in which Desiree occupied center stage. So then it became a game of connecting the pieces, pulling together so many disparate threads from so many other life stories until the beautiful and complicated picture that was Desiree's began to emerge.

The well-documented histories of Napoleon, Josephine, and Bernadotte—and their revolutionary and imperial power clique—provided the bones of the story, over which I was given free rein to imagine the flesh and the color and the heart of Desiree's. As I sought to craft this fictional world from the historical facts and legends, Desiree took shape as a leading lady with a will and an agency all her own. To return to the David tableau with which I began my search: her character not only appeared before my mind's eye, but in fact, it ended up stealing the show.

One of the criticisms leveled at Desiree by her Swedish court rival, the perspicacious Queen Hedwig Charlotte, was that Desiree was "a French woman in every inch." I am fortunate in my life to have many such "French women in every inch," most notably my one-hundred-percent-

French maternal grandmother, Monique LeBlanc Rowland, who helped me to understand what this meant (and who also, it must be noted, was the only family member who knew anything about Desiree at the time I set out to write this story). And even though several centuries separate them, Grandmère's stories of her convent boarding school upbringing directly inspired Desiree's time there in this book, particularly the feigned illness in order to binge on food and sleep in the sick ward.

Though so much of history has been written by and for men, I feel most passionately that women carry much of the heart and soul of so many of these great historical moments, and that their lives provide some of the most captivating and inspiring material for storytelling. On that note, I must point out that I broke out in full-body chills and spasmodic breathing when I uncovered that Josephine (the Queen of Sweden and Oscar's wife, not the French Empress) and another historic heroine whom I've had the great privilege of writing about, Sisi, were cousins! Both free-spirited and intelligent beauties from the royal Bavarian Wittelsbachs. Both pulled from their relatively low-key and bourgeois family circles to rule over vast kingdoms far from home. I like to imagine Desiree and Sisi—both queens whom I've come to love and admire, both fascinating and complicated women, both plucked from their ordinary lives to ride the waves of astonishing times—presiding together over a fantastic family reunion.

So, too, do I love the symmetry in the fact that Desiree and France's Empress Josephine—erstwhile rivals, reluctant friends, soul sisters in heartache and havoc—are joined forever through their many offspring and that their descendants still rule to this day, while the man between them—a man who was so obsessed with his own power and legacy that he left them both—can claim no progeny still in power. The current Crown Princess of Sweden, Victoria Bernadotte, has the middle name of Desiree; her sister, Princess Madeleine, has the middle name of Josephine. Unlike Napoleon, I don't believe that Desiree—or Josephine, for that matter—was ever particularly preoccupied with getting a crown or ruling for generations, but I'm gratified for them both nonetheless.

# Acknowledgments

There are so many people who made this book possible, and to all of them I say a heartfelt thank you, knowing even as I say it that it is not enough.

Dad, for that initial conversation and the tip that led me down the path of all things Desiree, I am so grateful. And to Mom, for always being such an enthusiastic and energetic cheerleader. On the topic of progeny and bequeathing to future generations, my parents love history and storytelling, and I'm happy to say that has carried to all of my siblings, who inspire and challenge me and who are my favorite people to join at a table and just talk, because we never know where it will go, but it will always be interesting.

To my in-laws and my second family of Levys, I love you all and I am so fortunate that you came in the package when I got Dave.

I am truly blessed to have such supportive friends and loved ones from childhood, school, college, my time working in news, my hometown community, as well as the wonderful network of pals and colleagues in the writing world and beyond—much heartfelt gratitude and appreciation to all of you.

To Lacy Lynch, Dabney Rice, and the team at Dupree Miller: thank you for your advocacy, expertise, enthusiasm, and humor at every turn on this fascinating and exhilarating road. Lacy, I would be hard-pressed to find someone who does more to support storytellers, and so this story of an incomparable woman is dedicated to you.

To Kara Cesare, it is my great fortune to call you both editor and friend. Thank you for believing in me, and for believing in Desiree. And to the entire team at Penguin Random House: you are not only the best at what you do, but you also infuse every step of the publishing process with your enthusiastic support and expertise: Gina Centrello, Kara Welsh, Kim Hovey, Jennifer Hershey, Susan Corcoran, Jen Garza, Michelle Jasmine, Leigh Marchant, Debbie Aroff, Taylor Noel, Rachel Kind, Loren Noveck, Jesse Shuman, Virginia Norey, and so many others, thank you.

To the book sales reps, the librarians, the booksellers, the book bloggers, the book club members, the filmmakers who bring books to the screen, and all of the readers: thank you so much for allowing this lifelong book nerd and in-my-head-story-maker-upper to call this work every day. I can never sufficiently convey my gratitude for what you do to support my books, or my joy that we get to connect through stories.

And finally, to Dave and my girls: you are my story. I thank God that we get to write it together every day. And I thank you for the love, laughter, support, and lessons.

I am indebted to many biographers, historians, editors, and memoirists—the individuals who distilled the complex and copious historical material that provided the inspiration for this novel. For the reader who would like to enter further into the fascinating world of the French Revolution and French Empire, here are some titles (fiction and nonfiction) to satiate the *encore:*

*Bernadotte: Napoleon's Marshal, Sweden's King*, by Alan Palmer

*Napoleon: A Life*, by Andrew Roberts

*Ambition and Desire: The Dangerous Life of Josephine Bonaparte*, by Kate Williams

*The French Revolutionary Wars*, by Gregory Fremont-Barnes

*French Revolutionary Infantry: 1789–1802*, by Terry Crowdy

*The French Revolution: A History*, by Thomas Carlyle

*The French Revolution and Napoleon*, by Leo Gershoy

*The Black Count: Glory, Revolution, Betrayal, and the Real Count of Monte Cristo*, by Tom Reiss

*Jacques-Louis David, Revolutionary Artist: Art, Politics, and the French Revolution*, by Warren Roberts

*Origins of the French Revolution*, by William Doyle

*La Révolution Française: Les Années Lumière* (film series)
*La Révolution Française: Les Années Terribles* (film series)
*A Place of Greater Safety*, by Hilary Mantel
*A Tale of Two Cities*, by Charles Dickens
*War and Peace*, by Leo Tolstoy

# About the Author

ALLISON PATAKI is the *New York Times* bestselling author of *The Traitor's Wife*, *The Accidental Empress*, *Sisi: Empress on Her Own*, *Where the Light Falls*, the nonfiction memoir *Beauty in the Broken Places*, and the children's books *Nelly Takes New York* and *Poppy Takes Paris*. Her books have been translated into more than a dozen languages. A former news writer and producer, Pataki has written for *The New York Times*, ABC News, *The Huffington Post*, *USA Today*, Fox News, and other outlets. She has appeared on the *Today* show, *Fox & Friends*, *Good Day New York*, *Good Day Chicago*, and MSNBC's *Morning Joe*. Pataki graduated cum laude from Yale University with a major in English. A member of the Historical Novel Society, she lives in New York with her husband and children.

allisonpataki.com
Facebook.com/AllisonPatakiPage
Twitter: @AllisonPataki
Instagram: @allisonpataki

# About the Type

This book was set in Albertina, a typeface created by Dutch calligrapher and designer Chris Brand (1921–98). Brand's original drawings, based on calligraphic principles, were modified considerably to conform to the technological limitations of typesetting in the early 1960s. The development of digital technology later allowed Frank E. Blokland (b. 1959) of the Dutch Type Library to restore the typeface to its creator's original intentions.